I0652963

# SINKHOLE

## by
## Ken Goldman

Copyright © 2017 by Ken Goldman

All Rights Reserved.

No part of this book may be reproduced, distributed or transmitted in any form or by any means without the author's written consent, except for the purposes of review

Cover Design © 2017 by Ben Baldwin

http://benbaldwin.co.uk/

ISBN-13: 978-1-947522-00-8

ISBN-10: 1-947522-00-0

This book is a work of fiction. Names, characters, places and incidents are either a product of the author's fertile imagination or are used fictitiously. Any resemblance to actual events, places or persons, living or dead, is entirely coincidental.

BLOODSHOT BOOKS

READ UNTIL YOU BLEED!

# KEN GOLDMAN

# SINKHOLE

# ACKNOWLEDGEMENTS

This particular SINKHOLE never existed in a vacuum. There are many people -- probably too many -- I'd like to thank. If this were the Academy Awards, I'm sure the orchestra would be playing me offstage.

At the top, my sincere thanks go to Pete Kahle for releasing SINKHOLE and its resident Wogslûk creatures for the world to see. Pete's attention to detail every step of the way kept me in the loop and on my toes. The man is the blueprint for what every editor should be.

Thanks also to cover artist Ben Baldwin for his nightmarish vision that horrifically captures the mood of my story. His cover gave me the creeps, and I wrote the damn book.

Credit also goes to publicist Erin Sweet Al-Mehairi for getting the word out to all you horror people.

Can't leave out my personal pals who religiously read my tales and are not shy about telling me what works and what doesn't:

Never a yes-man (or, in this case, a yes-woman), my good friend Marla Villari Gruber was the first human to sample SINKHOLE in its rough draft. As a teacher, she was never shy about sharing her opinions -- and she had many!

To my knowledge, Allen Essrig is the only person who has read every short story and novel I've written. Stephen King would call him my personal "constant reader." If ever a writer had a cheering section, Allen would certainly qualify as mine.

Thanks to friends Fern Saull, Ira Brown, Henry Barsky, Larry Arnoff, Andrea and Richard Frankel, Bill and Melissa Firman, and Cousin Andrea Eisenberg for allowing me to force my novels down their throats.There are others I could mention, but these are the ones I actually saw gag.

Thanks also to my older brother Marty (Historian and novelist Martin S. Goldman, an author in his own 'write'), whose talents have always set the bar high for myself. I think I'm almost ready for that high jump.

And of course, my great appreciation goes to you, my reader, whoever you are, for venturing to take this journey with me. But don't look down just yet. It's dark in that sinkhole.

Very dark.

Come with me and I'll show you...

**- Ken Goldman**

# PROLOGUE

## SPRING 2015: BED BUGS AND SLUGS

### *"You bite them right back"*

*New Glenn Echoes construction, Diamond Loop cul-de-sac 3 bedroom/2 full bath, 1410 sq. ft. 2 floor unit with sunroom view of large landscape area in front and generous rear garden area. Fully carpeted in spacious living room and large master bedroom*

—Real Estate Advertisement for *Diamond Loop* homes

The young realtor's business card read *Susan Donnelly* with a photo that belonged on a box of Ivory Snow. Accompanying the attractive couple through every room of the new home, Donnelly displayed her professional (and well-rehearsed) demeanor for the Colsons, Greg and Eden. For the full thirty minutes during her sales presentation, her smile never left her face.

"It's a new listing, the last available unit of twenty in this cul-de-sac, so this home won't stay on the market long. You've got all the amenities here—great neighborhood, convenience to shopping and theaters, and the schools are among the best in the state. Glenn Echoes Middle School's baseball team was the 2014 Jersey state champion. Does your son play?"

Susan touched all the bases. Of course, also during the middle school's championship year of 2014, a thirty-seven-year-old English teacher had molested his student of fourteen (making the unwise decision to rip off the girl's bikini panties in the school's empty parking lot after sundown, unaware of the night janitor's smoking habit). Even more unsavory, a few years earlier — and about six minutes from where the Colsons stood — some gun-crazed husband had followed his dinner by polishing off his wife and three kids. The guy had just finished his cheesecake when he put a bullet into their heads without leaving the table. His idiot lawyer blamed the man's sudden outburst on his type 2 diabetes and the cheesecake's high sugar level, but the man put another bullet into his own head shortly after.

Susan Donnelly knew of these incidents and many more, but pedophile educators and lunatic fathers don't encourage sales. Knowing her power points, she kept her presentation on task in fluid happy-talk, and it clearly was working. One look at Eden Colson told that tale.

"Our son is more into computers and writing, that kind of thing. Reads all the sci-fi and horror he can get his hands on, devours King, Asimov, and the classics like crazy, not to mention every sci-fi/horror movie, or TV show ever made. And he's into Rocky — that's his cat. She follows Zack everywhere. Did it from the day we brought her home. He's a good kid. Best in his class, his teachers say. And—" The young mother was babbling. Her husband gave her the look, and she shut up.

Susan didn't miss a beat. "Well, there's also a great tech program at the school. A computer club too. And there's a decent veterinarian over in Wellington. Cats, dogs, birds, even snakes — you name it. I'm sure Zack and Rocky will love it here. And so will you."

The pricey cul-de-sac's well-manicured lawns (and equally well-manicured housewives) meant Gregory Colson had probably been doing a little mental arithmetic. For the high asking price, Susan had to convince him that Diamond Loop was worth investing his savings in a thirty-year commitment. Unfortunately, she couldn't close the deal by saying what she felt like adding, but if Mr. Colson were anything like her former husband, and most other men...

# SINKHOLE

*(...and maybe you've noticed the women here in the Loop, Mr. Colson? Some married, some divorced, many willing and able. Nice to look at during a warm summer night's barbecue, eh? Maybe you could even do more than just look?)*

Greg exchanged another quick glance with his wife, but their mutual attempt at remaining cool and expressionless didn't work. Susan recognized an interested buyer's poker-faced ruse; it practically screamed "This is the place!" People didn't do cartwheels when they discovered a good match, not when an affordable mortgage depended on more subdued reactions. Usually they waited a day or two just to whittle away at the asking price. But Susan Donnelly knew how to play her hand too. Remaining cucumber cool, she felt certain Eden and Gregory Colson would high five each other the moment they were out the door.

That didn't happen. The couple waited until they were in the car. Greg stopped the Camry near the fancy Diamond Loop street sign that displayed red playing card diamonds on either end.

Like the realtor, Eden also had read her husband's muted reactions. "You think so too, don't you?"

Greg kissed her cheek. "Be it ever so humble..."

It's difficult to say when a house crosses the barrier to become a home. This takes time, and there is a breaking-in period required for both the walls and the people living within them to reach that special moment. Experiences fit into the equation too, whether they be births or deaths, or simply the measurement of a child's growth as recorded in the dated markings scratched into the woodwork. After the moving van has left and a family settles into their new digs for the first time, there is a special feeling about those events waiting in the future. Before life takes its natural course, those first few nights feel odd in this new and unfamiliar place. Perhaps that title of *home* is premature and undeserved during those early days, but there is not a species alive that doesn't desire a place it can

3

call by that name.

By early summer the mailbox at 613 Diamond Loop read COLSON. Before the couple fully unpacked cartons, Eden started her garden, and Greg busied himself turning the two-car garage into a one-car port, clearing space for his new work shop. Zack and his computer were never far apart, while Rocky seemed content basking in the nearest sun beam. The roof didn't leak, and the toilets didn't overflow. The house proved comfortably spacious and inviting, the neighbors friendly. Although the water pressure in the bathrooms seemed a little weak and the cold water sometimes dripped in varying shades of brown, that inconvenience appeared the worst of the anticipated flaws any new home might reveal.

Eden made the call to Glenn Echoes Department of Streets who forwarded her call to Reefe Water & Sewer Contractors. Supervisor, Fred Reefe, informed her that weak water pressure with chocolate sprinkles was apparently shared among the Loop's other residents, a problem not unusual for new housing units. The county had hired the private contractor, whose workers planned to dig through the asphalt entranceway, a job requiring several days to get at the water mains threading beneath Glenn Echoes.

"...and it could get noisy. Sorry if there's an inconvenience, Mrs. Colson, but something serious could come of a leaking water main if we don't nip it quick. I'm sure you don't want to be treading water in your garden. Anyway, the racket shouldn't last long."

Eden told Reefe she grew up in Manhattan, where car horns during the mornings seemed like birdsong. The man had a good laugh, and Eden hung up, humming as she returned to her flower garden. Today she would do a bit of digging herself. Gloves on, spade in hand, she broke ground for a new flower bed.

The damp soil churned a bit, turning over on itself. Something seemed to be in it. Eden's stomach also churned when she saw the slugs.

4

★ ★ ★

Zachary Colson prepared for bed, Rocky nestled closely alongside him. In his new home sleep came with difficulty, and once accomplished, he knew the nightmares would begin. Rocky helped keep the fear from completely overpowering the boy, but Zachary's night terrors continued to haunt him, and the furry warmth of a pet could do only so much. Watching *The Walking Dead* on his lap top may not have been the best idea.

*Walkers...and biters...*

His mother peeked into his room.

"'Night, honey. If those bed bugs bite, then you bite them right back." Since the family's arrival at Diamond Loop, Eden Colson had repeated some new variation of the bug theme practically every night at bedtime, punctuating the remark with a kiss on Zachary's forehead. She stroked the black cat's underbelly. "Night Rocky. You watch out for those bed bugs too, okay? See you guys in the morning."

"'Night, Mom."

Maybe he occasionally squirmed when she planted one on him, but Zachary didn't mind his mother's nightly kisses. He might even have admitted that he liked them.

But the thought of hungry bed bugs scared the shit out of him.

# PART ONE

## THE HOLE TRUTH

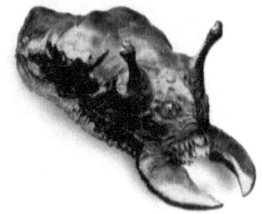

*"A hole is nothing at all, but you can break your neck in it."*

**- Austin O'Malley (author, 1858-1932)**

*"I almost wish I hadn't gone down that rabbit-hole—and yet—and yet—it's rather curious, you know, this sort of life!"*

**- Lewis Carroll, (author, 1832-1898)**
***Alice in Wonderland***

*"God not only plays dice, but also sometimes throws them where they cannot be seen."*

**- Stephen W. Hawking (Physicist, 1942 - )**

*"A big fuckin' hole it is, all right."*

**- Old Sam, Overland Stage Express Driver (1866)**

# CHAPTER ONE

ALONG THE SANTA FE TRAIL, 1866:
Melissa Monahan Riding the Westbound
Concord Overland Stage Express

*"You ain't goin' to like this part..."*

**T**he six horses were in full gallop now. Despite traversing hundreds of miles through dust and dirt, the harnessed beasts had somehow remained almost exuberant. Inside the small coach behind them, however, the four passengers were anything but. Sweating from the prairie heat, tired from the exhausting trip, tempers would have flared had any chosen to speak. Outside the coach, their driver's "Hey-ya! Hey-ya!" shouted to the horses were the only human sounds heard for hours.

*Eyes forward, say nothing. This abhorrent conveyance is only testing my endurance,* Melissa Monahan told herself. She sat unsmiling, averting the gaze of the equally uncomfortable young nun (not much older than her own nineteen years) seated directly before her, while thinking of the handsome *(and wealthy!)* cattle rancher whose name she would soon take, and who waited at her journey's end. An older woman sat alongside the nun. Wearing a ridiculous hat that looked like a fruit basket, she kept her nose buried in a tattered Bible during the entire trip. These two dour women Melissa had managed to tolerate for nearly nine hundred miles, but she took great pains not to look in the direction of the dark-haired stranger who sat uncomfortably close beside her, his leg brushing hers.

When she had attempted sleep, she knew the young man's eyes were on her, and although she would have admitted it to no one, she had briefly watched while *he* slept. Excepting the pleasantries of an occasional 'Good morning' or a comment on

9

the sweltering prairie heat, conversation remained minimal among the passengers.

*"Hey-ya!"*

Melissa's head ached with each snap of the driver's reins motivating the snorting horses, and the incessant clacking of wagon wheels became maddening. En route from Missouri to the newly acquired territories of New Mexico, the old reinsman had occasionally stopped in small towns to water the horses, sometimes changing them so that the animals would not drop dead in the heat. Meals were rushed and difficult to keep down. Five days into a miserable journey that would reunite her with her fiancé, young Melissa felt trapped inside some madly swaying pendulum. The stomach-churning motion of the coach nearly defeated her patience, and she felt certain this dusty trail's huge rocks would topple all six horses and the passengers in one great heap. She kept her lips stiffened and both feet firmly attached to the stage's unsteady flooring while her three traveling companions sat uncomfortably close because the wagon offered little breathing room. Most infuriating was the dark haired young man who seemed to enjoy the awkwardness of their situation. His leg against hers had not moved an inch. Melissa did the unthinkable and locked eyes with his.

He smiled and began a song to himself, *"'Buffalo gals won't you come out tonight, come out tonight, come out—'"*

"If you wouldn't mind—" Melissa pointed to his leg and did not include 'Please' in her request.

His smirk broadened. "My pardons, Miss, but it *is* tight in here, and I'm a bit wound up myself. Sorry if I was off key. However..." He attempted to cross his long legs, but somehow this brought him closer. "Better?"

Melissa said nothing, and a sudden side roll of the coach practically sent her into his lap. Burning with embarrassment, her polite smile melted.

"I'm to be Mrs. Christian McKenna, Junior next Sunday morning," she offered as her justification for the awkward moment. "His family owns the McKenna Ranch just outside of

Trementina."

"Well, then, hello, Mrs. Soon-to-be-McKenna. Benjamin Jamison at your service. Glad you decided to speak. And if you keep speaking, then I'll promise not to sing." The man offered his hand. Melissa stared at his calloused palm as if inspecting it for disease, but she took it lightly into hers.

"You have a deal, Mr. Jamison."

"Now that wasn't so hard, was it, Missy?"

He called her by the name only friends and family called her! *How—?* Realizing the term was generalized to include all young women, her face went crimson. "It's Melissa — Melissa Monahan, at least until next Sunday. Missy only to those who know me." This made the man almost double over with laughter. Even the young nun managed a half smile.

"A happy coincidence, eh, Melissa Monahan? Myself, I'm hoping to find some cattle work in San Miguel County so I can afford more than the suit and saddle I brought onboard. Is this your first trip on your own? I'm thinking it is, as you seem unused to the discomforts of stage travel."

Melissa straightened her posture for maybe the hundredth time. "I've experienced worse."

"Oh, worse it can be, all right. The Santa Fe is an old Indian trail, you know. Indians, they're common along this route. Brazen enough, they were, even to attack the military using the trail during the war, and they did the same to them Chinese immigrants building the new railroad. There's robbers too all along this route, and they know which stage is carrying the bank's money." The nun and the fruit basket-hatted woman looked at each other, the color gone from their faces. Turning serious, Ben leaned forward. "The Osage tribe, they're Sioux, the most savage of the bunch. Wouldn't hesitate to kill a woman or a child — no, not even a young nun such as yourself, Sister. One blow of an Injun's tomahawk and your brains, they'll spill right into your lap." He made a chopping motion with his arm.

Melissa flinched but managed composure. "I'm thinking you might enjoy an Indian attack, Mr. Jamison."

"No, Miss. I assure you, I would not enjoy seeing all that blood splashed. This is a new suit."

Melissa never would have admitted her racing heart had little to do with some savage Indian attack, feeling tempted to press her leg more firmly against Mr. Benjamin Jamison's. This absurd thought she quickly dismissed, and she saw the man grin as if he knew this.

Ben leaned close, seeming to share a secret. "I 'spect them Indians have their own bone to pick, what with the new rail-roads coming through these parts. Them rails will be chewing up the stagecoach business along the Santa Fe Trail, that's for sure. But stage robbers, they're a different breed from Indians entirely, and they're not above robbing entire trains. 'Course, the Overland Express is a whole lot easier than any iron horse. See, bandits in these parts, they're more interested in the West-bound traveler 'cause he's likely carryin' considerable cash, plus the Overland Stage carries quite a bit for the banks 'long its waypoints. And naturally, if a woman is pretty enough, them highwaymen, they take what they—"

The nun interrupted. "Mr. Jamison, I think you've said enough for—"

One of the horses whinnied loudly, and a rolling hell came on board. Taking a sudden wild turn, the coach careened precariously on two wheels, nearly going end-on as the driver outside reined in the screaming team.

*"WHOA, DAMMIT! WHOA!"*

All decorum lost, the women fell forward, and the old Bible went flying. Only Benjamin kept his wits about him as the wagon stopped, the team of horses still snorting and stamping trail dust. He rolled the window's leather shades, but no robbers nor Indians appeared anywhere in sight.

"Something's wrong." Gun drawn, he opened the door.

"You think you're going to need that weapon?" asked the fruit basket hatted woman.

"The Colt ain't called the Peacemaker for nothing. Don't you ladies move from here."

Melissa was having none of that. Straightening her

summer dress, she stumbled behind Benjamin towards the driver. The old man had tied the reins around his wrist and held his hat in one hand; the other hand covered the large black metal box at his side.

"Everyone all right back there?" He looked behind to check the luggage strapped to the coach's top. The traveling cases and trunks seemed intact under the drop cloth. Turning to Benjamin and Melissa below, he cursed and spit, pointing to a great cavity in the trail. "You see that damned hole? Sweet Jesus! I'm thinkin' maybe this was some bandits' crafty way of gettin' what's inside the bank's strongbox, but ain't no one around. Never seen nothin' like this on the Santa Fe. Thank Christ we're just a few miles out from the cut-off to San Miguel County."

Melissa showed the first evidence of her excitement. "Trementina is in San Miguel! Yes! That's where I'm headed!"

"Not goin' to be seein' Trementina any time soon, Missy, not with that damned crater in our path. Lord knows how deep it runs. Lucky the horses caught it 'fore I did, else we'd be lookin' up from its bottom right now — assuming a hole that size *has* a bottom."

Melissa strained her eyes to see through the raised dust. "A big hole out here? How—?"

Wiping the sweat from his forehead, the reinsman stared ahead. "A big fuckin' hole it is, all right. Were it nighttime, we woulda been swallowed in it for sure. Don't know how it got here in solid earth. But... see, there was somethin' else I seen, and... well, you ain't goin' to like this part."

"I'm not really liking much of any part of this trip," Melissa said.

The team of horse weren't enjoying it either. Each one snorted, several twisting their heads away from the chasm. Held securely in their harnesses, the animals seemed ready to bolt.

The old driver's mind seemed somewhere else. "Hole that wide don't make sense in these flatlands. Ain't many underground wells here, just dirt and tumbleweeds. And — well, I think I seen somethin' large crawlin' into that pit. Couldn't tell what, with all the dust and from this distance. Some animal, must be, but ain't much out here to feed no animals that size."

"Old man, this prairie heat can play nasty tricks with your eyes," Benjamin said. "Coyotes, maybe, or buzzards? There's food where there's people nearby."

"Maybe. Maybe not. Coulda been anything. There's herds of buffalo 'round here and some plant life to feed 'em, but I doubt there's any so mutton-headed to fall down some open hole." The old reinsman turned to the other two women poking their heads through the window. "You three ladies wait here while myself and this young man have a look, see there's no danger down there and if we can't get 'round this thing. Young Miss, if you don't mind holdin' the lines for a moment, 'case the horses get uppity."

"There's six reins here!"

"Six *lines*, Miss. I ain't askin' you to drive the team. Just hold 'em."

Hoisting Melissa to the driver's perch, he climbed down. A nod of understanding passed between him and Ben. The old man pointed to the rifle alongside his seat and Melissa handed it to him. The men approached the dark aperture with guns in hand.

The two women climbed from their coach seats, the nun's habit flapping in the prairie wind like the wings of a large bat. The other Bible-toting woman mopped her forehead with a handkerchief. "The old man says that hole coulda took the bunch of us, horses and all. Do you think it's safe for those men to—"

Melissa stared at the dark opening. It looked an acre wide. "I know if anything happens to them, that Bible of yours may come in handy. Indians and robbers are one thing, but some hungry pack of coyotes crawling from that pit is likely much worse."

"Coyotes don't live in pits," the nun said.

They watched the men circling the crevice, the old driver looking deep into it while scratching his head. He studied the terrain surrounding the rupture, figuring how to get an entire team of horses around it. There seemed more than enough prairie flatland to try.

The Bible clutched close to her chest, the other woman seemed reluctant to speak her thoughts. "That old goat said he saw something creep back into that hole. You don't think there's some kind of man-eating—?"

The nun pointed to the emptied bottles of whiskey alongside the driver's seat. "Apparently he's had himself some liquid companionship here — *rotgut*, the men call it. Under this hellish sun, that old man might've sworn he saw Satan himself crawling back to the underworld." Her unsmiling expression remained.

The same held true for the two men returning from their investigation. Ben looked to the reinsman before speaking.

"Old Sam here and me, we had a good look into that hole. That thing's deeper than either of us could make out, and my eyesight is sharp as a hawk's. Anyway, whatever come out is likely gone back. Don't know how far down it goes, but Sam can get the horses 'round it if the wheels don't stick in the dirt off the road. But, see, that ain't all of it, 'cause—" The driver shot Ben a glance and he shut up.

The nun caught this. "What madness are you gentlemen keepin' to yourselves?"

The old man looked like he could have used another swig from his whiskey bottle. "Sister, this trail leads straight into San Miguel County. There's fresh tracks stoppin' on the far side of that hole, and to someone who don't know better they may seem from wagon wheels. But they're all zig-zaggy, and they're leadin' right to that pit. They're too deep and too thick for wagon wheels, and they ain't no horse hooves nowhere around, neither, just them tracks alone headed for Trementina. Or headin' back into that damned hole. Maybe both, as the case may be."

Benjamin reached for old Sam's whiskey bottle and finished it off. "Damned prairie snails, is what I'm thinkin'. In these plains, them snails grow big as a barn! Don't have shells, just long slimy innards and sharp hooked mouths. Worse than Indians and robbers put together, and much uglier! And they love women — 'cause women, they're tastier."

Melissa knew when her leg was being pulled. "I think prairie snails have been chewing at your brain, Mr. Jamison,"

Ben grinned. "I figured it was worth a shot. And call me Ben, will you?"

The young nun wasn't buying it. "You men saw something inside that pit, didn't you?"

Sam and Ben looked at each other. "Just a whole lot of dark," the old man said.

Looking especially ridiculous beneath her fruit basket hat, the other woman raised her brow. "So? Tracks is tracks, don't you agree, old man?"

"Look, ma'am, maybe I'm gettin' too old for these long trips. Them tracks — likely they're just wagon tracks, like you say."

Ben helped Melissa from the driver's perch, holding her a moment longer than necessary. Surprising herself, she let him. "You believe that, don't you, Ben? A stiff wind could burrow into the trail to make thicker tracks from old ones, isn't that so? That could explain what's there, couldn't it?"

It didn't explain why the tracks ended at the hole, and a heavy wind would likely blow the tracks away, not make them deeper — and where *were* the horses' tracks? Melissa, needing to convince herself nothing crazy was going on, mentioned none of that. Ben pretended to agree with her, but he was no actor.

"I'm certain there's nothin' worth worryin' over. Next stop, the charming little town of Trementina!" His smile remained as he opened the coach's door. He didn't join the women in the cab; instead he seated himself alongside the driver and spoke low so the women wouldn't hear. "'Least, I hope there ain't nothing to worry over, considering the craziness we saw in that hole. You want some company, don't you, Sam?"

The old man picked up the reins and snapped them.

**16**

"Fuck yeah."

★ ★ ★

Old Sam got his team of six to perform some magic, and The Overland Stage Express sped double time beyond the chasm toward San Miguel County. The wheels bounced in the thick uneven trenches, and Ben climbed back into the cab to provide some weight. On its axle one of the rear wheels wobbled, but the Trementina blacksmith could tend to that. Entering the city's limits, Ben raised the leather shade to have a look at the late afternoon goings on in Trementina. Not much was happening. Melissa looked anxiously through the window.

"I don't see any people. Is that unusual?"

Ben surveyed the area. "Maybe something big is going on, but I don't see any sign of that. Christ, there's saddled horses just wandering the streets."

"Well, I'm certain of one man who will be out and about." Melissa searched for her fiancé on the stage platform. Turning to Ben, her expression told her thoughts. "I don't understand this. Christian promised he'd be—"

Sam pulled the team to the water trough, tying the lead horses to the hitching post. He stood outside the coach shaking his head. "Very strange. No station manager here. Ain't nobody in sight. Hell, always some folks come to meet the stage when she comes in, and there's someone to scrub the horses down and water 'em. No... wait a minute here. Missy, your man, is he kind of sandy haired, thin?" He pointed to a weathered sign that read **The Old Crow Inn** above a swinging door, where a young man exited wearing a canvas rancher's jacket. His eyes focused straight ahead as he approached, and he moved like some wounded soldier determined to follow his orders.

Melissa shouted through the opened window, "That's my Christian! *Christian! I'm here!*"

The young man's expression didn't change, but his pace quickened.

Ben stared at Mr. Christian McKenna and reached for his gun. "A little warm for Junior to be wearing that heavy jacket, don't you think? Your betrothed don't seem 'specially liquored, but something ain't right. That's blood — See? It's on his face. Don't go out just yet."

Old Sam extended his hand to the approaching rancher. "Damn, but we was worried there weren't a soul in this town. Glad I was wrong. One passenger here certainly is happy to see—"

From under his coat, the young man pulled a hand axe, and in one motion he buried its blade in Old Sam's brain. The man's head exploded in blood and he dropped to his knees.

*"What the fuck—?"* Ben went for his gun, but too late.

Tugging the axe handle free, McKenna again brought the blade down, halving the old man's skull to his nose. He hacked at him even after Sam clearly was dead, pulpy spatters of brain tissue spraying the women through the opened window. McKenna turned his attention to the coach door. A strange sound escaped his lips.

Ben's face contorted in confusion. "He's humming something..."

The nun backed away in her seat. "He's going to smash his way in!"

"I don't think so." Raising the gun, Ben steadied his aim.

Melissa managed, *"You —You can't! Ben, please, you—!"*

"No choice!"

The young man's axe swung and the door splintered at its handle. McKenna pulled the door wide, grabbing the shoulder strap of Melissa's dress. He tore the strap free and, steadying the axe, set his aim on his future bride.

*"Fucking bastard!"* The barrel of Ben's gun pressed against McKenna's forehead. He pulled the trigger and blew a hole clear through it, the bullet taking part of the man's scalp where it exited. McKenna's knees buckled, and he went down fast. Melissa tried pushing the door to go to him. Ben pulled her back, holding the sobbing girl in his arms.

"I don't understand any of this! Christian, he — he was going to kill me! He wasn't — *That man wasn't Christian!*"

The nun grabbed Ben's arm. "Where is everyone? There's

no people anywhere. Something terrible is happening here!"

Ben stroked Melissa's hair, and looked into her face.

"You okay?"

"No."

"Listen to me. Whatever happened here could've begun days ago. Folks maybe cleared out, or even worse. Your Mr. McKenna stepped out from that Old Crow place. Maybe some answers are inside that tavern."

"I'd sent a telegraph to him. I told Christian I'd be arriving on today's stage. But I didn't hear anything back. That was five days ago."

Ben checked his Colt's cylinder. "Any of you ladies know how to fire a gun?" The women looked at each other. "Yeah, that's what I thought. Okay, then, Miss Monahan. You're elected."

"Ben, I never even held a—"

"—You aim, you shoot. Squeeze the trigger, don't jerk it. That's all the schooling I can provide." He pulled some bullets from his shirt pocket, placed several in the chamber and handed the others to Melissa. "That's six bullets loaded, more in your hand. No reloadin' 'till you're done, and no warning shots, okay? Door handle is busted now, so anyone suspicious comes this way, don't ask no questions, you shoot to kill."

The nun sneered. "Oh yes. The Peacemaker."

Melissa took the gun. "What will *you* use? Anything could be waiting inside that tavern."

Climbing from the stage, Ben searched as far as he could see. Studying the rear wheel of the coach, he came around to where the two bodies lay. "That wheel's leavin' its axle in another mile or two. We're staying in Trementina, like it or not." He rolled McKenna's body over and searched beneath the rancher's jacket. "Missy, this sap-headed boyfriend of yours didn't seem to have 'nuff sense to carry a gun. I guess that's fortunate for us, all things considered. I don't think walking into the tavern toting old Sam's Winchester would be advisable either." He pulled the rifle from the driver's box and handed it to the nun, and she looked at Ben as if he were a madman.

Ben almost convinced Melissa he *was*. He twisted the dripping hand axe from the dead man's grip. "This will have to do. I want you to be able to protect yourselves with firearms. But no one leaves this wagon, not for anything."

The women watched as Ben headed for the tavern. "Suppose he don't come back," the Bible woman asked. "It looks so dark inside. Can't see a thing."

The nun took the book from her, opened it. Taking on the dour expression of a woman much older, she said, "Psalm 91, ladies. 'Those who go to God Most High for safety will be protected by the Almighty.'"

Melissa mumbled as if speaking to herself, "The Almighty didn't help those two men lying out there in the dirt."

Hiding Christian McKenna's axe beneath his suit jacket, Ben Jamison hesitated at the swinging door entrance to The Old Crow...

*...while on the floor inside the tavern, Hell has come to Trementina. Men, women, and even children lay in foul-smelling heaps along the floor and the balcony, their bodies gone ripe after several days following the town's personal Armageddon. More lay on the tavern's tables in the rear, and some on the staircase leading to the upstairs brothel. Out of sight from curious eyes, the corpses rest hidden in this place, one on top the other. The old public house has become a grotesque monument to a slaughter.*

*When the door to the old tavern swings open, from within the old public house the brief flash of sunlight shows a man standing there.*

*Inside, the Wogslûk stir.*

# CHAPTER TWO

## NIGHTTIME DIVERSIONS, JULY 2015: ZACHARY

### *"Serkers..."*

Straight from the shower, Eden Colson took another look into her son's bedroom before she called it a day. Zachary was in la la land, his cat Rocky at his side, and all was right with the world. The bed bugs would not be biting, at least not for tonight. Those ugly things crawling in the soil were another matter. Joining Greg, Eden sat on their bed.

"Water pressure is on the fritz again, and the shower is practically an ice bucket challenge — a dirty one. I think they're digging tomorrow because the township says if the pipes burst, then we'll be getting around here in gondolas. Water is being turned off tomorrow. No shower, no toilets."

"I'll pee early," Greg said.

"Before 9:00. Anyway, leaking pipes must have brought out the slugs. I saw dozens of them in the garden this morning — fat ones, if they *were* slugs. *Ugh!*"

"Not a conducive topic for bed time, my darling. Zack asleep, you say?"

Eden grinned and dropped her slug story. "Fair enough. Our son is out cold. I think it's okay for the adults to play. So, you up for it?"

Greg smiled. "That's one way to put it."

"I've got something to show you first. I'm not sure what to make of it. Hated to peek, but Zack left his computer on this morning. He's writing again, and I printed this from his Word file. I'm pretty sure he wouldn't want us seeing this." Eden handed a folded page to her husband.

**BOYS HAVE YERKERS, GIRLS DO NOT.**
**GIRLS HAVE SERKERS, AND BOYS DO NOT.**
**YERKERS AND SERKERS,**
**THEY'RE NOT THE SAME,**
**SERKERS AND YERKERS,**
**I WANT TO PLAY!**

Greg untied his wife's robe, allowing it to drop to the floor. "Yerkers and serkers. Not exactly Keats, but the sentiment is there."

"I'm just hoping it's healthy for a thirteen-year-old to notice the differences between himself and the female sex so early. I mean, a few weeks ago he was eleven. That's practically a baby. I saw him watching our neighbor, that Regina Campbell who always sun bathes in that string bikini. I'm sure you've seen her, the village slut."

Greg kissed his wife's cheek. "I'm sure he's noticed Mrs. Campbell. He's online enough to know what women like her are about. He has hormones, you know, and they're just kicking in. Like his old man's hormones right now."

"You know what I mean. Should he be aware of all the intricate details of the female anatomy this early? He hasn't even hit puberty yet."

Greg patted his wife's ass. "I'm still learning about that stuff myself. Look, our son is a straight-A student. I doubt Dr. Phil would worry about Zachary's sexual awakening."

"Dr. Phil would probably ask our son what a he thinks a serker really is. I'd like to believe we're more progressive than that. We never block any of those adult websites like all our friends do. Maybe we should?"

"A preemptive strike?" Greg's smile bypassed mischievous and turned shit-eating. He reached beneath Eden's night gown. "That online stuff wasn't available to me when I was a kid, and yet I still managed to have a good stash of old Hustler

Magazines beneath the mattress. My parents must have known, but they never said a word, and I turned out reasonably normal."

"The jury is still out regarding that, lover. Maybe I should check under our mattress, just to be sure."

"Woman, I'm thinking that as parents, we're way ahead of the curve. Zack seems trustworthy and mature for his age. I think we can allow for some preadolescent curiosity. I'll have a talk with him, okay?" Finding the moist spot between his wife's legs, Greg's hand worked its magic. Under her breath, Eden moaned while Greg looked into her eyes. "And speaking of serkers..."

"Women have 'em, men do not," she whispered.

Zachary didn't like fooling his mom, but some things she didn't need to know. When she looked into his bedroom for the second time (as she always did), he didn't want to worry her. There was little she could do to make sleep come anyway, and now he lay awake in the moonlight. Reaching for Rocky, he rubbed the cat's belly. She rolled over and continued sleeping, whiskers blowing with each breath. Zachary snickered because he had given his black feline a male name, and she would go through life never knowing it. But the image of those bed bugs quickly returned to sabotage his momentary time out. He knew he needed a better diversion or he would remain awake until dawn.

He didn't have to think hard. There was this girl — a woman, really — although Zachary didn't know how old she was. She could have been twenty or thirty; it was hard to tell with older people. But Taffy Licks wasn't really an older person, not like his mom and dad. Taffy was in a category by herself. He had seen some interesting YouTube videos of her expertly performing Miley Cyrus' twerking thing, getting into it a whole lot better than Miley ever managed. Alone in her room, and on her own private website, the girl got down and dirty, and Zachary was hooked. She hadn't been naked in any of her videos, although if he googled her name enough times, he felt sure he would discover videos on the 'adults only' sites in which she was. Picturing Taffy in her bikini briefs would do nicely to fill his thoughts as he lay in bed trying to sleep. Zachary closed his eyes — *and there she was!*

With the bed bugs vanquished, sleep came...

*"Hello Zack," dream-twerking Taffy says in a throaty whisper, and dream Zachary feels her warm breath close to his ear. Up close he sees her front tooth is a little crooked, but somehow this makes her even sexier. "This is just for you, sweetie," and with that, Taffy's exotic dance goes full tilt boogie. Her bumps and grinds are punctuated by snakelike slithers up and down a pole that miraculously appears from nowhere. Taffy's black silk pasties barely cover what Zachary has only imagined during his waking hours.*

*There is music too, but it isn't anything he hasn't heard before. A grin spreads across his face at what he is hearing. The words arouse him even more.*

### *"BOYS HAVE YERKERS, GIRLS DO NOT..."*

*The warmth is coming. He can feel it, whatever it is, and it feels damned good. Another minute or two and maybe...*

*But there's more. Taffy is on her back now, and she is undulating like a cascading wave slowly coming to shore. Every muscle in her body is called into play as she twists and turns, slithering on a pure white shag carpet, and somehow the pasties have disappeared and so has the bra, and now Taffy is naked and more beautiful than Zachary ever imagined.*

*"Do you like this, Zack. Do you? It's all for you, sweetie, all for you..."*

*Dream-Zachary reaches to touch her, just a quick touch of skin so impossibly white, impossibly smooth, especially ...* **down there!** *He has never seen that particular secret part of a woman, not close up and certainly not in the flesh, but he* knows what's supposed to be there. He knows...

But it isn't what Zachary thinks, not at all the way he pictured it. Something is there that looks like a gaping wound and it seems to be opening, growing. Whatever he expected, he didn't expect it to be so very dark and so very wide, and...

Something is crawling from it! No, there are many things there, and they're coming out of the woman, and they're large and dark, like...

**...LIKE BED BUGS!**

No, they're not bugs at all. They're long and slimy worm-like things, and they remind him of those slugs he has seen at the lake, and there are so many of them, little ones and big ones, and they just keep crawling out and crawling out...

"Make them stop! Please, make them stop!" dream-Zachary screams, but Taffy pays no attention. Worse, she's laughing like she's having the time of her life.

"I want to play! You and me, Zack!"

Those filthy things are filling the room while they're crawling all over his chest and his legs. They're covering every inch of Zachary's bare skin, even boring into it. He feels them squirming inside him, and still they're coming out of her, those slug-like creatures, by the hundreds they're slithering out of her...

They won't stop! They won't stop coming!

...the part of her that's open and so dark...

**...They're coming out of Taffy's serker!**

Far below the homes of the tree-lined Diamond Loop cul-de-sac, hidden from other living creatures and deep in the grottos and caves of their underworld, the Wogslûk lurk.

Hidden.

And in the dank emptiness, slithering in the foul stink of a buried world, they wait...

# CHAPTER THREE

## THE OLD CROW INN, 1866: BEN

*"The Devil will have to hold me back..."*

Hiding Christian McKenna's axe beneath his suit jacket, Benjamin Jamison hesitated at the swinging door entrance to The Old Crow...

The tavern's filthy windows allowed no light, and the darkness inside showed nothing of what awaited beyond its door. But the cloying stench emanating from the inn was beyond awful. Once, as a boy traveling the Western expansion route on the Missouri stage with his father, their driver came across a dead wild horse whose remains must have recently been picked apart by vultures or coyotes. The sight of maggots feasting on the rotted creature's rawboned flesh, and the horse's fetid smell proved too much for young Ben. He had gagged, then vomited his breakfast. The reek from that animal had imprinted itself forever in his memory, and the thought of it could bring on nausea.

During this late afternoon in Trementina, the smell drifting from The Old Crow Inn was much worse. Ben recognized that foul stink. This was the smell of death.

He didn't want to enter this place, but he knew he had to. Pulling the hand axe from his jacket he decided to keep it at the ready. He pushed open the tavern's swinging door, standing at the entranceway in the darkness. Only one candle flickered from the ceiling above the bar top in the rear, providing precious little illumination. The other candles and gas lamps must have blown out or been destroyed — most likely, purposely — but the darkness here seemed more than the absence of light. Ben felt a liquid sensation on his skin, that cold sweat that soaked your flesh when you entered a cave. He sensed that something shadowy and alive hid in here. Raising the axe, Ben moved forward not knowing what awaited his next step.

The gaseous smell knotted his stomach, but the lone candle revealed what he had already known, and it was all Ben needed to see. There were human remains everywhere. His eyes adjusted to the grey darkness, and now he saw their murky outlines. The twisted arms and legs in careless piles were unmistakable. Here lay the citizenry of the town of Trementina. The thing to do now was leave quickly and see to the women waiting inside the stage.

He heard something stir, and it was near. The mound of corpses shifted only slightly, like a heap of laundered clothing underneath which a prairie snake had been hiding. A man knows when he's being watched, and Ben had that uneasy feeling now. He had his proof with the reflected glimmer from the stub of candle that was mirrored in the red eyes studying him. Now there seemed many eyes blinking within the old tavern, but they avoided the glimmer of light. Ben could observe only the brief flash of something large and worm-like that crawled from beneath the corpses, causing the loose limbs of the dead to twitch with the movement. Some murky elongated thing curled and reshaped itself on the floor as it wriggled towards him. Closer now, it seemed huge, much too thick to be a prairie Rattler. Another one, smaller but fast, slithered not far behind. The two shadows raised their heads like coiled serpents. All this occurred within seconds. Ben slowly backed away, but he heard a skittering across the floor from behind. He was surrounded.

*"Shit...oh shit..."*

He swung the hand axe. With a liquid squish the blade connected with a substance soft and rubbery, but whatever it was, it suddenly twisted around his neck and held firm. Too slippery for him to grab, it tightened its grip on Ben's throat. He turned to see a large wormy thing approaching him. From behind he felt something sharp gnawing through his scalp, sucking at his skull and lifting him from the floor. Another flash fire of agony filled his brain, but he remained conscious as more of the cold things crawled over him in a slithering ambush. The axe fell from his grip.

One creature crawled into his mouth. No, he was wrong. It was crawling *out* of his mouth, from inside. The thing had bored through his skull. It felt too large, too thick for his mouth. Gagging, Ben heard his own jaw bone crack. Half detached from his face, his chin hung loose.

It was too late to scream.

Inside the coach, the three women sat as motionless as human stage props, beads of sweat glistening their foreheads. In this heat the harnessed horses needed scrubbing; they were snorting and restlessly stomping their feet. The coach shook with the motion.

"It's been an hour," the nun finally said. She had introduced herself to the remaining two passengers as Sister Margelle, mentioning she was traveling to the Sister Blandina Convent in New Mexico to do good works for the poor. This day's events had convinced her that some good works were needed here in Trementina. "It's been too quiet inside that saloon. We'll have to take matters into our own hands if Mr. Jamison has been detained. There may be people in there requiring help."

The old woman snorted, still clutching her Bible. "Detained? No offense, Sister, but I believe *detained* is the wrong word. Two dead men lay just outside this door. Mr. Jamison hasn't come out of that tavern, so he's probably dead too. As the three of us will be, if we remain here."

Melissa shook her head. "No! Ben told us to stay inside the coach, that we shouldn't leave, not for anything. I say we sit tight until he comes back."

Another pig-like snort escaped the old woman. "I don't think you understand, Miss Monahan. Mr. Jamison is *not* coming back. We haven't seen a soul leave that tavern. Something terrible is inside that Old Crow place, and we can't sit here waiting to find out what it is. Sister Margelle, do you agree?"

The nun nodded, but she didn't seem entirely comfortable with her assent. "I suppose this wagon can take us from here. There are other towns maybe fifty or a hundred miles from Trementina. There will be other travelers. Perhaps if that loose wheel holds for just a bit longer, we can find help, see what's going on. One of us can climb to the driver's box and grab hold of those reins. It can't be that difficult to get these horses moving."

Melissa shook her head. "I think we should wait. I have Ben's gun if anything should—"

The old woman set her Bible down on the seat. "You'll blow your own toe off before you shoot anyone with that! All right, then. I'm going into that old inn myself. But the Devil will have to hold me back kicking and screaming before I stay inside for more than a minute! Sister, you and the girl have got the old driver's rifle for company. Pray you don't have to use it." She took Ben's pistol from Melissa. Not allowing the other women to protest, she climbed from the cab. The fruit basket hat she wore looked more ridiculous than ever.

Melissa grabbed the nun's arm. "We can't let that woman go in there alone!" She moved to climb out too, but Sister Margelle stopped her.

"You wait here. I'll go. You keep that rifle handy." Clutching the Bible from the seat, she shouted for the old woman to wait for her. Melissa watched as together the two seemed to ghost-walk towards the tavern door.

As if awaiting their arrival in the fading light, a silhouetted figure appeared at the entrance. Melissa almost shouted to him. She stopped herself, watching as Ben Jamison emerged, slogging toward Sister Margelle and the old woman. Thick gouts of blood bubbled from his mouth and he had no expression, as if his face had folded in on itself like a busted doll's. There seemed something strange about the way he moved so stiffly, so purposefully...

*...like Christian!*

The two women froze where they stood. Melissa heard Sister Margelle holler out something as she raised the Bible high in the air. She couldn't tell if the nun were shouting some prayer or preparing to bring the Lord's book down on Jamison's head. The other woman raised the gun, pointing it at the approaching figure. She shouted something too, and this Melissa heard.

*"Stop right there, Mr. Jamison! Stop, or I'll shoot! I swear, I'll —"*

Melissa's eyes grew wide.

Ben didn't look right.

# CHAPTER FOUR

## MEN AT WORK, JULY 2015:
## REEFE & CO.

*"Darkness underground is a special kind..."*

As Supervisor Fred Reefe had insisted to Eden Colson, his men would be on site at the cul-de-sac at nine o'clock sharp Monday morning, and his company's pneumatic drills and power hammers sent asphalt flying at precisely that time. Reefe was also true to his word about the noise Eden could expect. The ear-splitting reverberations from the workers' power equipment fell significantly short of a symphony orchestra.

Reefe's team of six broke ground at the entranceway to the Loop. That meant no vehicles would be getting through to the homes along the cul-de-sac for at least three days. Commuting fathers and soccer moms would have to park their BMW's and family sedans in one of the other nearby loops of the Glenn Echoes developments. It would be a pain in the ass, of course, but the payoff would be shower heads that provided Diamond Loop residents with a lot more than the murky cold water dribbles they had been enduring.

Trained in the art of domestic etiquette, Eden greeted Reefe at the hole his men were drilling into the entranceway. The water in her unit had been turned off, as she had been informed, but the workers were welcome to iced coffee she had made earlier, she told him. She had already filled several pitchers for this occasion, plus she had bought some fancy Danish the men could enjoy inside her kitchen during their breaks. ("We're not talking Dunkin' Donuts here, Mr. Reefe," she had added with a smile that might have pissed off Greg, had he seen it.) The foreman responded that his crew would certainly take her up on her offer, and during their first day on the job, they did just that. Although filthy from their time below ground, and despite the occasional salty words (spoken not fully out of Eden's hearing range), Reefe's team otherwise had the polite and self-conscious manner of boys straight out of boarding school. The youngest worker looked to be in his early twenties. Introducing himself as Jessie, he must have said "Thank you, ma'am" a dozen times. Eden secretly thought that the entire crew, once cleaned up, could have come from central casting. Fred Reefe, although older, was no exception.

The builders' blueprints in hand, Reefe knew just where the Loop's water mains were located, but he didn't know what the problem with them was. Copper pipes were good to go for close to fifty years and they generally didn't leak, but sometimes their connections weren't as tight as they should be. A worst-case scenario was having to install new copper lines to tighten the whole network below. To know for sure, his excavation team would have some exploration to do beneath the Loop's entranceway. Fred Reefe hoped Jessie, the new guy, didn't mind crawling a little deeper than the job called for. Just because water pipes should be buried at a particular depth was no guarantee that Diamond Loop's construction people buried them at that depth. If those builders happened also to be cost-cutting idiots, they could have run those pipes close enough to gas lines to make the entire cul-de-sac go *ka-blooey*, turning manhole covers for five miles into metal Frisbees. Things like that didn't happen often, but they *did* happen.

By late Tuesday afternoon, Fred Reefe and his crew had excavated enough sludge to bring in the heavy artillery, a huge front loader the guys called Big Mama that would relocate a sizable portion of the dirt, creating small mountains of mud along the street leading to Diamond Loop proper. The tractor-like monstrosity dug out heaps of soil that had buried the miles of water pipes connected to the network of smaller ones leading beneath the Loop. The loader wasn't as noisy as the drills, but it was a lot more efficient at making a smaller hole into a chasm large enough to drive a good-sized truck through, which was exactly what the front-end loader was. The weak spots in Diamond Loop's water mains would not be hiding very long from Big Mama.

The uprights, extensive wooden supports, had been added to the sides of the excavation to make sure no man going into it would be climbing into his own grave.

"You feeling adventurous, Mr. Moss?" Reefe asked Jessie. "We've got one big hole here needs some investigation. Time to earn your stripes, young man!"

"Is that tour of duty in Afghanistan still in your blood, Fred?" Jessie asked, mock-saluting the former soldier. He looked to the other men. "What the hell. I know what a leaking pipe looks like." Straightening his hard hat, he took the high-powered flashlight from his utility belt and climbed upon the plank of the suspension rigging as two of the workers grabbed hold of the pulley that lowered him down. "I'll shout when I see something."

Jarmal Besser, who could pass for a clone of a young Denzel Washington, hollered into the hole, "Hey, Moss Man! It'll be easier if you pretend there's beer and pussy waiting down there for you!" That got a good laugh from the guys as Jessie disappeared into the excavation.

The first few moments inside a deep trench's dark world often sent icy fingers up Jessie Moss' spine. He was new at this, but he was getting better. Still, Fred Reefe's crew never missed an opportunity to go wise-assed on him about his inexperience, and even Reefe rode him on his boyish manner to the point Jessie knew he had to prove himself to these guys. One thing he knew about this pit: down here he would find no beer or pussy. He expected the antsy feeling would pass; he had been in ditches before, but this was one bastard of a hole. It seemed even deeper than Big Mama had dug, but that, of course was impossible. Other guys had been beneath the Loop, they had laid these pipes. This place was not unchartered territory. Jessie kept telling himself that as he climbed off the plank.

"Laying pipe," he mumbled to no one, and smiled. "Wouldn't mind doing a little of that with you, Mrs. Colson, and thank you very much, ma'am, for your hospitality." Jessie doubted his Julie would appreciate that thought having crossed his mind, but Eden Colson *was* one certified piece of ass.

Spotting the glint of copper above, he followed it with his flashlight. There were no leaks that he could see, but a whole network of pipe was down here to check out. Pulling a small hammer from his utility belt, he tapped the metal. Although the Loop's water had been turned off, a trained ear could sometimes detect when water was somewhere it wasn't supposed to be. More than likely he would find a leak near a bend, where one pipe had been joined to another. That meant he could be difficult to detect if the others were watching from above, but those guys would be coming down soon enough. Reefe preferred one worker at a time initially, so the suspension plank could be pulled back quickly, if necessary. The air got thin in a deep hole, and if a gas line had been accidentally disturbed...

Jessie didn't want to think about that, and he continued following the thick beam of his flashlight along the copper tube. He spotted a lump in the metal the size of a football, unusual because these mains were particularly strong to carry a massive amount of rushing water from the nearby storage tanks. The load of pressure required to supply several homes could have contorted older metal, but these pipes were new. Something from the tube's interior had created the bulge in the thick copper, but Jessie had no idea what it was. He touched the metal, first lightly with his fingertips, then he placed his palm flat against it. He felt the cylinder vibrate — no, it seemed more like the thump of something solid. The water had been turned off from the service line for Diamond Loop. There seemed no reason for running water to be traveling through the mains. Unless, of course, it was something else.

*"What the...?"*

A thick wad of mud from the pipe struck the back of his neck. Before Jessie could look above, something dark and wet fell on him. An elongated dripping hunk of black flesh hung over his forehead, but something snakelike also wriggled at his feet. He saw the pair of dark eyes for only a moment before another one — *whatever it was* — slithered up the back of his neck and chewed into his hard hat, tugging it from his head.

*"...fuck!"*

His hat flew off, the metal clanging against the water main. Turning its attention to Jessie's bare head, one of the wormy things sucked at his scalp like an insatiable leech. It felt heavy, thicker than a baseball bat and twice as long — too big for anything that should be lurking in this place. He tried aiming the flashlight at it, but the thing kept shifting away from the high powered beam. Flailing his arms he grabbed hold of any part he could, but the dark thing was too slippery. It eluded his grasp as if fish hooks held it fast to his head. He felt his scalp open.

A whispered sound reverberated inside his head. It made no sense, but he heard it repeat.

*"...Yoob...Die-em...Min...Yoob...Die-em...Yoob...Min... Yoob...Die-em...!"*

Something smaller slipped through his hair and squirmed through the laceration. Jessie felt the numbing sensation of the insides of his skull being siphoned out.

*That was impossible! He would have been a dead man!*

The flashlight dropped, and so did Jessie. He tore at the large thing still clinging to his scalp, finally managing to pull it free. It squirmed from his hand and bored through the underground mud like some great misshapen sand crab. But something remained squirming inside his head.

The flashlight's high beam still shone. Jessie pulled it from the dirt, aimed it all around. The hole's mud floor had filled with more slithering creatures of all sizes, maybe hundreds of them. They looked like water snakes from some prehistoric era, but Jessie knew these black things were not snakes. The light sent them skittering away. Managing to hoist himself back on the suspension plank, Jessie found enough strength to shout.

*"Pull me up! Pull me up!!*

Ten minutes later Jessie Moss hadn't stopped shaking. Fred Reefe was no doctor and not about to risk a law suit against the company. But inside the supply trailer he discovered the small medical kit's bottle of peroxide had gone practically dry, the kit painfully ill-equipped of any antiseptic cream or strips. The trailer had some running water from its own tank, and maybe a large butterfly bandage would do for now until the Glenn Echoes General ambulance arrived. Reefe cleaned Jessie's wound as best he could, applied the bandage to his scalp, and grabbed his cell to make the necessary call to Glenn Echoes General.

"You say something bit you? Like, a rat? Is that what I should tell them?"

"Don't know. Something small, dark. Really sharp teeth." The look on his supervisor's face caused Jessie to change his tone. "Fred, I just got spooked, is all. I'm feeling better now. It could have been a fucking bug that made me bump my head, for all I know. Really, let me get back to work. You don't have to make that call, okay?" He managed to quell his shaking to demonstrate his quick recovery.

Reefe wasn't buying it. "Not okay. You're hurt."

"Don't ask me to pussy out on my first day in the hole, Fred. Christ, those guys rib me enough."

Reefe held off on making the call to the hospital. He thought for a moment and dialed Eden Colson's number from his list of Diamond Loop residents, asked if maybe the woman had anything antiseptic or some kind of ointment or peroxide in the house. She countered that anything with alcohol wasn't always the best way to go because of the possibility of skin irritation, and that as a kid she used to do some work in a hospital. She seemed to know something about First Aid and offered to take a look at Moss. Reefe thanked her and made another inspection of Jessie's scalp. His bandage had absorbed the bleeding, but Reefe knew from his combat experience that head wounds could be tricky.

"I'm not really sure you're a hundred percent, Jessie, but all right. Are you okay to go over to 613 on the Loop?"

Jessie nodded, grinned. His eyes suggested he might certainly be interested in laying a different kind of pipe today. "Eden Colson. A fine woman, oh yes!"

Reefe smiled that the young man's hormones seemed to be in working order. "Mrs. Colson has some medical experience, she said. And one more thing — You're not pussying out on me, okay? I'll be over there in a few minutes, and if that wound looks worse, you'll be hearing some sirens soon. Agreed?"

Jessie nodded, and before Reefe might change his mind he headed out of the trailer. He chose not to tell Fred Reefe that he was feeling way off his game.

### 3:37 p.m.

Eden Colson took a moment to sit with her copy of Home & Garden. She craved a cup of coffee, but still no water came from the spigot, and she had guzzled the last of her bottled supply. She called from the kitchen to her son upstairs, "Off the computer, Zacker! I need you to bike to the Colonel's for a bucket of wings. Mom is too pooped to make dinner!" This was the truth. Reefe's men had been through her kitchen in various shifts, usually two at a time, and even during the longer lulls Eden felt the need to be on call as Diamond Loop's answer to Martha Stewart.

After his mother's several attempts to separate him from the Internet, Zachary came down. "Mac and Cheese too?" he asked.

"But of course. A real mess o' chicken and all the trimmings for Dad also, okay? We're way overdue for our heart attacks." She handed her son some bills, patting his ass as he exited through the screen door. The boy needed a little fresh air anyway, she told herself. Staring at the crumbs remaining inside the Danish boxes, she carried the emptied coffee carafes from the sink to the dish washer. Fred Reefe's workers must have downed enough iced coffee to fill her upstairs tub. She was hoping to do just that with a blessedly quicker stream of clean hot water right after the Colonel's chicken dinner with her family.

From the screen door came a weak "Mrs. Colson...?"

The young worker appeared for his third visit today, the cute one named Jessie, who reminded Eden of the "Happy Days" Ron Howard back when baby-faced Ron had hair.

"I'm sorry, Starbucks is closed for today, Jessie. I've run out of—" She stopped herself. The man looked sickly pale, and blood had started to seep through the butterfly bandage on his scalp. "My God, what happened to you? Mr. Reefe said you were hurt, but—" The words just slipped out, and Eden thought maybe this was what a construction worker looked like at the end of a hard day. Digging through dirt for eight hours could turn any man into a human mud puddle, but the blood dribbling from Jessie's scalp told Eden this had not been a typical day for him. He looked like one of those old photographs of a young soldier trudging home from the Civil War.

"A little accident, is all. Mr. Reefe wanted to call an ambulance, but I told him I'm okay, so he wanted me to come here to see if you might take a look, but — well, it looks worse than it is, really." He ran his fingers through his hair. "It's bleeding again, isn't it?"

His words sounded slurred, and Eden didn't think Jessie had made a very good judgment call not to beat a path for Glenn Echoes General.

"Nurse Eden will see what she can do. But I'm going to call Glenn Echoes right after, okay? Comprendé? Capisce?" She led the young worker to the upstairs bathroom, pulled out a wash cloth. Holding it under the sink for some warm water, she remembered the valves remained shut off. She made a goofy face.

"Sorry. Duh."

In the medicine cabinet, she found some antiseptic ointment and some gauze, and grabbed a handful of cotton balls. "This will sting a bit, and it isn't the best remedy because it can burn, but it'll have to do. Prepare to see some stars." She removed the butterfly bandage slowly. The blood from the wound had already coagulated, and Reefe's dressing adhered to Moss' thick hair like a sticky adhesive. She tamped his scalp expecting Jessie to flinch, but the young man didn't respond at all. Parting his hair with her fingers, Eden studied the laceration closer. The blood had slowed, but it hadn't stopped. "You know, this looks serious to me. It's small and that's why the blood is coming and going, but it appears deep. You're probably going to need a few stitches to close this baby." She cleaned the wound, pulling out some gauze and replacing Reefe's bloody bandage with a pair of super-sized Band-Aid pads to finish up. "I told Fred Reefe I worked in a hospital, but really all I was, was — well, I used to be a candy striper in high school. Men's boo-boos were my specialty, but I'm not really a nurse in any legal sense of the word." She expected another warm *'Thank you, ma'am,'* but Jessie said nothing. "You guys wear hard hats down there, don't you? How did this happen?"

Jessie seemed to fade out. "I saw things crawling inside that hole, Mrs. Colson, black things and slimy, like snakes. I told Fred I got bit, but he probably thinks I bumped my head like some dumb-ass rookie. Doesn't matter." He waited a beat and frowned like a kid spinning an incredible lie. His eyes beaded on Eden. "You don't believe me either, do you? Might as well say I spotted a dozen Iraqi terrorists in that hole, right?"

Okay, Jessie was young, new at the job, and probably something startled him alone in that pit. Eden didn't want to make it worse.

*(Oh, yes, I heard monsters are in town. Big ones wearing fezzes. Must be a convention.)*

"I believe anyone can get the heebee-jeebies doing what

**39**

you guys do. There are rats underground, probably all sorts of unpleasant creatures crawling from the sewers. Listen, Jessie, you're very pale. I think I should get you to the hospital."

"Thank you, ma'am." *(...and there it was!)* "...but no..."

Jessie's words slurred as if he had been on a serious bender. His head rolled, and Eden feared he might pass out any second.

"Jessie, have you been drinking?" She regretted asking this the moment she said it. Drinking on the job did not seem this young man's style, and Fred Reefe would have fired him on the spot.

"I'm sud'ly not feeling very good, Mizz... Colson. Dizzy..." He seemed some pathetic child telling his teacher his tummy hurt.

Eden's maternal instinct kicked in. "I'm going to drive you to Glenn Echoes General right now."

Jessie looked Eden up and down, focusing on her breasts — not like Ron Howard at all. Seeming to come out of one funk, he had gone into a new one. The change was not good.

"Nothin' from nothin' leaves nothin'. You ever hear that song?"

"What?"

"This song. Last hour or so, I can't get it out of my head." He hummed the tune as if this made perfect sense.

"Jessie, are you all ri-?"

"You are one fine piece of ass, Mizz Colson, you know that? Really great tits too. The best!"

The comment threw her. She managed a twitching half smile.

"Okay..."

"I knew the moment I saw you — I knew what I wanted to do with you." He locked the bathroom door, again checked out Eden's breasts. "The best. I really mean it."

The realization hit her, the idiotic thing she had done inviting into her home a complete stranger, no matter how boyish and innocent the guy seemed. Everything she had learned about a woman's vulnerability while in the house alone she had foolishly disregarded, and now here she was face to face with —

*...with what?*

"Jessie, listen to me..."

The kid — *and what was he, maybe twenty-three?* — clearly had lost his wiring. Eden had no time to process the moment before he turned to her, twisting her arm until she slid to the floor. He proved stronger than he looked, covering her mouth with one muddy hand. He wasn't gentle about it.

*"Mmmmmphhh!!!"*

"Really great tits, ma'am. I mean that." He reached for the zipper of her shorts. Eden shut her eyes. She tried to think, but only one thought came. The polite Jessie Moss was going to kill her right here on the bathroom floor, probably adding a sincere "Thank you, ma'am" after doing it.

*"Mmmmmmmphhhhh!!!"*

The back doorbell rang.

"Mrs. Colson? Are you in there?"

Eden recognized Fred Reefe's voice. Maybe the cavalry had arrived, but Jessie's eyes indicated that one sound from her would earn her a snapped neck, or maybe a sudden dunking in the toilet bowl until her lights shorted out. Maybe he would simply beat her to death with bare fists.

"Mrs. Colson, I thought I heard voices. Is Jessie Moss with you? I'm coming in, okay?"

Jessie gave Eden a *you'd-better-not-say-a-fucking-word* look. He left her sprawled on the cold tiles while searching through the bathroom's medicine cabinet, tossing pill bottles and shaving apparatus in the air like a mad man. Pulling out Eden's long nail file, he ran his thumb over the thin blade to determine its sharpness. It wasn't a weapon, but the metal blade could do serious damage. Holding it high like a butcher's knife, he made chopping motions with it.

Eden's mind raced. If she could get the cellular from her pocket without his seeing her, just punch 911...

*...but if he did see, maybe he would slice her neck to bloody ribbons.*

Securing the file in the short sleeve of his work shirt, Jessie turned ballsy. "We're in the bathroom, Fred! Me and the lovely Mrs. Colson! Tell Jarmal I found some pussy. Did you bring beer?" He was sweating badly, and his face had gone white. Blood leaked through the new dressing on his scalp, creating an elongated bloody Rorschach on his forehead. The kid looked about ten minutes to death.

Fred Reefe's footsteps stopped just outside the bathroom door. He knocked once. Then again, harder. "Are you all right in there?"

Jessie put his finger to his lips, warning Eden not to make a sound. She didn't take the advice. "You're not well, Jessie. That wound in your head, I think it —" (*No! Don't go there!* her inner voice told her.) "You don't want to do this thing you're thinking about doing."

"Mr. Reefe thinks I'm just a kid. So do you. Well, I'm a man, a fucking man!" He shouted at the door, "'Nothin' from nothin' leaves nothin',' Fred!"

His eyes, large and black, seemed vacant. Something maniacal had kicked in, and Jessie's former rules of behavior no longer applied. The thin bladed nail file that protruded from his shirt sleeve clearly was reserved for Fred Reefe's throat. Eden couldn't let that happen.

*Fred! Don't come in!*

Jessie turned to her. "This thing you don't want me to think about doing, Mizz Colson? Well, see, I'm thinking I really want to see you naked!" Slowly, forcing calm, he unlocked the bathroom door wearing one huge shit eating grin. "Hello, Fred..."

**4:01 p.m.**

It wasn't a hard bike ride, twenty minutes along tree-lined Apple Grove Way to the strip malls along Glenn Echoes Boulevard, maybe fifteen if Zachary really pumped it. The promise of the Colonel's wings with barbecue sauce proved a good incentive. The ride also gave him a chance to learn some of the goings-on around the Diamond Loop area. Maybe one of these days he would bike to the baseball field near the middle school, see where the kids his age hung out. He was getting a little bored, having made no friends in the new neighborhood. Rocky was a good companion, but she didn't quite cut it when Zachary felt like taking in a ball game or catching up on what new Hunger Game Katniss Everdeen was up to.

*...and wouldn't it be awesome to prove his mettle to all the kids in Glenn Echoes, in true Mockingjay style?* Zachary would have joined Katniss' rebellion with no hesitation, gladly risking his young ass so the bow-and-arrow wielding girl/woman could restore unity to the Capital, or whatever vague cause she was fighting for. He loved that Katniss character — but mostly he loved the way Jennifer Lawrence filled out her jump suit. Lately he seemed to be loving that sort of thing a whole lot more.

The Colonel's fast food place didn't look like it was going to be particularly fast. It was coming up on the dinner hour, and the line to the counter was long. What was it about fried chicken that turned practically the entire town ravenous at this hour? Zachary decided it was a stupid question. Maybe so much time on the computer had fried *his* brain, and maybe his Mom was right. He needed to get out more.

Some kind of ruckus was happening at one of the tables in the restaurant's rear section, enough for several in line to turn and check it out. Three older boys, probably high school kids, were harassing some girl who was seated alone. The boys blocked Zachary's view of her, and he couldn't hear exactly what they were saying, but their tone wasn't flattering. He couldn't hear the girl's words either, but she clearly wanted these boys to flake off. In typical *this-is-none-of-my-business* fashion, not one person inside Colonel Sanders' eatery made a move to intervene. Zachary placed his order, gave his name, and stepped out of line while the kid working the fryer did his thing. He took the moment to move closer to the girl's table.

**43**

Her face didn't register at first. She was pretty, dark haired, and very fair skinned, with a slightly crooked front tooth. Zachary had seen her before, but he couldn't place her. He knew her...

*"Damn...!"* he muttered under his breath. The recognition hit him like a thunderbolt. This was the girl/woman who appeared often on his laptop's screen, about whose gyrations and twerks he had spent hours watching and fantasizing, and whose appearance with a cast of crawling slugs also had inspired one mother of a nightmare. Here inside this Glenn Echoes franchise sat Taffy Licks in the flesh! What were the odds? He had to hear what these kids were saying to her; more important, he had to see Taffy up close.

The kid from behind the counter shouted "Zack, your order is ready!" He postponed his eavesdropping to pick up the large bucket of chicken wings, but there was no way he was about to leave. Standing close to Taffy's table, he pretended to count his change.

From Taffy, "Come on guys, just let me eat in peace, okay? You had your fun..."

A tall pimply kid wasn't taking the hint. "Just show a little tit. No one here will see if you flash one really fast. Come on, you do it online for the whole fucking world!"

From the fat kid standing next to him, "A little tit? No, man. She got BIG tits! I've seen 'em!"

And from a third, a kid with a huge nose, the ugliest of the trio, "Let's see how you eat those fries. I bet you stick one at a time in your mouth and just suck it in whole, right?"

Taffy tried ignoring them and kept eating, but it wasn't working.

Pimpled guy asked, "Does online whoring pay well?"

Fat kid: "Is Taffy your real name?"

Ugly Big Nose: "How much to suck my cock on YouTube?"

The three wouldn't quit, and they wouldn't leave her alone. Others inside the restaurant saw what was going on, but no one seemed about to step up to the plate. The image of Katniss Everdeen appeared in Zachary's brain, her bow held

**44**

straight and taut, her arrow with the red feather *(the exploding arrow!)* aimed directly at Big Nose. Zachary carried no bow and arrow, but he did have a bucket of the Colonel's chicken. He pulled off the lid and tapped the ugly kid on the shoulder. "Excuse me," he said, and when Big Nose turned, Zachary dumped the entire bucket of chicken wings on his head.

*"Who the fuck are you?"* The ugly kid shook the mess of chicken from his scalp like a big stupid dog shaking water from its fur. His two pals laughed. These other pricks must have been great friends. Zachary had no idea where his courage came from, but he was glad his sudden ballsiness had decided to show up now.

"Leave her alone, you shitheel! You're lucky I don't have more chicken for the rest of you!"

Taffy's hand went to her mouth. She seemed too startled to say anything. Zachary savored his Katniss moment with the full understanding it could be his last.

Fat boy claimed one chicken wing directly from his buddy's greasy scalp. "Five-second rule," he said and chomped into it.

Pimpled guy still was laughing. "Earl, you would eat food if you dropped it in the shitter."

"Your mother lives in a shitter, Nelson," was Fat Earl's clever rejoinder.

Before things got any uglier, the restaurant's manager stormed over, clearly pissed. This dispute would have to be taken somewhere else, he told them. He was built like a sumo wrestler and not about to take any crap from young assholes. The big nosed kid's humiliation proved a good inhibitor to potential violence rained down on Zachary's head. Grumbling their idiot protests to each other, the trio left, and the sumo manager turned his attention to the boy holding an empty bucket.

"You too, champ. This establishment is a family place and I don't want to see you in here anymore." He called for one of the servers at the counter to grab a mop and clean up the mess.

Finding her voice, the girl intervened. "Hey! This boy was

just trying to help. Those three goons were bothering me, and he was the only one in this whole damned restaurant who stepped up."

*This boy.* Zachary wasn't happy with the description. But Sumo man softened, not an entirely unexpected reaction since the request came from one beautiful young woman. He pretended to think it over, then said to Zachary, "Fine. Just no more trouble, okay DeNiro?" Pointing to a spot on the floor that the mop-up kid missed, he walked off. Zachary stood quietly, feeling uncomfortable.

The girl pointed to the seat facing her. "Hey, sit for a bit, okay? I want to know who my hero is. You're a little young to be taking on the big boys, aren't you? What's your name?"

Zachary's mouth went dry, but he sat. "I'm Zack Colson, and I'm thirteen." Putting it in those words felt really stupid, the kind of statement a child would make on Santa's lap. He didn't say anything about how he knew Taffy Licks. He didn't have to.

"Well, Zack Colson, I'm Tiffany Leone, and I'm twenty-three." She giggled at her own mimicry of his introduction. "...and I'm very grateful you were here to help thin the herd of morons. But you're going to need another bucket of the Colonel's finest."

"One of those boys called you Taffy."

The girl blushed and turned her attention to her chicken wing. "Well, see, that's a long story, Zack."

He figured she didn't want to pursue the subject. The truth was, she didn't look a whole lot like the girl named Taffy he had seen online. More student than seductress, this girl wore much less make-up and her hair was wrapped in a kind of pony tail, not cascading down her shoulders. She looked a little like one of those '60's hippie girls, but cleaner. He had just met her, but he knew he liked Tiffany a lot more than he liked Taffy.

Zachary watched the kid still mopping the floor. "I don't think this is what my mom meant when she asked for a mess of chicken." He looked inside the bucket. "I managed to spill out three orders of Mac and Cheese too."

That earned a giggle. Taffy/Tiffany reached into her pocket, pulled out a handful of singles. "Here. I do a little film work on the side to pay for my tuition. Nothing I'm ashamed of, but a bit risky with jerks who recognize me. I'm hoping to maybe get into investigative photo reporting, something like that."

"Like Lois Lane."

"Yeah. Like Lois Lane. Except I won't need Superman to rescue my ass all the time."

The girl stuffed the money into his hand. Zachary mumbled, "Okay. Thanks."

"I go to Glenn Echoes State for summer courses — film major, Journalistic studies, lights-camera-action, all that stuff. It can get expensive, and a girl has to pay her bills, you know?"

"Uh huh." Zachary knew.

"I guess journalism is just in my blood. When I went to Roosevelt High in Wellington I was mentored by Taryn E. Friedman, that sex bomb Channel 6 reporter that covered some crazy story about these local bird attacks back in 2000. A little before your time, I guess. Crows, like hundreds of them, went after people at the mall in Wellington and in the park there. No one could figure out why. Taryn quit the story. She didn't give a reason. Told me the whole thing freaked her out."

"Nature — it's weird, sometimes," Zachary said. "But I guess things happen for a reason, even the crazy stuff."

"Well, me, I'd never quit a story that juicy. So, are you from around here? I'm guessing you go to Glenn Echoes Middle? I used to go there myself — had tons of friends back then, but I was a movie geek, not much of a joiner. I live just off the campus now."

"My parents just moved to Diamond Loop. I'll be going to Glenn Echoes in September, but I haven't really made any new friends yet."

She touched Zachary's hand. "Well, you made a new one today, Boy Wonder. Come on, let's get you another bucket of dead chickens."

Ten minutes later he and Tiffany walked outside together. Zachary looked around to make sure none of the three older boys lurked near. It seemed they were gone.

So was his bike.

**4:02 p.m.**

Eden could only watch while Jessie Moss ranted. Fred Reefe had to know something was very wrong. He would be coming in even if he had to break down the bathroom door, and Eden knew when he entered, Jessie intended to sink the thin blade into the man's throat. Then he would turn his attention to her, rape her and probably kill her.

*Or maybe he would kill her first, and then...*

*(Shit...oh, shit...)*

*"Fred! Don't come in!"*

Moss stood behind the locked door while Eden lay on the cold tile. Her lips formed the words, *"Jessie, please..."* but no sound escaped.

Slowly, forcing calm, Jessie Moss unlocked the door. "Hello, Fred. Taking off early, are you?"

"Jessie, is everything all—-?" He spotted Eden on the floor shaking her head, silently warning him not to enter. One look at Moss must have told him that seemed good advice. "Jessie, what's happening here?"

Moss pondered the question. "Well, see... it's what's *about* to happen, Fred... see..." He reached for the nail file in his shirt's sleeve, held the blade straight out like a weapon. But his hand shook and he looked confused, suddenly uncertain what had brought him to this madman moment. He shut down as if an electric cord had been yanked from its socket. "I'm — I'm really sorry about this, Mr. Reefe." He studied the file, seeming to question how it got into his hand.

"Jessie, are you all—?"

He turned to Eden.

"Sorry, ma'am."

...and then he slashed the metal file across his own neck. He gurgled on the blood filling his mouth, founts of it spattering in thick lawn sprinkler spurts and pooling on the white tiles. Jessie's legs buckled and he went down, his face hitting the floor hard.

Reefe crouched quickly, turning Moss on his back and pinching fingers against the laceration. "Call 911!" he told Eden. "Jessie, can you hear me? Listen to me!" He got no response. "Just stay awake, Jessie. Don't you fucking let go!"

Eden placed the call on her cell and crouched alongside Reefe. She felt for a pulse. "He's still alive. Fred — Jessie, he — I don't know what happened. He just seemed to lose it, started talking crazy. He said he wanted to —" No, it was better to keep Moss' intentions to herself.

*"Unnnghh..."*

Reefe turned to Eden. "How about you? Are you all right?"

"He didn't hurt me. I'm okay." She put her ear to Jessie's heart. "He's still with us, but his beats are weak. Don't let him lose consciousness. If you can keep him from losing any more blood—"

Reefe's fingers still pinched the wound. "Afghanistan. Four years. You learn this shit." He lightly slapped Jessie's cheek. "Goddamn it, Moss, stay with us!"

The ambulance from Glenn Echoes General arrived minutes later than it should have; the large excavation at the entranceway had blocked its passage into the Loop. The two orderlies weren't pleased being inconvenienced with time so precious. They got Jessie on a stretcher, one of them maintaining the pressure on his neck. Explanations were given, but neither orderly asked any questions concerning what had caused the young man to do what he did; they asked enough to assess the damage, as if carrying out some kid who had sliced open his own throat happened every day. Eden figured the tough questions would come later when the police arrived, as she expected they would. She wasn't looking forward to that, having no idea what answers she could offer that would make any sense. The ambulance screamed from Diamond Loop, leaving her and Fred Reefe looking at each other without saying a word.

**5:11 p.m.**

In the kitchen, Reefe asked her again, "You're sure you're okay?"

"I'm shaken, but I'm okay. If you hadn't come —"

Eden found comfort with the return to some degree of normalcy, as forced as it felt. Any mundane activity beat having her name (and probably some awful photo) showing up on the evening news as some everyday housewife murdered in her own home. At the sink, Reefe scrubbed his hands and washed the caked mud (or maybe it was Jessie Moss' blood) from his face. There was something soothing watching him perform this routine.

Drying his hands, he turned to Eden. She blushed because he must have seen she was watching him. "Good thing we turned the water back on. But I'll have a hell of a time explaining any of this to my wife. My clothes look like I've been to a slaughter."

Eden touched his arm. "Don't go. Not yet, okay?" She hurried upstairs and returned with one of Greg's old golf shirts. "Can't let you leave looking like you've been working the guillotine. You're about the same size as my husband. I can wash your shirt for you."

"Thanks, but I should be getting home."

He slipped out of his work shirt. Eden promptly looked into her coffee cup as he did this, but she took full measure of how Greg's shirt looked on him. Fred Reefe cleaned up nicely. She owed this man big time, and she figured it wouldn't be inappropriate if she took the shot. "Will you stay and have some coffee? Just for a few minutes? I'd feel better with some company right now, until my son gets back. It's been a rough day."

"For both of us," he said. They sat at the small dinette table, saying nothing. Reaching into the pocket of his blood-soaked shirt on the floor, Reefe pulled out a Marlboro pack, asked "All right with you?"

She nodded. "You know, those things can kill you."

"Among other things."

They smiled at each other again and stared into their respective coffee cups. If Reefe saw the elephant in the room, he chose to ignore it, although the damned pachyderm was breathing heavily down Eden's neck. She was attracted to this man, plain and simple. But another matter was also on her mind. "Jessie told me he saw something in the excavation with him. Something alive — he didn't know what."

"Yeah, he told me he thought something bit him. I know he bumped his head because we found his hard hat with this huge dent. Banging your head on a pipe in the dark can frazzle your nerves. It happens. He'd had some experience with digs before I hired him, but it still gets creepy the first few times you're down there. Maybe the first hundred, because you never know what you're going to dig up. Darkness underground is a special kind, so even a spider crawling down your shirt can set off the ol' trypophobia big time."

"Who?"

"It's a fear of the dark, especially a fear of deep holes. I've read up on it. Some people won't ride subways because of it, or go through tunnels. You do this job long enough, you see jitters kick in with all kinds of guys, especially if something traumatic happens. Same thing can spook an otherwise sane kid when he hits the battlefield and discovers that war close-up isn't some John Wayne movie. His brain gets trip-wired once he sees his pal's head explode. It can happen any time, and it can happen fast. I've seen it."

"Well and good, Fred, but Jessie's head wound didn't look like a bump to me. Something sharp tore into that man's scalp. That would've scared the piss out of anyone."

Reefe dropped the Marlboro stub into his coffee, swished

it. "Jagged rocks, a pipe's torn metal, debris — there's sharp stuff in a hole. Worst case is rats that run along those water pipes. I've seen big ones, and underground a rat's shadow can look the size of a Labrador. Rodent bites aren't common, but they happen. A man gets scared, his head can play tricks. He'll swear he sees vampire bats down there, or whatever mud monster his brain conjures up. That could explain Jessie's irrational behavior. Maybe. Maybe not." Reefe averted Eden's eyes while he spoke. Maybe the man doubted his own explanation. Fred Reefe didn't seem the type to buy into mud soaked creatures of the dark. There was one way to find out.

Eden spilled out his coffee cup, filled another. "Since we're on the subject, I'll share a trick *my* head has been playing. The other day I was digging in my garden, and about a hundred slugs crawled from the dirt. Big suckers, too. At least, I think they were slugs. I guess there were really only a few because I covered them up fast — but they had these hook-like things in their mouths, and they were ugly enough to be slugs. Would your excavating nearby bring them out like that?"

"Slugs? I doubt it. Maggots have the hooks, not slugs. Slugs are usually found around water anyway. Salt water, fresh water, underground wells. Maybe, if one of the mains was leaking, but there wouldn't be many. We see our share of maggots depending on where we're digging and what kind of junk or dead rodent is underground, but slugs not so much. I hung some lights in the hole today after Jessie's accident, but nobody noticed anything like he told us, not from the surface, anyway. I wouldn't let my crew back into the excavation. What Jessie saw could've been anything. It's what I said, Mrs. Colson. In this line of work, you never know what you're going to dig up."

"Call me Eden, okay? And let's change the subject."

Following an awkward pause, Reefe's eyes went to the screen door. He seemed relieved to see the boy there. "We have some company. I wouldn't say anything to your son about today's adventure. Not yet."

Eden managed to force a composed smile for Zachary. He was carrying a bucket of chicken wings; alongside him stood a very attractive older girl. Fred Reefe grinned again, and she could read the man's thoughts. This girl accompanying her son would have easily opened the eyes of any thirteen-year-old male, especially one who recently had experienced the vague stirrings of the male adolescent horn-dog gene.

"Hey, Mom. This is Tiffany. She rode me home on her bike."

Eden nodded perfunctorily and turned her attention back to her son. "What about your own bike?"

"Long story, Mom. I think it was stolen."

Reefe kept his voice low. "Today's not showing much promise of getting better, is it?"

Eden made an angry-mom face. "Zachary, that bike was brand new! And you came all the way back on this girl's bicycle? You know how dangerous that is with the traffic?"

Tiffany extended her hand. "It isn't a bicycle, Mrs. Colson. It's my Harley. Plenty of room on the seat, and I made sure Zack held on tight."

(*'Girls have serkers, boys do not…'*)

Oh yes! Eden knew her poetic son most definitely was aware of that distinction as he held on to this girl's thin waist at 60 mph. She politely took Tiffany's offered hand. "Eden Colson," she said, and looked Tiffany over. Apparently, the Age of Aquarius was alive and well. "A Harley? You don't look the biker type."

Tiffany laughed. "I don't think of myself as a type."

Zachary gave the once-over to the stranger at the table sipping coffee. Reefe introduced himself as the supervisor in charge of the excavation and shook Zachary's hand, a no-bullshit gesture that treated the boy like an adult. Eden liked that.

"Your Mom was generous enough to invite my crew and me in for some coffee."

"Do you drive that big yellow tractor out there?"

"Sometimes. It's a loader. We call her Big Mama. Maybe when we're done digging I can give you a ride."

"Cool!" Again, Zachary looked hard at Reefe. "Isn't that

my dad's shirt?"

Eden's face reddened.

"It gets dirty digging down there. Your mother offered it, and I didn't want to sit in the family kitchen looking like a mud man." And to Eden, "I'll get the shirt back to you tomorrow."

She went for the save as Reefe picked up his bloodied work shirt from the floor. Fortunately, the darkened blood could pass for mud and Zack paid it no mind. "It's an old shirt, Fred. Greg doesn't even wear it anymore."

That seemed all the explanation Zachary required. He opened the Colonel's bucket, chose a wing to nibble on. He offered one to Reefe as the man headed for the door.

"Water's off again tomorrow at 9:00. You guys shower early," Reefe said. He took the wing.

"I'll write it down," Eden answered. She watched him as he left, her eyes staying on him. Zachary brought his mother back into the moment.

"Okay if Tiffany stays for dinner? I mean, she *did* give me a ride home."

"Mi casa, su casa, Tiffany." She mumbled to herself, "No one ever expects The Spanish Inquisition."

Zachary made a face. "What does that mean?"

"British humor on the element of surprise, which seems to apply here. It's from an old Monty Python bit."

"Who?"

Eden planted a kiss on her son's cheek. "It means that if you hitch another ride on Tiffany's Harley again, I'm grounding you until you have grandchildren."

Eden readily welcomed her return to normalcy, even if normalcy's price was a her son's stolen bike and his new girl pal who rode a hog and looked like she'd just returned from Woodstock. The aggravation of motherhood still beat having to deal with suicidal young men and God knows what was crawling beneath the soil of Diamond Loop.

Now if she could only get those ridiculous thoughts of Fred Reefe out of her head...

# SINKHOLE

## MONDAY

The small Wogslûk does not know this man-thing's living tissue is called a brain, that deep within its mysterious chambers are memories, logic and knowledge, that somewhere even deeper within him is something called a soul.

The Wogslûk knows only one thing.

It wants more.

# CHAPTER FIVE

## THE OLD CROW INN, 1866: BEN

*"...and dance by the light of the moon..."*

**B**en Jamison didn't look right. He didn't feel right, either. That tune, that damned tune kept playing inside his head. He didn't know why.

**Buffalo Gals, won't you come out tonight,
come out tonight, come out tonight...**

His jaw broken, he couldn't form the words, but they stayed with him. Standing in the shadows of The Old Crow Inn he watched the two women approach the tavern. The sun's grey luminescence blurred his vision, its diminishing warmth strong enough to bring heat to his flesh that he found strangely discomforting. Something inside him had been taken, something was changing. Much already had changed.

Moving closer, he saw the two women clearly enough to discern detail. The younger woman in black flowing robes held a square object with gold lettering Ben recognized. A book — no, the *Bible! S*he held it high like a weapon. The other, the older woman, held a real weapon. Ben immediately recognized it because he had held that weapon in his own hands. He couldn't remember the object's name but he remembered its purpose, understood that it was dangerous, and that the woman pointed it in his direction with the intention of killing him.

*"Stop right there, Mr. Jamison! Stop, or I'll shoot! I swear I'll —"*

Her shouts were now gibberish to Ben, a cacophony as

meaningless as the snorts of the horses harnessed to the stage nearby, but the woman's tone was unmistakably earnest. He sensed fear in her voice too. Ben knew she felt that fear because of him.

### ...won't you come out tonight?

"'The Lord tests the righteous, but his soul hates the wicked...'" the other woman in black robes threatened with raised voice, but she seemed to speak more to herself than to him. Her manner, although more calm than her companion's, hid her own underlying fear. He could sense her apprehension as if some force emanated from her. This woman's words also were gibberish, but Ben understood that underneath them was anger, aggression, but mostly terror.

He knew these feelings because he had experienced them inside the barely lit place from which he had emerged. He remembered holding something then... his own weapon — *No! It had been taken from another man, one like himself —* something sharp and capable of killing. The weapon had connected with a dark rubbery thing that was alive, but he had lost the weapon inside that inn, where...

*Yes! It was called an inn, and it was where the dark creatures were right now! He remembered! He had wanted to kill them because they wanted to kill him!*

*...Yes!*

There were many of them, and they had surrounded him, had taken something from him — squeezed it from his head like the juice from an orange. He was frightened then, but now his fear was gone. Those dark creatures — he knew nothing of them or what they were, only that they wanted him, at least an important part of him —

*...and now they wanted these women!*

### ...come out tonight, come out tonight...

Ben questioned none of this. That ability had been stolen

57

from him, and in that sense, he no longer was Benjamin Jamison. He barely remembered the name, and he retained only dim memories of most other things, excepting that tune that wouldn't stop echoing inside his brain. Other memories seemed unimportant. What mattered was the moment.

*"Don't set one foot closer, Mr. Jamison, or I swear I'll shoot you where you stand!"*

The elderly woman's hand shook, as did the weapon she held. He knew she was not used to killing and, uncertain of her ability, she would hesitate. She held her weapon straight out unsteadily before her, and this made it easy for him. His arm swiped at hers, sending the weapon flying into the dust. The old woman stared blankly at him as his arm swung again, the stiff motion not graceful but effective. His tightened fist connected with her face. Something crunched behind her cheek, and the strange multicolored object she wore on her head flew from it as she fell to the ground.

He chose not to kill her, although it would have meant nothing had he done so. He knew what they expected of him, those dark things waiting. Grabbing a fistful of the elderly woman's hair he dragged her through the dust back towards the old tavern and to the hungry creatures inside. There was not much to her. It was like dragging a person of straw. The tune in his head — he was beginning to like it. This was good because these were becoming the only words he remembered.

### *...and dance by the light of the moon...*

*"My Lord!"* he heard the woman in the flowing black robes mutter behind him...

...but the words of Sister Margelle seemed lost on the slogging man-thing that used to be Benjamin Jamison.

*"My Lord!"*

Still holding the elderly woman's Bible, Sister Margelle stood frozen watching Jamison as he dragged the poor woman into that godforsaken Old Crow place. The man's fist had knocked the old woman out cold. For one absurd moment, the nun had almost flung the Bible at him, hoping to strike the back of his head with several hundred pages of God's wrath. That would accomplish nothing except to cause him to relinquish his unconscious victim, then come for her.

*"You're not Mr. Jamison ...not Mr. Jamison!"* Sister Margelle repeated the words, attempting to convince herself. This was not the man who had sat alongside the attractive young passenger who blushed when he spoke to her.

The pistol the old woman had dropped remained in the dust. The sister saw it, and she knew she must act quickly. The man was practically at the tavern, and Sister Margelle had no intentions of following him inside. Nightfall was coming, and whatever lurked behind those swinging doors certainly loved the darkness. He wasn't that far off, and it would be an easy shot if she took it now. Scurrying to pick up the gun, she aimed it at his back. *The Peacemaker*, Ben Jamison had called his Colt, and now she pointed it at him hoping to shoot him dead.

"Lord forgive me..."

The sister's hand shook while her heart raced. She could do this, she told herself, she could shoot this man in the back because she had to. Needing both hands to steady her aim, she would have to toss the Bible in the dirt.

*Don't think... Don't think. Just drop the book, just do it and shoot...*

She could do neither. Standing with the fully loaded pistol, instead Sister Margelle watched the man drag his victim into The Old Crow Inn, watched as the two disappeared into the darkness.

"Fool! Cowardly fool!" she muttered to herself. The nun had no time to ponder her inaction. The Monahan woman remained aboard the stage and there were decisions to make. Two men's bodies lay outside the cab, blood caking the dirt. Already the flies had come to feast, and maggots would not be far behind, another of this day's sickening events. She returned to the coach to find Melissa Monahan in tears.

"I wanted to shoot Sam's rifle, but I was afraid I would hit you! I'm sorry. I'm so sorry!" The young woman spoke through nearly uncontrollable sobs. "No, that isn't true! I was scared, too damned scared to fire a shot! I mean, that was **Ben**!"

The nun shook her head. "I was frightened too. Too frightened to pull the trigger. And that man wasn't Ben. Not any more than your Christian was the fiancé you knew."

Melissa's sobs returned. "I don't understand any of this! Sunday morning I was to be a bride, I had a home in San Miguel County, a new life. Now Christian, Ben, and that old woman—we didn't even know her name! Sister, I don't understand what's happening! What sin have I committed to...?"

"He was trying to say something."

"What?"

"Mr. Jamison, when he dragged off that woman, he was groaning some tune under his breath. I think his jaw was broken and he couldn't speak."

"That's — that's what Christian did! He was humming something when he broke into the carriage. This is insane!"

"We can't stay here, Melissa. The danger, it's too great. These horses have rested, and we can pull this stage out of Trementina if we hurry. We have only minutes before full dark. We must leave now!"

"The carriage wheel is almost off its axle. We won't get very far."

"We have the pistol and a rifle. We have to try!"

Screams came from within The Old Crow Inn. They were weak, but the shrieks were a woman's.

"It's her!" Melissa said. "She must have regained—!"

As quickly as it began the shrieking inside the inn stopped. Maybe she had fainted, but that seemed unlikely. "The old woman is dead," Sister Margelle whispered. "Probably Mr. Jamison too, or what was left of him. We can't stay or we'll be joining them. You know that as well as I." She turned towards the old tavern. The purple twilight allowed no clear view, but something large appeared at the swinging doors.

"What *is* that?" from Melissa.

"That's not a man. It's on its belly!"

"It's too dark. I can't see what—"

Other misshapen shadowy things crawled from the tavern into the dusty street. Grabbing Melissa's shoulder, the nun forced a whisper. "They must have been waiting for nightfall. There's twenty or more — the dark things old Sam mentioned. The old man was right!"

"They look like snakes."

They're not snakes!"

The harnessed horses saw them too, and the stage shook with their restlessness. The rear wheel would not hold if the team of six did not calm down. Nearby, the slithering shadows seemed thick as tree trunks, and they kept coming. Melissa opened her mouth but brought her hand to it to stop herself from screaming.

That would have been a very bad idea because now there were many more than twenty, and whatever the dark creatures were, they were slithering towards them.

*Unused to sun, they do not like the light. But the sun has gone, and the night welcomes them.*

*They sense the two who sit close together in darkness are alone and afraid.*

*These are women things, weaker in strength.*

*This is good.*

*The Wogslûk move nearer.*

*If they act quickly, they can have them both...*

# CHAPTER SIX

## GLENN ECHOES GENERAL
## JULY 2015, NIGHT: JESSIE

*"Ear worm..."*

The attractive young woman who introduced herself as Julie Bowes had dropped everything, rushing to Glenn Echoes General to be at the side of her fiancé, Jessie Moss. She had been spared details of Moss' attempt to take himself out of the game, although Head Nurse Christina Dougherty had asked the requisite questions regarding Moss' emotional state with the intention of her own personal follow-up and an at-the-ready listing of phone numbers for future therapy. For the time being, the medical staff's all-purpose and vague explanation of 'work related injury' sufficed, and it wasn't a complete lie. Dougherty offered the comforting "We're doing all we can" answers for Julie and sent the woman on her way when visiting hours were over. Studying Moss' test results, Dougherty felt uncertain she had given the young woman the most accurate response. Then, again...

"This can't be right..."

Patient Moss had been admitted to the Emergency Unit for a self-inflicted wound to his neck, but his blood loss had been quelled by immediate and constant direct pressure to the punctured carotid artery, and the patient was taken to the hospital's trauma center. The wound was sutured; Moss' airway wasn't severely blocked, and endotracheal tubes seemed to have done the trick. Not quite stable, the patient was far from healed because another injury required immediate attention. His scalp's deep laceration had received timely first aid, but the wound required surgery, and chief surgeon Dr.

Ahmad-Kabar would do the honors. An emergency CAT scan came first. Here Nurse Dougherty observed a problem for which twenty years at the job could supply no answers. Near the midnight hour she called for Dr. Ahmad-Kabar to have a look at the results.

"At first I thought it was a smudge, some sort of false read with the CT scanner, so we did the scan again. I wanted you to see this, Doctor." She said no more, allowing the hospital's chief surgeon to examine the computer screen and draw his own conclusions from the elongated dark spot inside Moss' brain that looked about the size of a cigarette.

Ahmad-Kabar studied the scan, removed his glasses, put them on again and looked more closely.

"This was taken in the last hour?"

"During the last thirty minutes. I wasn't sure the scanner was operating correctly, but a second round of tests confirmed it. I'm not sure what — I mean, I've never —" She collected her thoughts. "What's your opinion of this?"

The doctor shook his head. "This spot in the skull cavity seems to have moved from one scan to the next. That would suggest —" He seemed to shrug off his own analysis as utterly ridiculous. Nurse Dougherty finished the doctor's sentence for him.

"It would suggest something alive is inside that man's skull. Something that's still there and is moving." Trying to make her own tentative analysis sound matter-of-fact, she failed miserably.

Like Dougherty, Ahmad-Kabar seemed to doubt the evidence of his own eyes despite the computer image before him. "There's no indication of subdural hematoma. His skull was entered without fracturing. This man's brain should be submerged in blood, but there's not a trace of swelling or fluid. Something of that size in motion inside his skull would cause massive cranial injuries. He should have died hours ago."

"The patient is stabilizing. We've given him blood. He's very much alive."

"I would like to see that for myself, Christina."

At 12:17 a.m., the two visited the ICU to have a closer look at Jessie Moss. Dr. Ahmad-Kabar believed that observing his patient in the flesh often proved more reliable than anything showing on an imaging screen or an x-ray. That opinion was about to change.

At 12:24, Nurse Dougherty noted on Moss' chart that his vital signs had stabilized, that his EKG measured a general regularity of beats per minute for someone who had been approaching death's doormat hours earlier. Although still pale from blood loss and heavily sedated, Jessie Moss seemed to have avoided Code Blue Territory. This much was encouraging. The rest, the unanswered questions, were not.

By 12:31, the doctor shook his head, a response reserved for when a patient irreversibly had reached his expiration date. Ahmad-Kabar's tenure at Harvard Medical School had supplied no better answer than Nurse Dougherty's certificate from Princeton. The thought almost made the woman smirk, a reaction she quickly restrained.

"There's no more we can do here, Christina. Keep an eye on him. We can run more tests first thing in the morning." The surgeon handed his clipboard to her and started out, but Dougherty's words stopped him at the door.

"Doctor!" It was all she said. It was all she had to say. She waited a moment for the surgeon's response from Moss' bedside because something truly insane had just occurred.

"That's not possible. This man is heavily sedated."

"With Propofol infusions. I administered them to him myself."

The sound was unmistakable. Unable to speak, Jessie Moss was humming something. Ahmad-Kabar moved closer and reexamined the man's pupils.

"He's in REM sleep. Dreaming. Is that a song of some sort he's... singing?" Ahmad-Kabar asked, struggling to find some sort of explanation, logical or otherwise. "I'm unfamiliar with American—"

"I'm not sure. It's probably just gibberish." Dougherty didn't look convinced.

**64**

"Probably. Keep a watch on him. Inform me if anything changes." Dr. Ahmad-Kabar didn't add another word. Seeming confused or just plain embarrassed having found no sane explanations, he shook his head one last time and left Dougherty alone with her patient. She remained studying him, trying to make sense of a night that had gone completely off the rails.

At 12:53, Jessie Moss' eyes snapped open. He stared at the nurse alongside his bed. She looked back at him, unsure if she should call for Ahmad-Kabar again, unsure if she should even speak. "Mr. Moss. Can you hear me? I'm Christina, your nurse. Nod your head if you can hear."

He struggled against his pillow but managed only a croak that somehow transformed into mumbled words.

"What? Mr. Moss, I can't quite understand what you—"

He mumbled a string of mush words. The nurse had a thought. What was that slang term for a song that annoys the crap out of you because you can't get it out of your head? Until this moment Christina Dougherty believed the term was only a hip buzz word for the kids of the new millennium, not a real thing. But right now, her patient demonstrated a very real thing having itself a fine time inside his skull. "Ear worm," she muttered to herself.

Jessie Moss looked at her with unblinking eyes. His ludicrous sing-song tone could not have been more out of sync with his circumstances, but his words were clear enough even if they made no sense.

*"'Nothin' from nothin' leaves nothin'...'"*

By 2:17 a.m, Jessie Moss finally slipped back into sedated unconsciousness. Dougherty had rounds to make, and the night nurses could look in on him while she was gone. The halls fell silent, the patients' rooms dark. Occasionally an orderly's cart interrupted the quiet or nurses carried whispered conversations, but the night staff heard no sudden screams of ambulance sirens. Time undisrupted was rare for Glenn

Echoes General, the calm deceptive. Patient Moss slept un-watched for only a few minutes. That was all the time that was needed.

Jessie's head twisted on his pillow. Even in medicated slumber, his body twitched like an arthritic old man's. His face seemed a melting wax sculpture, and slowly his mouth opened wide in a silent scream. Had anyone been there, it would have appeared his curled tongue had gone coal black and peeked from his mouth like a snake's forked tongue. But it wasn't his tongue that slowly crawled from between his teeth and slid down his chin. The slug-thing wriggled along the pillow and fell to the floor, quickly disappearing in the HVAC vent in the corridor.

With no slithering demons to jar him awake, a more restful deep sleep finally came for patient Moss. Nightmares don't haunt a man whose own soul had been so efficiently removed

Small and ravenous, the Wogslûk had taken from Jessie Moss what it needed.

# CHAPTER SEVEN

## DIAMOND LOOP - JULY 2015:
## FRED REEFE

*"If Jessie is still Jessie..."*

Two dozen new single homes comprised the development called Diamond Loop, the Colsons' home at 613 having been built and sold last. Addresses ranged from 600 to 623, and each house had its unique features as well as its unique residents.

In the spoon-shaped cul-de-sac, the housing followed a straight line on either side of the street. This handle of the cul-de-sac led from Apple Grove Way, (so named for the nearby apple orchards, a pleasant remnant from Glenn Echoes' old farming days). At the far end of the Loop, the street split into an elongated oval; a small beautifully landscaped island stood in the oval's middle. Addresses 612 to 617 were the furthest from the excavation, and included the Colson home along with the homes of other families and married couples.

Diamond Loop and its residents would have fit nicely into a Rockwell painting. Here was a friendly street, filled with perfunctory 'good morning' greetings and comments about the weather, an agreeable place to live just as realtor Susan Donnelly had described. It was too new a development for any serious feuds to have broken out among the neighbors, certainly not before they got to know each other better.

The pit at the Loop's entrance didn't fit the picture. Cordoned off by several sawhorse barricades, its flashing yellow warning lights were surrounded by fluorescent tape with the single repeated word DANGER. These warnings blocked vehicular access from Apple Grove Way to the Loop itself, a circumstance meant to last only a few days. Below ground, unknown to the cul-de-sac's residents and the work crew, there was more damage to the pipe system than Reefe Water & Sewer Contractors had anticipated. That would mean more digging, more searching for the problem.

### MONDAY P.M. — TUESDAY A.M.

Immediately following Jessie Moss' accident, Supervisor Fred Reefe had refused any of his crew access to the excavation until he had a look for himself. Moss had insisted something inside the hole attacked him, and the badly dented hard hat that Reefe discovered indicated that maybe his new worker had seen something that shouldn't have been there. Attaching a dozen high-powered lights along the wooden upright supports, Reefe had detected nothing suspicious.

But he had heard something. He inspected the pipe line, tapped it and listened closely. Something skittered inside the water main, but he heard another sound too.

*"What the—?"*

The tubular copper line was wide enough for a small animal to have gotten in somehow, maybe a rat or a squirrel. That meant the water main had a serious break. He pressed his ear against the pipeline to be sure, tapped it again.

A whisper from inside the pipe.

*"...Yoob...Die-em...Min...Yoob...Die-em..."*

*"...the fuck...?"* Reefe muttered.

No rat, no squirrel, and there seemed more than a few of them, whatever 'them' was. Maybe he had heard some echo coming from somewhere above? Sound sometimes carried from the surface to the underground, and the pipes could have been a conduit for surface noise. Reefe considered the possibility and quickly dismissed it. His rational self knew that wasn't likely. He listened again.

*"...Yoob...Die-em...Min...Yoob...Di-em...Min..."*

It seemed a kind of chant, like the dwarves in "Snow White" singing on their way to the mines, *"Hi Ho, Hi Ho, it's off to work we go."* The words he heard were garbled mush, and making the connection to some Disney feature seemed ludicrous. But another thought occurred.

Maybe Jessie Moss had heard this too. Being the new guy, Moss had shown he didn't want to look bad in front of the crew by admitting he'd been spooked; similarly, he couldn't be ingloriously carried off to the hospital because of a 'fucking head scratch,' as he called it. Reefe's suggestion had sent Moss to the Colson woman for some first aid, since Eden Colson appeared the most obliging among the Loop neighbors, and she seemed to like Jessie. Reefe had headed to 613 shortly before the work day was done, expecting to tell Moss what he had heard inside the hole, maybe compare notes. And then the craziness began.

*[Die-em..Min...Yoob...]*

What the hell did that mean? The bigger question was, from what source had that sound come? Alongside his sleeping wife, Fred Reefe played the moment over inside his head.

"Barb? You awake?"

*"Unngh..."*

He wanted to share with her, but thinking it over, how could he? Any sane person would have thought he had gone mad. What followed soon after his experience in the pit made things infinitely worse.

"Hello, Fred," Jessie had said, pretending he was going to follow up with a chummy "How you doing?" But that didn't happen, did it? Barb sometimes told him he seemed too tough with the new guys, and the kid had been hurt because Reefe had sent him into that hole alone. In retrospect, maybe he *had* been too hard on Moss. He wouldn't blame Barb if she called him on it, but she would never lay that guilt trip on him.

*"Unnnnghh...What?"*

"Nothing. Sorry, honey. Go back to sleep."

Reefe replayed the day's events. He had left the excavation early to check on Jessie Moss, told the crew to clean up the area and call it a day. Moss had greeted him inside the Colson house, friendly as a damned cub scout just before he tried for a healthy slice of his own jugular. And just what was Moss planning regarding Eden Colson? *That* sure as hell wasn't cub scout behavior.

*("Tell Jarmal I found some pussy. Did you bring beer?")*

Fred Reefe tried connecting the dots. It wasn't easy. Nothing that happened Monday seemed to connect. What was it Eden had shared with him afterwards?

*Slugs!* She had mentioned unearthing a shitload of them in her garden, *("...about a hundred crawled from the dirt. Big suckers, too...")* but Reefe had shared nothing with her of his own experience in the hole. Maybe he should have. Reefe's first impulse *was* to tell someone.

Leaving the Colson home, he had almost called the Glenn Echoes County supervisors who hired him. But clearer thinking made him decide that would be a foolish move. A worker's injury on his watch was bad enough; in the morning, he would report it because that was his responsibility, and if it was a bad call not to send Moss immediately to the ER, he would have to face the firing squad for that one. But large whispering slug-things crawling inside the pipeline? Reporting that would serve no purpose except probably to get him fired for either being drunk or crazy. There could be lawsuits against the company too if the Loop's residents believed sewer creatures were bathing in their drinking water because his team had somehow fucked up. Reefe decided to keep mum until he knew more, and he hoped he had made the right call. Tomorrow his crew would again explore those pipelines for damage because there was a schedule to meet. He would warn his men to take extra care to avoid further injuries. When the time felt right, he would speak to Jessie.

"...*if Jessie is still Jessie,*" he mumbled to himself.

Maybe he would find logical explanations, maybe in the morning he would decide how rat-fucked it was believing in sewer slugs that were trying to communicate with him. He spent the rest of the night thinking about what he knew for sure.

**FACT:** Something very bad had happened to Jessie Moss inside that pit.

**FACT:** His head wound was more serious than 'a fucking scratch.'

**FACT:** Less than thirty minutes from the hole, Moss, a personable guy, suddenly turned on Eden Colson, practically raped her, then calmly tried cutting his own throat.

**FACT:** ...therefore, whatever physically hurt Jessie Moss had also caused some serious trouble to his thinking, and that trouble began inside the excavation.

**FACT:** If trouble were brewing under Diamond Loop, then this was only the beginning.

And there was one more fact. Reefe whispered the words aloud.

*"Yoob-Die-em-Min-Yoob.-Min..."*

This had become a mantra inside his head, a damned ear worm. It meant something. It had to mean something...

The dots connected. And then he had it...

*"Yoob-Die-em-min-yoob-min...Die-men-yoob...Die-amond-yoop..."*

He almost shouted, *"Yes! That's it! Diamond...Loop!"*

It had to be! That was what he heard! What else could it be? *Diamond Loop!* He didn't know what sort of muddy creatures had spoken it or how they had managed even to say it, or why they chose these words — but that had to be what they said, assuming these *were* words and not a bizarre mush of random sounds.

Fred Reefe felt convinced he had broken the code.

But Fred Reefe was wrong.

*They know no sun, no light. Only darkness and dirt is theirs.*

*And the female Ri, from whom the Wogslûk have learned.*

*She knows the sounds the man-things speak, and the Wogslûk try to make words from them.*

*"Yoob...Die-em...men...yoob..."*

*Among themselves they whisper. Under the ground, to the man-things, they curse.*

*"Yoob...Die-em...men...yoob..."*

*It is not quite speech, not speech as Ri speaks it, but it is close enough and they understand the meaning.*

*"You die, human..."*

# PART TWO

## WILD SLUGGOTS

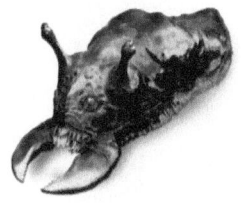

*"He would pore by the hour, o'er a weed or a flower
Or the slugs that came crawling out after a shower..."*

**- Rev. R.H. Barham (English Poet and Dramatist, 1788-1845)**

*"Silently and after dark, when you're tucked up, sleeping tight, they wriggle in and set their mark, waiting long into the night."*

**- Judy Darley, "Slugs Slither Slowly"**
***Remember Me to The Bees* (2013)**

*"If you have to hate anything, let it be this slug, a cruelly destructive pest if there ever was one."*

**- Eugene N. Kozloff,**
***Plants and Animals of the Pacific Northwest* (1976)**

*"Beware the Jabberwock, my son! The jaws that bite, the claws that catch!"*

**- Lewis Carroll, "Jabberwocky"**
***Through the Looking Glass* (1871)**

*"We create our own monsters..."*

**- Zachary Colson, age 13**

# CHAPTER EIGHT

## THE WESTBOUND CONCORD
## OVERLAND STAGE EXPRESS, 1866:
## MELISSA AND SISTER MARGELLE

*"A goddamned psalm for the hopeless."*

The purple twilight allowed no clear view, but when night came to Trementina something appeared at the swinging doors of The Old Crow Inn...

The two women knew that at least four people lay dead, two inside the inn. Two more lay in the dust outside the coach in which Melissa Monahan and the young nun, Sister Margelle, sat in paralyzing terror, expecting they were next. The women watched something large slithering from the tavern; then it seemed there were a hundred of them. Melissa opened her mouth but stopped herself from screaming. They were trapped — she and Sister Margelle — and in a few minutes the Overland Stage Express would serve as a casket on wheels for both of them.

"They look like snakes. They're on their bellies..."

"They're not snakes!"

The nun's insistent response left no doubt, but whatever the dark creatures were, they were coming for them. She handed Ben Jamison's pistol to Melissa, picked up Old Sam's rifle for herself. Melissa held the gun close, remembering Ben had entrusted her with the weapon just hours earlier, during the moments when the world she knew abruptly stopped making sense.

"There's too many of them. We can't kill them all!"

Melissa's observation didn't prevent her from steadying her aim. From the opposite seat, Sister Margelle did likewise. Neither woman had ever fired a gun in her life; now both faced an army of creatures spawned from some immense hole along the Santa Fe, nameless slime things hunting them for reasons neither woman could begin to understand.

The nun bit her lip as she steadied the rifle's long barrel along the window's rim. Her finger touched the trigger. "Maybe a few shots will scare them off. Then we can pull this wagon out of here, if that cursed wheel doesn't fly off. Mr. Jamison said shoot to kill. The old man's rifle has more range than your pistol. I'll take the first shots."

"Even if we hold them back — even if I *can* manage to get to the driver's box, Sam used six reins just to move this thing. I have no idea how—"

"That's the least of our problems," the nun said.

Outside in the darkness countless eyes shone red and intense, as the creatures-that-were-not-snakes surrounded the stage. Melissa hastened to the other window. From opposite corners the women readied their weapons. Sister Margelle recognized the crawling slime-things' tactic.

"They're spreading out, forming a circle around us like Indians do before they attack. My God, they're smart!"

Melissa spotted one moving closer, a large wormy thing that advanced more quickly than any four-legged animal could. Steadying the pistol, she got a good view of the dripping black creature nearing the window.

"Look at its mouth! It's got hooks like a maggot."

The sister took in the image growing nearer. "And tentacles like a slug's. They're too large to be either. I don't know what these things are!"

A small black slug-thing the size of a finger wriggled up Melissa's forearm. She tried to flick it out the window, but its hooks dug into her flesh. Crushing it with the butt of the pistol, she mashed it into a dark jelly until she felt sure it was dead, picked bloody chunks from her arm, and tossed them out. A red blotch puckered near her elbow.

"They're sending in the smaller ones first, like pawns in chess! My God, they *are* smart!"

Sister Margelle shouted, "Never mind that! Look at the window!"

The distraction had given a slug-thing the opportunity to hurl itself against the wagon. Several feet long, its head huge, it thumped powerfully at the door while its hind section snapped at the air like a leather strap. The lock had been smashed by Christian's axe, and Melissa kept tugging to keep the door closed.

"I can't hold this! If another one comes — *Sister, they're too strong!*" Point blank, she fired between the creature's eyes and saw its head explode in black goo. It folded over on itself, falling into the dust still squirming. Melissa's stomach churned as another approached. *"I can't do this, Sister. I can't—"*

The nun fired, and a second creature splashed inky globs of matter, hurling backwards with the rifle's blast. Those behind stopped cold, but only for a moment. Sister Margelle fired again. "They turned away, but I don't think we can hold them off for long. They seem put off by the flash of gunfire."

The retreat didn't last. Others closed in, and if some were shot, there would be more that made it through. Neither woman mentioned this fact, but each understood it. Melissa managed to pick off another one, but there were more of them than she had bullets. She pulled those remaining from her dress pocket and reloaded.

The sister turned to her. "We have to leave!"

"We can't go out there! There's too many!"

"We can't stay!" She fired again and another creature whirled in twisting spirals, curling and kicking up dust in its death throes. Sister Margelle's eyes said it all. If they stayed they were sitting ducks, but once out of the carriage they were even more vulnerable. Mumbling words Melissa couldn't determine, Sister Margelle prayed for some divine intervention. Melissa doubted the hand of God would appear from the night sky to carry the coach to safety. What did appear were more slime things.

*And then a small miracle...*

A divine intervention came that very moment, but it didn't come from the hand of God. It came from the horses.

The team of six had been frightened by the slithering things surrounding the coach. They had snorted and stomped, and the carriage shook so perilously it seemed it might topple over. The fired guns made matters worse, and the two lead horses bucked and pulled against the hitching post. The slug-things showed no interest in the harnessed team; their focus remained on the women.

The team of six had been strong enough to pull over 3000 pounds a thousand miles; an old wooden hitching post was no match for them. They wrenched the whole thing free, snapping the rotting wood in the process. The entire coach moved backwards, spilling the two women from their seats.

Melissa's fears now turned to the new threat. "The horses! They're going to run! That loose wheel will never hold. We'll be killed!"

Clutching the old Bible in one hand, steadying the rifle in the other, Sister Margelle's prayers grew louder. "'The Lord is my shepherd, I shall not want...'"

"Not that one, Sister! That's a goddamned psalm for the hopeless!"

"Which is what we are..."

Loud squealing came from nearby. Melissa chanced stretching her head through the window.

"The two horses out front, they just stomped a couple of them! Those things are backing off. The horses are scaring *them!*" The nun mumbled some bible nonsense and crossed herself. Melissa kept the pistol trained outside but already the slug-things had retreated. "It may be too early for thanking God just yet, Sister. I don't think the horses are calming down."

Several of the team whinnied and tried to buck, but confined to their harnesses, the entire team could only stomp. Freed from the hitching post, they charged forward as if some phantom driver had whipped the crap out of them to move. More likely, the slime things had ventured too near, and the horses knew better than to stay in this place. Imprisoned inside a stagecoach behind six runaway horses, tossed like children's toys within their confined space, the women had exchanged one method of dying for another.

All color left Sister Margelle's face. "The wheel..."

Melissa could feel the unsteadiness of the coach as it bounced in every direction. The rear wheel wobbled on its axle, and the increasing speed of the horses meant it was not going to make it much further. The broken door opened and slammed shut as the two women huddled close. With one bad roll of the stage both would tumble through the opening.

An unsettling thought occurred to Melissa. The horses were headed further west, but what if another huge pit waited along the trail? In this darkness the entire team would plow them right into it, and if its depth were anything close to that of the other, that pit would swallow the horses, the stage — *everything*. Even worse, if there were another crater, suppose more of those things were waiting inside it? Catching her breath, Melissa spoke first.

"Maybe I can climb to the driver's box. If I can just stop the team, or at least slow them down—"

"Yes! Yes, please try!"

If she did make it to the driver's seat, Melissa had no idea how to halt six horses in full gallop, but she put that out of her thoughts also. She had to consider the moment, and doing nothing meant death for them both. Where she found such insane courage, she hadn't a clue. Maybe Sister Margelle's call for divine intervention had something to do with it. Or maybe people just grasped at anything when they were trapped inside a runaway stagecoach with nothing left to lose. It didn't matter. Stuffing the pistol inside the deep pocket of her dress, she managed a reassuring nod for the nun.

"I guess it won't hurt if you say a prayer for me, Sister."

"I'll say one for both of us."

Climbing out, Melissa held to the swinging broken door for leverage, reaching for the side rail at the top of the stage to pull herself up. It wasn't an easy climb. The carriage careened as if at any moment it might separate from the harnessed team and send the wagon speeding into oblivion. A canvass drop cloth covered the passengers' bags. Grabbing hold of the material Melissa belly flopped on the lumpy covering on the stage's top; splaying herself like a spider, she held on tight. The horses showed no sign of slowing down, and the stage bounced crazily. Melissa crab-crawled towards the driver's box below. One good bump would send her flying, but luck had been with her this far. If the wheel held a little longer, then maybe...

But the rear wheel shimmied badly, and it would fly off any minute. Melissa kept belly crawling toward the front of the stage. If she could drop into the driver's box, she could grab hold of the lines and hope for the best. With both hands she grabbed the side rail preparing to swing herself down. She stopped when she saw the pair of glowing eyes staring back at her from the driver's seat. Reflected off the early moonlight, they were blood red.

*"Shit!"*

Never in her life had Melissa spoken the word aloud, but this moment warranted it. One of the slug-things — a very large one — must have crawled onboard, terrifying the horses even as they hurtled along the dark trail. Melissa pulled out the pistol. On her belly, and holding the gun in both hands, she aimed for the creature's head.

*"Just stay put for a few seconds, you bastard. Just stay put..."*

It didn't. The black thing saw her, coiling snakelike and rising high in the driver's seat so that they were almost eye to eye. A hard roll of the coach knocked Melissa sideways. Grasping at the canvass she lost her grip on the gun, and it rolled along the cloth. She grabbed for it, but too late. It toppled over the edge and disappeared.

*"Fuck!"* This was another word Melissa had never muttered aloud. The dark thing crawled towards her, and the words just escaped. *"Fuck **you**!"*

Its mouth hooks opened. Like twisted swords pointed at her throat, they snapped as the slug-thing lunged. When first she had seen these filthy things Melissa had stopped herself from screaming. She knew it would do no good then, and she knew this now.

Melissa screamed anyway.

# CHAPTER NINE

## SOME TAFFY LICKS, JULY, 2015: TIFFANY AND ZACK

*"We create our own monsters..."*

She could do this, Tiffany Leone told herself. July's rent was overdue, and the guy waiting for her under the sheets seemed decent looking enough. Climbing into the stranger's bed, she giggled as her jeans dropped to the floor. "I don't know if I should be here. I mean, I hardly know you," she said, because that was what she was supposed to say. Her short breaths worked their way into her words in the same manner breathy (and breasty) Marilyn used to speak, back in the day. Tiffany almost felt like improvising a chorus of "Happy birthday, Mr. President."

"The name's Tom. I really like your tits. What more do you need to know?"

Succinct and to the point, but she wasn't fooling anyone about why she was here. Words spoken during these moments had little value anyway. The muscular stud looked maybe thirty or older, and she hoped he wouldn't be using her body as a bench press. He very gently assisted Tiffany in removing her tube top. Why should she resist? She had come this far, here in what clearly was a very upscale penthouse apartment, complete with a view of the skyline of exotic Wellington, New Jersey. Tom took her face into his hands, kissed her gently. Had they been in practically any other circumstance, the gesture would have seemed sweet.

"You like?" he asked.

"Mmmmmmm," she responded, getting in a little tongue action with their next kiss. She flashed a very broad grin at Tom

Whatever-Your-Real-Name-Is, whom Tiffany had met less than an hour earlier. He pulled away the sheets to allow a better view of her. The guy looked like he spent half his life pumping iron, and in another minute he would be pumping her. She wasn't looking forward to him hoisting his weight on top of her, but his kisses kept coming, and soon he would be advancing to the next step. She wasn't looking forward to Tom's doing *that* either.

Yes, this guy really did seem to like her tits. He focused most of his attention on them for the next few minutes, biting, sucking, nibbling, kissing — practically *eating* them. It amazed Tiffany how creative a man's mouth could become during moments like this. Of course, soon she would be returning the favor. Quid pro quo, as the lawyers called it, although in Taffy Licks' case it was more like tit for tat. She went with her instincts, squealing with pleasure and moaning with delight. Tiffany was good at this. She had to be. She was getting paid for it.

"I want to fuck you into next Thursday," Tom told her.

"Words every woman wants to hear," she answered.

Of course, 'Taffy' was the one doing all the work, in a manner of speaking, anyway. Tom seemed excessively eager as he climbed on her, and his considerable manhood was finding its way inside. The bearded guy holding the camcorder moved in for a tighter shot, but this wasn't what Tiffany had signed up for. She pushed Tom off and positioned herself upright in the bed, addressing the wannabe director standing in the shadows behind the camera man.

"Hey! Wait! Wait! No insertion, you said! You were going to use another girl!"

From across the room a man's voice answered, "Come on, Taffy, dammit! We're rolling! This is working!"

"Not for me it isn't!" Tiffany crawled out of the bed and pulled the top sheet over herself. "You told me there would be a body double for the close up insertion shots!"

"Fuck! Cut! Hey, Tony! I said 'cut,' asshole!" Ed Coombs, the greaseball who liked to think of himself as the George Lucas of YouTube porn quickies, stepped out from behind Tony holding the camcorder. "I'm paying for an hour of your time, Taffy. This is part of the package."

She wasn't risking much by walking. Coombs' entire video catalogue included only one other effort, the direct-to-garbage-pail video, *"Star Tricks: The Wrath of Cunt."*

"Stuff your package!" Tiffany almost giggled at the unintentional double entendre, but stayed on task. She reached for her jeans on the floor, wriggled into her tube top. "Just give me what you owe me. I'm done for the day." She turned to her partner, who remained on the bed with his arms folded. "Nothing against you, Tom, all right? This is business. Maybe in some other circumstance—"

"My name is Bob."

Tiffany smirked. "Of course it is." She turned back to Coombs and held out her palm. "Five hundred for the shoot. Cash. That was the agreement."

"You're holding up the production, sweetie. Don't play Cuntzilla with me. We only have this apartment for the afternoon."

Tiffany didn't care about that. Ed Coombs' version of "We" included a meager staff of three: Coombs himself, the bearded Tony with the camcorder, and some bald continually smirking horn dog working the sound. They were probably former fraternity brothers, or something equally creepy. Her palm went out again.

"Fine," Coombs said. He dug into his dirty jeans and rifled through a stack of bills, pulled out a few, and handed them to Tiffany. She counted through some twenties.

"There's only a hundred here."

"You want to get back into bed for the rest?"

She stuffed the cash into her pocket. "You're a bastard, Ed. You knew my terms. You've always known them. No hard core shit. You're a real bastard."

"And you, Miss Taffy, are wasting our time. We all have our bills to pay, don't we?"

Tiffany performed some mental arithmetic. Tuition for

those summer film classes was steep, as was the Glenn Echoes apartment rental fee. Her cameras weren't going to pay for themselves either. "Damn you..." she mumbled under her breath. She slowly dropped her jeans to the floor again, and Tony with the camcorder stepped closer as she removed her top. Tiffany forced a smile and climbed back into the bed. This smile was less convincing than her previous effort.

Her musclebound partner again wrapped his arms around her. "Welcome back."

Tiffany's fingers threaded through his hair as if the two were longtime lovers.

"Okay, Bob. Where were we?"

"Tom."

"Of course."

This wasn't looking like a good day, and Tiffany needed some diversion to get the bad taste of Ed Coombs out of her mouth. Unfortunately, the same thing applied, more literally, to Bob/Tom, or whatever her ersatz bed partner was calling himself today. For that she required a little excitement — and some Juicy Fruit.

Tiffany climbed on her Harley and checked her cell for the time. It was still early. Carrying her small camcorder inside the bike's glove box (should anything worth recording pop up), she could work on her film project with plenty of daylight to interview random citizens of Glenn Echoes going through their work day. A message from Zack Colson appeared on her cell's screen. The kid, who yesterday had stepped forward to defend her honor at the local KFC, had texted some urgent news.

**Cops here talking to my mother for some reason. Big secret. Mom seemed upset, wanted me to go out & disappear. WTF? Something weird going on IMO????? So? Want to come over & play Five-O?**

Zack's message was well timed. She could get some work done

on her project while checking out what had gone down around the Colson home. Tiffany knew how to get people talking, especially men people. Taffy had taught her that much. Something serious must have occurred if Glenn Echoes' finest were speaking with Eden Colson. She punched the keys to her cell.

**Hopping on chrome pony right now. Will be there 30 mins. Got school project u can help me with & I can help u/w weird stuff happening at home. Ur mom won't want u near the big bike. Go to hole. Will meet u there. Book 'em, Danno.**

Tiffany fired up the Harley and headed for Diamond Loop.

The huge yellow loader was busy at work. Tiffany spotted Zack a short distance from the excavation. He seemed interested in the dig and stood taking photos with his cell phone when she pulled up. The sight of him absorbed in this activity verified that the two of them shared the investigative bug. Tiffany knew they were going to get along just fine. She waved, and he came over while she remained on her Harley.

"So what am I missing here?" she asked.

"Just taking a few shots of these men at work. Got some of the hole too, close as I could get, anyway. You never know when you might find something. The workers, they're having trouble locating the bad pipe. They had to make a bigger and deeper hole than they'd expected, so they're really busy today." Zack looked around as if to determine that what he said next would stay only between them. "Something happened here yesterday. The men are acting hush-hush about it, but someone got hurt. I think there's more to it than that. I heard the police questioning my mom about it when I left."

"Hurt? How? Why your mom?"

Zack looked towards the excavation. "It happened inside

the hole. Something bad. That guy who got hurt came to my house, asked my mom to fix him up 'cause she was friendly with the work crew, and later they took him to the hospital anyway. That's all one of the workers would tell me. I don't know what happened at my house, or after that. I don't think anyone here knows either, except for Mr. Reefe, the supervisor you met. He was at my house too this morning, talking to the cops."

Tiffany smiled. "Maybe I can find out something. Which man talked to you?"

"Good looking guy working the tractor. Guy's name is Jarmal — should be Denzel, don't you think? The tractor's name is Big Mama. Remember Mr. Reefe said when they're done plugging up the hole, maybe he'll let me ride on it? That'd be cool."

Tiffany climbed off her cycle. "Well, maybe I can show Mr. Jarmal something more interesting than Big Mama. You wait here."

Watching Tiffany walk towards the hole Zack called out, "He won't let you ride, you know!"

She smiled. "There are much better rides than Big Mama, Grasshopper!"

Tiffany allowed the dark hair of her pony tail to cascade to her shoulders, and standing near the yellow warning tape she let Taffy come out to play. Flashing her YouTube smile at the tractor's driver, she knew nature would take care of the rest. The behemoth loader pulled in reverse to hoist another mound of dripping mud, and at the helm Jarmal noticed Tiffany. Any man with a working set of gonads couldn't miss her.

"You shouldn't stand so close, Miss!"

"It's okay. I'm behind the marker here. See?" Tiffany didn't move from where she stood, knowing this would probably piss off the man at the wheel. That's what she was going for.

"Really, Miss. For your own safety, back away a little, okay? There's heavy equipment here. Nothing to see."

The guy really did look like Denzel Washington, with a

little of The Rock thrown into the mix. "That's a really deep hole, isn't it?" She backed off three steps, counting them aloud and smiling at her own thought.

*(C.T. 101, Taffy Licks, Instructor...)*

Wiping sweat from his forehead, Denzel/Jarmal returned to his manipulating the tractor through lumps of piled dirt, but his half smile suggested Tiffany had scored a direct hit. The guy wouldn't be driving the dirt loader all afternoon, and she could wait. She saw Zack watching. He gave her a knowing nod of approval. Ten minutes later the tractor stopped a safe distance from the excavation's slope. Tiffany reached for her camcorder as Jarmal hopped off, making sure he saw. Whether through curiosity or something more basic to the XY chromosome, he approached all smiles.

"You know, I look a hell of a lot better when I haven't been playing in the mud. You the paparazzi or somethin'?"

Tiffany checked the display lens to study the shots she took and held the camcorder for him to inspect. "Nope. Just your garden variety college student taking a film course, recording a really nice looking guy doing his thing. Is that okay?"

"Very flattering. If I was white, I would be blushing right now. But like I told you, ain't nothing but dirt to see here."

She laughed, pretending to give Jarmal the once over. "Oh, I wouldn't say that. Okay if I ask you a few questions? This project for my class, it's about men at work, that kind of thing around Glenn Echoes. Mostly outdoor stuff, down and dirty sweaty stuff."

*...and smile.*

"Well, I guess I sure qualify for that. I can spare a couple of minutes, 'long as you don't mind if I eat my lunch while you ask. It's in my truck. We're on a tight schedule here. Five minutes, okay?"

"Deal."

Tiffany walked him to the dusty pickup at the curb. As they passed, Zack pretended he was absorbed in the digging. She gave him a quick wink.

Reaching into his truck, Jarmal pulled out his lunch pail, looked into the brown bag. "Tuna fish. Damn! Second time this week my wife packed that. The Colson woman, she offers the crew these fancy-ass cakes and coffee. Might go over there later, next break. Nice woman to do that. Classy, you know? That's her kid I seen you talkin' with. You want to know why we're digging here, I suppose?"

"Sure. Why not?"

"Township suspects a small leak in the water pipes, but a small leak has the nasty habit of becoming a big one. If this was winter, probably you be talkin' to me here wearin' a snorkel."

Tiffany went for it. "You mentioned something about the Colson woman. Did you know the police were with her and Mr. Reefe this morning? I'm told one of your crew went there after his accident yesterday. Would you know something about that?"

"That don't sound like no class project question to me. You sound more like a reporter."

"Just curious, is all. It's part of my assignment to ask questions, and I like to touch all the bases for my three credits. Think of me as Barbara Walters with great tits."

He grinned. "Pretty outspoken, ain't you? Well, I don't know that much. Just that the new kid, Jessie, he got hurt down in the excavation late yesterday. He's young, inexperienced. Probably just bumped his head. It happens."

"He was okay enough to stop into the Colson house, but he went to the hospital after that."

"Yeah, well, I guess he got hurt more than he thought he got. Occupational hazard. Like I said, it happens."

"Police don't come unless there's suspicion of some sort. Seems something serious happened at the Colson place that Mr. Reefe knows something about."

Jarmal bit into his sandwich and dropped his Denzel charm. "This is information you need for some homework assignment? I'm thinking, no fuckin' way. Barbara Walters, my ass. Are you from the Department of Safety and Health? Listen, Mr. Reefe, he's a decent guy, anyone will tell you. Accidents happen, ain't nobody's fault. Talk to him yourself. Nothin' here for you to—" He shut up fast.

The time had come for Tiffany to up the ante. Looking like she might be about to burst into tears, she waited for Jarmal to take a swig of his Pepsi so he wouldn't miss her expression.

"I'm not here to dig up dirt on Mr. Reefe, or on any of you guys. But, see, I need to know the truth because Glenn Echoes General won't tell me anything. See, I'm Mr. Moss' ... I'm *Jessie's* fiancé. I'm a film student, I didn't lie to you about that, but I just want to know what happened to Jessie yesterday at Eden Colson's home. Everyone is so silent about it, and...and...*I just have to know what happened!*" It was a wild shot in the dark and an Oscar worthy performance. Jessie Moss was the new guy, so Jarmal probably knew very little about him. You mix in a little truth with a big fat whopper, and *voila!* the worst horse shit sounds credible. Tiffany even managed a single tear.

Grinning again, Jarmal wiped his mouth from his messy sandwich. "You Julie? Yeah, Jessie mentioned you to us. Said you two 'sposed to get married 'round Christmas. Listen, I hear he'll be fine, I can tell you that much. But, see, there's more—"

Tiffany wiped away the tear. "What really happened to him, Mister—?"

"Call me Jarmal. See, I wasn't sure until I seen it this mornin' with my own eyes, but down there in the excavation, down deep in the pit where it's very dark—" He whispered the rest as if sharing a secret. "See, there's monsters down there, Miss, just like Jessie told us. Big 'uns that took a chunk out of his scalp. I seen a dozen of 'em early this mornin' just crawlin' around in the mud, some kinds of monster water bugs or snails, maybe cockroaches, I dunno, but they looked the size of big dogs. No, bigger! Nasty things. Ugly. The others and me, we 'gots to keep dat devil way down in the hole' like that 'Wire' song says. You can't tell no one this, hear?"

"You mean Jessie said something alive inside the hole bit him?"

"Oh yes! Bit me too, and a few of the others. Lord, I think

I may be growin' hair where it sho' ain't 'sposed to be. Oh, Lordie, Lordie!! Ah thinks I becomin' one o' dem!! Ah thinks — Why ah thinks you changin' too, Miss Julie! 'Cause yo' sho' don't look like no Miss Julie to me! And I don't recall tellin' you Jessie's last name!"

The man suddenly had slipped into Stepin Fetchit mode, and Tiffany knew her mask had been yanked off. Her 'Taffy' alter ego evaporated on the spot. "Okay, okay. I see where this is going. You don't have to go all politically incorrect on me."

"That's good, Miss Whoever-you-are. 'Cause, see, Jessie, he was very proud of his woman. Gave us vivid descriptions whether we wanted to hear them or not, showed us a shitload of photos from his phone too: Julie and him on the beach, Julie and him at Christmastime, Julie and him huggin' and kissin', the whole nine yards. So, 'less you managed to go from blonde to dark, and your eyes from deep blue to brown, I really don't believe you're Jessie Moss' intended. I'm no fool, Miss... Miss ...Who the fuck *are* you?"

Tiffany forced a weak smile. "Okay, you got me. So, no monsters?"

"No monsters. And I'm gettin' back to work if you don't mind. This sandwich is done, and so is my patience. But you are one fine lookin' young woman, I'll say that for you, whoever you are. It's been fun, but before I go, maybe you want to 'fess up?"

Taffy clearly had abandoned ship. "The name's Tiffany, a friend of Zack Colson's — a friend of his mom too, I guess. Look, he just wanted to know why the police were questioning his mother this morning. I'm sorry about all of this. I didn't mean—"

"Forget it. 'Least you helped me keep down this shit tuna. Anyway, time's come for me to get down and dirty again, so if you'll excuse me..." Tiffany watched him hop on Big Mama without looking back. This wasn't a good day for Taffy Licks, but Tiffany had another ace to play. She found Zack perched on the driver's seat of her Harley.

"So?" he asked. "What did you get from the big guy about

the cops visiting my house?"

"I learned the man hates tuna. But I did get some dirt about Jessie Moss, your mom's visitor, and I think it's enough that maybe we can find out more. You feel like exercising your acting chops? I promise you shits and giggles."

Zack's excitement showed. "I'm in! I think I may have some dirt too. I took some photos — of dirt!" He laughed.

Tiffany flashed her choicest smile his way. "You and me, we're on the same page, Boy Wonder. Now get your ass off my bike."

The two visitors arrived at Glenn Echoes General by mid-afternoon. At the sign-in desk the young 'nephew' of Jessie Moss did the speaking, although both appeared visibly upset about their favorite uncle's condition. Dried tears streaked the boy's face (or maybe it was just dirt), and accompanying him was his 'older sister,' a very attractive dark haired girl in her early twenties. She appeared equally affected by her Uncle Jessie's accident, although sunglasses hid any indication of recent sobs. Each affixed signatures to the visitors' sheet with the surname Moss — Zeke and Taffy Moss. The woman at the desk asked no questions; neither did any of the nurses along the way. It was that easy.

The trick now was to figure what to say to Mr. Moss when they arrived in his hospital room as complete strangers. Tiffany didn't want to freak the guy out, but something very suspicious had occurred at Diamond Loop, and patient Moss definitely had been involved.

Hospital staff had removed him from the ICU because his condition had significantly (and somewhat miraculously) improved during the night. He would remain under close observation for a few days, of course, but today Moss was both awake and speaking. He had company too. Tiffany Leone was about to meet the blonde and blue-eyed fiancé whose identity she had borrowed less than an hour earlier.

A nurse was just leaving, and Julie held Jessie's hand

when Tiffany and Zack entered. Patient Moss looked as if he had spent the previous night relaxing at the spa instead of recuperating in Intensive Care.

"Can I help you?" Julie asked.

Zack spoke first, not shy concerning his reasons for this visit. "Hi, Mr. Moss. I'm Zachary, Mrs. Colson's son. My friend Tiffany and I won't be staying long. We wanted to see how you were doing, and I—"

Tiffany added, "— but mostly, we have some questions. The other men at the site were concerned. I imagine they'll be along after working hours."

Moss stopped her there. "Who are you? I don't know either of you."

Julie proved more civil regarding the intrusion. "Jess has been through a lot these past few hours. The nurses say he's doing much better, but they don't want him tired out, okay? So thank you for coming, but—"

Tiffany didn't have much of a window. "Mr. Moss, I know you received a head injury yesterday in the excavation, but I see you have dressing on your neck as well." She said no more, expecting the man to fill in some gaps. Instead Julie spoke again.

"Who *are* you, and why is this so important for you to know? What happened yesterday is a private matter. You're not family."

"I'm a friend of Zack's — and I know you're Julie. The Reefe crew mentioned your name. Yes, I realize it's a private matter, but I think we're on the same team, you and me. See, the police were at the Colson home today, and I think Mr. Moss can clarify what happened yesterday, since he was there. I'm sure there's a good explanation, don't you agree, Mr. Moss?"

Jessie shifted in his bed, but he seemed okay with the question. "I remember some of it. Weird stuff, like a bad dream — like I was watching someone else go through it, as if I wasn't in control, or part of me wasn't there. I said some crazy shit to the guys at the site, and I was rude to Mrs. Colson. She invited the guys in for coffee and cake, a real nice woman. I remember that much, and I'm sorry about my actions. I intend to apologize to everyone, especially your mother, Zack."

Julie seemed confused with the new information. "Rude? Crazy shit? You didn't mention anything about a Mrs. Colson."

"I got hurt in the hole, like I told you. I fuzzed out after that. I guess I may have said some things out of line. I was dopey."

Julie squeezed his hand, held it close to her. She gave the go-ahead nod and Tiffany spoke up.

"Start with what happened inside the excavation, if that's easier."

"It's going to sound like I've lost my mind. In a sense, I think I did — for a little while. I mean, Mr. Reefe and the guys will probably tell you that much. Maybe I was hallucinating. But, see — I don't take drugs, maybe a beer now and then, a little weed..."

"Well, who doesn't?" Zack interrupted. The three looked at him, and he shut up.

"I didn't really see what was there in the pit, not well, anyway. There were a few of them, black things, different sizes, but it was dark and I dropped my flashlight. Hard hat fell off — I heard it hit the pipe. Then something tore into my scalp. Claws or teeth, I don't know, chewing through my hair. It hurt like a bitch, and things went blurry."

Tiffany exchanged confused glances with Julie.

"Well, thinking it over, it was probably only a rat, maybe a squirrel. A large rodent down below can give you the creeps. In the dark I guess my mind played tricks on me, and that enclosed space just made it worse. I yelled for the crew to pull me back up, and I must've told everyone crazy shit about what bit me. I was scared, probably a little stupid. Mr. Reefe saw me bleeding and wanted to call an ambulance, but I went to Mrs. Colson instead. Your mother is one hell of a woman, Zack. She fixed me right up, at least 'till I got here. But she probably got scared because I wasn't making sense. Fuzzy, like I said."

"What did you say to my mother?" Zack asked.

"I don't remember, but I must've really frightened her.

That's how I got this other wound, the one in my neck. I know I bled a lot, but it wasn't as serious as it looked. Neither was the head wound. I was damned lucky. No severed arteries, no brain damage."

Julie allowed Jessie's hand to drop to his lap. "You told me you got that neck wound in the excavation. Another bite, you said."

Tiffany and Zack exchanged glances. Something didn't feel right here. "You got that neck wound at the Colson house?" Tiffany asked.

Collecting himself, Jessie shifted in his bed. "Mrs. Colson, she grabbed this nail file, 'cause I must've been ranting. I have no idea what I was saying, but I guess she thought I was threatening her, and she—she—"

Zack shouted, "My mother would never do that! She didn't do that! I *know* she didn't!"

Tiffany interrupted. "Is that why the police were speaking to Eden Colson this morning?"

Julie went for the save. "The neck wound was suspicious. The nurses told me they weren't sure what caused it, but they had to report it. It's hospital policy."

Jessie spoke up. "Listen, Zack, I'm not going to press charges, all right? I'm fine now, and I know your mom probably just panicked—"

"What did you say to the Colson woman?" Julie asked. She didn't attempt to lower her voice.

"I was goofy — the head wound, you know? And I guess I—I guess I—okay, I mentioned how I thought she was a very attractive woman. I mean, because she was so nice to me, you know? Maybe I acted inappropriately, frightened her, I don't know. It's like I told you, it was like I wasn't there, that it was someone else, not me talking — Nothin' from nothin' leaves nothin'..."

The two young women looked at each other. Julie spoke first. "What?"

"You know, from the song." Jessie hummed the tune, then smiled. "Remember? Billy Preston, the '70's? Casey Casem's top forty? They're both dead now, you know. They're nothin'..."

The man's non-sequitur sprang from nowhere. Julie whispered to Tiffany, "I think he needs some rest. You should leave now. Wait outside the room for me, will you? We need to talk." Wiping a rogue curl from Jessie's forehead, she spoke close to his ear, "Get some sleep. I'll be here. I love you, okay?"

"Okay." He shut his eyes.

Julie waited until he seemed asleep, then whispered to Tiffany, "I'm not so sure he's fine."

Zack remained agitated. *"Listen. My mom, I know she didn't—"*

"We'll be right outside the door," Tiffany said.

Outside the hospital room Zack calmed himself. "My mother, she feels bad when she swats a fly. She couldn't have done what Moss said she did. He's lying, Tiffany."

"Open mind, okay? The guy might have had some kind of memory loss, or his brain got rattled by the accident. Maybe he doesn't even know he's lying."

"He knows! He doesn't care. Jessie Moss is interested in saving his own ass! That man did something to my mom, or tried to! You don't think she—?"

"We'll find out. Mr. Reefe might know something. It's why the cops wanted to talk to him — or maybe *he* wanted to talk to *them*. Maybe your mom was defending herself. The only other answer is that Moss cut *himself* with her nail file, and that means he went out of his way to get his hands on it. If that wound was self-inflicted, there's got to be a reason why."

"I think I know the reason," Julie interrupted, closing the door to Moss' room carefully. She looked around as if making sure no one could overhear her. "Jessie caused that neck wound himself. I think he tried to do something terrible to your mom, Zack, but a part of him couldn't do it, even if another part of him *wanted* to. I know him better than anyone. Jessie is a decent guy."

"Look, Julie, Zack and I aren't saying your guy is at fault

here. Like you say, I think he wasn't rational, wasn't himself. That's probably all that —"

Julie shook her head. "Something very screwed up is going on. Listen, I'm going to share something with you, okay? Make of it what you will."

"We're listening," Tiffany said.

"I told Jessie I love him just now, and he said — he said, 'Okay.' But that's not what he says whenever I tell him I love him. *Never!* See, what he says is 'Ditto,' like Patrick Swayze said to Demi Moore in *Ghost*, remember? It's like our joke. Jessie always answers 'Ditto,' and he does the air quote bit with his fingers. And I say 'Ditto' too when he tells me he loves me. It's our thing, even after we have an argument. We've been doing it for years!"

"He's been under heavy medication," Tiffany said. "He admitted to being fuzzy from the wound, and adding the meds to that, he's probably not remembering real well."

Julie seemed close to tears. "No, Jessie would never forget that! Besides, there's something else that's strange."

"That he attacked my mother?" Zack asked. Tiffany shot him a dirty look. Julie seemed too lost in her thoughts to notice.

"This nurse named Dougherty, she attended Jessie last night. She didn't say much about the neck wound; she didn't know much. But this morning she told me that whatever had attacked him in the excavation wasn't very large, and she thinks the scan they did showed that it somehow bored into his skull like a corkscrew. She had no idea what it was; neither did his surgeon. She showed me the latest CAT scan from this morning, and that was even more strange. There's no sign of internal damage anymore! My God! Something tore into Jessie's skull yesterday, and today he's fine? Dougherty said it's some kind of medical anomaly, that there are rare cases of patients healing quickly, even overnight. It's in medical journals, that's what she told me, like with those old-time tent preachers and their laying-on-of- hands when someone is sick or wounded. The 'Thank you, Jesus, I'm cured!' bullshit. Mind over matter sometimes can heal a patient, she said, like a placebo sometimes can work. But I doubt that works with serious lacerations."

"Regeneration," Zack said. "It's like when you cut a worm in half and two worms grow back. Some lizards lose tails and then grow new ones. You can cut a starfish into five pieces, and you'll have five little starfishes. And human skin cells stay alive for weeks after a person dies. It's as if you don't die all at once." The two young women looked at him. He shrugged. "I read a lot, okay?"

Julie kept looking back at the hospital room. "You know that song he quoted, '*Nothing from nothing leaves nothing...?*' After you left, Jessie hummed it in his sleep."

"It's the medication, Julie, that's all it—"

"No, it isn't the meds! He always turns off the radio whenever that idiot song comes on, says it's got the dumbest lyrics he's ever heard. Jessie hates that damned song! I know that for a fact!"

This whole thing was tearing Julie apart, and Tiffany felt maybe she was going at this all wrong. "Jessie admitted he was acting crazy yesterday, mentioned he hasn't been himself. He's aware of his strange behavior. Maybe we should give him the benefit of a doubt."

Zack shook his head. "No! Can't you see he's looking for a way to cop out? He's nothing but a lying —" Julie's expression stopped him. The color had disappeared from her face.

"I don't think so," she muttered to herself.

Tiffany placed her hand on the girl's shoulder, her sympathetic best friend she had known for ten minutes. "What are you saying?"

"I don't know what I'm saying. None of this makes any sense. Look, I'm sorry. I can't talk about this anymore. Thanks for coming, both of you, okay?"

"You got a cell phone?" Tiffany asked. Julie held it out, and Tiffany punched its keys. "My number, if you need to talk. Okay?"

"Okay. Thanks." Julie returned to Moss' room, closing the

door behind her.

Tiffany's lips mouthed a silent *Fuck!* "You know what, Zack? I think what Julie wanted to tell us is something she can't admit to herself. Hell, I don't blame her." She stepped far away from Moss' room, and Zack followed. Out of anyone's hearing range, she still whispered. "Her man has his own excavation going on inside his skull. Medical anomaly, they tell her. That explains nothing, and she knows it!"

"Regeneration, like a worm — but human!" Zack said. "It was on an old *Doctor Who*."

"Riddle me this, Batman. You ever hear of a rat chewing all the way into a living man's skull, and he's alive to tell the tale? I doubt that's possible. Something bit Moss, all right, but it wasn't any rat, not a squirrel, or a great white shark. Whatever took that bite took something from him and then left the premises, and it took more than his scalp. I think Julie is telling us the man inside that room no longer is Jessie Moss. Not the man she knew, anyway. But I don't know if I buy that. He seemed perfectly lucid to me, disregarding his homage to Billy Preston."

Zack looked around, made certain no staff person stood nearby. "Maybe it's like a new worm is growing, but it's inside his head — like another brain replaced the one that got busted? Pieces of his old one are there, and the song helps him connect to what he remembers, like some kind of trigger, because he remembers some stuff, enough to show he's still who he was. Maybe it's not really his own brain any more. Like *The Invasion of The Body Snatchers*, or an episode of *The Bachelor*."

"Could be — if this were a bad science fiction movie."

Zack mulled his thought over. "You know what this means, don't you?"

"That Jessie Moss is regenerating like a human Tribble? Maybe by tomorrow there will be ten of him. Fascinating, Captain."

"Dial that down a little. We're in the real world here."

She turned serious. "Okay, then. We have impulses that

we have to keep in check, don't we? I mean, if we could just let them go, just act on our basest instincts —"

"We create our own monsters, Tiffany."

Tiffany's eyes drifted back towards the hospital room with the closed door. "If you're right, and I'm not saying you are, but if you *are* right — it means that Jessie Moss is no longer in control of Jessie Moss, and that girl in there could be in some serious danger from that man who looks like her fiancé, but really isn't. Shit!"

"Ditto," Zack said.

# CHAPTER TEN

**THE GARDEN OF EDEN, July, 2015:
EDEN AND REEFE**

*"...speaking of going back into the dirt..."*

**E**den Colson never intended to cry. She usually appeared much tougher, and the sobbing-little-girl bit wasn't her style. The tears just happened, and (thank you, God!) Fred Reefe was with her to allow them. She would never have admitted it to anyone, but Greg wouldn't have understood those tears. Eden hadn't told her husband about Jessie Moss, convinced he would probably overreact and do something stupid involving further police investigation and lawyers. It was the way Greg thought, and although his heart was in the right place, vengeance was not what Eden wanted. Both Reefe and she agreed that Moss needed help, not a criminal record.

Fred Reefe understood Eden's need for his support during the officers' visit. Reefe may have lacked Greg's urban sophistication, but when the two officers' questions proved too much for her, the man knew when a woman just needed to be held. For almost an hour, senior officer Detective Michel Kearne and his younger partner *("Hello, I'm Officer Ed...")* fired their questions.

—*"Mrs. Colson, did you, however innocently, flirt with Mr. Moss, maybe toy with him?"*

—*"...and exactly why did you decide to invite a stranger upstairs when you could have treated his head wound in the kitchen?"*

—*"...and just how did Mr. Moss come to possess your nail*

*file inside your bathroom?"*

 —*"Did he speak crudely to you? Did you to him?"*

 —*"...and exactly where did Mr. Moss touch you?"*

*"And another question, if you don't mind, Mrs. Colson..."*

Polite as hell, the two men were, yet their questions made Eden feel increasingly dirty. She insisted Jessie Moss' wound was self-inflicted, but somehow the truth did not have truth's ring. The older cop asked the questions, the younger one (a rookie, probably) simply took down Eden's responses, remaining quiet except for one damning question:

*"You invited Mr. Reefe's men into your home, including Jessie Moss and Mr. Reefe here, while your husband was out and you were alone, isn't that correct?"*

The unspoken implication was clear...

*(...and pardon my bluntness, Mrs. Colson, but didn't you bring this on yourself because you're really just a bored and lonely housewife looking for a little excitement that got a bit out of hand?)*

"He made advances, yes — but nothing more..." Eden answered. "I was scared, but he didn't hurt me. He told me he thought I was attractive and, well..." Eden watched the young officer scribble away at his pad. "He said he wanted to see me without my clothes." This would be the most she would admit to Jessie's remarks.

Both officials looked at Eden. She half expected one to add, "Well, who wouldn't?" but neither said a word. The older cop had questions for Fred Reefe also, but these seemed significantly less offensive: about Moss' relationship with the other men, about his work record, whether he had shown any signs of instability before or after the time spent in the excavation, and about how the young worker received the head wound that sent him to Eden Colson's door.

Reefe kept his answers succinct also. "Jessie removed his helmet — don't know why. You get sweaty down there and sometimes you need to wipe the sweat from your eyes because it's so damned hot in a hole during the summer, and there are sharp rocks there, and..."

Blah, blah, and blah...

"Are you all right, Mrs. Colson?" from Officer Ed, the silent partner.

"I'm — I'm..."

Supervisor Reefe had remained cool throughout, but Eden broke down in sobs, her body shaking in his arms. The two officers glanced at one another; Eden could have sworn she saw the younger one smirking. The older cop asked one last question, and it was the expected whopper.

"Any idea why Jessie Moss would suddenly, out of nowhere, decide to slash himself in the neck with *your* file?"

Drying tears, Eden said, "None whatsoever. He seemed embarrassed, maybe suddenly realized what he was doing. Look, officer. I don't want to press charges, all right? I'm sure Mr. Moss was experiencing some side effect from his head wound, maybe trauma from whatever he'd experienced in the excavation. He had a nasty cut, seemed disoriented—"

Reefe added that the young man had no criminal history, that Jessie's erratic behavior likely wouldn't repeat, and that until yesterday he was an exemplary worker. He didn't want this smudge on Moss' record to follow him for the rest of his life. Hearing both Fred Reefe and Eden Colson's statements, the younger officer closed his note pad, and that seemed to be that. No Columbo-like "Just one more thing, Ma'am" intended to incriminate her, no lecture regarding the inadvisability of inviting strangers in for coffee and Danish. The law officers thanked the two for their time and were gone.

Eden waited until the squad car disappeared from the excavation site. She turned to Reefe with the tone of a woman at confession. "I'm so embarrassed. I didn't mean to do the ugly cry. Hell, you'd think those men believed that I plunged that file into Jessie's neck myself!"

"They got your statement, and that's what they came for. I appreciate your not pressing charges, Mrs. Colson. Jessie Moss is a good kid; his brains got scrambled, is all. His fiancé phoned, told me he's going to be okay. Kind of a miracle, but a miracle is what we needed to make all this go away. I'm thinking it has."

Eden chose not to admit her real reason for not pressing charges, although she did believe Moss had suffered *something* caused by the accident. She had a more personal motive for her lenient decision. Fred Reefe hadn't asked her to forgive Jessie Moss, but she knew this was what he wanted her to do.

"Some coffee?" she added, again the gracious host.

"I have to be getting back to the site, Mrs. ... *Eden*. There *is* one thing, though. You mentioned the other day about your garden, said you saw a load of slugs while you were digging? I heard some strange thumps coming from inside the water pipes yesterday, also some kind of chittering, and I'm worried that we may have a bigger problem with the water lines than I thought."

"Come see for yourself. I'll grab my garden tools."

Eden Colson's garden really wasn't much of one, not yet anyway, and there were still tangles of weeds. But it seemed large enough for several flower beds and some roses, and by midsummer the place could look decent if she were diligent enough to tend to it. Eden dug into the hole she had started days earlier. She had avoided returning because of the slug-things, but Reefe's presence made that fear go away. The two went at the hole for several minutes and they created a sizable hollow, but not one slug appeared.

"I don't understand. The other day there were dozens of them." Eden dug some more.

"You seem disappointed."

"I wasn't exaggerating, I swear, Fred. There were dozens, at least I think there were, because they moved so fast. Fat and ugly things, the size of knockwursts, the biggest damned slugs I've ever seen, if that's what they were. They skittered back into the dirt when I dug them up. I guess they stayed there."

Reefe got to his feet, clapped some dried mud from his palms. "And speaking of going back into the dirt — Anyway, let me know if you see any more."

"I'm sorry to have wasted your time. You want to wash your hands first?" It was all Eden could think to say, and she felt like an idiot the moment she said it.

"No water, remember?"

Eden blushed. "Oh, right. Guess it's silly to wash up anyway, doing what you do, right?"

Another smile. "Right."

She removed her work gloves, showed her palms. "Clean hands, see?" She slid open the screen door, and Reefe followed her into the kitchen. "About that coffee. It's already made, just have to heat it—"

"Thanks, no. Oh, I just remembered. I have Greg's golf shirt in the truck. I can get it—"

"Don't worry about it. I'll get your work shirt back to you soon as I can clean it. No water, remember? And Greg would be suspicious if I loaded the washer at night. We have this routine, you know, like..." She shut up. Trivialities after recent events seemed especially trivial.

Their silence was short but awkward as the two stood looking at each other. Eden felt another heated blush. She knew Reefe had to have noticed.

"I have other work shirts. Thanks. I really appreciate —"
*Awkward as hell...*
"I guess I'll just let you get back to—"

He touched her cheek, lightly ran his finger along it without taking his eyes from hers. In one sudden motion he pulled Eden to him and kissed her. It happened fast, and she was caught off guard. The kiss lasted longer than she should have allowed, and Eden pulled away, looked at him. She said nothing, just kept looking into his eyes. She would have lost herself in those eyes had he not spoken. He looked like a man bracing himself for a powerful slap.

"I'm so sorry. God, I don't know why I — Look, I didn't mean — *damn!* I got dirt all over your—"

She put her finger to his lips, whispered, "Shut up."

This time she made the move. They kissed again.

Taking his hand, Eden led Fred Reefe upstairs.

Closing the bedroom door, Eden locked it. Not that it would have made any difference had they been discovered together. She and Reefe managed to keep as quiet as they were able, discounting the unmistakable sound of skin slamming against skin. Although not silent by any means, the two achieved some restraint silencing the screams and moans that came with sudden lovemaking. Passion, once let loose, has the nasty tendency to dull clear thinking; their cautious attempts at self-control also would have made no difference if they were discovered.

What *did* make a difference was the closed bedroom door that muffled the liquid mushy sound that came from the hallway bathroom. That door had been kept closed also.

Inside the bathroom was proof why earlier no slugs had crawled from the garden soil. The dark creatures — creatures that were really not slugs at all — had gone somewhere else. These were the smaller of the Wogslûk, but every bit as deadly as their larger brethren, and dozens slithered like dark sludge emerging from the open cavity of the Colson family's bathtub drain.

# CHAPTER ELEVEN

## THE WESTBOUND CONCORD
## OVERLAND STAGE EXPRESS, 1866:
## SISTER MARGELLE AND MELISSA

### *"Make it fast and painless..."*

**S**ister Margelle had a secret.

During the spring of 1827, Margelle had been born to Jacob and Jenny Mallory, an identical twin arriving six minutes and thirty-three seconds behind her sister, Nancy Beth. The girls' father often joked of the differences between his two daughters: Margelle, from the day of her birth, seemed reluctant to enter the world, foretelling his daughter's general attitude. In contrast, Nancy Beth came out swinging, and Jacob insisted the infant screamed bloody murder while her sister didn't even cry. Margelle always hated that story.

The sisters seemed twins in name only. Whereas Nancy Beth rarely appeared without a broad mischievous grin, Margelle found little humor in anything. The sisters seemed years apart rather than minutes, even dressing differently: Nancy Beth the perpetual tomboy in split skirts (suitable for riding side saddle with the local youths), Margelle preferring long dowdy dresses that displayed not even an ankle, "the youngest old lady in St. Louis," as her male classmates called her. During the twins' adolescence, when the boys came calling after church, Jacob had no doubt which of his daughters would be enjoying a picnic that Sunday afternoon. Even when Nancy Beth begged her sister to come along (to the sadness of whatever male held the picnic basket), Margelle stoically refused.

Fate dealt a cruel hand shortly after the girls turned

*sixteen. Within days of each other, the two became stricken with scarlet fever, Nancy Beth the first to take to her bed — but only because Jacob insisted. When Margelle fell to the illness also, the sisters lay side by side in their small cots, the doctor standing between them shaking his head. Their fever worsened by the day, and it did not look good for either of them.*

*Kneeling between his daughters' beds, Jacob reached to hold each girl's hand. "Will you pray for your sister, both of you? God will surely hear your shared appeals to Him." The girls gave him their word that each would pray for the other. Once alone, Margelle listened as Nancy Beth said her evening prayer.*

*"Please, Lord, if you must take one of us, take me," Nancy Beth whispered, hands clasped tightly, her eyes turned up-ward. During that moment Margelle could not have loved her sister more, but she did not want to die.*

*Margelle's own prayer she kept to herself, muttering so quietly she knew Nancy Beth could not hear. "Please Lord, if you must take one of us, take my sister, as that is her wish..."*

*Nancy Beth Mallory did not live to see the next morning.*

*The twenty-six-year-old Sister Margelle never talked about her twin, never even mentioned her. No one who knew her at the Convent Loretto learned much about Margelle's past. She volunteered nothing about her twenty-six years to the Mother Superior with whom she had a distant relationship at best. She certainly shared nothing about the pact with her God that she had made.*

*There came another pact shortly after the diggers lowered young Nancy Beth into her grave. Now alone inside her room, the surviving sixteen year old prayed again. "If you choose for me to live, Lord, I swear on my own soul that I will do your work for the rest of my days."*

*Margelle's recovery was both surprising and swift. Many close to Jacob and his wife called it a miracle. The young girl felt certain it was. Whether through the love of God or the burden of a soul heavy with unrelenting guilt, Margelle*

*Mallory entered the convent soon after.*

...but now, so close to what seemed certain death, the sister questioned if she had dissatisfied her Lord in a manner for which she had not atoned.

Driven by a team of runaway horses the inside of a speeding stage seemed less a place for prayer than for action. The coach's broken door slammed open and shut, and Sister Margelle cowered in her seat as her fellow passenger climbed to the wagon's top with hopes of reining in the six panicked horses. A stranger days earlier, now the nun's life depended on Melissa Monahan's grit. How that young woman would stop the team of stallions was anyone's guess, but the only other choice was for both to die. The coach's rear wheel had held longer than Margelle thought possible, but the women's luck couldn't last much longer at this speed, and prayer was not her best option.

She could not climb out of the coach as Melissa had. A nun's habit seemed unfit clothing for that sort of activity, and once caught in the rushing wind her robes could send her catapulting from the stage to a very messy end. She chanced leaning through the window, stretching herself partially through to catch a glimpse of Melissa in the driver's box. Her blood froze that instant.

Sister Margelle couldn't see it clearly, but she recognized the creature by its size. Even in night's darkness, the murky silhouette appeared huge. Somehow one of those hellish slugthings had gotten onboard. Margelle saw only the hands of the young woman above the coach, but she was holding to the side rail with both of them, and that meant Melissa was *not* holding the gun while that dark creature wriggled from the driver's box toward her.

If she did nothing, the sister knew Melissa would die, and that meant they both would die. Pulling herself back into the carriage, Margelle reached for the rifle. She had never handled a gun, and if firing it after one shot involved more than pulling the trigger, she had no idea what to do next. She might have only the single shot, and to hit her target she would have to do more than simply lean through the window. Leaving the coach would be a huge risk, but she had an idea.

From outside she heard Melissa shout into the wind, *"Fuck you!"*

She acted quickly. The crucifix at the sister's neck contained a long and thick chain. It could withstand pressure, but Margelle didn't know how much. She was thin, didn't weigh much, and she would need only a minute or so, but she had less time than that to make her decision. Removing the chain she slipped the loop around the swinging door's handle; the other end she fastened to her arm. Grabbing hold of the rifle she allowed the door to support her weight and kept her footing inside the coach for balance. With her arm harnessed securely, she located the dark shadow in the rifle's sight, a difficult task to perform with the careening coach's sudden shifts.

She heard Melissa scream. With no time to think, with hardly enough time to take aim, Sister Margelle squeezed the trigger.

Melissa could smell the damned thing, it was that close. Thick as a tree trunk, it had the raw stink of river scum. Its mouth hooks opened and closed, huge twisted swords snapping at her throat, eager to grab her. She screamed, knowing it would do no good, wishing for some of Sister Margelle's belief in divine intervention. The slug-thing's hot breath almost wilted her skin, and in another moment those hooks would sink deep into her throat. All the while the horses did not slow one bit. Tonight, death had many choices, but Melissa's choices had run out. She shut her eyes.

*"Make it fast, please... make it fast and painless..."*

She recognized the sound of a single rifle shot. It reverberated inside her head, but she welcomed it as she would have welcomed the hand of God. Melissa opened her eyes in time to see the creature thrash in sudden agony, but it remained near enough to do serious damage. She kicked at it, kicked hard with every ounce of strength she had. Squealing, it made an aborted lunge for her, but with one last kick it spilled from the coach's top. Melissa watched it spin over on itself, disappearing in the trail's darkness. Below, she saw Sister Margelle still holding the rifle. A bizarre sight, a nun with a weapon, but no less bizarre than what the sister had shot. The nun maneuvered herself through the broken door of the coach, her crucifix catching a shimmer of moonlight, a strangely spiritual image in the midst of madness. Maybe this wasn't divine intervention, but it would do.

Dropping into the driver's perch, Melissa grabbed the reins. There were six lines, and she grabbed all six. Six horses, six lines, probably one for each of the team. That made sense. She held three in each hand, pulled each one and hoped for the best.

*"WHOA! WHOA! DAMMIT!! WHOA!!"*

The horses whinnied, the two in the lead pulling back the hardest. The rear wheel spun off its axle and disappeared from the coach. Dragging in the trail dirt, the careening carriage bumped wildly and threw Melissa from the seat. Grabbing the stage's long brake lever, she could only imagine what Sister Margelle below was going through, assuming the nun hadn't been thrown through the busted door into some ravine, her body ripped to shreds.

The two women had certainly gone beyond their allotted quotas for miracles, but another one arrived when the horses slowed their pace. The drag of the stage proved a phenomenon in itself, its missing wheel affecting the harnessed team. Violating every rule of gravity, the coach did not turn over while yanked along practically sideways. Covered with a cloud of trail dust the horses came to a grinding stop.

Maybe there was something to be said about the hand of God. With no breath in her, Melissa sat exhausted at the driver's perch, its seat slanting crazily because of the missing wheel's support. She dropped to the dirt and peered into the stage. Sister Margelle crouched inside, her body hunched while clutching her crucifix. Its thick chain, wrapped around the door handle and her arm, probably had saved her. Melissa could only marvel at what the sister had done. "You're all right?" Margelle only nodded. "I suppose I should give thanks to Jesus, eh, Sister?"

The nun looked up from what seemed a very deep prayer. "No, I suppose *I* should give thanks to *you.*"

"I think we owe each other those thanks," Melissa said. She looked into the distance of the Santa Fe Trail disappearing into the darkness. "Now comes the hard part. We have to figure where we go from here."

"Anywhere that isn't here will be a good start." The nun climbed out from the coach. "Grab your bags from this damned stage. We've got a long ride ahead of us. We'll unhitch the horses, bring them together. Mr. Jamison's saddle is onboard. We can share it."

"Suppose there are more of those things out there?"

Sister Margelle clutched the rifle and held it close. "I'm suddenly feeling a whole lot more confident."

Melissa smiled. "Amen to that."

Selecting one of the lead horses, they rode slowly with the remaining five in tow behind. At every turn the darkness threatened, but the animals would sense danger before the two women did, and the team appeared all right. Melissa hoped the horse they shared didn't drop dead from exhaustion. They changed horses every few miles.

How long they would travel there was no telling, nor where they were headed or whether another town were nearby. Total darkness made it impossible to know if they passed any cattle ranches or even a trace of human life. Margelle held onto Melissa's waist, her head occasionally drooping so she could doze leaning against her companion's back. In the morning the women could properly rest. The slug-things, if they were out there, didn't seem to love the sunlight.

Through the night, they spoke little or not at all. As sunlight appeared through the horizon, Margelle finally broke the silence.

"We haven't answered the obvious question, you know."

"There's about a hundred obvious questions. Like when do we get to pee?"

"Okay, there's that. But — just what *are* those creatures?"

Melissa had no idea, but she considered the sister's concern. "Ben joked about prairie snails. Those ugly things *did* look like snails without shells, didn't they? There must be all kinds of creatures that no one knows about living under the ground in these parts. Reptiles, insects, things digging through sand and dirt. Probably those slug-things burrowed out through that hole in the trail; they had a look around, found a few things they liked. Maybe the bastards will crawl back like ants after a picnic, and that'll be the end to it."

"Maybe," Sister Margelle said, "but entire towns don't disappear in a few days. Those things, whatever they are, somehow made off with every living person in Trementina, and they seemed focused on wanting us too. I don't think they were just after food, either. You saw what happened to your fiancé — to Christian, and to Mr. Jamison. They weren't themselves any more, like a piece of their brains had been sucked right out of their skulls. Those men *were* bleeding badly, right? Those slug-things did it."

"Right." Melissa shook her head. "About Christian — Sister, you know, I've been so concerned about saving my own skin these past hours, I haven't given a thought to him. He was going to be my husband the day after tomorrow. My God, what kind of woman am I to—?"

"You said it yourself — that wasn't your Christian who killed old Sam and tried burying his axe in your skull. And that wasn't Mr. Jamison who dragged that old woman into the tavern. But if that's so, if Christian and Ben no longer were Christian and Ben, then who *were* those men? Whatever happened to them, it happened quick."

Melissa considered this too. "You called those slug-things

smart because they seemed to know what they were about, how they circled the stage, sent the smaller ones to us first, like pawns in a Chess game, you said. Maybe — well, this will sound crazy."

"After these past twenty-four hours, nothing will sound crazy, Melissa."

"I'm thinking — well, it's just a possibility, but maybe those things absorbed some kind of intelligence from the townspeople, and the more they absorbed, the smarter they got. It wasn't food they wanted, not food for their bellies, anyway. They took something from Christian and Ben without killing them right off. Sister, if that's so, then those creatures had the entire town of Trementina for their schooling!"

Margelle squinted at the morning sun. "I doubt those 'prairie snails' will be quoting Shakespeare any time soon if they were looking for book intelligence from these locals, but you may have a point."

"Do you think you killed that one on the stage?"

"He won't be joining his friends for breakfast, you can be sure of—" Margelle stopped talking, shielding her eyes from the morning sunlight to make certain that what she saw was there. "There's a fence up ahead! It's a ranch... with a signpost! There must be people!"

The signpost shook on rusty hinges above a gate, but no words appeared painted on it, only the boldly printed letters **McK** — the kind of symbol appearing on a branding iron. This had to be a cattle ranch.

Melissa stopped their horse at the gate, studied the signpost. "Can it be? Those letters —- *McKenna!* This could be Christian's ranch — well, Christian Senior's, his dad. Christian told me the cattle ranch wasn't very far from Trementina. We have to go inside!"

"No argument here," Margelle said. "Maybe there's food! I'm ready to eat one of our horses."

Melissa dismounted. The front gate was closed but not bolted, and the large ranch house sat only a few yards from an empty corral. Off to the side the ranch hands' bunkhouse

**114**

seemed deserted, and its windows were smashed. Margelle climbed from the saddle. The women glanced in all directions.

"You see any cattle? Any livestock? Stables look empty too."

"I don't see a thing, Sister. Nothing."

The nun pulled the rifle from the saddle scabbard. "Whatever the reason for that is, it can't be good. Let's have a look."

The house doors were unlocked, but furniture had been piled to the door, another bad sign. Melissa pushed past it. One look inside the parlor revealed the place recently had been occupied, although whoever left recently had no intentions of tidying up. A cigar gone to ash rested in a coffee cup on the small table by the fireplace, and a lamp lay broken on the floor. That broken lamp spoke volumes. Someone wasn't around to pick up its pieces.

"No fancy curtains, nothing on the walls. No woman's touch here, that's for sure," Sister Margelle whispered. "And the furniture at the door — someone may still be inside."

"Christian's mother died a while ago. There's just men here — or there *was*." Melissa called out, "Hello? Anybody here?" Nothing. "It's me, Melissa Monahan. Christian's fiancé? Any McKennas here? Hello?"

A loud thump came from the back room. The two women looked at each other.

Margelle whispered, "There *is* someone in the house! Take this, just in case." She handed the rifle to Melissa. "Your turn. I fired one shot."

Melissa cocked it, looked inside the chamber. "It's a Winchester, Ben said. There's about fifteen rounds, give or take."

"Good enough," Margelle said.

The two women approached the closed door of the back room.

Soaked in blood, the lone Wogslûk lay in dirt. With the

morning light came much worse pain. It understood pain; it did not understand death.

Not yet...

*It struggles to remember.*

*(The woman-thing fights, kicks, hurts. Then — a noise from below, more loud than the crack of a rock. More pain. Much blood. Then dirt...)*

*The pain inside its head is terrible, and there is tiredness.*

*Powerful tiredness.*

*Until this moment it has understood nothing of pain, of endings.*

*Of death.*

*The Wogslûk is afraid.*

# CHAPTER TWELVE

## Diamond Loop, July 2015:
## MEET THE NEIGHBORS

*"...like sand through an hourglass..."*

Along the Diamond Loop cul-de-sac, mailboxes lined up before each home in perfect symmetry like those all-looked-the-same little boxes made of ticky-tacky, as the old folk song went. But that was where their similarity ended. Some were adorned with painted birds, others flowers. There were happy 'Have-a-nice-day' faces, big red Valentine hearts, and a few displays of abstract nonsense Jackson Pollack would have had difficulty making sense of. Many boxes were plain and grey, exhibiting only names and numbers of neighbors who preferred to remain unseen and unheard. Paired with the welcome mats at the residents' doorsteps, these postal boxes were a stranger's first indication of what to expect of a Diamond Loop homeowner when the front door swung open...

★ ★ ★

### 608 Diamond Loop : The Campbells

Like the peacock's plumage displayed on her mailbox, Mrs. Regina Campbell's beauty bordered on overkill. From the time she was a child, people commented how she seemed almost too stunning, that opinion persisting as young Gina blossomed into womanhood. Unfortunately, Regina Campbell was living proof of beauty's being only skin deep. The adolescent girl broke more than a few hearts, and stomped on many. Older and wiser, she had learned to focus more on men's bank accounts, and those she broke also. In her mid-thirties

**117**

she met shipping magnate, Harry Campbell, while standing by a nude ice sculpture of some Greek goddess at a local politico's Manhattan dinner party. Years later Harry would consider how that statue's ironic symbolism reflected his marriage.

Certainly, her first two husbands would have agreed that Gina's appreciation of them was questionable, and her third spouse seemed well on his way to that persuasion. Harry had no problem with the arm candy his trophy wife provided, nor with the eighteen years' difference between them. He assumed that Gina felt content with the jewelry, the open credit card accounts, and the sporty new BMW in the driveway of her suburban Diamond Loop home that went nicely with their Manhattan condo and the shore house for weekends in the Hamptons.

It wasn't that Gina didn't appreciate her husband's thoughtfulness, and as long as the goodies kept coming, Harry's generosity seemed enough to keep the woman's restlessness in check. She did love the gifts; she simply didn't love Harry. The man hadn't cheated on her, hadn't gone bald or gotten fat, and he hadn't once staggered home drunk nor raised a hand to her. Never insisting on putting a baby inside her, Harry wasn't even half bad in bed. The simple fact was that Mrs. Regina Campbell had become bored, the quintessential desperate housewife for whom the afternoon soap operas and exorbitant shopping sprees were not enough to fill her day. But Gina saw some potential in something that *was*.

The Diamond Loop excavation certainly proved a pain in the ass because of its daily shutdown of water, but the men working that hole showed some promise. The crew was a visual smorgasbord for those Loop wives whose estrogen still bubbled hot. For Gina, it didn't take much detective work to learn that Eden Colson had been entertaining those workers from their first day on the job, luring them into her home with Danish pastry and iced coffee. Gina recognized a like-minded woman despite Eden's June Cleaver demeanor. Watching the Colson home, she made note of how the supervisor of Reefe Water & Sewer Contractors spent an excessive amount of time there. This morning he visited again when, for some reason, the police came calling. What interested Gina most was that Fred Reefe remained after the police had left. She had watched as the Colson kid went off with some older biker girl, and that meant Eden and Reefe had remained alone for some time. Something was going on inside that house, something requiring a visit from men wearing badges, and whatever it was, it beat *Days of Our Lives* by a mile. And if Gina's suspicions were correct about Eden's handsome gentleman caller, well, then...

*"Like sand through an hour glass, these are the days of our lives..."* she mumbled, grinning to herself.

Gina often had exchanged meaningless pleasantries with Eden Colson, in the mornings waving from her back patio as if they were old pals. Running into each other at the Shop Rite, she had even shared details of upcoming barbecues and neighborhood festivities, housewifery bullshit about which Gina couldn't have cared less. But the channels of communication had opened and she could stop in to say hello, maybe share some gossipy girl-talk. Since Fred Reefe had not left the Colson home, she knew her visit would prove interesting.

Gina slipped into a pair of hip huggers most women past thirty would have had difficulty getting away with. She brushed her hair (counting to thirty strokes, as was her ritual), then headed to the bathroom for a quick freshening up. The water remained off, but a little cosmetic handiwork was doable. With a strategic floral spritz of Shalini behind each ear (and one between the silken skin of her girls), she checked her image in the bathroom mirror. Yes, she was good to go, but for one delicate matter.

It was a less than feminine consideration, but she had been out earlier to ask about the excavation's progress. The morning had been humid, and Gina had perspired a little. Those nasty lady pits required a few delicate scrubs. The water wasn't running for a shower, but her trusty baby oiled loofa remained damp enough to do the trick. Pulling the shower curtain, she reached for the pink sponge.

Something long and black slithered along the shower head. Having no time to react, Gina managed a gasp. As if it saw her, the dark thing's mouth hooks extended and opened wide.

Curling itself, the small creature dropped into Mrs. Regina Campbell's scalp.

### 617 Diamond Loop: The Hunters

A 1960's-style peace sign adorned the family's mail box, although neither Paul nor Gloria Hunter resembled anything close to '60's hippies. Their teenaged son, Denny, however, was another matter. He had slapped the peace decal on the box during the family's first day at their new address. Paul had managed to talk him out of another decal, that of Frank Zappa giving the finger.

The remains of a shared joint lay in the misshapen ceramic ash tray Denny Hunter had made for his mother when he was a cub scout. His artistic attempt wasn't a bad effort creatively speaking, not for a ten year old, but on this afternoon Denny would have been hard pressed to come anywhere close to duplicating it.

"We're like Romeo and Juliet, bumping uglies behind my parents' backs," he whispered into the ear of his sixteen year old girlfriend of two weeks, a pony tailed nymphet named Heather Cooper. He had a good high going, but not all of it was owing to the weed.

"No. Like Bonnie and Clyde," Heather answered, "raiding your mother's freezer for popsicles." The adolescent lovers laughed, then continued making out on the couch like ferrets in heat. It was a hot and sweaty session because Denny had turned off the air conditioning. He had read online that when girls felt warm they also felt horny, and while his parents were at work the house would remain empty for the entire afternoon. With a little luck he and Heather would be hitting his sheets within the half hour, sweating themselves into a foaming frenzy.

Heather's warm tongue tasted like the cherry popsicle they had shared from the freezer after smoking, and the sensation sparked the boy's hot-wired hormones tenfold. He set about dutifully slipping his hand beneath her tube top. She moaned a little, pulled Denny to her, and squirmed herself under him. Denny knew that once he reached into her shorts there was a good chance they wouldn't make it to the sheets, that they would be doing the wet nasty right there on the living room couch. Thinking that over, some rationality returned. If he happened to spill himself onto his mom's brand new upholstery he would have some explaining to do, and he knew enough about what could happen if he spilled himself into Heather.

"Wait, let's stop for a minute, okay?" he said between hot breaths.

Heather grinned but made no effort to roll down her top. "You know, that's supposed to be *my* line." She wrapped her fingers around the back of Denny's neck, manipulating a milky white breast close to his mouth.

"No, really. Let's go to my room — you know, to do this right."

"You have a way with words, Dennis Hunter." This time Heather *did* roll up her tube top, her girlish modesty returning the moment she left the couch. The two bee-lined to the stairs.

Heather sat on Denny's bed. "A little hot in here, don't you think?"

"What I think is, it's about to get a lot hotter." Denny removed his shirt, and again Heather's tube top came off, this time with no assistance required from him. He was accurate about the temperature. The two were happily bathed in sweat within minutes.

During moments of teenaged passion, neatness never counts for much. Cut-off jeans and tossed underwear lay in a haphazard pile alongside the bed while Denny and Heather body slammed for the next hour.

Neither noticed the small dark slug-like creatures that

crawled along the bed posts to join them.

★ ★ ★

## 610 Diamond Loop: The Brimleys

An American flag provided the background to the Veteran of Foreign War sticker affixed to George and Anna Brimley's mailbox, and rightfully so. George Brimley had served in Viet Nam, and on April 30th 1975 during the fall of Saigon, just as that cursed war was nearing its end, he took a bullet in the spine for his efforts. Decorated by his country with the Medal Of Honor, the same country he had served so honorably could find no place for PFC George Brimley in its work force.

*(At ease, soldier, and have a good life...)*

Brimley had managed to keep his legs; he just couldn't use them anymore. The GI Bill covered just so much, and for months he found himself slopping meat and potatoes into his plate inside several Philadelphia soup kitchens. But on April 1st, 1976, Anna Sobielsky, a twenty-four year old immigrant from Kiev, came into George Brimley's life.

Pretty in a subdued way, Anna spoke broken English as she scooped a ladle of potato soup into his bowl at a local veterans' kitchen calling itself the Cornerstone. George couldn't speak a word of Russian, but somehow, against all odds, love happened, although not right away. It took an hour.

As he sat alone, Anna walked over to him during her break. *"You...you...I...know...you not able..."* she managed, blushing with embarrassment.

"I'm sorry," George said, ridiculously pointing to his mouth and ear. "I can't understand what you're trying—" He smiled and shrugged.

Frustrated, the girl scribbled something on her note pad and pointed to the heavyset cook behind the counter. She called him Yuri, indicating the man would know how to decipher what she had written. Smiling with shyness, she returned to serving the other men waiting in line. George looked at the piece of paper.

**122**

*Мы наме есь Янна. И ам аваре юг лежа ноу лонгер ворк, вот юр смеле дух. Плеасе вайт фор тэ. Иль бе финишед суонк, окай?*

"Yeah, that helps," he mumbled to himself.

Maybe she was too shy to communicate in any other way. For all he knew, maybe the girl was telling him she noticed something hanging from his nose. This *was* April Fool's Day.

The cook was Russian himself, and George figured this Yuri guy probably was instrumental in acclimating Anna to the strange culture that was America. Handing him the slip of paper George felt his heart race, but he knew better than to set himself up for disappointment. Before the war he had been engaged, but his returning home in a wheelchair altered circumstances significantly. His high school sweetheart offered tearful excuses worthy of an Academy Award, but anger was never part of Brimley's repertoire. Wishing his beautiful Felicia well, he knew he would never see her again.

"So, what is the girl telling me?" he asked the cook. The man grinned as he read the note to himself.

"You know, Anna, she is my niece. She has been in this country only one month."

"Yes, I figured that. So, the note?"

Another grin, broader. "She says, *'My name is Anna. I know your legs don't work, but your smile does. Please wait here for me, I will be finished soon, okay?'*"

Until that moment George Brimley's life had been pitifully short on miracles, but now one had presented itself. With Anna in his life, he searched day and night until he found simple janitorial work at the Philadelphia Exchange. During lunch breaks, reading the big wall of ever-changing numbers, he discovered that he had a talent for recognizing when to buy, when to sell. George took some of his paycheck to invest in a new computer company called Apple, managing to turn a little money into a lot. Shortly after marrying Anna Sobielsky, he opened a hardware store; a few years later he turned it into a local chain. As Anna learned English, he learned some Russian. There was money, there were children, and years later there were grandchildren. Maybe a cold war was going on between their countries, but you could never tell that by watching the two of them.

...and now there was Diamond Loop. George's plan was to buy the spacious cul-de-sac home as an investment for his eldest son, live in it for a short while, then retire happily at the Jersey shore with Anna. His being confined to a wheel chair had done little to slow the man down even as he neared seventy, and he looked forward to living by the ocean where he could fish off some pier at sunrise, then relax with his wife sipping margaritas while overlooking the Atlantic.

During the early afternoon hours Anna took the SUV to pick up some deli in Glenn Echoes so the two could share sandwiches and lemonade together on the enclosed back patio. Often, as he relaxed alone, the blonde woman who lived at 608 would wave to him as she sunbathed. She had once asked to see George's impressive collection of rare guns, and he had shown her the old Johnson Flintlock pistol he had purchased from the Cole McKenna estate. He laughed when she was afraid to hold it, but women seemed to have a natural aversion to guns, and Anna never came near his collection. Seductive as Regina Campbell was, slim-waisted leggy types could never compete with Anna. Still, George always waved back and smiled his best neighborly smile at her, then returned to the highlights of the latest Phils game on his lap top. He expected any day the Campbell woman would remove her midriff top as she lay on her patio chaise just to see if he were watching, but this noon she was nowhere to be seen.

Anna had parked near the excavation because, for the second day, there was no access to the cul-de-sac. It wasn't a long walk from the site, but approaching the patio she appeared pale and moved slowly. George attributed this to the heat, but the couple were at the age when the slightest ailment could lead to a screaming ambulance siren.

"Everything all right, sweetheart? You seem to be a little

peaked."

Anna put down the large bag from the Glenn Echoes Deli. "Some roast beef, some corned beef. Today you get to pick." Almost as an afterthought she added, "Very strange thing, George. At the big hole, I mean. I seem to have been—"

*(Strange theeeng...seeem to have beeen...)*

Her thick accent didn't conceal from George that something was wrong. One close look at his wife verified it. A thick bubble of blood beaded at her hairline.

"My God, Anna! You've cut yourself! Your head, it's bleeding!"

She wiped at the small scratch, studied the smear of blood on her fingers. "Something in the car, just now — it was in the visor, I think. I don't know. Some big insect, maybe a dragon fly or something. Couldn't see. Probably flew off when I left the car. Don't worry, it isn't bad. I can put something on it and make your lunch in a few moments, okay/"

*(Eeesn't bad ... Som-theeeng... )*

George wriggled uncomfortably in the wheel chair, pissed because he couldn't manage any other movement. "*Not* all right, Anna! If something bit you, you have to—"

"Not bitten. Just — just cut, is all. Don't worry, George, I know what to do. You enjoy the sunshine." She disappeared inside, and George watched her go up the stairs. He called to her.

"Anna, I don't care about the damned sandwich! I think we should take you to the doctor!" He reached into his pocket for his cell phone, remembering he had left it charging in their bedroom. *"Damn!"*

His wife remained upstairs and silent even when George called to her, and he was beginning to worry if maybe Anna had passed out. On humid days like this the bugs were biting, all sorts of the nasty bastards. Anna was strong for a woman in her mid-sixties, but there were wasps and bees, and probably ticks from the woods carrying Lyme Disease too, and if something *had* bitten her —

Anna appeared before him, and she was smiling — sort of.

She had placed a single Band-Aid on her cut and the blood seemed to have stopped.

"You're okay?"

She handed him a paper plate containing his sandwich packed thick with lunchmeat, the plate surrounded with chips, as Anna always prepared it. She forgot the pickle, but George chose not to mention this.

"I'm okay," she answered. Her mood had changed considerably, but to *what* George wasn't sure. As if the past ten minutes hadn't occurred, she muttered some tune in Russian and her head bobbed like a child's as she sang.

" *s 'dnjo:m razh'denija, s 'dnjo:m razh'denija...*"

It took a moment before George recognized the tune. He stared at Anna hard. "Isn't that 'Happy Birthday?'"

"It is!" She laughed as if preparing to surprise him with a cake.

"But my birthday isn't until October."

She laughed again. "I seem unable to get this tune out of my head. Eat your sandwich, Georgie."

*(Eeeet, Georgeee...)*

Anna hadn't called him Georgie in years. He used to love when she called him that, but today it sounded peculiar, although he didn't know why. He took a bite of his sandwich.

*"Ey up to Leh ESD sandweech, Geirgie?"*

"I'm not up on my Russian today, Anna."

She was all smiles. "I asked if you liked your sandwich, Georgie?"

Something inside the thick layers of roast beef felt squishy, like one of those candy gummy bears his kids used to love, but much thicker. Probably an anchovy, he told himself. He knew Anna meant well, and it was never his style to complain. It stuck to his dentures and it wasn't something George wanted to chew for very long. Swallowing, again he chose not to mention this. Once down his throat he felt it move.

Anna continued to sing.

## **613 Diamond Loop: The Colsons**

Appropriately, Greg and Eden Colsons' mailbox featured one long stemmed daisy with several cartoon bees buzzing near its petals. Eden enjoyed working in her garden and looked forward to starting this new one. Today, however, the Colson mail slot more appropriately would have displayed the decal of creatures significantly uglier than the smiling bees, because Eden's bathtub rapidly was filling with them. Two or three at a time they crawled from the drain, and they kept coming as if from some busted garbage disposal that continuously regurgitated its contents.

The drain gave off a slight slurping sound as the slug-things squeezed through, but Eden heard nothing. For the first time during her thirteen year marriage she shared her bed with a man who was not her husband, and her racing thoughts were miles removed from the bathroom. She enjoyed the raw sex (and that *was* what it was; Eden was not kidding herself that it was anything more), and it wasn't until the deed was done that genuine guilt kicked in.

Fred Reefe reached for his pack of Marlboros. Eden stopped him.

"Please, don't. My husband doesn't smoke, and the smell of a cigarette—"

"I hear you." A thick silence followed. Then, "Look, Eden, I know we shouldn't have, okay? No excuses. This thing, it just hap—"

She put her finger to his lips. "I'm not sorry, Fred, but there won't be another time. I've never — I mean, you have a wife, I have a hus—" Eden almost choked on the word. "Christ, maybe I *am* sorry. I don't know what I feel. Mostly shitty, I guess."

He answered with an unconvincing nod of agreement. Pulling the covers off he reached for his clothes. He stopped dressing to touch Eden's cheek.

*"'Of all the gin joints in the world, she had to walk into mine...'"*

**127**

The man was charming as hell, all right. Eden wasn't looking for drama, and Fred mercifully offered none. She needed to smile, and she did. "Worst Bogie impression ever."

"Well, back to the basics of real life. Mind if I use your bathroom?"

"You know where it is." Eden thought her remark over. "...and *that,* folks, has got to be the understatement of the week."

Eden dressed, put herself together as best she could, and returned to the kitchen. She knew Fred Reefe had taken a huge chance spending time away from the water main project, and she wouldn't ask for more of it. Their interlude had not called for basking in lovemaking's afterglow; to expect that seemed not only stupid, it was asking for trouble. To even think of it as lovemaking seemed ludicrous. They had fucked, she had enjoyed it, and that was that.

Reefe joined her in the kitchen, but something was wrong.

"Your husband — Greg, he barbecues, right?"

The question threw her. "What?"

"Lighter fluid. Where does he keep it?"

"We have a gas grill. Lights itself. Fred, what—?"

"Hairspray. You have that? That'll work."

"In the bathroom."

He headed back up the stairs. Confused, Eden followed. At the closed bathroom door he stopped her. "You don't want to see this, Eden. Trust me."

She was not the woman to say that to. Pushing the door open, she stopped where she stood. "Oh my God!"

The tub had filled with them, stacks of slug-things crawling over one another in thick tangles. Clotted together, it was difficult to tell where one ended and another began. They were plump and much too long, and probably they weren't really slugs. Eden didn't know what they were.

"I don't think any got out of the tub, but they're trying," Reefe said. He pulled a can of hairspray from the cabinet, broke off the nozzle, then found Greg's container of mousse. He handed the can to Eden and squeezed out the entire tube of hair gel. "Spill the whole fucking load on them, soak the bastards!"

Eden put her hand over her mouth and gagged, but she kept dousing them. *"Jesus! Where did they come from? How...?"*

"Maybe from your garden. Probably from the busted water mains. But I know where they're *going!*" Reaching for his book of matches, Reefe lit one. He flung the match on the squirming pile and pulled Eden back.

The entire mound ignited with a loud *POOF!* From inside the tub, an erupting volcano bubbled, then burst, a raw sewage stink filling the air. The slug-things snapped like popping corn, rubbery bits of burning flesh surrounding the room with black firefly particles. Smoldering, some scaled the side of the bath. Reefe soaked them and lit another match. The fatter ones popped open, spurting black goo that smeared the porcelain with blobs of spilled ink. Thick sludge dripped towards the floor.

Eden hid her eyes while Fred watched the lumpy stack sizzle until it no longer moved. What remained resembled a small mountain of black mud. Reefe stepped closer.

"I think we got all of them. Are you okay?"

Eden was shaking badly. "I'm very far from okay."

"Must be a nest nearby, some kind of larvae. More of a pain in the ass than dangerous, probably. Slugs are a nuisance, is all." Reefe said this more to himself than to Eden, and his eyes averted hers.

"You don't believe that any more than I do. Did you see those hooks on them? Those things aren't garden slugs — maybe they're some kind of hybrid, a crossbreed of maggots or snails, or God-knows what lives underground. You know what I'm thinking?"

"Time to call the exterminator?"

"Besides that."

Reefe knew. "Jessie Moss. He said something bit him."

"I saw that man's scalp, Fred. Something sharp chewed into it, maybe something with hooks like—" She indicated the smoldering mush inside the tub. "...except bigger. A whole lot bigger. The ones here could squeeze through the pipes, and *these* weren't small, not like regular slugs — Christ, suppose there *are* nests of them?"

Reefe ran his forearm across the sweat beading his forehead. "Right now, your tub is the only casualty. It won't matter. You won't be needing it because I'm shutting the water off for a long time on this whole fucking block."

"There has to be more of them. Mine can't be the only home those things have decided to visit."

Reefe's expression told Eden he was thinking the same thing, maybe something worse if there were details he wasn't sharing. But under his breath he muttered only one word.

*"Shit..."*

It was an accurate word to describe Eden's disposal of the little suckers. There wasn't enough water pressure to send their fried remains down the toilet to their watery grave; instead, Eden filled several Hefty bags and tossed the dark pile of sludge in the garbage, and while doing this, she echoed Fred Reefe's one-word sentiment.

★ ★ ★

## MORE NEIGHBORS

**605 Diamond Loop:** Seven-year-old Robbie Lewis plucked a wormy creature from the toilet bowl and laughed. He pocketed it so he could toss it into the crib of little Emma, his baby sister.

**615 Diamond Loop:** Ester Gold, an eighty-three year old invalid living with her daughter, noticed something very long and dark crawling from beneath her daughter's kitchen sink. She immediately clutched her chest. The thing made it up Ester's leg before she hit the floor.

**620 Diamond Loop:** Retired cop, Sergeant Wally Smith, after devouring a huge cheese steak and napping on the living room couch, awoke with a terrible ringing sensation inside his ear and a strong urge to sing *God Bless America*.

...and back at **613 Diamond Loop:** Zachary Colson's cat, Rocky, although getting up in years, was not so old her hearing had gone bust, and her sense of smell worked just fine. She sniffed the air, then the kitchen floor, her paws scratching at the tile. Her ears perked sensing the practically inaudible buzz that came from below.

*"...Yoob...Die-em...Min...Yoob...Die-em...Yoob...MIn...Yoob...Die-em..."*

Fred Reefe headed back to the excavation. He had been gone too long, but his crew knew the police had questions about Jessie Moss and hopefully that eliminated suspicions about his extended visit to Eden Colson's home. The police cruiser had pulled away well over an hour earlier, but if none of his team mentioned this he certainly wasn't going to. Besides, he had a lot more on his mind right now, assuming he hadn't lost it.

He called for his crew to shut down operations and come together for an update. Jarmal Besser jumped off the driving pad of Big Mama, three more guys climbed from the hole, and two men quit unloading new copper pipes from the truck, all gathering before Reefe like scouts at a campfire. Never having been called together in the middle of the work day, no one doubted the man had serious business to discuss.

"First off, I wanted to tell you I spoke to the hospital and they should be releasing Jessie later this week. He's made a remarkable recovery, his nurse told me. He'll need some rest, but he's going to be okay."

The men nodded and smiled, but this wasn't why Reefe called them together.

"Okay, now the serious stuff. I'm afraid we have a bigger problem than we anticipated with the water lines. There's been an incident at the Colson place, and I'm worried it won't be an isolated situation. We must have disturbed a large nest underground, and the Colson home — and probably others — have been infested. I'd say they were slugs doing the dirty work, but

I'm not sure. Whatever they are, they seem to have gotten in through the plumbing. What's important is, we have to locate the source of the problem before we turn the water back on, and I'm expecting some pissed off homeowners."

"Slugs don't nest," Jarmal said. "They bunch together to keep warm, kind of in clumps, but they ain't like bugs in hives or nests." He looked around, saw some of the men smiling. "Hey, I'm educated, okay? Not like you guys."

Reefe added, "Okay, perhaps not slugs. Maybe they're something else, I don't know what. Prehistoric gophers or pissed-off groundhogs, whatever. The important thing is, we have to find out where they are and what damage they've done. We'll smoke them out before they do any more harm, or before the residents' lawyers smell lawsuits. So, I have to ask if you've seen any unusual activity in the pit."

The curly haired Stallone loving Tony Marchetti spoke up. "I saw Carl here picking his butt, but I wouldn't call that unusual. May have to report unsanitary working conditions to Local 732 if you keep going at your ass in the crawlspace, Carl."

Carl wasn't appreciative of the comment, particularly because it was true, but he had something to add. "Yeah, Fred, me and the guys saw something down there. We were going to report it soon as we came up. See…" Looking at the other two, he waited for the go-ahead nod from them. "Those pipes leading to the Loop are done for. I mean, like you said, we're going to have to replace much more than we figured."

Reefe hesitated before he replied. "See, that's got me stumped. The Glenn Echoes mains are older, but the Diamond Loop system is relatively new. These homes were just built."

Carl didn't appear any more in the know than Reefe. "Yeah, well, I have to agree that if the water is turned on any time soon around here, you're going to see a fucking geyser — probably more than one. And, something else." Carl again looked at the other guys. "Those Loop pipes, they're not shoddy or poorly connected, but in some places those new ones, they're torn clear through — punctured is more like it. It's amazing any water got through at all, but what didn't is leaking along those lines as if that copper's been gnawed. A hundred rats the size of St. Bernards couldn't do that kind of damage, and unless we start some powerful digging, the soil beneath them new homes will soon look like one big mud puddle once water is back on. That dampness won't be good for the homes' foundations, don't matter how solid they are, and it's going to invite sink-holes and termites."

"Shouldn't we tell the residents?" from Jarmal. "They're goin' to have questions when the water's off longer than we told 'em."

"We'll tell them when we know what's doing this. Those pipes are meant to last something like fifty years." Reefe's color left his face. It probably would be a bad idea to mention the barbecued slugs or maggots or whatever the fuck crawled into Eden Colson's bathroom; worse, that yesterday he thought he had heard the vicious little bastards babbling war chants, and that Jessie Moss was the first soldier to fall. That could start a panic among the homeowners, maybe get him a ticket to a rubber room. Probably both.

*On the other hand...*

Reefe's thoughts ran wild. Those smaller things he had deep fried, as dangerous as they appeared, couldn't have done the damage to the lines the men reported. It would take something bigger — much bigger.

No, not something — Some *things*.

*(...the size of St. Bernards!)*

But these weren't rats. Rats didn't have teeth long enough to puncture new copper pipes. Christ, what did? The answer came to Fred Reefe, although it was anything but logical.

*(...large slug-like creatures with maggot-like mouth hooks, that's what!)*

Someone called out, "Did I hear somebody mention law-suits?" The female voice came from behind a dirt mound un-loaded from the pit. Reefe turned.

Stepping out just beyond the yellow taped warning was the girl Reefe recognized from yesterday in Eden's kitchen. Eden's kid stepped out too. Tiffany Leone and Zachary Colson stood behind the DANGER signs and the several saw horses, a safe distance from the excavation, but well within hearing range of the Reefe Water & Sewer crew's conversation.

Reefe noticed the girl was holding a small camcorder. He mouthed a silent "*Fuck...*"

"A little warm this afternoon," Tiffany said. "Kind of makes you feel a bit SLUG-gish, don't you think...?"

She and Zack sprinted to her Harley and were off.

# CHAPTER THIRTEEN

## THE McKENNA CATTLE RANCH, 1866
## MELISSA AND COLE: THE ATCHISON,
## TOPEKA, & THE SANTA FE

*"...that's what I call 'em in my head..."*

Around late 1865, Porter Monahan found himself in trouble. For years, his chicken farm had housed healthy and well-fed birds always fat for the slaughter, the hens good egg-layers until their clutches turned skimpy and they met the axe. Business had been especially profitable because a few healthy roosters could put an entire coop of hens in the family way, and the farmer rarely had to replenish his broods anywhere outside his own hutches. But, during the fall of 1865, an avian sickness spread through the coops, and Porter's birds were dropping fast. Unless the man could start paying his bills in chicken feed, he knew soon he would financially find himself as sick as his birds. He kept this information from his wife and his three daughters, the prettiest being nineteen-year-old Melissa.

Monahan's keeping mum was a good thing, particularly because Melissa had developed a taste for the finer things, and her father knew she would not give up that predisposition easily. Even the best of the Missouri farm boys did not cut muster with his daughter, although her younger sisters had no problem accepting invitations to barn dances and church socials. Melissa was not saving herself for Jesus or any nonsense like that, but she certainly was saving herself for someone damned close.

Sure enough, that man showed up. More precisely, the man's father, Christian McKenna Senior, showed up. Owner *of the McKenna Cattle Ranch far off in New Mexico, Christian Senior had a serious legal issue with the new Santa Fe railroad that soon would be coming to the coveted flatland of his very profitable enterprise, and he had no desire to see tracks laid through his front door. The New Mexico territories were indeed new, and McKenna had secured property rights to his land quickly, but now those rights were jeopardized. Even good property lawyers rarely had connections with the Federal government, but Porter's brother, Marcus Monahan, did have that connection. The man had friends in high places, and Marcus' signature on a legal deed held federal weight — even against the expanding railroad, as rumor had it.*

*It was to Marcus Monahan's Kansas City office that Christian Senior and his son traveled for some serious legal assistance at precisely the same moment Porter had visited the city to inquire about his prospects for a bank loan — and he had brought his daughter, who seemed little interested in her father's reasons for the inquiry. Rather, Melissa's interest sparked for those men who owned property, and she never missed the opportunity to visit the business offices where official looking forms were signed by well-dressed young men. Dropping in on her uncle on the day of the senior McKenna's visit, Melissa Monahan struck gold.*

*Christian Senior had brought his handsome twenty-one year old son on the trip because the young man soon would inherit his father's ranch and both knew the importance of developing business savvy. The times were changing with the Western expansion, and there was money to be made, but a foolish transaction could mean there was money to be lost. Christian Junior proved to be a fast learner concerning the accumulation of wealth. That aspect of his character applied also to the young man's accumulation of women, and few failed to yield to Christian's charms. In that respect, he and Melissa Monahan were much alike. Their meeting was for-tuitous, their mutual attraction instantaneous.*

*Just outside her Uncle Marcus' office, Melissa stared at the young man seated at the table with his father. She smiled*

*Politely. He smiled back. Every few minutes Christian's eyes drifted to where Melissa stood, and the smiles continued, Melissa's accompanied by hand-covered giggles. When Christian excused himself from his father's business talk, he walked over to the young woman, but she spoke first, a well-rehearsed smile firmly in place.*

*"It certainly took you long enough to come over. My feet were getting tired standing here."*

*The girl was direct and to the point, and Christian could not have been more pleased. "Well, then, I suppose we should find ourselves a comfortable place where we can sit together." Introducing himself, he offered his arm and she took it.*

*The days that followed featured buggy rides to the hidden caves near the ferry crossing on the Kansas River, and eventually stolen water-soaked kisses beneath the falls at Alcove Spring. Christian informed his father he would be staying in Kansas City for a while, after the man's business had been successfully completed. The senior McKenna grinned, quickly visiting Porter Monahan to confide to the chicken farmer that he had a good feeling their two families would soon be joined. Weeks later his son confirmed that feeling in a telegraph stating that Christian had found himself a future wife and would be sending for her soon upon his return to Trementina. Porter envisioned a comfortable life for his daughter in which she would truly delight; Christian Senior envisioned the stability of his son's having his own family when he inherited the profitable McKenna Ranch. As Melissa prepared for her stagecoach trip upon the Westbound Concord Overland Express, no one in either family foresaw anything but a happy ending for the handsome couple.*

*Certainly no one foresaw that in a few weeks' time Christian McKenna Junior would be coming after Melissa Monahan, his lovely wife-to-be, with a hand axe.*

## COLE McKENNA

Melissa Monahan and Sister Margelle stood exhausted just outside the McKenna Ranch.

"You see any cattle? Any livestock? Stables look empty too."

"I don't see a thing, Sister. Nothing."

A warm morning had arrived, and there was bright sun. This was good; the slug-things seemed to hate the light. Once inside the spacious McKenna home, Melissa and Sister Margelle stood together studying the interior. The furniture had been pushed to the door, a broken lamp lay in pieces on the hardwood, and on the table an untended cigar had burned to ash.

As the nun had said, the place lacked a woman's touch, and even though she intended the understatement, her comment put it mildly. It seemed some wild animal had run rampant through the place, but Melissa suspected something much worse.

"Christian's mother died a while ago. There's just men here — or there *was*." Melissa called out, "Hello? Anybody here? It's Melissa Monahan, Christian's fiancé...?"

A loud thump came from the back room, maybe the sound of feet hitting the floor. Someone was in the house with them! Margelle had experienced enough gunplay to last a lifetime. She handed the Winchester to Melissa, and the two women approached the closed door of the back room.

"Who's in there?" Margelle called out. "If you're not a McKenna, I'm letting you know we're armed. We have guns!" That wasn't entirely true. Margelle had nothing. There was only the rifle in Melissa's hands and whatever bullets remained in the chamber. "Mr. McKenna? Are you in there?"

A boy's voice answered. "Don't come in! I have my father's rifle, and I swear I'll shoot you dead!"

Melissa forced the fear from her voice. "I'm Melissa. I was supposed to marry Christian McKenna this Sunday. Do you know who I am?"

The door opened a crack, then wide. It took a moment for the image to register. A boy of about thirteen stood there. He held a rifle whose barrel was almost as long as he was tall.

"I know who you are. My brother, Christian, he told me about you. I'm just playin' it safe, is all. I thought you may be one of the bad ones. I ain't shootin' nobody."

*One of the bad ones.* Melissa didn't have to ask what the boy meant. She placed her rifle on the floor, and he did the same. "We didn't mean to frighten you. Christian didn't tell me he had a brother." She felt her face burn with the admission. "I guess he didn't tell me much about much. We only knew each other a few weeks, and ... Well, maybe we didn't really know each other at all."

"It don't matter, Miss. Really. I'm glad you're here. It's been bad being alone these past few days. I come out to get food from the kitchen when I'm hungry, then hole up in my room the rest of the time. You've been outside, so you must know why. Anyway, I'm Cole." Extending his hand he looked at the nun. "God himself must've sent you here, Sister."

Margelle smiled. "The Overland Stage sent me here — myself, and Miss Monahan. At least most of the way. You want to tell us what's going on? Excepting you, there's not a soul to be seen. Trementina looks like a ghost town." She said nothing about the slug-things and the craziness of Christian's death. Whatever the boy knew, he would speak about it soon enough.

Cole bit his lip. "That's because by now Trementina prob'ly *is* a ghost town. I 'spose those townsfolk that's missing must include my brother, 'cause he didn't leave here in the best of shape. I know my father is most likely dead. Do you know if my brother—? Is Christian dead?"

Melissa leaned close to him. "What went on here, Cole? Will you tell us what happened to your brother and your father here?"

"What I know sounds crazy enough, but I figure you know that, if you been on the trail. Miss Monahan, I see your dress strap's been torn and your dress is a bit bloodied, and I'm guessin' you've had a rough few hours. But first, I need to know about Christian, all right? I know he planned to meet your stage in town, but he didn't leave here with what I 'spect was good intentions."

The women looked at each other, since Christian was the reason behind the damage to Melissa's summer dress. Margelle gave her the nod to tell it all.

"It's going to sound crazy, Cole, like you said. I guess that's because it *is* crazy."

"You women hungry? It's best we talk while we got the chance to eat. The people, the bad ones, they can come any time. I seen them from here, out on the road. But those other things, they come out at night, you know."

"Those other things?" Margelle's expression revealed she already knew.

"Yes, Sister, and I know you've seen 'em. Miss Monahan, you tell it first. All of it. I can handle it now. First, I'll fix us something to eat, then we can talk."

Over plates stacked with scrambled eggs and warm corn bread, Melissa started. "There were four of us passengers on the Overland Stage Express coming out of Kansas City. Sister Margelle here, an old woman, a man named Ben, and myself..."

She told it all, the slug-things included, and the wild stagecoach ride that brought her and the young nun to this place.

Cole listened without saying one word.

## DEEP HOLES AND SLUGGOTS

Their story told, the women sat quietly as the boy took it in. He didn't cry over Christian, not so much as a quivering lip. He didn't seem shocked or even surprised hearing of his brother's shooting death. But Melissa hadn't cried either.

Cole finally spoke. "So them sluggoty maggoty things been crawlin' through the Trementina streets too? Yeah, I seen 'em. Wild Sluggots — that's what I call 'em in my head, 'cause I don't know how else to peg creatures resembling slugs and maggots pushed together."

That meant those dark creatures had made it this far from Trementina, maybe a good five miles — further, measured from the hole along the Santa Fe Trail. Melissa attempted to appear calm when she spoke. "Tell even the worst of it, okay? I know it must be diffi—"

Cole stopped her. "— Not so difficult, Miss. I need to tell somebody that won't think this is just a whopper some dopey kid made up. My brother and my father, they're gone. I got nobody will believe any of this, 'cepting those that seen it for themselves like you two. Not certain I believe it myself."

Sister Margelle touched the boy's shoulder. "From the beginning, okay?"

Cole McKenna clearly was raised right. He placed the dishes in the sink and poured cups of steaming coffee for his guests. Pulling the curtain, he checked through the window to have a look at the acres owned by his father. Seeing nothing disturbing, he was ready to talk.

"I've been learning the ropes 'bout cattle ranching from my father. And Christian, he knew all 'bout the business end of cattle drives and the best markets for beef. I guess the railroads would've helped with the transporting end, so long as them engines weren't chugging through our acreage. That was what Pa worried most about when he and Christian traveled the prairie with the Longhorns, moving our cattle to the territories. Other hands helped, of course, but Christian and Pa, they always oversaw the drives. A few days ago not far from here, that's when they noticed the hole."

"The large hole along the Santa Fe near Trementina?" Margelle asked.

"Cattle drives don't use main roads, Sister. No, this hole was maybe ten miles out in the grasslands. Didn't see it myself, but Pa said it was the biggest damned pit he'd ever—" Cole looked at the nun. "Sorry, Sister. I mean it was a real big hole."

Melissa muttered to Margelle, "That means there's another one. Maybe more."

The nun responded, *"Damn!"*

"It was big, yes Ma'am, in the middle of nowhere land and close to an acre wide, my pa said, and deep like there weren't no bottom. It proved treacherous to just about every man on that cattle drive. Some cattle was lost, but something in that pit scared the others, and our steers went charging like bulls. They took two cowboys with 'em, 'cause no man can stop a wild herd of cattle when it gets moving. My father and Christian, they was on the drive's back end, so they weren't hurt. Pa said our entire herd took off hell-bent for the plains. Animals sense when something's amiss, and even the horses knew that hole weren't right. They must've bucked like crazy to throw both my father and Christian from their saddles, not to mention every one of the cowhands, and them men are skilled riders. The horses run off scared too, and there weren't no calling them back. Men without horses ain't worth spit driving cattle, and the entire herd stampeded off, maybe a hundred head. That weren't a good day for the McKenna Ranch, but not the worst of it — not even close."

"Did your father or Christian see any of those ... those sluggots?" Melissa asked.

"I know they looked into that hole after some of the cattle went down, but it must've been late morning, and I've learnt them sluggot creatures do their work only when it comes dark. It had to be a long walk back to the ranch since there were nowhere else for them men to go. Darkness was coming on by the time Pa, Christian, and maybe ten of our cattle drivers come back hauling the bodies of two more, which must've slowed 'em down. They was off in the distance, and when I seen them, I know something awful must've occurred on that drive. I don't see cattle or horses, and there are dead men being carried. My heart nearly pushed through my chest 'cause I didn't know what was what, so I run out to meet them. Our housekeeper, Miss Betty, she tried to stop me, but I wouldn't have none of that."

"Betty?" asked Sister Margelle. "She lives in the house here with you?"

"Yeah, after Ma passed she took over the household

chores. I'll get to that part. Anyway, I'm running crazy towards Pa and Christian, but when Pa sees me he's gesturing and shouting to get back in the house quick, and I know that look on my father's face when he means business. He never said later if they'd seen anything inside that hole. I'm thinking it's more likely they did, but his first consideration was he wanted all of us safe in the house. And Miss Betty, she's hugging me tighter than my own ma ever done, while my father and the others are off in the men's bunk quarters. The two bodies was left there with the remaining cattle drivers, and him and Christian entered the parlor exhausted, burnt from the sun, and all sweaty from their long haul on foot. Pa locks the door, not saying anything, and I never seen him so old. My brother, he's not looking real good either."

Melissa stirred her coffee cup without looking up. "But they were okay when they returned here, you're saying? You didn't see anything wrong with them except they were tired?"

Cole shook his head. "Worse than tired. Them two can take a week's cattle driving with less than five hours sleep at night, and they don't look anywhere near as beat as I seen that moment. They was scared too, and it takes a whole lot to scare a McKenna man, that's a fact. I'm thinking they seen something in that pit, prob'ly the same thing you both seen in Trementina. Maybe worse. It sure was enough to scare off the horses and our cattle. Anyway, that night Pa tells me in the morning he'll go into town, send a telegraph to the dead men's kin, if there were any, 'cause he couldn't do no more. And I'm thinking how that bunkhouse weren't going to be the most pleasant place to sleep that night. Pa told me what he felt like sharing about the hole and the animals running off, saying how maybe some cattle could be recaptured with fresh horses and new men, and so I'm thinking the worst is over. Shows how little I knew then."

Melissa's coffee had gone cold without her taking a sip. "Cole, I think a few days ago we all knew a lot less — about everything."

"Well, Miss, I discovered pretty quick how little *I* knew...

"Pa kept first watch by the door that night, staring through the curtains for reasons he wouldn't say. But I guess the day's exhaustion must've got to him and he nodded off without finishing the cigar intended to unwind him. Around midnight it started. All this screaming and cursing is coming from the men's bunkhouse with things crashing against the walls and through the windows like some awful fight is going on inside. There was gunfire too. The noise wakes up everyone, and Pa tells us to wait in the house while he goes check it out. No moon shone, and the lights in the bunkhouse was out, so it was too dark to see much through the windows there, but me and Christian are trying to figure what the ruckus is. We seen only the shadows, but what followed — *Jesus!* I apologize for saying our Lord's name like that, Sister. It's just that what I seen was so awful."

Margelle touched his hand. "Cole, if you would rather not—"

"No, Sister, I want to tell all of it. See, Christian was worried about our father, and he decided to see what was going on inside the bunkhouse, even though Pa didn't want him to leave Miss Betty and me alone. There was this sudden silence in the bunk, like whatever brawl was going on had just stopped cold. So, Christian, he grabbed his gun, told me and Miss Betty not to move one inch, and headed out, 'cause that silence seemed worse than anything. He didn't know what waited — I mean, how could he know?

"Miss Betty, she started to cry. Kind of more like a whimper 'cause she didn't want to upset me, but I know she was scared. 'Cole,' she says, 'You're going to have to be a man tonight, all right? I don't have a good feeling about this. Promise you'll be a man for me.' I wasn't certain what being a man in this situation called for, but I went for my father's rifle since I figured protecting her and myself was a big part of it. We waited a while, heard some more gunfire in the bunkhouse, some men shouting too, and I can see shadows of the ranchers inside. When the bunkhouse door swung open, Christian comes out staggering bad, like he's just been in the worst

**144**

barroom brawl of his life. 'Wait here,' I told Betty and headed outside.

"I'm calling to my brother when I see my father step out, and Pa's yelling to me, *'No, Cole, no! Stay back!'* Christian, he's gripping a small axe and he's hurt. Close up I see his nose is bleeding bad, and he's saying my name, *'Coh-el...'* like he's contemplating what to do next. But then Christian turns, 'cause something huge and black is sneaking slow and quiet behind Pa. My blood went cold that instant, and I pointed to it, and my father tries shooting the damned thing — but it's too fast and wraps around him like a snake. It took only seconds 'fore half his head is inside the thing's mouth, these twisted hooks sunk into his scalp, and I'm watching streams of blood drip down his face. I start to go after it not having any idea what to do if I catch up with it, but the thing moves so damned fast dragging my father past the coral, then disappearing past the gate. Christian, he's watching this sluggot carry him off, but he's doing nothing at all. I'm telling you, it was too awful..."

"You saw one up close? The ... sluggot?" Margelle asked.

"One of many, Sister. Another comes out of the dark, slinks right past Christian as if he ain't there, and stands there just looking at me. This one's even longer and fatter than the first, twice the size of any cobras I seen in my school books. My brother, he pays no attention to that sluggot— Christian is coming for *me*, moving slow and strange, and with his axe raised high enough to split my skull in two. I'm thinking there weren't no way out with both him and that sluggot coming after me! Jeez, my own brother—"

Cole turned away from the women, embarrassed at the momentary deficiency of his manhood.

Melissa spoke up. "Yes. I know all about that part, Cole. Your brother wasn't himself any more. Whatever made Christian *Christian* got sucked out by one of those things. May-be a small piece of him was left, enough to remember you and enough to slow him down with the memory, but only for a short while. The man holding that axe no longer was your brother, no more than he was the man I was supposed to marry."

**145**

"I suppose that's true, Miss Monahan. It's just hard to swallow. Anyway, that sluggot wriggled right past Christian, being more intent on having *me*. I managed one shot but couldn't take time to aim, and it missed. I'm setting up for a second chance when Miss Betty comes up behind me, and that woman drags me back into the house even while I'm kicking and screaming not to let Christian remain there with them slime things crawling all around. She pulls me inside, tells me, 'Your brother — something's wrong, Cole, and he won't be of any help against whatever that slithering thing is." She went to shut the door, but that damned sluggot pushed itself into our parlor. Betty, she's standing 'tween me and that thing, arms outstretched and waving like she's about to yell' *Shoo!'* or something ridiculous like that. She tells me to get into my room and not come out, no matter what. 'Let me get one more shot at that thing!' I told her, but she grabbed my rifle and says, *'Go! Now!'*

"'Course, the rest I didn't really see. My door was shut, but I heard rifle shots — and Miss Betty's screams. I knew that thing was on her, 'cause I heard it thrashing in our parlor, busting the lamp and turning over furniture. But Miss Betty weren't no match for it. It got her clean, 'cause later I didn't find blood on the floor. Then it dragged her off — I knew that without seeing it, and I'll admit that my eyes was shut tight. When I found the nerve to return to the parlor, she was gone. From the window I seen my brother was gone too, them sluggot things as well. They must've carried off our cowhands with 'em, or maybe those men staggered off stupefied like Christian, I don't know where."

"Probably into one of those holes," Sister Margelle offered.

Melissa shook her head. "I don't think so. You and I, we saw Christian come out of that tavern in Trementina. And Ben, he took the old woman in there too. You saw what happened to them, Sister. They were alive when they went in, but I doubt they stayed that way."

Margelle considered this. "The slug things took them to

The Old Crow Inn! Of Course! They're smart, and they couldn't leave bodies scattered everywhere where others might find them. To cover themselves, that inn was their repository for the dead. Yes, that makes sense!"

Cole shook his head. "Wouldn't that hole you saw be the more logical place? Or the one that took our cattle and our ranch hands?"

Melissa thought otherwise. "Not if those things use those pits for some other reason than coming and going, or for hiding human remains. Back on the stage I had the feeling Ben and Old Sam saw something in that trail hole, something they weren't comfortable sharing. Maybe your father and Christian saw the same thing too, Cole. Maybe it *was* bodies, but I'm thinking something maybe worse, something they decided it was better not to tell us."

"Miss Monahan, Sister... Speaking of holding back, there's something else I should tell you, something you likely figured already."

"Cole, Sister Margelle and I can handle anything you have to tell us." Melissa tried not to let the lie show on her face.

Cole didn't question her response. "See, I don't think my father and Christian was killed by them sluggots, not right away, in the strict sense. I mean, I seen my father dragged off, but his legs was still kicking, and Christian, he must've just wandered off and followed the trail to Trementina to finish what started at our ranch. I heard those men in the bunkhouse — the screaming and shooting. But what I seen through the windows weren't just sluggots' shadows. I think them creatures sneaked into the bunk long before the men saw them, likely while they was sleeping."

Sister Margelle's face went pale. "Of course those slug things killed them! They were in the men's bunkhouse, you said, who knows how many?"

"I know that. But what I seen through the windows told a different tale. The lights was out and I seen only shadows and shades, but I know what I seen. Axes raised, rifles too—-" Cole turned to Melissa, whose face had gone ashen. "Haven't you

**147**

figured it out, Miss? Those men inside the ranchers' bunk-house, my brother Christian included — Miss, them sluggots was inside, all right, maybe a dozen, and I'm sure they swallowed bits of those men's scalps while paying their visit. But those men, our cattle drivers, my brother — You should've seen his face, Miss. My own kin, and he was about to bury that axe in my brain."

Melissa knew that expression Cole had seen on Christian McKenna's face. She'd seen it herself.

Cole leaned forward. "Sister, Miss Monahan, don't you see? Them slimy things, they're smart, smarter than some regular slug or maggot that's got mud for brains. Them things are thick skinned enough for bullets not to do much damage, but they must know there's more of us than there is of them, 'least around these parts. I'm thinking, after doing what they come to do, them sluggots was just watching the rest of the night play out, 'cause those men — *they was killing each other!*"

Margelle and Melissa exchanged glances. The nun spoke first. "That means anyone we see around these parts —"

"Can't trust nobody," Cole said. "But those men went to Trementina for a reason, probably killing along the way, and taking them bodies along. Maybe their brains didn't work for them anymore, maybe after them sluggots had no further use-fulness for them, *then* those creatures finished them. Maybe they ate them!"

"The Old Crow Inn!" Margelle said. "That's where the men went. That's where those sluggot things still are, gathering everyone in the same place! Thing is, I don't have any idea what those creatures are getting from all of this. Why not just kill those men when they had the chance? Or —" The nun prac-tically gagged on the word "—or *eat* them?"

"They're smart, remember?" Melissa said. "There must be something in it for them."

Cole nodded. "Sister, Miss Monahan — what's important now is we know where they are and whatever people they dragged into that old tavern. They're probably waiting for whoever else comes into Trementina, and another stage will be due any time. It's still early morning. There's too much light for them to be out." He picked up the two rifles from the floor, another from the wall. "Maybe when we find them—" He handed the rifles to the women. The boy's newfound determination seemed misplaced, maybe even crazy.

"Guns won't do it," Melissa said. "There's dozens of them holed up in that place!"

Cole thought that over. "There's plenty of gas lamps in town! We'll empty them inside that tavern, and we'll visit the holes too, burn them things to toasty crisps!"

Melissa shook her head. "There must be more holes than those two. Dozens, maybe a hundred in the middle of nowhere. Who knows how many? Even more may be opening as we speak! There's no certain way we can track them all down!"

Cole's brow knit and the blood seemed to leave his face. "Track 'em...tracks...! *Jesus!* It just hit me! I think I know what brought them holes here and set them sluggots crawling out. It can't be anything else! It's the damned Atchison, Topeka and the Santa Fe that my father and Christian traveled to Kansas City to keep from our door!"

"The railroad?" Melissa asked.

Cole slammed his fist on the table. "Damn right, the railroad! Transcontinental, people are saying. There could be hundreds of them holes because them railroading bastards have been laying tracks Westward for months, just blasting through whatever's in their path. There's talk them tracks will be reaching the Pacific in the next few years, opening sluggot holes anywheres along the way!!"

Sister Margelle put her hand over her mouth. "My God! Those railroaders use black powder — *nitroglycerin!* They're blasting their way through the plains for over a thousand miles!"

Cole cursed under his breath. "...all the way to the coast. Maybe my father was right. Men wanting to move faster, leaving one place behind for another that ain't no better than the first. He never liked seeing the old ways die out, the railroads ripping apart the land and people's lives."

Melissa remained skeptical. "I don't know, Cole. A million things could've brought those things to the surface, not just the railroad."

"A constant round of close-by explosions could only happen along where them tracks are laid. I'm betting them holes are a stone's throw from where new tracks are going down! I disagree with my father's fear of progress — that's a whole other matter. But maybe he had a point he didn't even know he had. I'm thinking those creatures broke ground near wherever those disturbances occurred, just come up from below and worked their mischief, 'cause them railroaders practically sent for them. Trains leading further west are a poor exchange if it means them explosions are unearthing more than a thousand miles' worth of sluggots!"

"A thousand miles — *and counting!*" Melissa said.

Sister Margelle's face appeared more dour than a nun's three times her age. Turning to the window, she seemed to speak to the morning sky. "There's a thousand miles of tracks out there with more to come, and maybe hundreds of those crawling slime things anywhere along the way!" She turned to Cole. "You think you're really going to do this, do you? Hunt them down? There's three of us, maybe hundreds of them — and that's not counting the unfortunate people they've met up with! They're squirming killing machines!"

Melissa nodded agreement.

Cole's tone no longer sounded like it belonged to a kid. "I'm sorry, but it seems we got no choice — and if you consider it for one minute, you'll see we don't. I'm not liking this any better than you, but it's not open to debate. So, I'm thinking you women might need some rest before we head out?"

"Sister Margelle and I haven't slept in two days. Do you need to ask?"

Cole half shrugged, but he had made his decision.

"Then you two better get some rest. You got an hour..."

# SINKHOLE

Behind the McKenna Ranch, near a deep well, sat a rusted water pump. Old, its handle a little loose, the pump otherwise worked fine for quenching the thirst of the McKenna household and the ranch workers. A single liquid drop appeared at its nozzle.

So did an elongated black creature with its mouth hooks extended.

# CHAPTER FOURTEEN
## Diamond Loop, July 2015: BLOCK PARTIES

### *"In my own house!"*

### TUESDAY P.M.

On what seemed a typical summer's day (excepting the volley of the jackhammers breaking more concrete near the cul-de-sac's excavation), a humid July afternoon came to Diamond Loop...

— **At the excavation:** The crew of Reefe Water & Sewer Contractors chose to dig a larger hole, tracing the homes' ruptured water lines while hoping to discover the source of the extensive damage. The new dig required further ruin to the Loop's asphalt entranceway and maybe to some residents' driveways. But doing anything less risked a water main break that could rival Vesuvius, possibly resulting in the entire development's sinking into an ocean of mud. For the next several days Big Mama would have her work cut out for her.

— At **608** Diamond Loop Mrs. Regina Campbell, after freshening up inside her bathroom, scratched her scalp, having developed a throbbing headache. Postponing her surprise visit to Eden Colson (and to Fred Reefe, oh yes!) she decided to take a nap. Awakening feeling energized, she belted out Madonna's "Like a Virgin" while she searched through her kitchen drawers for her sharpest bread knife. The song seemed appropriate because, in one respect, Regina Campbell *had* been touched for the very first time, and her scalp itched because of it. Still wearing her hip huggers that seemed tattooed to her ass, her come-and-get-me attire was not the only surprise she had planned for her husband.

— At **617** inside the Hunter home, adolescent lovers Denny and Heather topped off their afternoon delights in Denny's bed with yet another shared joint. While reclaiming the sheets their passion had displaced, Heather noticed trickles of blood along her partner's forehead. Giggling, she traced the stream with her finger, then licked it off. Similarly, Denny spotted a thin rivulet threading down the back of Heather's neck, but too wasted to mention it, he chose instead to finish their shared doobie while taking in the wonders of his ceiling fan. Feeling no pain while flying high on their euphoric combination of weed and sweaty sex, neither expressed concern or even questioned the appearance of blood. Instead, the young couple shared a repetitious chorus of *Excuse me while I kiss the sky,* the single line sung poorly a dozen times over until the two fell into a funk more stupor than sleep. While Heather snored softly, Denny experienced an intense dream in which his father grounded him for life. Even while he slept, Dennis Hunter despised his parents.

— At **610** Anna Brimley seemed all smiles. "I asked if you liked your sandwich, Georgie?" she spoke in her thick accent. She softly sang the Happy Birthday song in Russian as she watched her husband finish his lunch. George Brimley made a sour face getting the last of the lunchmeat down, but that anchovy Anna had tucked between the thick slices really hadn't been an anchovy at all. She suspected George had recognized that, because his sour face had become a grimace. Even while watching him, Anna knew she loved this man more than anything else in her world. It was his disability she hated, confining him to that cursed wheelchair and confining her as well. She hoped that her little treat would make it easier on them both for what she had to do.

— At **613** Eden Colson stared at the charred porcelain of her brand-new bathtub, muttering "Shit" no less than a dozen times. She didn't blame Fred Reefe for the damage; he had to destroy those crawling little suckers. But Eden worried how Greg was going to take this. She decided not to tell her husband about Reefe's part in the slug-things' funeral pyre, and she suspected Greg's call to their lawyer was a given. Hoping they had managed to burn every slug-thing that had got through her pipes, Eden decided some garden work would do her good. Along with her decision to sleep with another man today, this was Eden Colson's second mistake.

★ ★ ★

Tiffany Leone pulled her Harley into the parking lot of the baseball field near the middle school. In the stands, she and Zack examined her video. It was all there on Tiffany's camcorder: Supervisor Reefe's talking about the strange invasion at the Colson home, and the construction crew's warning that the Loop's new copper water pipes appeared dangerously close to bursting. Something had chewed through them, something more destructive than "a hundred rats the size of St. Bernards." The soundtrack of Tiffany's video of Reefe and his men resembled some badly dubbed 1950's Japanese B-movie about giant insects created because of atomic bomb testing. But this wasn't post-war Tokyo; this was today at Diamond Loop in Glenn Echoes, New Jersey, and this was real.

"Those things were in my house!" Zack said.

Tiffany connected the dots. "I think whatever the construction crew thinks is down there are the same things that attacked Jessie Moss, and I'm thinking they took a piece of him with them. Julie told us Moss wasn't himself today, and Reefe clearly didn't want your neighbors to know about what's happening in that pit. What we have here, my friend, is a story the old-time news men used to call a scoop."

"In my own house!" Zack repeated. *"Fuck!"*

Tiffany connected more dots. "Your house is one of the

homes furthest from the excavation site, but Reefe mentioned those slug-things made it there, probably through the pipe lines. That means they probably visited other Loop homes along the way. That's why he wants the water kept off. Jesus, Zack, this is bad!" She thought for a moment. "Didn't you tell me you took some photos of the hole with your cell phone?"

Zack pulled the cellular from his pocket. "I didn't see much — just the hole and the men in it. It was lit with those lamps they put down there."

Tiffany examined the dozen photos on the screen, going back and forth among them. "How far apart were these taken? An hour maybe?" Zack nodded. Tiffany enlarged the focus of two photos, the first and the last. "Look at the pipe in the last photo, Zack. It's after the men were out of the excavation. That Jarmal guy on the loader was digging a wider hole at the time, but those men must have spotted this afterwards."

"Yeah, Jarmal yelled at me to step away 'cause I was getting too close when I snuck past the yellow tape." Zack examined the narrow pipe in both shots and turned to Tiffany. "The water pipe — it's *bent!* That bend isn't there in the first shot!"

"Put two and two together, Zachary. This isn't rocket science. Reefe mentioned new copper pipes should last fifty years. Something small enough to wriggle through that water line was also strong enough to bend it in a few minutes. His crew said there may be much *bigger* ones down there!"

Zack couldn't take his eyes from the screen. "I have these dreams sometimes about bed bugs, 'cause my mom is always telling me not to let the bed bugs bite. What *are* those things in that pit? Giant fucking piranhas? Slugasauri?"

"Maybe something a lot worse. The thing now is, what do we do with this information?"

Tiffany and Zack looked at each other. During the past few hours a new boldness had entered the boy's way of thinking, and those nightmare bed bugs could go to Hell. Katniss Everdeen had nothing on Zachary Colson.

"You still feeling adventurous, Miss Lane?"

Tiffany had to smile. "I'm with you, Jimmy."

The developers of the Diamond Loop homes knew exactly where to dig when burying the extensive water lines for the rows of new houses, but these weren't the only lines that threaded beneath the cul-de-sac. Anyone who held a blueprint of the Loop's complex systems knew this. Should questions of danger arise, reflective warning signs had been placed in various locations throughout the subterranean world beneath the Loop for those professional excavation workers who ventured down there.

Terrible damage had been done to the mains. Water had been the Wogslûk environment, and they were drawn to wherever it was. Signs of warning meant nothing to them — the pipes were what mattered. Pipes carried water; more importantly, the pipes were the network that led directly to hosts.

A good distance from the water mains lay another section of lines. Closer to the surface and constructed of steel, these seemed stronger and thicker than the others. Recognizing an additional access to their hosts' dwellings, the larger of the Wogslûk had not yet gnawed at the metal, although they had grown strong and their mouth hooks were very sharp.

Under the ground, many glow-in-the-dark yellow signs were posted beneath the Loop area. The print appeared big and bold for those construction teams intending nearby excavations, but to the Wogslûk the warnings remained meaningless scribbles.

# DANGER!
## HIGH PRESSURE
### NATURAL GAS PIPELINE

# PART THREE

## DOWN, DOWN, DOWN

*"Some mysteries bite and bark, and come to get you in the dark."*

— **Dean Koontz, DARKFALL**

*"There are some secrets which do not permit themselves to be told."*

— **Edgar Allan Poe, THE MAN OF THE CROWD**

*"We do not see things as they are. We see them as we are."*

— **THE TALMUD**

*"Let's go kill us some Wag-sloogs..."*

— **Cole McKenna**

# CHAPTER FIFTEEN

## The Old Crow INN, 1823-1825:
## KATIE McGILLIS

*"I take what's mine..."*

**F**ew citizens of Trementina knew for certain when The Old Crow Inn was built, but no one doubted it had been among the first structures to appear on the town's main street — its *only* street. The early pioneers' thirst proved a powerful incentive to create a local watering hole, although during the tavern's first years it existed only as a large tent in which the beer seemed about as tasty as warm piss. But from the time The Old Crow proper was constructed by a ragged assortment of German, Irish, and Chinese immigrants, the inn fulfilled its purpose. The new Americans fought daily, and no one seemed to understand anyone else, but somehow the tavern got built. Its original proprietors recognized that certain needs exceeded the male patrons' thirst for cheap whiskey, and the Crow's hastily constructed second floor served that need as well. It became a brothel.

Few of the early pioneers passing through Trementina settled in the town, or anywhere close by. As late as 1849 the Gold Rush to California made the small borough little more than an overnight stopover that offered some liquid invigoration spiked with a quick trip up the stairs for some adult entertainment. Regarding that, the ladies of The Old Crow Inn of 1823 never disappointed.

One Miss Mellie Carter selected her girls carefully, keeping them well dressed and well fed. Sweet Annie, Wicked Alice, Irish Polly — these women knew the game. More importantly, they knew their men, at least the types of men who came through the inn's swinging doors. For the unmarried women of San Miguel County, life didn't offer much else in the way of opportunity. If you weren't a wife, a teacher, or a nun, then you were a prostitute, and that about covered your options. Miss Mellie didn't much care about a woman's past.

Hearing the calling at twenty-three, Katie McGillis ("Kat" to the clientele) seemed to appear from nowhere one day. The girl had no family, no past she was willing to speak about, and she found gainful employment with Miss Mellie Carter at The Old Crow. Except for a crooked front tooth, the dark-haired young woman was beautiful enough to have a line of men waiting nightly inside the tavern for her favors, because nighttime were the only hours the woman worked, and no one saw her at all during daylight. Known for her ability to tie the stem of a maraschino cherry with her tongue, a man couldn't help but wonder what other tricks that tasty gobbet could perform. Kat's customers received their answer once her bedroom door closed and money exchanged hands. She was young, and she remained employed with Miss Mellie for only a short while, but no man leaving her bed ever complained to the management.

Kat couldn't count the men who climbed those stairs. She didn't know many of them, and most she never saw again. But not all of her partners were clients, and like most women of the shadows, she had her secrets. When her belly grew during the late summer of 1824, she had no idea what manner of visitor had put a child inside her, nor had she any notion of how to care for a helpless infant. This didn't change when, during the following spring, she gave birth to a girl for whom she hadn't even selected a name. She often joked how she felt relief she'd birthed a human baby, but secretly she feared for the child's doubtful lineage, feared also for what the infant might grow to become in her mother's questionable environment. Certain she was unsuited to raise a child, Katie McGillis was clever. The idea that occurred to the young mother would have appeared outlandish to anyone in a town more civilized than Trementina, but to the early settlers who called San Miguel

County their home, her offer seemed perfectly reasonable.

Daily at The Crow, Stud Poker was the game of choice, and for a few coins a man could pull up his chair to acquire a decent pile of chips. Once Katie McGillis had reclaimed her shapely figure, she sweetened the pot considerably by offering a full evening of her favors to the man whose chips stacked the highest by nightfall. But it was the woman's second frivolous offering — an offering created by fear soaked in alcohol — that raised the stakes considerably. To the man whose winnings bested the others, Kat offered free and clear her infant daughter. For several male patrons whose wives proved either barren or too old to produce offspring, the offer seemed too good to pass up. Given the times and place, the law had nothing to say of this, and cards were dealt with the sheriff's deputy himself seated at the table. Kat stood by, blinking back tears from her eyes as she held her infant.

Also at the table sat one Cade O'Brien, a foul mouthed drunken lout whose luck at cards often proved either astounding or questionable, depending upon the value a man put on his own life. Cade was both ugly and mean, and you didn't want to question the aces he held. Although he had broken many men's bones during those brawls he had initiated, O'Brien never had killed a man, but that event's occurrence seemed only a matter of time.

Kat could tell by the look in Cade's eyes that he held the final winning hand, but even if he hadn't, she knew the man could bluff the devil himself. Watching every player at the table fold, the young mother felt her heart do the same. This was not the man she wanted to see walk off with her child. Clutching the infant close to her, she shook her head in defiance.

"I'll be good to my word regarding my favors, Mr. O'Brien, but I'll not let you walk from this room with my infant in your arms as I have promised my child a decent home." She turned to the other men, her Irish blood near full boil. "Mine was a foolish offer made from a woman feared of motherhood, no more than that. I'll do what must be done in my bed, but I'll not give my child away!"

O'Brien's eyes gleamed like a snake's. Collecting his cash from the table and scooping it into his hat, he turned to the woman. "As you can see, Miss Kat, I take what's mine, whether cash or flesh. I'll certainly accept your favors now; the child I'll take later. Cards were dealt, I have won, and even the promise of a drunken whore must be honored."

Placing the infant into her bassinet, Katie stood firm. "I sincerely doubt you know much about honor, Mr. O'Brien. I apologize if you mistook the muddle-headed ramblings of an inebriated woman as gospel, but I have changed my mind. Even had I not, I would choose to burn in hell before I allowed a man like you to care for my daughter, although I have no doubt you would sell her to whomever offered the highest bid." The remark caused a murmur among the patrons, and one of the older poker players was foolish enough to let a laugh escape. The man covered his mouth, but too late.

Cade O'Brien was not one used to humiliation, and he didn't take Kat McGillis' remark well. But to become the recipient of another man's laughter seemed even worse. He turned to the offending card player. "Old man, I know of only one way to make that smile disappear for good." Reaching for his holster, he stood in place as the tavern's patrons scattered for safety. The offending man remained seated alone at the table. Although elderly, he didn't seem much experienced in the matter of looking down the barrel of a gun.

"Now, just hold on a minute, Cade..."

"Old Pete doesn't even have a gun!" Miss Mellie shouted. "It ain't a fair—"

Momentarily forgotten, Katie noticed one of the men's rifles leaning against the card table. The gun had been left unattended, but not for long. She grabbed it and came up from behind Cade O'Brien.

"Old Pete has no gun, but *I* have," Kat said, poking the rifle's barrel into Cade's back and speaking with an authority that in no way resembled a woman's manner. "I think you may want to drop yours now. Slowly, please."

Cade held his weapon at his side, but he didn't drop it.

Instead he took several paces forward and placed it into the infant's bassinet. He turned to Katie with a toothy smile.

"Think your young daughter here will feel a bit curious 'bout that strange new shiny object laid alongside her, maybe want to play a bit with it?" His smile melted like dripping wax. "You don't want to fuck with me, Miss Kat." He walked towards her, grabbed the barrel of the rifle. "No, Miss Kat. You certainly don't want to fuck with—"

Katie McGillis couldn't say what made her squeeze the trigger. She hadn't thought she could do it, hadn't consciously intended to. It took only a moment to blow a hole clear through Cade O'Brien's belly and send him rocketing clear across the room, where he lay on the sawdust floor soaking in his own blood. Without looking at the man she killed, Katie reached into the bassinet to retrieve the man's gun. She handled it lightly, as if it were something poisonous, dropping it at the dead man's side. Before she could reach for her infant, the sheriff's deputy stood before her, his weapon drawn.

"Jesus, Kat, what did you do? You saw the man was unarmed!"

Her hands covered her mouth as if horrified at her own actions. "The man was not fit, he was not fit!" the woman muttered through splayed fingers, her eyes on her child.

The young deputy seemed apologetic even as he led the infant's mother from The Old Crow, and in under ten minutes Katie found herself behind the bars of a small cell.

No jury heard the young woman's case; there was only Trementina's sole magistrate, an old man named Malcolm Tate bordering on senility who epitomized the image of the hanging judge. Tate muttered something about justice and the law to the townspeople who had arrived for another county hanging on August 3, 1825. Asked about whether she had any final words, Katie replied, "For my infant daughter, a good father is all I ask, please — and a good name." With the noose tightened and the hood placed on her head, the sheriff's deputy smacked the horse beneath her, and Katie McGillis became the first woman in San Miguel County to swing from the town's lynching post. Her feet kicked for a few seconds before her neck snapped, but the townspeople stood quietly until her limp body was cut down.

Excepting Miss Mellie Carter, few tears were shed for Katie McGillis, but the child she had left behind had need of a parent. The Old Crow's proprietor was an immigrant nearing thirty, an Irish widower named Aidan Hannigan who'd had an eye for the pretty Katie despite her chosen profession. Far too devoted to his late wife's memory to enjoy another woman's pleasures, now the man felt responsibility for the hanged woman's infant. He immediately had the girl christened Riona Hannigan, and from the day of the young mother's hanging, Aidan happily called Katie McGillis' child his own daughter.

Shortly after Riona's fifth birthday, during the spring of 1830, Aidan watched the child at play near the stagecoach's terminus. He regretted the absence of other children in San Miguel County because there were not many companions for a little girl in the dusty town of Trementina. She contented herself with a makeshift game of jacks fashioned from small stones she had dug from the streets, and Aidan smiled seeing the girl so happy with so little. She must have wanted more stones with which to play, and so she dug into the dirt near the vacant stagecoach depot. Darkness was coming, and the street had emptied except for those men entering the tavern. Only Aidan Hannigan saw what occurred in the next instant.

It happened fast in the near dark, so fast that Hannigan didn't trust his own eyes. But a second glance assured him. Where his daughter played, a great hole had opened, and something shadowy and alive peered out. In another moment little Riona Hannigan was gone, and so was the hole.

The Wogslûk had come calling.

# The McKenna Ranch: 1866

Cole McKenna prided himself on his intuition. The boy could sense the presence of a prairie rattler before the slithering bastard made a sound, and he could shoot it dead from twenty paces. His father often told him he had the sharpened senses of a cat as well as the stealth of one, and both comparisons were true. Young McKenna could sense when there was danger even in silence, because not all silences were the same. Cole knew some silences whispered death.

While Melissa Monahan and Sister Margelle slept soundly in Christian McKenna's room, Cole understood it was unmannerly to interrupt the women's sleep. But manners would have to be set aside if the two were in danger. His senses kicked in powerfully enough to convince him that they were. He stood by the bedroom door where the silence inside seemed somehow unsettling. Cole entered the darkened room.

The single sluggot was much smaller than the behemoths he had seen crawl from the bunk house, but significantly larger than anything that ever had emerged from the mud by the lake. The ugly worm-like thing was stealthy in its own right, having somehow made it into the house and to the women's bed, where Cole caught it slithering along the Monahan woman's bare shoulder. The boy didn't have much time before it was on her face, and he could see that its extended mouth hooks clearly meant business. To awaken the woman would be unwise if her sudden movement caused the thing to sink its hooks into her flesh. Those mouth hooks were long and sharp, and they could do serious damage.

Cole backed off and went into the kitchen, returning with a large glass jar. The sluggot was smart enough to move slowly not to awaken Melissa, but Cole knew how to play the same game. He approached the bed, but his footsteps, light as they were, awakened Sister Margelle. Placing his fingers to his lips, he mouthed *"Shhhh!"* and gestured not to move. The nun's eyes opened wide as she followed the boy approaching the sluggot, the opened jar in both hands.

In sleep, Melissa's body twitched. The movement was slight, but it was enough to cause the sluggot's hooks to open wide. Cole had no choice. He flicked his fingers at the thing and sent it flying to the hardwood floor.

"You ain't goin' nowhere, you little fucker!"

It tried scurrying away, but Cole was fast with the jar and placed it over the sluggot, shaking the creature inside and twisting the lid to capture it. Melissa awakened and sat up, her hand over her mouth.

"My God! You caught one of them!" She practically jumped from the bed. "Look, Sister! Cole got one of the small ones!"

The slug-thing wriggled inside the jar, trying mightily to gnaw at the thick glass. It threw itself against the enclosure like a wildly fluttering bird, but it did no good. Cole pulled out a pocket knife and punctured holes into the lid.

"I want to keep this bastard alive. Anyone doubts our story, we got our proof right here." He turned to the nun. "You came here with horses, did you?"

"Coach horses. Six of them. Got a saddle on one."

Cole smiled. "That's good. I'll saddle up another two, stable the others. It's a few miles to the town, and there's a stage coming in. You may want to exchange that nun's habit for some travelin' clothes, Sister. You too, Miss Monahan. Miss Betty was about your size. I'll get some of her clothes for both of you." He placed the glass jar on the night stand.

Alone, the two women sat alongside each other on the bed. Sister Margelle looked troubled, and she spoke low. "I'm beginning to believe that my doing God's work means He isn't going to be doing any of it Himself. Do you think going back to The Old Crow will do any good? Those things — the sluggots, like the boy calls them — they can be anywhere."

Melissa picked up the jar, surprised at its weight. She watched the dark slug creature fling itself against the glass. Shaking the jar, she sneered at it.

"Well, Sister, at least we know where one of them is."

# Trementina

The trip into town proved mercifully uneventful. The ruined stagecoach, its rear wheel gone, remained where it had come to its grinding halt along the trail on the previous night. It seemed untouched, and Melissa didn't know if that were a good or a bad sign. No one had picked it clean, but the absence of other people anywhere was disturbing. The driver's strong box, intended for delivery to the Trementina bank, remained where Old Sam had left it, in the driver's perch. Cole shot the lock open and stuffed his backpack with its cash.

"For the bank's coffers, where it's 'sposed to go," he told the women. Melissa didn't doubt the boy's good intentions, but she felt uncertain if the town would have much use for its bank anymore with possibly all of its citizenry dead.

Further along the trail she searched for the large slug-thing she had shot the night before, but it must have crawled off. Maybe the vultures had made a meal of it, although Melissa doubted it was a very tasty one. Part of her felt relief the three of them didn't discover the remains. It wasn't the sort of thing about which she wanted any memories.

Approaching the town shortly after noon, they stopped their horses. The air thickened with bellows of black smoke that scorched the sky, and even from a distance the smell of its vapors surrounded them. It seemed as if the entire town of Trementina was burning.

"There's trouble," Sister Margelle said. "Someone in town set that blaze."

Melissa saw it differently. "No, Sister. Don't you see? That means there's someone in Trementina that's still alive! Hell, we were intending to torch The Old Crow place ourselves!"

Cole had his rifle at the ready and suggested the women do the same. "Ain't never a good thing to see an entire town in flames, even if there weren't much there to burn. It's a safe bet that whoever set that fire intended to see an end to Trementina, at least a good part of it. We'll make our entrance into town slowly, ladies, very slowly."

The smoke remained heavy, and the three paused often to allow the air to clear before they got closer to the town. Trementina was never much of a town to speak of anyway, a place filled with mud in the winter and dust in the summer. It contained a handful of wooden shacks that passed for a bank, a livery stable, a ramshackle church (with broken stained glass), a two story uninviting hotel, and a barber shop that also housed a Western Union. On the town's edge, the sheriff's office and jail seemed an afterthought. The whole place barely covered a half mile, but in its center near the stagecoach terminus was The Old Crow Inn, the largest of Trementina's structures and probably its most important, and the old tavern was in flames.

None of the three said a word as they approached, watching the smoldering Old Crow crumble. Apparently someone had done their work for them, and probably for the same reason. The fire clearly had started at the inn and spread to several adjoining structures, and it had been recently set. Since the slug-things were not likely to have ventured out during bright sunlight, they probably had remained inside the inn and had burned to cinders with it.

*Probably..."* Melissa muttered to herself, hoping it were true.

Cole's thoughts seemed elsewhere. He pointed to the bench at the stagecoach terminus. An old man sat alone seeming oblivious to the smoldering ruins of the town, his face and clothing blackened with the smoke. He must have seen the three of them, but he didn't make a move. Dismounting, Cole approached the stranger, motioning for the women to stay behind.

The elderly man noticed the boy for the first time, but he didn't get to his feet. Dwarfed by the long bench, he looked about ten minutes past death. "Had to do it," he muttered with a thick Irish brogue. "No choice, no choice..."

Cole sat alongside him. "You set this fire, old man?"

The stranger was muttering as if Cole weren't there, and he didn't turn to look at him. "Gas lamps. Not hard to do. Those creatures, they were everywhere."

"Creatures?" Cole asked, but he already knew. The old man looked at him as if knowing he didn't have to explain.

"I knew they'd be back. Saw one near forty years ago, and

I knew time would come I'd be seeing more again. Didn't think it'd come to this, but I should've known."

Under ordinary circumstances the man's ranting would have seemed insane, but Cole knew he wasn't. "You're alive. Don't see evidence of no one else here. How...?"

"Hid in the upstairs room of The Crow while those things went and did what they did. Long time past, it used to be Katie McGillis' room, where she —" He was rambling, and he shut up for a moment. "My own place, and I had to burn her down! Fire, it spread to the other structures too. Never meant for that to happen."

"You owned The Old Crow?"

The man nodded. "Proprietor for these forty-some years. Watched it built before this town was even a town. Hell, I helped put up a couple of its beams."

"About those creature things you mentioned..." Cole left the bench and reached into his horse's saddle bag to retrieve the glass jar. The sluggot inside spun and turned over on itself. Cole held the jar for the stranger to see. The old man's jaw went slack.

*"My God! Yes! That's one of 'er! Those I saw were much bigger, but damn, that's one of 'er!"* He noticed the two women approaching and removed his hat. "You've seen them too, then? The big ones?"

"We've seen them," Melissa said. "All of us have. Seems there's not many town folk alive left to say that."

The man pointed to a spot in the dusty street near where he sat. "Long time past, right there is where this hole appeared — just opened right before my eyes. One of them things — a bigger 'un — grabbed my young daughter, took her under, and then the hole, it just closed up and disappeared with not a trace it'd been there. Not a trace of my Riona neither. It was like that creeping thing picked her out special and just took her under. Thirty-five years it's been."

"The other people here," Cole asked. "Do you know what happened?"

"I know what happened, you're damned right I know what

happened! Whole town went crazy with killing, *that's* what happened! From what I determined, them things sucked the brains out of people I'd known for years, just found them during the night and did their work on 'em. Seemed everybody turned murderous and come dragging others into my inn. Saw through the window what they did! Them dark creatures inside, they finished them off, every last one. I heard it all. Between them maggoty sluggoty things and the crazy folk they left in their wake, it was a damned slaughter, and no one was left standing! They dragged them bodies through the street and piled them inside the Crow, is what they did! Those bodies, they're all burned to ash with the rest of those creatures."

Cole spoke up. "Those *creatures,* wild sluggots is what I call 'em. I lost my father and my brother to them. I'm figurin' their remains was in that human pile inside the Crow. Prob'ly hundreds of other sluggot bastards are still crawling around near here. Seems they got reasons for what they're doing, but maybe not. I don't much give a damn."

The old man's thick Irish accent repeated the new word, and somehow saying it back, it sounded like *sloogs*. "Yes! That's what they are, the devils! They're damned Wag-sloogs, like you said! There's got to be more, and I want to kill every last fucking one!"

*(...ev'ry last fooking woon...)*

"As do we," Cole said. "And I may know a way how." He extended his hand. "I'm Cole McKenna. This woman here is Melissa Monahan, and here's Sister Margelle."

"You're a McKenna? Your brother was Christian? He frequented the Crow, you know. A good man, he was. I saw when he went for the noon stage yesterday, and—" The stranger chose not to complete his sentence. Instead, he turned his attention to the sister. "You don't seem like a nun to me, Miss Margelle. I mean, the skirt..."

The sister blushed. "I'm thinking I stopped being a nun several hours ago, Mister...?"

The old man forced a smile for the first time. "Hannigan. Aidan Hannigan, at your service. And if I'm going to hell for

**170**

the evil I did today, Sister, I have to tell you, it was worth it."

Melissa spoke up. "The sister and I were on that stage you saw through your window. Another stage is due here soon, isn't that right? There'll be more people coming."

"There's been no Western Union for days now, so there's no one from the outside knows what's what here. The stage, she's due about 3:00. Assuming she makes it, people arriving here won't be happy with what they find. I think them things have been coming out at night, so I'm not expecting a warm welcome for any visitors."

Cole still held the glass jar. He studied the struggling creature inside and turned to the old man.

"Well, then, Mr. Hannigan, let's go kill us some Wag-sloogs..."

# CHAPTER SIXTEEN

## IN THE LOOP: JULY 2015

*"Something here is very wrong..."*

### 608 Diamond Loop: The Campbells

**H**arry Campbell considered himself a connoisseur, and in most respects he was. He knew his cigars. *("Screw Cuba — The Nicaraguan **Oliva Serie V Melanio Figured** makes any Cuban stogie taste like a Tootsie Roll.")* He knew his whiskey. *("Yeah, I've had that Macallan 1946. At $460,000 a bottle, I'd taken only a sip, but I swear I would prefer another one over a young Liz Taylor's snatch.")* And, yes, he knew his women. *("My wife, Regina — she can be a cunt, but I never tasted a better one. Sweet as vanilla ice cream, I swear it!")*

Harry's description of Regina was on the money. Eighteen years her senior, he didn't kid himself about his beautiful bride. She was on the money too — *his* money. But a good stiffy was very forgiving, and just looking at her could get Harry Campbell's withering manhood on the dance floor and ready to boogie. Even better, Regina could achieve that small miracle without her husband's requiring any pharmaceutical incentives. Although his marriage had seen better days, the sad fact was that Harry loved the woman, and when Gina chose to share her favors, she could suck the chrome off a Buick. On those memorable nights, Campbell was again a horny lad in his twenties nursing a serious hard-on to rival any frat boy's.

Arriving home, Harry said hello to Eden Colson, who was just leaving. He didn't question the Colson woman's visit as she acted the social director for the entire cul-de-sac, although there seemed a discernible nervousness in Eden Colson's demeanor. Inside, Harry detected the aroma of Gina's lasagna. His wife had some Italian blood in her, and while her talents in the kitchen didn't match those in the bedroom, she was no slouch at the oven when she set her mind to it. For some reason, today she had. Harry figured maybe she was buttering him up for another shopping spree, but that was okay if it meant that later beneath their silk sheets he would be enjoying some of that vanilla ice cream.

The table was set, and candles were lit. Gina had even worn her long silky fall that made her resemble a twenty-year-old Playmate, complementing her golden locks and almost completely covering her scalp. Harry was no dope; something was up. Removing his tie and jacket, he took a seat. "This looks like you've been cooking all afternoon. Is the IRS auditing your expenses, or have you been possessed by Julia Childs? And your hair...?"

"Couldn't wash it. No water, remember? And I wanted to look beautiful for you."

Gina smiled as she poured Harry a red burgundy. She said nothing more, but for some reason she was singing Madonna's "Like a Virgin." Campbell grinned because his wife's virginity had probably disappeared the day she hit puberty. She sat across the table and pointed to her wine glass. Harry poured. Regina reached for his hand, caressed it.

"I don't get it," Harry said.

"Do I need a reason? I just love my man, is all."

Campbell hadn't heard his wife say that in as long as he could remember. He knew Regina had chosen those hip huggers because she knew he loved how her ass stretched latex to its limit. The throbbing in his pants began immediately, and he no longer gave a sweet damn about his Gina's motives. She drank the wine down and served him a heaping mound of lasagna, waiting for Harry to dig in. The man went at his dinner like a ravenous wolf. He put away two helpings and still had room for dessert, but he suggested they skip coffee.

"You don't mind if I leave the dishes 'till later?" Gina asked.

Harry didn't mind at all. Regina took his hand and led him up the stairs to their bedroom even before the sun had set. Clothes flew off, and Gina thrashed on top of him cowgirl style. It didn't take long for Harry to get his rocks off.

He didn't notice as Regina reached beneath the mattress for her bread knife. Smiling while showing teeth, for the second time Harry Campbell's stunning wife got his rocks off.

They were on the floor.

## 617 Diamond Loop: The Hunters

Denny Hunter was a damned good shortstop for Glenn Echoes High, but at bat his abilities bordered on astounding. His batting average at .300 rivaled legends like Shoeless Joe Jackson, and he was aiming for Ted Williams territory and possibly even the immortal Babe's by the time the college recruiters came to call. Dennis could tell you nothing about why Hester Prynne had earned her scarlet letter, or why Jay Gatsby had a permanent bone-on for his Daisy Buchanan; he knew nothing of plane or solid Geometry, even less of Algebra. Denny did, however, know how to smack a baseball sky high, and...

...he knew about pussy. Concerning the many mysteries of a young girl's ripening cunt, Dennis Hunter could speak volumes, and on this hot summer's day Heather Cooper could happily validate his talents. She could validate also young Hunter's ability to roll one bomber of a joint that would have sent Jerry Garcia's head spinning.

The two were flying quite nicely by late afternoon. Following what sounded like a shot, there seemed some sort of commotion was going on outside in the street, but they paid no attention to it. Despite the dried blood caked on Denny's forehead and on the back of Heather's neck, they sang together in bed, kissing the sky for almost an hour while oblivious to the world. They continued their mutilated Purple Haze lyrics (and frame of mind) as they dressed and headed down the stairs into the family room. There, Heather sucked on her third popsicle, occasionally holding it in front of her, twisting it before her eyes to admire its beauty.

"Your parents are coming home soon? Your father picks up your mother at work, doesn't he? Do you think I should leave before they see how wasted we are?"

Denny thought Heather's question was hilarious. He laughed for a solid minute.

"Hell no. Hell no. Hell — *NO!*"

Falling into each other's arms, both cracked up for no sane reason. Dennis grabbed Heather's face, looked into her eyes.

"So, you ever see me hit a homer? I hit something like thirty least season, you know. Or maybe it was a hundred. Or ten. Fuck, maybe it was soccer."

They howled with laughter for another minute. Still giggling, Heather said, "Yeah, I watched you knock a few balls into the stands, just like... like... Oh, fuck, Denny, I don't follow baseball, but I'm sure it was like somebody important."

"Well, then, let me show you how it's done." Dennis pulled two bats from the closet and handed one to Heather. It was heavy and she immediately dropped it. Giggling as she picked it up, she pretended to lick it like a popsicle — or something considerably sweeter, to Dennis' way of thinking.

"Remind you of anything?" Heather asked.

More laughs followed. "No, really. Let me show you..." He pointed to the fancy table lamp his mother had purchased on special order from somewhere in Europe. Stepping up to the end table, he rubbed his hands together as if he were on the field. He went into his batter's stance, taking the requisite few practice swings before he smashed the glass lamp into a hundred sparkling cinders. Turning to Heather, he sang *"Where have you gone, Joe DiMaggio...?"* taking a deep bow while Heather applauded. He crouched again and aimed his bat, this time for the curio."... *Joltin' Joe has left and gone away!"* he sang, and sent a dozen expensive figurines flying. Laughing hysterically, he suddenly stopped and put a finger to his lips to silence Heather's accompanying snickers. There were voices outside.

"Your parents?" Heather asked.

"They had to park down the block 'cause of the excavation. *Shhh...*" Still holding the bat he went to the door, motioning for Heather to take the other bat and stand on the opposite side facing him. Maybe she would even decide to help him out.

The door opened. Dennis smiled as his parents entered. They appeared confused.

"Hi, Mom. Hi, Dad."

"Hello, Mr. and Mrs. Hunter."

Dennis waited for his father to close the door. Nodding to Heather in silent agreement, he raised his bat. Glenn Echoes High's star hitter prepared to demonstrate to the still giggling Heather Cooper how to smash his parents' heads clear out of the park.

## 610 Diamond Loop: The Brimleys

*"Ey up to Leh ESD sandweech, Geirgie?"*

*"I'm not up on my Russian today, Anna."*

*Anna was all smiles. "I asked if you liked your sandwich, Georgie?"*

Forty years of marriage demonstrated that it had never been George Brimley's style to complain, but he clearly did *not* like his sandwich. Choking, he dropped it on the patio floor. *"Anna! I can't breathe! There's something in my throat. I can't — I can't...!"* He tried to cough but gave it up. Instead, he gagged and convulsed violently in his wheelchair.

"Don't try to talk, Georgie. Just let it go down. It will go down..."

*(Eeet weeel go down, Georgeee...)*

His wrinkled face turned blue, and something seemed to bubble the flesh of his neck from the inside. Anna's Russian schooling had taught her that the skin's blue coloring meant oxygen wasn't reaching her husband's blood and cardiac failure would follow unless she took immediate action. She knew CPR; she also knew the Heimlich maneuver. Years ago Anna had learned both when she was sixteen. At the time, these were modern life saving exercises every Russian student knew, and she still remembered them. Maybe there was enough time to —

Anna knew she wanted to help, she knew she *could*, but something inside stopped her.

A brief moment of clarity came to the elderly woman, and she spoke close to her husband's face. *"Ya lyublyu tyebya, Georgie.'* You know that means I love you, yes? I always have. I want you to understand that. It's just that what I'm feeling inside me, please understand, it's just that... *Damn! Damn!"*

Anna shook her head, realizing she couldn't fathom her own reasoning. A network of cobwebs had somehow got into her brain, clouding every rational thought. She had an insane urge to sing that birthday song again, but she shook the words from her head.

...*Her head* — it had hurt like a demon earlier, but now she felt fine. She pulled off the Band-Aid that adhered to her hairline. Feeling for some evidence of a wound, she felt nothing. How could any laceration, even a small one, heal so quickly? She remembered something near the excavation had bitten her before she could see it, something that had been inside the car.

Terrible thoughts crept into Anna Brimley's brain.

*(My husband's legs, they will not move. They will not ever move...)*

*(My own life to consider. My own life, what is left of it...)*

She shook more cobwebs free and kissed George's cheek. Already, his skin felt cold, but George's eyes remained open wide, and they were looking at her. His lips formed two soundless words.

*"Anna... Why?"*

It was a good question, one she had asked herself. The answer came quickly. It crawled from her husband's ear.

The small dark creature hung there. Like a tiny snake its head twisted upwards, seeming to take full measure of the woman. Before Anna could react, it fell to the patio's concrete and disappeared in the surrounding grass. Anna's head was hurting again, but in no manner that she ever had experienced. It felt like television channels changing inside her brain — clarity one moment, complete disorientation the next. She told herself nothing she was seeing could be happening.

*"Kahk vahs...?"* (What...?)

And then, a shock...

George's color had returned to normal, but little else Anna watched could be called normal. Her husband struggled to stand as if he had forgotten his legs hadn't worked since the fall of Saigon. He seemed to have recovered in only seconds, but like herself, he also seemed to find no comfort in his recovery.

*"Anna..."*

She stared at him. "Are you all right, George?"

"No."

Anna knew he would say that. "Something here is very wrong, George. I deceived you, fed you something that was not good for you. I don't even know why I did that. And a moment ago, from your ear..."

*"Anna, something terrible is happening... I feel it..."*

Her next words came as if she could not spit them out fast enough. *"I hate my own thoughts! I hate that your legs are useless dead things! I hate myself for hating!"* She covered her mouth as if her words were too repellent to express. Brimley nodded with dark understanding, and why not? So often he seemed to share the same mind with her. Anna loved her husband too much to allow any despicable thoughts regarding his disability, but today she spoke those thoughts, horrible and shameful thoughts growing stronger by the minute. She couldn't stop them, and she knew very soon she would act on them.

*"Anna..."*

"Wait here, George. Please." She disappeared inside. When she returned to the patio she held the antique Johnson Flintlock pistol, among the most valuable in her husband's collection. "I don't know how to load this. Do you have —?" She pretended not to know the American word for bullets, but of course George had to know she did.

She understood her man didn't need to hear her reasoning, didn't need to ask her intentions. He always knew she hated to be near his antique guns, yet here she was holding one. She remembered that bullets had come with his collection. They were very old, and she worried they wouldn't work. He must have known why she handed him the pistol, but she told him anyway, "I want you to load your gun, George."

She wheeled her husband to his study where he kept his assortment of old Western pistols and rifles mounted, and where, until today, she rarely ventured. Inside one of a dozen drawers, he located a small box.

"Load the gun, George."

"Anna, I can't do this. Maybe the feeling will pass."

She put a finger to his lips. "There is no other way. If we wait..." She put her hand to her temple. Her head was throbbing again. "The feeling is too strong!"

"Then I'll go first!" George placed the gun into his mouth, but hesitantly withdrew it. "I can't."

"It happened so fast, this thing inside. A lifetime of love for you, and in a handful of minutes it's leaving me. I don't want to be like this!"

George spit his words like some poisonous venom. "Every time I see you look at an able-bodied man, I hate you a little! My God, how could I ever want to hurt you? But Goddammit, I know I *will!*" Brimley's lips tightened as if he were at war with himself. He forced a half choked "I loved you from the day I first saw you, Anna."

"I know." She extended her hand for the pistol, and George gave it to her. The woman turned to glance through the window of the study. Outside no one was nearby, and the sporadic pounding of the jackhammers at the excavation was loud. That was good. She raised the old pistol to her husband's forehead and saw the wild look in his eyes, knowing hers probably appeared the same. Waiting for the jackhammering to start up again, she whispered, "Ya lyublyu tyebya, George..."

Two shots rang out from 610 Diamond Loop, less than a minute apart.

No one heard them.

### 613 Diamond Loop: The Colsons

Eden Colson felt dirty. Her morning had been filled with accusatory police questioning and clandestine sex. *(No, damn it, it was adultery!)* She had topped it off with a tub full of repulsive God-knows-what slime creatures. Maybe those slug-things were her divine punishment for her sin of having fucked up...

*(... No, of having fucked Fred Reefe, of Reefe Water & Sewer Contractors!)*

Working with some real dirt seemed fitting for a woman whose hands felt like they would remain forever filthy. She decided to go after the thickets of weeds that seemed determined to ruin her garden, just as she had gone after those dark things crawling from her drain that seemed determined to ruin her life. Summer rains had nourished the thick tangles. Healthy and strong, the weeds twisted along the yard's edges in dense tuffs. Eden's hoe whacked away, and at least she felt some satisfaction denying those flower-killers the opportunity to strangle the remaining beauty from her world. She swung the hoe like a pissed off Grim Reaper.

Eden played the morning's events on an endless loop inside her head. A few weeks living on the cul-de-sac and here she was, no better than her bottle blonde neighbor, Regina Campbell, who steamed her bikini briefs for anything in pants. A fat lot of good all that private parochial school education did for the virtuous teenaged Eden Gallagher, she thought. Today the nuns at Sacred Heart of Jesus would have branded a scarlet "A" into her tits.

The hoe struck something soft hidden inside the thickets. Eden hacked at it again before sensing the concealed thing was alive.

"Shit! If that's you, Rocky — Like today hasn't been bad enough." Zachary's cat often slipped out of the house whenever there was traffic moving in and out, and if Eden had just smashed her garden tool into the cat's head—-

It wasn't Rocky. Eden saw the feline staring at her from behind the sliding screen door, and Rocky's fur raised. The cat must have sensed something in the garden had gone gonzo. The thick plant patch moved again. Eden pushed the hoe through, poking at something that felt squishy, and she readied herself to haul ass back inside. Whatever it was, it grunted with the nudge. Eden froze where she stood. An eye the size of a baseball blinked from behind the tangles. Two long hooks the size of twisted garden shears emerged snapping at her through the brush. Eden's first instinct was to back off fast, but no...

The thing bit into the handle of the hoe and snapped it in two. Eden dropped the useless handgrip.

*"A quick photo, you bastard,"* she mumbled. Reaching for her cell phone, she said *"Smile!"* and took the picture just before the twin hooks lunged for her.

Eden picked up the hoe's handle as she stepped back, but with the weed patch thinned, the exposure to sunlight seemed more of a threat to the hidden creature than did the broken garden tool. It disappeared beneath the soil with the efficiency of an earthworm, but Eden knew this thick-as-a-hydrant creature was no earthworm. Those hooks, the red eyes, its size...

(*...like some python. No, more like an anaconda!*)

She knew it was neither. Smaller versions of the same creature had slithered from her bathtub's drain, but this thing seemed prehistoric. Eden hurried into the house and shut the sliding door behind her, locking it. Trying to summon a rational thought, she could make no sense of what she had seen. She studied the photo on her cell's screen. The thing half hidden in the bushes looked like a cheesy Hollywood CGI effect. Then she remembered...

*"Fred! Damn..."* she muttered to herself. Reefe was in the excavation, and she had to show him the photo. He had

watched those slug things crawl from her drain, and he knew what had happened to Jessie Moss. He and his crew had to get out of that hole. Probably every neighbor on the Loop would have to leave too. Eden didn't want to create a panic, but she couldn't wait either. Zack and Greg would be returning home soon, and no way would she allow her family to stay home while more of those things were slithering below the cul-de-sac. *Probably from the water mains,* Fred had mentioned, but had he known about those filthy things' big brothers? Well, now she had the photo —- *she had proof!*

The day's drilling had concluded as Eden headed for the excavation. She stopped cold when she saw Wally Smith emerge from 620, his movement a drunken shamble. The retired police sergeant was beyond corpulent, and he couldn't run carrying so much weight. For some reason Smith was singing a slurred *God Bless America* at the top of his lungs.

**"...Gah bless 'Merica, Lan' ' dat I love...."**

It took a moment for another image to register. Smith was waving a pistol into the air and shouting, "Gah Bless 'Merica, Mizz Colson!" then started again.

**"From th' mountains, to th' prairies., to th' oceans, white wit' fohhhhm..."**

A small laceration at the man's temple leaked blood, as if something had bored into it. Eden had the sinking feeling that maybe something did.

He pointed the gun at Eden.

*"Mr. Smith, what—?"*

The man started another drunken patriotic chorus.

And then came the shot

★ ★ ★

## MORLOCKS AND ELOI

Tiffany Leone's camcorder had captured the excavation workers' suspicions — suspicions that weren't good. Zachary Colson's photos of the damaged water line didn't indicate anything good either. Here was proof that the unsettling events

182

beneath Diamond Loop might soon be getting a lot worse. Seated in the stands of the middle school's athletic field, Zachary flashed his best balls-out smile.

"You still feeling adventurous, Miss Lane?"

Tiffany had to smile back. "I'm with you, Jimmy." Headed for the Harley, she handed Zachary his helmet. Frowning, he didn't put it on.

"Do you really think, if you cracked up this bike, that wearing this thing would help?"

"We're in Jersey, kid. It's the law. Put it on, or we don't move." She slipped hers over her head and waited. Tiffany's solid black helmet (with a bright yellow lightning bolt on either side) made her appear more like her tougher alter ego, Taffy Licks. Zachary understood his new pal preferred that he knew nothing about her secret identity.

He shrugged, but he put the helmet on. "I've been thinking. Jessie Moss had to have had a worker's helmet down in that hole — a hard hat. But something down there chewed through to his skull anyway."

Tiffany thought that over. "Maybe he took it off."

"Or maybe something knocked it off."

"Mr. Reefe said something had gnawed through those copper water lines, so who knows?"

Tiffany revved up the engine, its four-stroke twin cams performing on cue, although all Zachary Colson knew of Tiffany's Harley was he liked the way it went *Va-room! Va-room!* She told him to hold on, and Zachary was happy to wrap his hands around Tiffany's waist.

"Where to, Cub Scout? It's getting late."

"I'm thinking I'd like to take a look around the excavation later, after the workers leave. But I want to stop home first before my dad gets back from work, make sure that my mom is okay. You know, with those things we heard Reefe mention seeing in our house, I may have to kill a few creatures before dinner. It's the American way."

"Roger that, Grasshopper." Laughing, Tiffany peeled out, and Zachary never felt more cool or more fearless. This girl had the kind of laugh that made him wish he were ten years older. Conversation became difficult with the bike's roaring, and he had to practically yell.

"What ever happened to Davidson?"

"Who?"

"Davidson! You know, this bike is a Harley-Davidson, but no one ever calls this a Davidson. So I was just wondering—"

That laugh again. "You're a really strange kid, Boy Wonder."

Zachary took that as a compliment. "Something else has been on my mind, Tiffany. I mean, something that's really bothering me. Promise me you won't say I'm crazy."

"I'll wait until you prove otherwise."

"Well, see, I've been thinking about Morlocks."

"Morlocks? You want to explain that?"

Zachary held tight as Tiffany took a sharp turn towards Glenn Echoes Boulevard. "I read about them last year in English. They're creatures in *The Time Machine*. H. G. Wells wrote how, a few thousand years into the future, people have evolved into two species that are sort of human but not too bright, the Eloi and the Morlocks."

"Kind of like Democrats and Republicans."

"Worse. See, the Morlocks live underground, and they come up at night and eat the Eloi. And I was thinking, maybe Wells was saying that eating Eloi made the Morlocks smarter, or something like that. The Eloi were civilized and more human looking, and they lived better. That's why the Morlocks ate them. They were jealous, wanted what they had."

Tiffany shouted over the engine, "Yeah, I read that book too. The Eloi just sort of accepted it, and they let the Morlocks come and get them. They were pretty stupid. I think that's what *eloi* is supposed to mean. Maybe ol' Herbert George thought they were even more stupid than the Morlocks. So?"

A daredevil on the road, Tiffany zipped past a dozen cars. Zachary held tight and leaned close to her back. "I was just wondering if maybe people today are used to acting like we're the Eloi. People just accept all kinds of shit happening, but they don't do anything except carry signs and occasionally riot. Suppose those slug-things in the hole are jealous and are coming for *us? Mankind On The Menu,* the ultimate reality show!"

Tiffany stopped at the light, turned to him. "Damn, you really *do* read too much, Zachary Colson. Do you really think you are what you eat?"

"Maybe if what you eat is brains."

*"Ugh!* Change the subject."

Still holding Tiffany's waist, Zachary felt her shudder. He tapped her shoulder.

"Light's green," he said.

It didn't seem a good idea for Tiffany to ride the Harley anywhere near the excavation site considering her secretive cam recording. She changed her mind when an ambulance passed by with siren screaming and stopped near the Diamond Loop cul-de-sac entrance. The excavation had emptied too, a clear indication that something had gone very wrong at the Loop. Tiffany took her chances being spotted if Reefe's crew were near, and she pulled up close to the ambulance. She watched two attendants jump out with a stretcher and an oxygen tank. The men rushed on foot into the Loop area because there still was no direct access to the homes.

Tiffany turned to Zachary. "There's a crowd gathering. What is it about human suffering that brings people out of their homes like roaches, having to see?"

"Guess that makes both of us like the roaches." Zachary noticed the construction team were part of the gathering. He jumped from the Harley and charged ahead with Tiffany close behind. The two guys from the ambulance broke through the cluster, and Zachary spotted his mother standing in the middle of the street. For a moment he stopped and just stared. Fred Reefe was holding her.

*"Mom!"*

Pale and shaking badly, his mother looked at him dully

but didn't respond. Tiffany caught up in time to see a heavyset man lifted into the stretcher, although the attendants were having trouble hoisting him. The guy was huge and half of his face had been blown off.

"Gross," Zachary said.

"What's going on?" Tiffany asked a woman.

"It's one of the neighbors. Mr. Smith, I think. He shot himself right there in the street. Happened just a few minutes ago, and that woman there saw it." The woman pointed to Zachary's mother.

An attendant in white pried the gun that remained clenched in the man's hand and handed it to the three-piece suited crime scene investigator. The man slipped the weapon into a plastic bag. The two ambulance workers looked at each other, and one shook his head. The other pulled a sheet over the guy's face, but he was bleeding so badly the blood leaked through the material. There seemed no reason now to rush back to the ambulance, but they did anyway. The vehicle pulled away. There was no siren this time, but in a few moments there certainly would be another one when the police arrived.

Tiffany put her hand on Zachary's shoulder to hold him back. "Listen, Zack, your mom looks shaken up. Maybe you'd better not—"

Zachary wasn't listening, and he ran towards his mother. Her face was buried in Reefe's chest. The man was stroking her hair, holding her much too close.

"Mom, are you okay?" For the first time since this morning Zachary Colson sounded like the thirteen year old kid he was. His mother looked at him but said nothing. Fred Reefe spoke for her.

"Zachary, your mom's had a bad shock. She'll be okay, but right now she's trying to pull it together. Give her a few minutes, okay?"

"Okay, but quit holding her like that!"

Tiffany appeared and stood next to Zack. "Why don't you explain what's happened, Mr. Reefe? To both of us, okay?" She spoke like she knew more than she was letting on, and Fred

Reefe must have known she did. He whispered something to Eden Colson. Another woman neighbor put her arm around Eden while Reefe ushered Zachary and Tiffany from the crowd to a spot near the Colson house where they could speak in private.

"Okay — it's Tiffany, right? Well, Tiffany, I think, considering what you two overheard earlier today, maybe we should share some observations, don't you think? Zack, your mother has had two close calls these past two days, and what happened with Mr. Smith you may already have figured is very similar to what happened yesterday with Jessie Moss. I know you both went to see him. The desk nurse told me the two of you visited Glenn Echoes General this morning, although the names — Zeke and Taffy Moss? It *was* you two, wasn't it, Zachary?"

Zack shuffled his feet and nodded. "Your worker, the loader guy, Jarmal, he told Tiffany that Mr. Moss got hurt in the hole yesterday, and then went to visit my mom. Mr. Moss did something to her, didn't he?"

Reefe spoke low like a man at holy confession. "Okay, I won't lie to you, Zack. Mr. Moss tried to hurt her. He wasn't thinking clearly. Same thing seems to have happened with Mr. Smith just now. Both men — well, see, I think both men hurt themselves rather than hurt your mother. I don't know what changed their minds. Conscience, maybe some sense of what they were doing. But what set them off to begin with, I haven't a clue."

Tiffany looked around, making sure no one stood near. "I think you *do* know what caused that craziness, don't you, Mr, Reefe? I mean, why both men seemed to have suddenly gone off their nut? We overheard you talking to your crew, remember?"

Zachary seemed distracted. The image of Reefe holding his mother wouldn't leave his head. "My mom, she'll be okay, right?" Not happy with Reefe's hesitation, he wondered if the man's stalling had nothing to do with Jessie Moss or Mr. Smith, and everything to do with the way he had been manhandling his mom.

**187**

Reefe continued, "Sergeant Smith pointed his gun at your mother, then stuck the pistol into his own mouth. That's what Eden — your mom — told me. Zack, that's a heavy thing to see happen. Your mother just needs some time to come back. She'll be fine."

Tiffany didn't want to drop the other topic. "Jessie Moss and Mr. Smith. What do *you* think happened to them to make them act like that?"

Behind Tiffany, Eden Colson appeared. She held out the display screen of her cell phone.

"*This* is what I think happened to those two men..."

"Eden, are you—?" Reefe shut up and looked at the image on the phone's screen. Tiffany and Zack looked too, then looked at each other.

*The large crimson eye hidden in the weeds, those hooks...*

Zack practically shouted, "I was right! Morlocks!"

Reefe turned to Eden. "Where did you take this?"

"That thing was in my garden less than an hour ago. Those slug-things crawling from my drain earlier looked like smaller versions of *this* thing. I think they got to both Jessie Moss and Mr. Smith. You saw what happened to Jessie, Fred. Hooks that size could've done that damage and had some bizarre effect on him. That's the same crazy look I saw in Wally Smith's eyes, and I noticed his head was bleeding too, just before he—" She looked at her son, allowing the rest of her sentence to disappear into the wind. "*I'm* all right, Zack, so don't worry about me. But, I'm not sure about..."

"...but you're not sure about our other neighbors. That's what you wanted to say isn't it, Mom? Because those things you saw took healthy bites out of two people you know. Do I have that much right? Is that what's making people around here crazy?"

A siren screamed, and sure enough, the police were pulling up at the entrance. Two officers climbed out of the cruiser, the same two who had visited Eden earlier.

Tiffany studied the dispersing crowd of Loop residents. "These folks look okay to me, Zack. Cops won't find much here." That wasn't entirely true. The infant daughter Betsy Lewis held in her arms squirmed and growled as if at any moment she might go for her mother's throat. Tiffany saw this, but she figured any baby with a wet diaper would react the same.

Zack turned his attention towards the surrounding homes of the cul-de-sac. "Maybe the folks out here are okay, but what of the people *inside* the homes, the ones who *didn't* come out to see Mr. Smith's showdown? When something like this happens on their own street, people are always curious to see the blood and guts, right? It's what people do, like fucking ghouls."

"Zack, *language!*" from Tiffany. She turned to Reefe and Eden Colson. "...although I think Zachary has a point. What about the people who *aren't* here? Maybe some slug-things like those you saw went calling on other homes too." She looked at the crowd, saw the two officers questioning some of the neighbors. "Maybe Jessie Moss and Wally Smith are just the beginning. Mr. Reefe, you were going to inform the residents that their water would remain off a while longer, weren't you? Well, then...?"

Fred Reefe considered this. There really was no other option.

"All right. Maybe it's time we knocked on a few doors."

## THE WOGSLûK

*Beneath Diamond Loop, sounds like words.*

*They're not words. Not really.*

*"Yoob...Die-em...men...yoob..."*

*They're guttural clicks and liquid gulps, attempts at simple articulation.*

*Beneath the streets, the high pitched sounds go unheard. It is doubtful they would be understood anyway.*

*But whether large or small, every Wogslûk understands.*

*"Yoob...Die-em...men...yoob..."*

*They make the sounds, sounds learned from one belonging to a long time past.*
*A female.*
*And human.*

# CHAPTER SEVENTEEN
## PLAINS AND TRAINS, 1866:
## TRACKING WAG-SLOOGS

*"A place where it's dark all the time..."*

C reated from a mixture of saltpeter, charcoal and sulfur, black powder made a damned good (and dangerously unpredictable) explosive. The highly volatile powder cost many rail workers their limbs and lives, a genuine occupational hazard for those Chinese immigrants laying rails westward. The powder grew scarce during the War Between The States because the mixture was also used in muskets for gunpowder. Of necessity, California built a Power Works factory in 1864 to meet the railroaders' growing demand. The builders stockpiled maybe a hundred thousand 25-pound powder kegs of the material near the sites where tunnels were anticipated and where mountains required blasting. Tons of black powder remained unguarded, often stored in rows of covered wagons or deep within the tunnels already built. That meant the explosive became accessible to anyone crazy enough to want to pilfer the stuff.

*"Well, then, Mr. Hannigan, let's go kill us some Wag-sloogs..."*

Young Cole McKenna was literally playing with dynamite's older cousin. He knew only one thing: There were shit wagons of wild sluggots to hunt and kill — Wag-sloogs, as the old Irishman, Aidan Hannigan, mispronounced them — but *demons* was probably more accurate. Cole wasn't naive enough to think he could destroy them all, but he could certainly blow to smithereens a few nests of the slimy bastards, maybe enough to stop them from spreading. He knew where to find them too, as he had told Sister Margelle and Melissa Monahan.

*"I know what brought them holes here and set them sluggots crawling out. It can't be anything else! It's the damned Atchison, Topeka, and the Santa Fe. I'm betting them holes are a stone's throw from where new tracks are going down!"*

Studying his captured creature inside the glass jar, Cole offered his plan of goosing the Wag-sloogs from their holes with the plentiful supply of flammable liquid taken from the town's gas lamps. But the elderly Aidan Hannigan had a few ideas of his own as he and the three strangers sat by the stage depot in the deserted Trementina.

"I doubt gas bottles will do much more than barbecue a few of them creatures. Oh, them gas lamps worked fine burning down The Old Crow and killing a few of 'em trapped inside. But you'll need something's got considerable more poop if you want to kill a whole damned colony of those bastards. I'm thinking some black powder might do the trick, blow your Wag-sloogs clear back to Hell where they belong. Them railroaders nearby have enough of that powder to drill through several mountains of rock, which is exactly what they use that stuff for. Toss that stuff into a 'sloog hole, and it's nap time for anything inside it."

Cole liked the idea. "I got money in my backpack can pay for some powder under the table if we find them railroad camps. Found it on the empty Overland stage the ladies was on, and planned to give it to that bank near The Crow, but that don't seem probable now that Trementina's turned into a ghost town."

Melissa had other thoughts. "Mr. Hannigan, you're saying you plan to set off explosives you know nothing about? Railroad men know where to place that powder, and still there are many who manage to blow themselves to pieces. Powder is unstable. You'll kill us all."

Hannigan removed his hat. Maybe it was a show of respect for the woman; more likely it was because of the heat. "Miss

Monahan, I'm willing to take that risk, and I'm not asking you to do the same. I've lost a daughter to those things — my only daughter even if her blood wasn't mine. My young wife back home in Ulster caught the fever before I could send for her, and here in Trementina my Riona's natural mother was hanged. She had no other father but myself, and I watched one of them filthy creatures take her from me 'cause I was too damned scared to do more. I knew the day would come I'd find them again, even if it was them that found *me*. So you see, I have a personal stake here."

Melissa didn't budge. "And I lost a man who was to be my husband, Mr. Hannigan. I don't think explosives are a wise thing to fool with. There must be a better way to—" She looked to Sister Margelle for some support, but the nun didn't seem much of an advocate. The riding clothes she wore didn't make her appear much of a nun either, but she still spoke like one.

"You lost a wife to the fever, Mr. Hannigan? As a child, I lost a sister — a twin sister, lost to that scarlet illness. We both suffered it, and when I survived I swore to serve my Savior as best I could. I'm thinking maybe this is a way to do so. I'm not sure the church would favor my thirst for those creatures' blood, but you may count me in."

"That's good," Hannigan said. "Today's stage is an hour overdue, and I'm thinking I may know why. We ought to saddle up, go look for it. General store here has plenty of foodstuff — can last us several days. I'll pick up a load of matches and some thick cord can serve as a decent fuse, 'case we choose to do some blasting while Miss Melissa here watches from a safe distance."

Melissa saw she was overruled. "All right, then. But maybe first we should find that pit we passed coming into town. That's where those things came from. The stage could've been delayed a while there. Ours was."

Cole seemed satisfied. "Then we're agreed on this, Miss Monahan, Sister Margelle?"

"Excepting for one thing," the nun answered. "From now on, it's just Margelle..."

★ ★ ★

## 'SLOOGS

Some daylight remained, and that meant hopefully some security also because Wag-sloogs disliked the light, and none of the four trackers knew how many lurked along Trementina's outskirts. So far they had discovered no sign of the gaping maw that had stopped the women's coach along their way into town, nor any indication of the noon stagecoach that had been due. No wheel tracks nor any signs of horses' hooves other than their own appeared along the trail either. The open prairie's light winds could not have blown those remnants away so quickly.

Searching the dusty roadway, Melissa shook her head. "We're past where our stage stopped yesterday. I don't understand. That hole was huge. Where is it?"

Margelle slowed her horse and the others followed. "I don't like this. Nothing would stop the afternoon wagon from arriving on schedule unless something got in its way. Maybe another crater opened up further. Or maybe something else stopped the stage?"

"Indians? Robbers?" Melissa sounded almost hopeful.

"Yeah, maybe Indians or robbers," Cole repeated. He unpacked a pair of binoculars and scanned the terrain. "I see something off the trail ahead in the brush. Could be a wagon. There's horses!" Hannigan had a look also and agreed something was there.

Rifles at the ready, the four rode on to discover what each had feared. The stage due for Trementina remained off the trail, perfectly intact. It had been ditched in tangles of brush far off the road, its six horses still harnessed and snorting like mad. The doors on each side swung in the breeze, and the baggage on top remained untouched. The passengers were gone.

Hannigan looked over the empty coach and frowned. "Them things, they made off with the people, same as they done with my Riona. Probably dragged them poor folks clear out of their seats and down one of them holes in the dust, then closed it up clean like a grave. I seen it happen forty years ago. That hole just filled up fast, like someone stuck a big plug into it. I'm thinking we ain't about to find any of them Wag-sloog devils, not if we're looking just for them holes, 'cause they don't seem to stay open for long. They're too smart, them creatures are! But we can be smarter!" He turned to Cole. "Can you maybe think like a Wag-sloog, boy? Let's assume you were like your little friend in the jar and not fond of the daylight. Where would you figure you'd go to hide yourself?"

Cole didn't have to think long. "A place where it's dark all the time, like that Old Crow Inn or like the underground, but close enough to the settlements since that seems to be their huntin' grounds.

"Right you are, but there's not an inn to be found for miles on these open prairies, and underground is damned risky when you come up and you don't know where you are. Think what *is* out here that's dark and where them railroad men are blasting away disturbin' them 'sloog creatures?" Aidan Hannigan clearly knew the answer to his own question, but he waited for young McKenna to confirm it.

"The tunnels through the mountains! Them places are always dark, and railroaders' explosions must be bringing them creatures to the surface! And there's people there. Prey!"

The old guy patted Cole on the back. "Your father would be proud, boy."

Melissa again turned skeptical. "A dozen explosions are likely needed to get through just one of those mountains. Those tunnels aren't the smartest places for those creatures to nest if they prefer remaining in one piece."

Margelle had her own opinion. "You saw the mouth hooks on those bigger ones. I'd say those hooks serve more than one purpose. The ground inside a tunnel must be dug thorough enough to lay those railroad tracks, so it would be simple work for those ugly things to burrow through. They're good at disappearing quickly into the dirt, wouldn't you agree, Mr.

Hannigan?"

"I'll search for them damned holes before they close if it takes the rest of my days. But right now I know where we can start." Aidan Hannigan had reached his decision. Searching the empty stagecoach he found a woman's hat and studied the small spatters of blood that freckled the seats. He pointed these out to Cole and the women. "Whatever happened here, it happened fast. Maybe some shots was fired, but apparently none of them creatures was wounded enough to stay behind. These horses seem unharmed. That's good. We can use 'em and this stage" Already the man was tying his own horse to the back of the coach.

"What exactly do you have in mind, Mr. Hannigan?" Margelle asked.

"We have some decent transportation right here, ladies. We can rotate these horses with our own when they're tired, and feed them some of our own foodstuff 'till we get back to town. A team of six will cover a lot more miles than any single horse can. We should be good for a few days, and this wagon will do just fine for transporting a decent load of black powder we can purchase with the boy's cash. Them new railroad tracks ain't too far off from here, maybe a couple hours' ride if we travel by night, and I know every trail in this area. We'll follow them to the mountains, locate some of that blasting powder, and then do that Wag-sloog hunting we came to do, at least young McKenna here and myself. You women can decide what you prefer. I'll hold no grudges."

Melissa caught Aidan Hannigan's eye. Watching the old man climb into the driver's perch, she wasn't happy with any of this. "Give us a moment, will you?" Melissa took Margelle aside and spoke low. "There's a good chance that old man is just plain crazy. I'm not real comfortable with having another confrontation with one of those filthy things, especially over a pile of explosives. You?"

"I have to agree with the old man. You've seen what's happening around here. If we don't look for those creatures, they're going to come looking for *us* — and for any other poor souls that set foot into these parts. That's not a prospect I care to think about. There's no turning the other cheek here." Margelle forced a smile. "...and that's the last biblical reference you'll be hearing from me."

"But there are so many of those things. Hundreds. Probably more under the ground."

"Exactly." Margelle tied her horse to the rear of the stage and climbed into the carriage. "Coming?"

Melissa spoke low. "You're certain you're through with being a nun, Sister?"

"Absolutely."

"You took your vows?"

"Screw my vows. I'm creating some new ones of my own."

Tying her horse to the stage axle, Melissa whispered to her companion, "Then, fuck it," and climbed in.

★ ★ ★

## EXPLOSIVE SITUATIONS

*In April of 1866 a leaking crate of nitroglycerin arrived at the Wells Fargo office in San Francisco. Concerned about the leak, an employee grabbed a hammer and chisel to open the damaged crate. That proved to be the last thing the man ever did. The resulting explosion leveled the building and killed everyone inside.*

*Nitroglycerin was a new kind of explosive, and black powder, while not as effective, was considered by the railroad financiers and executives to be their incendiary device of choice for blasting through the numerous mountains to lay tracks. Black powder was significantly slower, but it was safer.*

*The dangers of nitroglycerin did not matter a bit to one Frederick Gibbon, the efficient and time-conscious overseer of the New Mexico leg of the proposed AT&SF railroad stretching across the prairies and through the mountains of the American West. One formidable mountain in particular, the Donner Summit, proved especially stubborn regarding black powder's effectiveness. Concerned with time lost, Gibbon notified his Panama connections, whose more volatile pro-duct, during transit, recently had blown fifty men aboard the freighter* **European** *to bloody bits and pieces. Again, this mattered little to Frederick Gibbon, who cared only that his product was effective. With some creative modifications applied to his shipment order, black marketed nitroglycerin replaced the less efficient black powder in the crates he received, and no one was the wiser — including his 500 immigrant workers. Unmarked crates of the explosive were piled ten feet high and hidden inside the tunnel's two entrances at a safe enough distance from the blasting not to send any Chinese workers on their way back home through the Earth's core.*

*Common practice was to blast from both sides of a mountain, meeting somewhere in the middle. Although this saved time by having two teams working simultaneously, this meant the workers' night camps were often on either side of the lengthy Donner Summit. For safety reasons their makeshift bunks were at some distance from the crates of blasting powder piled on both ends near the entrances. Many of the Chinese workers, seeking more comfortable accommodations, chose whatever lodgings were available in nearby settlements. This meant that during the night few of the workers bunked close to where the explosives were stored. Crates of blasting powder weren't the sort of thing that attracted thieves, but for anyone who wanted to lay their hands on the combustible stuff, thievery wouldn't be difficult...*

During this hot July midnight, thievery seemed especially simple. On the western slope of the Summit, sixty-three rail-road workers had gone missing. The Gibbon workers' site was deserted when the re-routed stage (two women, a boy, and an elderly driver) pulled up. Removing the gas lamp from the coach and looking about the workers' camp, Aidan Hannigan turned to young Cole McKenna.

"Looks like you won't be needing that black powder money you're carryin', since it appears there's not a soul here to purchase it from. Ain't no thief, but seems stealing is our only remaining option." Raised honest, Cole McKenna would have protested, but old Hannigan had his mind set on a plan. "Bring your little pal in the glass jar," he told the boy. He gave no explanation, but Cole carried the jar in his back pack as the elderly man led the others on foot through the abandoned camp. Some tents had been torn, and sleeping cots were strewn about. It didn't take much reasoning to determine that something terrible had happened here. Hannigan seemed strangely pleased. "We've come to the right place. 'Sloogs been here too. I'm thinking this may be the same story for the next twenty miles, and there's not many on the outside who'll know what happened here any time soon. 'Specially with them rail workers being mostly Chinese and having no connections with the territories."

Melissa scanned the empty tents and ramshackle sleeping quarters. "This is crazy, you know that, don't you? Those things killed everyone here, probably dragged them from their beds! There had to be a whole colony to do this. How are we supposed to—?"

Cole interrupted. "Some lamps are still burning. Them 'sloogs stopped here this night. They're close by, maybe bunched together inside the tunnel — or under it. And if they're inside, that means them blasts through the mountain haven't hurt them any."

Hannigan considered Cole's point. "I doubt any powder's been tossed directly into their living quarters. Blasts inside that tunnel prob'ly did nothing more than scatter them back under the ground like roaches." The old man gathered three flickering lamps from several of the surrounding bunks. He handed one lamp to each. "This is the Donner Summit, tallest mountain in the area. I'm betting there's enough black powder in that tunnel to finish off a mess of them and their nests if we can find them."

Melissa's jaw dropped. "You're going to blow up that

tunnel? My God! If that doesn't kill us, or if those creatures don't, the railroad people will!"

Aidan Hannigan said nothing. Rifles in one hand, lamps in the other, the three followed him to the tunnel's entrance. Tracks had not yet been laid, but there was a flattened roadbed that led into the cavern. The tunnel must have gone close to a mile depending on how much had been completed. There was no way to tell from the outside.

Margelle stopped cold at the entrance, aware of Melissa's staring at her as if expecting some sanity to prevail. "I don't know about this, Mr. Hannigan. We're dealing with something we understand nothing about. You don't know explosives, you don't know those creatures. Maybe we should see if there's other people anywhere who can help with —"

"There *ain't* no other people! It's got to be us!" He stared into the blackness of the unfinished tunnel. "Can't see no crates in that darkness, not from here. Blasting powder might be further inside close to where them workers last finished."

"How can you be sure there's explosives in there?" Melissa asked.

"I can't. But it's the most likely place for at least some of that stuff, ain't it? Look, I don't plan to blow us up, 'case you been wonderin', Missy. A crate or two of powder that we can carry out should serve us nicely when we find more holes. There's got to be some of them pits in these parts that we'll discover open." The man sounded less than convincing. Holding his lantern in front of him and with his rifle at his side, old Hannigan entered the mouth of the cavern. He turned to the others. "'Sloog tracks is still here in the dirt. A lair's inside, I've no doubt. I can do this alone if I have to."

Cole looked at the women who stood firm. He stepped forward. "You don't have to, Mr. Hannigan."

Margelle bit her lip, the lapsed nun inside her at war with the more sensible woman who was scared to death. Her reaction came slow, but she stepped forward too. "The more rifles the better, right? I mean, just in case."

Melissa didn't budge. "This is breaking the law. You'll

need someone to stay behind here if anyone comes, right? You never know... *isn't that right?"*

Hannigan's expression remained passive, impossible to read. "Nope, you never know, Miss."

Melissa watched the three disappear into the tunnel's darkness. She turned to look at the empty campsite, its few lanterns casting ghostly illumination over the deserted place. A cold wind sent an ice floe up her spine and she muttered to herself, *"This is crazy... This is crazy!"*

It *was* crazy. Those 'sloogs, as the old man had christened them, were nearby, there was no doubting that. And if the creatures waited hidden in the tunnel's darkness, then they were right at home inside there — and anyone inside with them was dead.

*Crazy... Completely crazy. Yes, but.....*

It seemed just as crazy to remain standing in the darkness alone.

Melissa shouted, *"Hey! Wait up!"*

Four lanterns sliced sickly beams through the dark, but they didn't illuminate much. The tunnel was cold and unfriendly, the crunch of boots on soil echoing in its chambers. Aidan Hannigan led the way, but the group seemed three blind people led by an equally blind fourth who was also maybe a little insane. The mouth of the tunnel disappearing behind them, they followed the curve of the burrowed roadbed. Their few words reverberated off the walls of rock, echoes growing louder the further into the guts of the tunnel they went.

"We could go to jail for this," Melissa muttered as they pressed forward. "And if you happen to locate the explosives you're hoping to find, Mr. Hannigan, you'll bring this whole mountain down on us. I'm not here because I want to be here, I just want you to know that."

The old man smiled. "Breakfast with Jesus would suit me just fine." He stopped and shone the lantern as far as it would go. "Ladies, I believe I see a load of crates piled neatly along the walls straight ahead, and I'm betting they ain't Christmas presents." He quickened his pace, with Cole close behind.

The crates were kept at a safe distance from wherever the workers intended to blast next, but close enough to be handy, just as Hannigan had figured. Holding his lantern at a safe distance from the incendiary contents, Cole studied the stacks. "These should say *Explosives* or *Danger* or something like that, but they're not marked. Could be anything inside. Can't imagine it would be anything but blasting powder, though." Some lettering on each box seemed to have been hastily scratched out. He blew dust from the wood of the top crate. "Letters here been rubbed with something coarse, maybe a rock. Looks like the word *Panama*." He ran his palm against the grain. "Definitely *Panama*. Far as I know, black powder don't come from no Panama. Learned in school they used it during the war. Plants for the powder were in Boston, and there's a new one in California. The stuff is domestic, nothing foreign. No need to go very far for it. There was tons of it available for the war." He looked at the old man. "Mr. Hannigan, there may be something else that's not black powder in here."

"One way to find out." He set about prying the crate open with a rusted hunting knife, but that did little. Picking up a large rock to smack the knife's handle, the man's hand shook badly. Cole stopped him and took the rock from him.

"Trust me, Mr. Hannigan, you don't want to use this 'less you're planning on sharing a drink with your maker." Tossing the rock aside, Cole removed his backpack and unsheathed a hunting knife almost twice the length and thickness of the old man's. "This may take a little longer, but I'll get this bastard open, you can bet on—"

A sudden shriek echoed through the tunnel. The four froze, then looked at each other.

Margelle whispered, "They're in here with us."

Another shriek echoed even louder, and an answering **Scree! Scree!** came from inside Cole's backpack. He placed his lantern in the dirt and removed the glass jar. The small

Wag-sloog inside wasn't so small any more. It had grown to almost twice the size it had been hours earlier, its echoing cries deafening enough for the two women to cover their ears. To Melissa it seemed the same sound her father's chickens made when they met the axe. Its mouth hooks snapped at the glass as it tried to escape.

Melissa's eyes widened. "My God! It's grown too large for the jar! It's going to break right through that glass!" Her words barely spoken, she watched a spidery crack in the glass thread along the side of the jar.

Hannigan studied the creature Cole held. "The others must sense we've got this one captured. It's trying to let them know he's here! I think we'll be having company..."

The ground shifted, as if the vibrating dirt suddenly had softened and turned rubbery. Thrown off balance, Melissa went pale.

"They're under us! Can you feel it?"

Hannigan turned to Cole. "They're coming, just as I figured they would. We have the advantage, but only for a while. We have to act fast."

The boy quickly placed the jar on the ground and saw it tip over then roll in the dirt with the creature's weight. He bent to retrieve it, but Hannigan stopped him.

"No! Let them bastards come for it! Get that crate open!"

Not knowing what else to do, Cole went at the large wooden container with his knife, twisting the handle to pry it open with as much caution as he could manage. Miraculously, the top loosened, and he yanked hard at it with both hands. Hannigan pulled at it too. The lid slid off the same moment Melissa screamed. She pointed at the flatbed roadway dead ahead.

*"The dirt is opening..."*

Something from below sucked the soft earth in a spiral like water traveling down a drain, the small vortex rapidly growing larger. A pit emerged, its maw expanding and drawing closer to where they stood. The ground felt as if it could give at any moment, swallowing all of them. Hannigan unraveled the spool of cord to create a fuse that led to the opened crate. He pushed the makeshift fuse deep inside the powder, tamping it tight. Cole studied the contents of the large crate.

"That powder's colorless, not black! Ain't black powder 'sposed to be *black*?"

Hannigan continued unraveling the cord. "Doesn't matter! They'll be coming to say howdy any min—"

Close by, the first Wag-sloog crawled from the expanding hole, blood-red eyes catching the lanterns' fire. The thing was huge as a bear, and staring at the four, it slithered towards the old man with its head raised cobra-like. Hannigan's hands deep in the powder, he had no time to retrieve his rifle. He felt the hot stink of its breath as it coiled above him.

*"Shit..."*

From behind a shot rang out. The creature's head exploded in spatters of black ink, but it kept twisting on the ground before it lay dead. Melissa stood behind the others with her rifle still smoking. She'd been hasty but accurate. Her words came without expression.

"I got him..."

Cole had planned to take that shot, had taken careful aim, but the Monahan woman got there first. "There's gonna be more," he said. "I'm thinking maybe the thing to do now is leave, Mr. Hannigan. It's too late to deposit that powder into that hole. You said that's the only way to be sure..."

"Maybe I can do that."

Cole shook his head. "No disrespect intended, but you can't just drop that whole opened crate down there. It'll spill all over, practically useless 'less you got some container to hold it. Anyone who knows fire crackers knows that much."

Hannigan considered Cole's point. "We got a container, you bet we do. It's laying dead right in front of us. They's plenty of rocks 'round here. Lemme see..." He found two rocks curved like scoops. Filling each with the blasting powder, he handed one to Cole. "Let's get this done quick, as I'm expectin' them visitors soon."

"Mr. Hannigan, that's just plain crazy," Margelle said.

"You can't—"

Cole had no choice but to follow the old man, and the two approached the dead 'sloog. Aidan Hannigan certainly was shooting in the dark with his plan, but craziness seemed to be the day's order.

"Hold open the thing's mouth, will you?"

Cole looked like he might lose his breakfast. "I don't know about this, Mr. Hannigan."

"Don't you turn candy-pussy on me now, boy. We've come this far. Hold open its mouth!"

The overturned creature's open wound leaked some gooey dark substance. The mouth remained intact, but its hooks looked sharp enough to slice off a man's limb like loose meat. Pulling at the jaw and opening the mouth wide, Cole gagged.

"Oh Christ, it stinks!"

Hannigan poured the scoops of powder into the dead 'sloog's gullet and retrieved some more. Cole looked over towards the two women and shook his head, appearing helpless to do anything but follow the old man's orders. He watched Hannigan pour two more heaping loads of powder into the creature.

"Now comes the hard part, Mr. McKenna. Grab the head. I'll take care of the ass." They dragged the creature as it still drizzled blood, its weight making it a difficult task. It felt soft and slimy, more like worm flesh than a snake's. "Count of three, and into the hole with this fucker."

*("...intoo the howl with this fooker. Woon...tooo...")*

Hannigan counted and they pushed the creature in, waiting for the sound of it to hit bottom, wherever bottom was. They heard nothing. Cole somehow found the piss to look into the chasm. He saw Hannigan doing the same. They stared at each other.

"Do you see what I see, old man?"

"Can't be. It's reflections from them rocks, is all, some trick of the eyes. Has to be, all them shiny rocks and who-knows-what that's down there."

"That's not rocks down there, you know that as well as—"

The ground felt unstable. Turning to sand, the precipice surrounding the hole loosened beneath their feet, and they moved quickly from it. Discussion of impossibilities would have to wait. Hannigan returned to the crates of explosives. "If I can set this top one off, these other crates will catch too, as will our friend we just dropped into the hole. That'll take care of the entire colony, goodnight and amen."

"It'll probably level the whole damned mountain," Cole said. "We don't need to use all this! We'll never make it out before it blows!" Shrieks came from the pit, louder and closer. Cole tried reason one last time. "They're coming. Let's get the hell—"

The pit expanded considerably, two huge heads emerging. They stared at the four strangers, their machete-like hooks opening wide. Hannigan turned to the others. "Rifles will stop one, maybe three, but shooting won't do much good if a dozen of 'em come slithering from that hole in the next minute. Hold your fire for now, okay?" He grabbed the jar containing the 'sloog, twisting the top open. He turned it upside down and shook it. Cole reached to stop him.

*"What are you—-?"*

"...buying some time. Get out of here! All of you!"

The released 'sloog dropped to the ground and skittered towards the pit, squirming into the hole as the larger two emerged. Throughout the tunnel, ear-splitting shrieks reverberated, a convoluted language of endless squeals. Holding the spool of cord, Hannigan spoke quickly. "Run like you never run before! Don't wait for me." He reached into his jacket and set about unraveling more cord from the spool for his fuse as he backed away. Cole grabbed the spool from his hand.

*"You* go. I'll be right behind, okay? I can hold 'em off..."

The old man made a silent protest, but Cole McKenna meant business. With no time to argue, Hannigan told the women to get moving and he would follow. "Go! Just go!" He handed Cole his matches. "Okay, then, Mr. McKenna. You'll need these." He patted the boy's shoulder, and disappeared in the dark.

Standing alone, Cole watched the 'sloogs crawling closer while his lantern flickered. If he lit the fuse now, he knew the old man hadn't set enough cord for him to make it out of the tunnel before the crates blew, but if he dropped everything and ran, the creatures would overtake him. Either way, he was a dead man.

*Like Christian... like his father...*

"Shit..."

He needed to fire his rifle, but he would have to let go of the gas lantern and pocket the spool of cord for a steady shot. The decision was made for him when the lantern picked a terrible time to quit, leaving Cole in pitch dark. Unable to see anything, he knew the 'sloogs were near and slithering closer, their mouth hooks readying to slice his throat to ribbons. Fumbling in the dark with his rifle, he fired blind.

Nothing. Not a squeal of pain from either of them. The flash from the report caught the two creatures for a moment in the boy's sight, but they were fast and shifting too quickly in the dirt for him to hope for better luck with a second shot. He hesitated, listening for their silent approach, and took the shot anyway. The rifle's crack reverberated inside the tunnel and inside Cole's head.

His intuition had not failed him. The echoing shrieks were those of pain. He had hit one of the filthy things dead-on, and the other stopped cold. McKenna enjoyed only a moment's confidence. The remaining 'sloog squirmed near enough for him to smell its swamp-like stink. Resisting the urge to cut and run, Cole remembered the slithering fucks hated the light, and he had the old man's matches! As he lit one, his jaw dropped.

There were now maybe a dozen more crawling from the pit. Worse, the hole had expanded, a widening maw ready to swallow him if he remained. That meant more 'sloogs would be coming for him, maybe an entire army of them. The ground shook with their numbers, a small earthquake rumbling beneath him. The match went out.

*The match...*

Cole managed to summon some rationality. Hadn't he

stayed behind the others for a reason? Reaching into his pocket for the spool while stepping backwards, he unraveled the cord. He couldn't see the creatures, but that raw fish smell filling the tunnel meant there were many more. Another lit match proved him right. Their bloody eyes glowed red in the firelight, and a whole nest of the bastards would soon be on him. The match light wouldn't last long. He backed away.

"Demons and fire go together, but maybe you ain't really demons, hey? Maybe you're just fucking overgrown slugs after all!" He was ranting like a madman, and he knew it. Cole moved faster, the match light holding them back, but only a little. Another match flickered out and left him in darkness.

He had a hard decision. If he lit the fuse now, the fire would keep them back long enough for him to run. But he would be running in complete darkness inside a twisting cavern. Too young to call himself a betting man, Cole knew he was about to become one. Surprised that his hand shook so badly, he stuck another match and set it to the cord, holding the glowing fuse in front of him like a weapon.

*"Stay back! That's it, you bastards. Stay back..."*

His hand felt the heat of the traveling flame, and he dropped the cord. He backed off with only a minute or two, at most maybe three. The fuse popped and fizzed as the flame sped along its trajectory towards the dozen crates of explosives, more than enough to turn the Donner Summit into several miles of pebbles. The 'sloogs shrieked but wriggled away from the flame. Satisfied, young Cole McKenna half smiled as he turned and ran.

In the pitch black of the tunnel, he immediately slammed face first into the rocky wall and passed out cold.

# CHAPTER EIGHTEEN
## GLENN ECHOES GENERAL: JULY 2015
## JESSIE LOVES JULIE

*"Dit...Dit..."*

Glenn Echoes General Hospital's head nurse, Christina Dougherty, looked over Jessie Moss' latest CAT scan and didn't know whether to consider his recovery a medical phenomenon or to question her own eyes. She believed she had seen evidence of severe head trauma less than twenty hours earlier, made infinitely worse with the astounding CAT-scanned image of something worm-like inside his skull. But that thing, whatever it was, did not show up in the morning's scan. Not to mention Moss had entered the ER with a serious (and potentially fatal) self-inflicted throat laceration, and she had the computer images to prove this too. Others on the staff had seen the seriousness of Moss' condition. His was a case that doctors called, for want of a better term, a medical miracle, a one-in-a-million inexplicable overnight recovery. Moss' rally was even more remarkable than those patients declared clinically dead who, twenty minutes later, opened their eyes and asked what's for breakfast. But Moss had suffered two physical and quite visible injuries — nothing any faith healer or even the world's top surgeon could repair in the time his contusions had disappeared almost entirely. There was no explaining her patient's recovery, which would have been miraculous had it taken months, let alone hours. Shaving cuts took longer to heal.

That anomaly inside Jessie Moss' skull had vanished without a trace. The sutured wound at his throat had not completely healed, but by morning it could have passed for a bad scratch. The sutures themselves appeared useless remnants. All evidence of the Jessie Moss who had entered Glenn Echoes late yesterday afternoon, the young construction worker who had seemed minutes from being a dead man, was gone.

Dr. Ahmad-Kabar's corroboration of Dougherty's findings supplied no answers for her either. The chief surgeon seemed adamant about keeping the records of Moss' recuperation between them for reasons the head nurse could only guess. But the doctor did have his reasons. After all, his accomplishments had been written up in many major medical journals, and there was a good chance someone hearing the story of patient Moss would discount those close-to-miracle surgeries the good doctor *did* perform. In the post 9/11 world, an Indian surgeon had to be on his toes for those out to criminalize him. The man in no way was interested in being denounced for delusions of grandeur, and there were many in the field who would have happily branded Ahmad-Kabar an overzealous opportunist. He preferred to remain a doctor of surgery, not one who doctored CAT scans, demonstrating some misplaced God-complex that would make him Time Magazine's Person Of The Year.

Head Nurse Christina Dougherty was not a religious woman, but if Dr. Ahmad-Kabar preferred to see the will of Allah in any of this, it was in her best interest to keep her thoughts to herself and her mouth shut.

Tiffany and Zack's visit having ended hours earlier, Jessie Moss awoke and turned to his fiancé. Although now he appeared almost the picture of health, he wasn't happy with their visit, and he didn't seem happy with Julie either. She smiled at him, but it seemed forced.

"You're awake. How are you feeling?"

Moss grunted something unintelligible, then frowned at her. "What was that drop-in all about? I don't even know those people, and that little prick blamed me for trying to hurt his mother. Like I could ever do something like that! And that skank with him—-"

Julie's silence spoke volumes. She squeezed his hand. "You said you weren't yourself after your accident in the excavation. You admitted that you were talking crazy to Mrs. Colson. They just wanted to know the truth, Jessie. So do I."

"Here's some truth for you. Look at this damned hospital gown they've got me wearing! My bare ass is freezing! That's enough to make anyone say anything. Whatever I said to those two about Eden Colson meant nothing."

"Be serious. You know that's not true."

Jessie pulled his hand from hers. "You believed that little shit, didn't you?"

"Jessie, I believe something bit you like you said, a rat or maybe a rabid squirrel. You were hurt bad. I can't explain this sudden recovery, but I know you haven't been yourself. There's probably been some internal damage. How could there *not* be? Nurse Dougherty said you had a serious head injury, and maybe that affected what happened between you and Mrs. Colson. Just understand that I'm here for you, no matter what—"

Jessie's face reddened. "...no matter what I've done? Is that what you're saying? Christ, Julie, if we can't trust each other, we've got nothing, and nothin' from nothing leaves nothin'!" He grabbed her hand again and squeezed it hard, watched her face grimace with the pain, then hummed that irritating tune again.

"You're hurting me — Jessie, please, that hurts!"

Christina Dougherty entered the room, and Moss quickly released his grip. The nurse kept silent and placed a thermometer into his mouth. Moss continued humming even with the instrument below his tongue.

Dougherty showed no expression, but her brow raised. "That's a tune I've heard you going at a few times, Mr. Moss. Do you know you muttered a few bars of that ditty last night shortly following your surgery? Your doctor and I heard you sing it. Most people fresh out of the O.R. are so heavily sedated that they don't speak for hours, sometimes days." She didn't ask why he now hummed the tune, didn't ask if Jessie had any recollection of his bizarre nocturnal behavior. She removed the thermometer. "Ninety-Eight point three. Normal, Mr. Moss."

"Normal, you say? Do you really think I'm normal, Nurse? My loving fiancé here doesn't."

Dougherty's lips tightened and she took the shot. "No, Mr. Moss. In medical terms, I don't think you are."

Hers was a bizarre response that made Julie uncomfortable, but Nurse Dougherty's words encouraged Julie's own. "You're right, Jessie. I don't think so either."

"Well, that's great. That's just great! Fuck both of you!"

The two women stared at each other. Julie shook her head for the nurse to see. "That's not... he's not like this. Nurse Dougherty... Christina... I'm so sorry." Dougherty said nothing and left. Julie turned to Jessie, brushed some hair from his forehead. "I love you, you know that. I want you to be well. I love you so much, Jessie..."

Moss' mouth twitched as if he tried to make sense of what was happening to him. For a moment he softened and muttered what sounded like a word, but wasn't.

*"Dit...Dit..."*

Jessie Moss was trying to say *Ditto,* but Julie could see that memory had disappeared.

Some time later Moss awakened from a succession of naps. He had no idea how many hours had passed since Dougherty's visit, but time was difficult to measure while he was confined to a hospital bed and medicated into a stupor. Julie remained inside his room, but she had fallen asleep in the chair. Having to visit the bathroom for a piss stop, Jessie saw no need to alert her or any of the staff. The bed pan wasn't his preferred option, and he felt perfectly capable of taking the ten steps to the toilet on his own. He unhooked the pinball game apparatus attached to his wrist and entered the bathroom while that damned hospital gown hung uncomfortably on him like a sheet on an unmade bed. Dropping it to the floor he relieved himself, then stared at his naked image in the bathroom mirror. His hair was a mess and he needed a shave. Jessie Moss knew he looked like someone who belonged in a police lineup, someone who had done exactly what that little Colson shit had accused him of doing. He stared at the image closer.

"Nothin' from nothin'," he muttered and shut up fast. He hated that song, had always hated it. Why were those lyrics ringing in his ears almost constantly? It seemed something from his memory was trying to break through, that the words somehow opened up a passageway.

"...*DITTO!*" He spoke this aloud to his mirrored image. *That* was the word he was trying to remember. It was *Ditto*, and Julie was the woman he loved and whom he was going to marry and whom... and whom...

*(Kill her bloody dead, claw her accusing eyes from their sockets, rip her lying tongue from her mouth, kill the bitch a hundred times over and leave her in the dumpster!)*

Where did that come from? He loved Julie, dammit...

*(...killherkillherkillher!)*

That thing in the excavation had taken something from him, something important and good, sucked it clear out of his brain like a Hoover. Enough of his memory remained to understand the stranger he was becoming to himself, enough of him was still Jessie Moss. He had to keep telling himself that. But that other part of him, this *new* part that had replaced the wounded Jessie, what *was* that? He had no idea, but he knew he hated that other self.

Nurse Dougherty was right. Julie was right. That new part that had sprouted overnight, that healed flesh all shiny and new as if he had been rebirthed — it was not *him!* At least, *The Jessie-That-Once-Was* knew that. This new part was something else, something awful that wanted to hurt, wanted to kill someone, anyone...

...everyone!

*...especially Julie!*

...just like he'd wanted to hurt *(no, kill!)* Eden Colson too — after fucking her, of course.

*("Thank you, Ma'am")*

Why?

The answer came to Jessie that instant. That awful part of him didn't care, it didn't feel, and it most certainly didn't love, because that better part of him had been surgically removed.

No, that wasn't true.

*It had been eaten.*

*("...Yoob...Die-em...Min...Yoob...Die-em...Yoob...MIn...Yoob ...Die-em...!")*

"Sorry... Sorry..." he muttered to Julie, who slept just beyond the bathroom door. For that moment he was Jessie again, but he knew the moment would slip away. Already the once familiar lyrics were fading. "Nothin'...from..nothin'..." he forced himself to say, but he couldn't remember the rest, although he knew the rest was so simple and so idiotic. How could he not—?

It didn't matter. That other *Jessie-That-Was-Not-Jessie* was coming back. He could feel him taking over. He couldn't allow that. Looking at the flimsy hospital gown on the floor, he picked it up, twisting it into a long cord and tying one end of it to the shower head. He turned over the tall trash receptacle, dragged it to the shower stall, and stood on it, tying the other end of the gown tightly around his throat.

Jessie smiled. He remembered!

*"...is nothin'!"* he shouted. He remembered something else. He *did* love Julie, loved her more than anything. He would never hurt her, *couldn't* hurt her. His fingers twisted into an air quote and he whispered a raspy *"Ditto, Ditto, and Ditto!"*

Hoping this time his effort would succeed, Jessie Moss kicked the trash receptacle out from under him. His body twitched as he swung from the shower head, but he remained alive long enough to hear his own neck bone crack.

# CHAPTER NINETEEN
## DIAMOND LOOP: JULY 2015
## NEIGHBORHOOD WATCH

*"We're selling Girl Scout Cookies?"*

The ambulance from Glenn Echoes General required no screaming siren as it carried off retired — and now *ex*pired — police sergeant Wally Smith. The sergeant had finished singing a rousing chorus of *God Bless America* before wrapping his mouth around his revolver and blowing his jaw completely off his face. This he did in full view of Mrs. Eden Colson, who had believed Smith's bullet (for reasons only the sergeant knew) was intended for her.

The events in Diamond Loop had turned squirrelly for Eden and those cul-de-sac residents who had come out of their homes to watch the aftermath of Sergeant Smith's dramatic exit from the world. Some talked with the police officers investigating the scene, and no doubt the two men would have a few questions for Mrs. Eden Colson.

Standing before the Colson home, Tiffany repeated Zachary's question to Supervisor Reefe. "What about the people who *aren't* here? Maybe some slug-things like those you saw went calling on other homes too. Maybe Jessie Moss and Wally Smith are just the beginning. Mr. Reefe, you were going to inform the residents that their water would remain off a while longer, weren't you? Well, then...?"

Fred Reefe considered this. "All right. Maybe it's time we knocked on a few doors. I think, to play it safe, we should team up. Eden with me, Tiffany, you're with Zack, okay?"

Zachary liked the idea of teaming with Tiffany. But remembering the questionable way Mr. Reefe had comforted his mother, he felt less enthusiastic about Reefe's choice for *his* team.

Still, it seemed a good idea at the time.

"Mrs. Colson, a word with you, please?" Detective Mike Kearne stopped Eden and Reefe on their way to the neighbors' homes while the officer's young partner again stood quietly, a repeat of their morning visit to her.

Fred Reefe wasn't happy with the interruption. "Officer, Mrs. Colson has had a very difficult couple of days."

Kearne offered a sympathetic smile, but then went for the jugular anyway. "It's very unusual that, during a twenty-four hour period, a woman is attacked by two different men who are strangers. Mrs. Colson, your neighbors tell me you were the last person Sergeant Smith spoke to before the incident. What exactly did he say to you?" The law officer's question had the tone of an accusation.

"Have I broken any laws, Detective?"

"No, Ma'am. But it's important you answer the question."

"Fine. Mr. Smith was singing *God Bless America* for some reason. You know, 'From the mountains to the prairies...' I don't think he was singing to me, particularly."

Kearne scribbled the late sergeant's non-sequitur without any response to suggest Smith's behavior was that of a nut case. "Did Sergeant Smith appear drunk to you?"

Eden hesitated. "He had this deep cut in his forehead that looked pretty bad. He was a little incoherent. Maybe he was drunk. I don't know." She watched the officer jot that down, but she didn't add that some wormy slug-thing probably had chewed Smith's brains clear out of his skull. Between Wally Smith and Jessie Moss (and who knew how many others?) those creatures probably had themselves a damned feast. Eden couldn't share that information without expecting her own sobriety test, maybe then finding herself in the back seat of the officers' patrol car. Yeah, her neighbors would enjoy that. Then, again...

She had the photo in her cellular! Proof! The two cops would have to believe that, wouldn't they? She considered this, even reached into her jeans pocket, then had second thoughts. How would that photo prove anything about Smith's decision to put a gun's barrel into his mouth? She looked to Reefe who seemed to read her mind. Almost imperceptibly, he shook his head. Not a good idea, at least not yet. Someone was sure to say the monster hidden in the bushes was probably a neighbor's St. Bernard.

Officer Ed, the young cop, spoke up. "Mrs. Colson, did you say anything to Smith? Maybe offend him in some way?"

Brought back from her thoughts, Eden resented the implication that she was somehow at fault. "No. Nothing. He just came at me, kind of shambling. But the sergeant was a large man. He didn't move fast. I was just there, is all. Ask anyone who saw."

"No neighbors claim to have seen the actual shooting."

"It's pretty obvious what happened, isn't it?"

Officer Ed remained expressionless, as if Eden were talking herself out of a ticket for jay walking. But Kearne had another question ready. "Were you going somewhere in particular when you and Sergeant Smith met on the street?"

*(Why, yes. I was going to inform Mr. Reefe here that I had a photo of some slug monster in my garden. You know, just your garden variety slug the size of a Doberman and probably longer than a garden hose. Want to see?)*

"My car is down the block because of the excavation. I was going to do some shopping. Pick up a few cases of water because the lines have been turned off."

*(Liar! Liar!)*

More notations on the officer's pad. "Sergeant Smith pointed his gun at you before he turned it on himself?"

"I really thought that he — that he was going to—" For that moment Eden almost lost it, but she brought herself back. "Yes, he pointed the gun at me. Some suit took it when they put him on the stretcher. I don't know what he did with it."

The questions continued and Eden answered them, but

looking occasionally at Reefe, she knew the man was pissed at the pummeling she was receiving. Seeing this, something else disturbed her more than the endless interrogation and the day's bizarre turn of events. Her son was an intuitive kid, and Eden noticed his curious look when Reefe had held her. Now a terrible thought occurred, and she couldn't shake it.

Hours earlier she had slept with Fred Reefe, fucked him six ways from Sunday.

And Zachary knew.

Tiffany Leone had her own suspicions regarding Eden Colson and Fred Reefe, but right now that wasn't a concern. Some house calling *was*, but she wasn't looking forward to this part.

"Are you friendly with any of the neighbors here, Zack? We should start with them, don't you think? You'll be able to tell if someone has gone gonzo if you knew them before."

Zachary nodded. "What are we going to say? That we're selling Girl Scout cookies?"

"We'll smile sweetly, then tell them giant brain-eating slugs are living under their homes."

"Really?"

"No, dope. We'll say their water will be off a while longer, that Mr. Reefe asked us to spread the word. And we'll keep our eyes open for the crazies, maybe any sign of slug bites or radioactive gila monsters. After the day's events, nothing will surprise me. So, kimosabe, where do we start?"

Zachary looked towards the mailbox with the American Flag and the VFW sticker. "610... the Brimleys live there. George, he's a nice old guy, always says hello, and he's home most of the time. Got wounded in 'Nam, uses a wheelchair. His wife made me a lemonade last week and told me his story. Anna, she's Russian and hard to understand, but she's okay. They're often both outside on the back patio, doing whatever old people do."

"We'll use the front door. More polite." They headed up

the Brimleys' walkway and Tiffany rang the bell, then knocked. There was no answer. "Okay, then, back patio it is."

One look at the elderly couple's lanai told the tale. A mostly uneaten sandwich lay on the ground already covered with ants, and a full glass of lemonade remained untouched on the parson's table where George Brimley's wheelchair must have been. The sliding screen door was half open.

"Not good," Zack said.

"So, do we go inside? It's too quiet in there. This may be a job for the CSI people."

Zack stared at the ant infested roast beef. "You see Ted Danson anywhere? I vote we go in." He didn't wait for Tiffany's response. "Coming?"

Inside the kitchen, Tiffany called, "Mr. Brimley? Mrs. Brimley? Anyone home?"

Zack muttered, "Not good, Tiffany. Definitely, not good."

The living room was empty, the door to George Brimley's study closed. In silent agreement, Tiffany pushed the door open while Zack continued muttering. He was right. What awaited inside George Brimley's private study was not good.

The small room appeared spotlessly clean excepting the freckles of blood spattered across the wall like bad modern art. Old George Brimley sat collapsed in his wheelchair while his wife sprawled crab-like at his feet. Blood dripped over their jaws, and an ancient Western-style pistol from the wall collection marked 'From the Cole McKenna Estate' lay close to Anna's outstretched arm. An old box of bullets had spilled to the floor. Apparently, kindly Anna Brimley had done the honors to her husband first, maybe nervously spilling the box after loading her pistol, then blowing a hole clear through his head before helping herself to the same.

Tiffany fought an urge to woof her breakfast. "She shot her husband, then herself. Why? Jesus, Zack, I didn't really think we'd find — *this*. We have to tell those officers. This is serious shit."

"What do we tell them? That we broke into the Brimleys' house for no apparent reason? Cops will find these two soon enough. I think the thing to do now is leave before they find *us*."

Tiffany shook her head. "We can't just lea—" She stopped herself, her face pale with a realization. "The other houses! This can't be the only home where something nuts has occurred. Something very fucked is happening on this street, Zack."

"Don't touch anything. You can play Nancy Drew if you want, but I can't unsee this. I'm out of here!" Without looking back, Zachary headed the way they came in. Tiffany closed the study door with her elbow and followed him, again carefully closing the sliding screen door halfway as they had found it. If no one noticed them going inside the Brimley house, once back on the street maybe they were home free.

The neighbors had dispersed and relative calm seemed to have returned to the cul-de-sac. Eden Colson and Mr. Reefe were not around either. The thought of what they would find in the residents' homes made Tiffany shudder. "So the adventure is over for you?"

Zachary hadn't shown any real fear until this moment. "There are two dead people in that house, Tiffany, and we're the only ones who know they're there. I never signed up for this!"

"Well, here's more bad news, Zack. There are more people like the Brimleys on this street, and maybe in other places around Glenn Echoes too. And we may be the only ones who know what's happening — and *why* it's happening." Tiffany thought that over. "No, I'm pretty sure Mr. Reefe and your mom know something. The point is, we may be the only ones who can do any—"

Tiffany's cell phone chirped. Zack watched her face go white with a succession of "Oh my God!" and "I'm so sorry" responses, finally adding "If there's anything I can do..." She turned to him. "That was Julie from the hospital. She's in pretty bad shape. Jessie Moss hung himself in the bathroom an hour ago." She shook her head. "I think this pretty much says it all. The question now is, what are we going to do?"

"We're going to tell the cops, that's what! About everything! Slugs and all."

"I guess you're right. I just hope they don't include us among the nut cases on this block." Tiffany looked around. "I don't see those two officers, but their squad car is still here. They must have gone house calling too. God knows what they'll find.

Detective Mike Kearne and his partner, Ed, noticed the mailbox at 617 before the Hunters' home.

"A peace sign. You don't see much of these around anymore. You picky about hippie eye witnesses, Ed?" The senior officer rang the bell. The officers had no reason to enter with guns drawn, at least Kearne believed they didn't. When the door swung open he saw how wrong he was.

Two adult bodies lay twisted on the floor, their heads soaking in thick ponds of blood. The couple's faces were as thoroughly pulverized as smashed cantaloupes. No peace-and-love '60's hippies here.

On opposite sides of the door young Dennis Hunter and his pretty girlfriend, Heather, greeted the officers with broad toothy smiles and dripping baseball bats. Kearne went for his gun, but too late. Heather stepped up to the plate first, smiling one lovely smile as her bat sent the detective reeling to the floor. He flopped like a hooked trout, again reaching for his gun when his partner fell on top of him. Dennis stood over them.

"Foul ball!" He took another swing and Kearne's skull cracked like a walnut. It took a little longer for his partner. "...and two men out!" Dennis added, blood drenched and still pounding away.

The teens' game shifted quickly from baseball to human whack-a-mole.

Still shaken, Eden Colson could have used another few moments in Fred Reefe's arms. Thinking that wouldn't be a good idea should Zachary see, instead she shared a serious concern with Reefe.

"My husband knows nothing about any of this, but I'm sure he'll be cursing out the realtor who sold us on Diamond Loop."

Reefe's lips tightened with the thought. "I wouldn't blame him. But I guess that depends on how much you tell him."

"Fred, what happened between you and me, that's one and done, and Greg doesn't need to know. But he'll see our scorched tub, he'll certainly hear about Wally Smith and my part in that whole thing, and if any of this gets leaked to the news, our home becomes worthless overnight. That can come back to bite *you* in the ass too. I wouldn't want that."

Reefe looked hard at Eden. "I was going to keep this to myself, but that girl who hangs with your son, Tiffany — she and Zack overheard me telling my crew about those things in your tub and how they've been screwing up the water mains. Your husband won't be the only one asking questions. I have the feeling after we visit a few homes here, the shit is going to hit more than one fan."

Eden had a terrible thought. Her next-door neighbor, Regina Campbell, had her nose in everyone's business on the Loop. She had sniffed around the construction site in her tight shorts and bare midriffs, assuring herself that every man in the cul-de-sac area enjoyed ample viewings of her shapely ass. Yet the woman did not appear outside after the shooting, and this wasn't like her. Eden decided that the Campbell house should be the first stop — but it would be better if she paid her visit alone. Reefe agreed, insisting to remain close by. He would allow her five minutes inside the Campbell home because who knew what waited beyond the door of 608? That concern had not escaped Eden as she headed up the walk.

Gina answered the doorbell looking like an expensive call girl in her lush blonde fall and her pink hip huggers. The woman and her husband probably played some interesting games once the lights were out, but Eden figured that was none of her business. What *was* her business was whether something from the garden had paid the Campbells a visit. Maybe Regina was too busy fixing herself up to notice anything going on in the street, and with all the noise from the excavation possibly she hadn't heard Smith's gunshot. Eden composed herself and flashed a high voltage smile.

"Hey, neighbor. Whatever you're cooking smells damned good."

Regina looked curiously at her. Although the women had been cordial on the street, neither had ever paid a visit.

"Hi, back. I've been busy all day preparing lasagna for Harry. And preparing myself for him too. You like?" She twirled like a runway model, ridiculous behavior but nothing out of the ordinary for her. "So, to what do I owe the honor, Eden? I was hoping you might stop by some time, but right now isn't good."

"Okay, understood. I wanted to ask if you've had any kind of problem with your garden? The workers will have to keep the water off for the next few days because of some sort of trouble with the mains. It'll be a necessary inconvenience, and the supervisor asked me to pass this on to the neighbors." She said this as if the lines had been rehearsed.

Regina flashed an ever-so-slight smirk with Eden's reference to Fred Reefe. "A problem in my garden? What kind of problem?"

Eden managed a semblance of coolness. "Oh, you know, an unusual presence of mud or bugs, that sort of thing. Pests can sometimes get into the water pipes and into the home to shower with you when the water is back on." She winced with her own words.

"No bugs, no mud, no problems. Well, except that the low water pressure keeps our toilets from flushing right. We may have to resort to chamber pots." Regina giggled. Ditzy, to be sure, but the woman always seemed that way. She apparently had no idea of the drama that had occurred earlier, and Eden had no intention of telling her.

Eden thanked her neighbor for her time and left, running into Harry Campbell on the walkway. Campbell smiled back, they exchanged hellos, and that covered the social amenities. *Seems normal here,* Eden though, and waited for Reefe in the cul-de-sac.

Inside 608 Diamond Loop, a cheerful Regina Campbell greeted her husband's return home with some good wine, several tasty servings of her expertly prepared lasagna, capped off with the promise of an evening of hot fun. "You don't mind if I leave the dishes 'till later?" she asked following dinner, as she led Harry to their bedroom.

"More surprises?" he asked.

"You have no idea," Regina said.

At seven years, Robbie Lewis was one little monster, but his baby sister, Emma, counterbalanced her brother's bratty ways. The infant had a sweet disposition, rarely cried, and she ate what she was supposed to eat without any of her Gerber's smearing the kitchen walls.

Today, inside 605 Diamond Loop, all that had changed.

Betsy Lewis noticed Robbie had remained inside his room all afternoon, unusual for the boy who was hyperactive and usually a handful. But with his iPad along with his collection of a hundred video games, her son had plenty to keep him busy, and Betsy relished the brief respite from Robbie's constant need for her attention. The respite was short lived. Baby Emma seemed uncommonly cranky and restless, scratching and biting like some kind of ravenous animal. Betsy didn't notice the small squirming worm-like thing Emma had left in her Pampers.

The afternoon incident on the cul-de-sac worsened the infant's behavior, and Betsy retreated back inside with hopes of her daughter going to la la land inside her crib for her usual nap time. But despite the mother's well-rehearsed lullaby, Emma had no intention of going sleepy-bye. On every other day the Disney ditty "Let It Go" worked wonders, and Betsy knew every word of the damned song because Robbie and Emma had watched the *Frozen* DVD about a million times. Today, however, little Emma required the more traditional maternal approach.

Removing the infant from her crib Betsy rocked her, but that just increased Emma's screams. The young mother had quit wearing her bra, and lifting her spittle covered t-shirt she gently pressed her child's head close to her chest.

Betsy whispered, "And that, my little one, despite my husband's opinion to the contrary, is why God created tits." Emma hungrily locked onto her mother's breast. Nursing her child usually did the trick, but today that proved one huge mistake. The woman shrieked in pain.

At that moment, for Betsy Lewis, the song "Let it Go" took on a whole new meaning.

Fred Reefe rang the bell at 605. Betsy Lewis didn't answer, but he had seen the woman go inside carrying her infant. Excepting the child's restlessness, nothing seemed out of the ordinary. He figured the Lewis woman probably didn't want to be bothered. He approached Eden returning from the Campbell house. "I should be getting back to work. We'll knock on some more doors tonight. I'll be there with you."

"You're going back into that hole? Knowing what I saw in my garden? What we *both* saw in my bathroom?"

"It's what the township is paying me for. I'll see you after 5:00. And if we discover anything strange, then we can show that photo you took to the authorities. I think we need some credibility before we ask anyone to believe in garden monsters."

Eden thought that over. "No, Fred, we shouldn't do this together. Greg will be home soon. I don't feel like making any more explanations than I'm going to have to make to him. I can go on those house calls alone. Any problems, I'll call."

Reefe agreed. For a moment Eden thought he might kiss her on the forehead, forgetting they were standing in the cul-se-sac and that Zack could reappear at any moment. Instead he just squeezed her hand and headed back to the excavation site. Watching him go was probably not the thing to do, if anyone saw. Eden watched him anyway.

Zack and Tiffany approached from across the street. "Mr Reefe left?" her son asked.

"Big Mama calls, Zacker. How do you and Tiffany feel about some pizza for dinner? I haven't had time to work my usual magic in the kitchen. I'll even let you hitch a ride on your friend's hog to pick up a couple of pies." She reached into her pocket and handed him a few bills, her smile's wattage turned all the way up. "Pepperoni and anchovies, okay?"

"'Kay," Zachary said, adding nothing more. Tiffany offered Eden a shrug.

Wearing her painted-on smile as she walked back to the house, Eden Colson made certain she closed the door behind her before she broke down and cried.

## THE WOGSLûK

*It isn't a throne upon which the woman sits, but deep under the earth, the large rock is the closest thing to it, and she is the closest thing to a queen.*

*They have chosen her, and she has learned enough to understand them. Young in appearance and startlingly beautiful, she calls herself Ri, and when she speaks the Wogslûk listen.*

*They know little of her language, yet they grasp the meaning of what she tells them. There are words understood that go beyond words spoken.*

*She knows what they require. She knows their pain, their confusion. They are like children in a strange world they cannot understand.*

*They act because she tells them to act, they believe because she wants them to believe, and on this day she utters a single word to them.*

*She utters, "Tonight..."*

# PART FOUR
## Queen Ri

"*I am a queen, and I demand to be treated like a queen.*"
— **Sheila Jackson, American Congresswoman**

"*All things truly wicked start from innocence.*"
— **Ernest Hemingway (1899-1961)**
*The Garden Of Eden* **(posthumous publication, 1986)**

"*I am and not, I freeze and yet am burned,*
*Since from myself another self I turned.*"
— **Queen Elizabeth I Tudor, (1533–1603)**
*Her Life In Letters* **(2003)**

"*Wag-sloogs. A filthy sounding name if there ever was.*"
— **Aiden Hannigan (1866)**

# CHAPTER TWENTY

## THE DONNER SUMMIT: SUMMER,1866
## GROUND BREAKING DISCOVERIES

*"This ain't no reg'lar hole..."*

I n the complete darkness of the unfinished railway tunnel, unknown to his three companions, young Cole McKenna lay unconscious. The three made it out, but McKenna hadn't joined them. He had set the fuse to ignite enough explosives beneath the mountain to kill every Wagsloog in their lair, but also enough to bury any other living thing within miles under the rock slide that would follow. There remained little time before the lit fuse would reach the piled crates of blasting powder, and if that happened too quickly, old Aiden Hannigan knew (as did the two women) that they might as well mutter what prayers they could for the McKenna boy and for themselves.

Just past the mouth of the tunnel Melissa Monahan halted her escape and made a sudden decision, having no time to consider its rationale or its consequences. Margelle stopped too and called to her. "Keep running, Melissa! The summit will blow any minute!"

Still breathing heavily, Melissa shook her head. "You two go on. I'm going back in to find Cole. He said it would just take him a minute—"

Aidan Hannigan turned and grabbed hold of her arm. "I can't let you do that. The McKenna boy knew the chance he was taking, and that was the choice he made. His wasn't a foolish decision, but going back inside there *is*."

Melissa had no time to argue. "That boy is the brother of

**229**

the man I'd intentions to marry. I've got my weapon handy. I'm going!" Old Hannigan's grasp couldn't hold her. He saw that the light inside her lantern had extinguished, rendering it useless, but his and Margelle's lanterns had practically no life left in them either, and they had no time to get them going again. Melissa didn't seem to care and tossed hers aside, selecting to return to the tunnel's entranceway with only her rifle for company. The darkness quickly swallowed her.

Hannigan muttered, "Damned foolish woman picks now to turn courageous. We can't stay, Miss Margelle. That mountain's going to scatter boulders for miles. Them rocks will be coming at us like buckshot."

"We can't just leave the two of them inside there!"

"We've no choice! What can we do that they can't do for themselves? We may have time to make it to the stage..."

Margelle seemed about to follow her friend, but Hannigan's reasoning (and a firm grip) pulled her back. The two managed a sprint beyond the railroad workers' abandoned camp site when Hannigan's age caught up with him. His knees buckled, and he stopped cold.

"Are you all right?"

The old man tried catching his wind. Turning toward the summit, he looked uneasy. There had been no explosion, nothing but the night's stillness.

"Guess the fuse didn't take, or maybe the McKenna kid never lit it. Miss Monahan and the boy, I'm expecting they'll be safe — assuming no 'sloogs spoil their reunion. We'll wait a bit, just to be sure, and go back."

"Thank you, Mr. Hannigan. We'll get those slime creatures next time."

They waited, waited some more. If the McKenna boy had failed, maybe it was for the best, Hannigan figured. "All right, Miss Margelle. Let's go get our two companions while we—"

—and then, the world cracked in two. The rumbling at first seemed like a ferocious thunder clap, the roar from the mountain's interior reverberating throughout the passage. Seconds later additional crates of powder detonated inside the tunnel, setting off new explosions as they blew. The moonlit sky filled with rocks that rained to the ground with heavy thumps.

*"Get down!"*

The impact knocked Margelle off her feet. She struck the dirt face first, her splayed fingers locked behind her neck as her arms covered her head. Whipped up by the explosion's force, clouds of dust filled her throat, and she coughed mightily.

One explosion ended, another began, and the cycle repeated, rocks hurtling through the sky in a thunderstorm of stone. The two held to the shaking earth as if the rumbling ground might fling them to the heavens. A painful shower crashed down on them, and they shielded themselves from the battering with faces buried in cold dirt. The explosions kept coming, each additional blast more powerful than the one before it. The mountain's apex blew like a volcanic eruption, with a barrage of huge boulders darkening the moon like giant moths, chunks of rock large enough to squash anyone below flat.

Margelle squinted through the dust towards where the Donner Summit had stood tall moments earlier. The mountain had caved in on itself, a rocky monument half gone in minutes. The sight was enough for the former nun to rethink her failed relationship with her God and beg forgiveness. She didn't. Instead, she cursed.

*"Cole... Melissa... in there..."*

Covered in dirt, the old man lay motionless. Margelle crab-crawled to him, shook him. "Mr. Hannigan? Are you all right? Mr. Hannigan?" She shook the old man harder. *"Mr. Hannigan! Please... Please..."* This wasn't a prayer, but it sounded close to one.

The dusty air cleared a little. The ground leading from the tunnel transformed into a terrain of unsteady lumps that rose and fell like ocean waves. Something below sucked the dirt into a huge vortex that swirled in a maelstrom of dust and sand. Another crater was opening. Instinctively, Margelle crossed herself, the nun inside her soul awakened.

Hannigan's body twitched, his eyelids flickering as he struggled to pull himself up. He was alive, but not by much. Getting him halfway to his feet Margelle pointed to the dark aperture in the earth. She didn't need to say a word as another shadowy abyss expanded before them.

"That ain't no reg'lar hole..."

"I know."

Hannigan's breathing remained labored. "I can't run no more. You have to go!"

"I can't do that!"

"You have to! You don't know what I seen inside that other hole! You have to go now!"

"You saw something?"

"Dammit! Go!"

"No!"

The man's mouth opened, but no other words came. He could only stare at what emerged from the huge tear in the earth. Silhouetted against the dusty sky, dark figures appeared in the moonlight. Heads visible first, a dozen 'sloogs wriggled clumsily like overgrown rattlers from the crater and crawled into the dust. Huge creatures they were, longer and thicker than any snake by a mile. Sniffing at the filthy air, they scented the two nearby. A solid dark wall of rubbery slime slithered toward them.

"These bastards must've crawled back into the earth when the explosion hit! A ton of powder, and we didn't kill them all!"

"They don't die easy, do they?"

Hannigan pulled Margelle to him, burying her face in his chest. "There's more coming. Keep your eyes shut tight, just keep them shut." He reached for his rifle in the dirt, steadying his shaking hands to take aim. "I can bring down one, maybe two, but—"

Margelle pulled away and grabbed the other rifle from the dirt. "Maybe three or four," she said, and took her shot. The firearm clicked dully. She cocked it, aimed again. Nothing.

"All that muck kicked up from the explosion clogged the cylinders." Hannigan cursed under his breath and pulled the trigger of his own weapon with no better luck. He grabbed the rifle by its barrel, got fully to his feet, and swung it like a club at the nearest 'sloog. The thing's reflexes were too good. It backed off unharmed, then came at him again. Margelle's eyes searched the old man's for answers. He offered only one. "There's no need for us both to be worm food. I can hold 'em off while you make a run for it." He poked the creature with the rifle's stock. It slithered backwards, but another readied for a strike. Others were gathering behind. A sharp mandible narrowly missed the old man's leg.

"I'm not going without you!"

"Find the stage. The horses are there. Go now!" He poked at another 'sloog. *"Now!"*

Margelle saw that the old man meant business. She got to her feet and ran. Hannigan waited for her to put distance between them. He looked behind, searched all sides. In a tightening circle the creatures were surrounding him like a war party.

"Wag-sloogs. A filthy sounding name if there ever was. Fuck all of you!"

*(Fook all uff yer...)*

"I got something you want? Something you need, maybe? Okay, then..."

*(Soomthin' yer wont...)*

He tossed his rifle to the ground. Falling to his knees, he followed the advice he had given Margelle. Eyes shut, he waited for the bloodbath to begin. Like the tunnel explosion that had bided its time, Hannigan sensed by their fetid smell that the 'sloogs circling him remained very near but motionless, as if they too were waiting. He ventured having a look and saw what had to be an apparition conjured from his heated brain. A young woman stood between him and the surrounding creatures. He heard her speak, but it wasn't to him. Palms outstretched, her arms straight out before her...

"Stay!"

The 'sloogs froze in place. Some backed off.

Wearing a ragged mud covered dress that looked like it

once hung on a dirt farmer's clothesline, the woman could not have been more than twenty, but she seemed to have the presence of someone older. Maybe she had climbed from the deep hole, maybe by some miracle she had emerged alive from what remained of the fallen Donner Summit or had simply appeared from nowhere. It didn't matter because there was something else, something familiar about her. The realization struck the old man like a thunderbolt. He expected the woman's image to vanish, some ethereal spirit here then gone — or maybe never here at all, a ghost only inside his head. But she remained standing before him, beautiful and unreal.

...except she *was* real.

"My God!"

She would have been close to forty, not possibly this young. He had gone mad, Hannigan felt sure of it. Or, maybe this was his death, nature's final ludicrous joke on a lonely old man. But no, here he was, still alive and breathing. And here *she* was.

The Wag-sloogs slithered threateningly on all sides, but none defied the woman's command. Beautiful and strangely poised for one so young, she stepped closer to Aiden Hannigan but did not touch him. She simply looked at him.

"Hello Father," she said.

*"Riona..?"*

Mouth hooks — huge curved ones — sprouted from the corners of the young woman's lips. A trick of the eyes, Aidan Hannigan told himself. All that dust from the explosion, the crazed imaginings of an aged mind... what he saw had to be an illusion.

It wasn't.

"Goodbye, Father," the woman said.

## Spring, 1830: RIONA

*It had happened fast in the near dark, so fast that Aidan Hannigan didn't trust his own eyes. But a second glance assured him. Where his daughter played, a great hole had opened, and something shadowy and alive peered out. In another moment little Riona Hannigan was gone, and so was the hole...*

Riona would remember nothing of the terror she had felt. It was better that she didn't, considering it would be the last day the five year old would spend among those of her own kind. This day initiated a new life for the girl, a rebirth that would soon bond her to her strange captors who hadn't known this would be a rebirth for them as well.

The transformation of Riona to Ri was not a simple one...

First came the screams — the worst kind of screams, those of a terror-stricken child. The ground had opened while some dark creature had snatched her, the very stuff of children's worst nightmares. Fortunately, the girl had not remained conscious long enough to experience the intentions of the others who lived below. Beneath the ground the combination of stifling heat and paralyzing fear had caused Riona to pass out.

The Wogslûk studying the child recognized what they had captured. Here was one untouched by the detritus of human experience, yet easily capable of becoming like them. She was a blank slate, but a necessary link to the man-things in ways she could not know.

*She was special...*

A silken web spun tightly around her cocooned Riona in a great chrysalis. Occasionally, she awoke in utter darkness to discover herself mummified, her arms and legs unable to move, her throat too raw to scream. She went unfed, but food was unnecessary. This was not intended as some grotesque ritual of death. This was a metamorphosis; more than that, an evolution.

Emerging, the girl's physical features remained unchanged, but her insides were another matter. The transformation complete, the child crawling from the thick pool of larvae remained human in appearance only. She didn't fear the dark creatures, not any more, as she spoke her first words to them.

"I'm Riona Hannigan."

They answered as one voice but without words, and somehow, she understood their response echoing inside her head.

*No, you are not...*

*"There are more things in heaven and earth...*
*Than are dreamt of in your philosophy."*
*—- Hamlet, William Shakespeare*

### Summer, 1866: MELISSA AND COLE

Melissa didn't expect the darkness inside the railway tunnel to prove so unrelentingly black. Earlier, she'd had the luxury of her own lantern and those lamps held by her companions, but now she had no illumination to guide her through, and the twisting cavern seemed devoid even of shadows. Like a blind woman, she felt her way by following the jagged walls of rock, aware that the fuse Cole had set could reach the blasting powder before she reached *him*, and that would bring the entire Donner Summit down on both. Worse, she could come face to face with Wag-sloogs, as the Irishman, Aiden Hannigan, had mispronounced Cole's name for them. It seemed a foolish name for the creatures. She had believed this from the first, because it made the filthy bastards appear about as threatening as prairie dogs. Now if any of them were near, they had the advantage of darkness, and Melissa would have only her sense of smell to warn her. Those blood thirsty 'prairie dogs' might be crawling all over her at any moment.

She considered calling out to Cole but knew that wouldn't be the wisest decision. She would have to depend on discovering the glow of the lit fuse and hope the boy was near and that the fuse was long. In this darkness McKenna could pass right by her without even knowing she was there. Melissa chose to put these fears somewhere else as she slipped further inside the tunnel, the pistol in her hand.

The ground felt unsteady, the solid rock below her slightly giving way with the pressure of her weight as if a great emptiness had opened just below her feet, leaving the surface above vulnerable to complete collapse. That chasm they had seen earlier likely had expanded to allow more creatures, and it probably was still growing because the ground kept shifting. That meant Wag-sloogs (she didn't know what else to call them) could be near. She would have to find Cole quickly. If she didn't, she had serious problems.

Rounding a sharp curve, Melissa spotted the flickering firelight of the fuse. It sputtered and seemed to go out, then started again, significantly slowed by the ground's unsteadiness. In the darkness, she saw only the slowly advancing sparks of fire along the fuse, but there was no sign of Cole. She risked calling his name, keeping her voice low.

*"Unghhh..."* The sound came from the other side along the rocky wall. It was hard to make out. It could have been some echo or something much worse.

"Cole... is that you?" She shoved the pistol under her belt. Arms outstretched, she traced the opposite wall with open palms and almost tripped over the boy who lay prone and barely conscious. She shook him, but he hardly stirred. "We don't have any time. You have to get to your feet!" She turned to look at the fuse. For a moment it had seemed to have flickered out, but now it sprang back to life. Melissa pulled him up, difficult because his legs had gone limp. She slapped him. "Cole, we have to get moving!"

"Miss Monahan...?"

Struggling with the boy's weight, she almost smiled. "I think you can call me Melissa now."

*"I... I ran... into the damn wall... What about the fuse...?"*

"It slowed down a bit. I thought maybe it went out, but then it picked up again and it's not far from the powder keg. You did good, Cole."

"Margelle and Mr. Hannigan...?"

"They're fine. We're not." She released her grip on him. Cole seemed wobbly, but he came to his senses quickly enough to notice what Melissa hadn't.

"The hole keeps getting bigger. Them kegs of powder could fall in — the fuse could go out."

"It won't. But we can't stay. 'Sloogs, remember?"

They backed off slowly, but the yawning pit opened only a few feet from where they stood, the ground slanting sharply. Melissa reached for Cole trying to maintain balance to avoid toppling in.

There was something else, something in the cavernous fissure before them. Light, bright as the sun, emanated from far below.

*Blinding light, gleaming in the pitch darkness above...*

Cole held tight to Melissa. "Mr. Hannigan and I saw this too. I thought it was some kind of reflection, some illusion, but now it's even brighter. Light down there can't be possible..."

*"That's no illusion. It's possible because there it is!"*

"Them 'sloogs hate any kind of light. Why would they come from a place so damned bright? And where are they now...?"

Melissa pulled Cole back, but the cavity was expanding too quickly. "We may be about to find out..."

The pit could swallow them whole, its walls expanding and contracting in a chewing motion like an enormous mouth. The ground dipped sharply, then disappeared, the unsteady shelf suddenly pulled from beneath their feet at the same moment the fuse reached the crates of blasting powder. The deafening explosion brought a world of stone toppling around them. Cole grabbed Melissa's hand.

*"Don't let go!"*

*"I won't... I won't!"*

The fissure swallowed them in its glaring illumination, and the two toppled into a seemingly bottomless hole that was really not a hole at all.

They could hear the explosion from above as they fell...

*Brightness, darkness, then brightness again...*

# SINKHOLE

*It seemed a bad dream, the one where you're just free falling into a vast open nothingness. You're tumbling head over heels, dizzy with the plunge, but the velocity just increases and your heart races while you keep tumbling down and down and down. You know you're going to hit bottom* **(there has to be a bottom!)** *but no, the drop continues and you keep falling through the air like a dead weight, plummeting through blinding light and pitch darkness into an abyss that seems endless, and somehow you feel smaller as the chasm expands and its boundaries disappear until you're no longer falling so much as floating through what feels like the starry night sky, spiraling as weightless as a feather with no sense of any direction at all, not up, not down. And finally there is a bottom, although it seems more like a soft landing at the end of a long journey, almost a kind of sleep...*

Incredibly Melissa's fingers remained entwined in Cole's. By some miracle of nature their drop came to a painless end without so much as a bruise. The two simply had arrived together in a dimly lit place with no rational explanation of what had happened or where they were.

Numb and semiconscious, Cole released Melissa's hand. His boots felt soaked, his clothing damp. He got to his feet. Silently, Melissa got to hers. Amazed he hadn't broken every bone in his body, Cole turned to her. "We're alive? We should be dead ten times over from that fall." He shook the cobwebs from his brain. They were inside some kind of cave or tunnel. "Feels like we landed just outside the gates of Hell."

"It's wet and smells awful enough. There's light up there." Melissa pointed towards the high ceiling at what appeared to be several grates leading to the surface. "That looks like sunlight. But that's crazy. Feels like we tumbled a hundred miles in the opposite direction from the sun. None of this makes any sense!"

"It didn't feel like falling, not after a while, did it?" Cole said. "Like there weren't no gravity pulling. I don't get none of this either, but I felt sure we were goners, Melissa. I guess what's important now is we're here, wherever 'here' is."

"You tell me. I don't see any sign of the hole that got us to this place. You'd think it'd be up there." She pointed above them.

Cole studied the ceiling. "Above's solid, unbroken excepting them grates. At least there's no 'sloogs around. I guess that much is good. This ain't no place put here by nature, that's damned certain. Maybe that's good too. It means we ain't alone."

Melissa pulled her pistol from her belt, grateful she hadn't lost it in the mad tumble to this place. "I smell the stink of them creatures, or something damned close, Cole. Keep your eyes open." She looked above. "Those grates are too high to reach. We'll follow this corridor we're in, see if we can find some way back."

Cole drew his pistol, looked around. "I'm not sure there is one, Melissa. That hole must've plugged itself up just like the one you saw on the trail."

"There must be clusters of them. They may not stay open long, but we know there's other ones. Whatever got us here will get us out. You able to walk?"

"Through this muck I think the best we can do is slog." Cole shouted, *"Anyone down here? Is there anyone here?"*

Melissa joined in, *"Hey! Anyone? Anyone, please..."*

They heard only their voices echoed. Kicking at the ankle deep water he shouted, "Shit!"

*...Shit...Shit...Shit...*

"Okay, Boy Wonder, we're alone and it looks like we have some slogging to do."

He looked confused. "Boy Wonder? That's funny. Who's that?"

Puzzled over her own words, Melissa shook her head.

"I don't have the slightest idea."

# CHAPTER
# TWENTY-ONE
## DIAMOND LOOP AND BELOW: JULY 2015
## MUD AND BLOOD

*"You only fear what you don't understand..."*

### THE COLSONS AND COMPANY

**A**t the kitchen table with the Colson family, Tiffany Leone prepared to enjoy several slices from two large pizzas. Not so enjoyable were the subliminal images the pies suggested. Like some Rorschach in tomato sauce, mental snapshots flashed inside her brain of George and Anna Brimley soaked in blood, and brain matter splashed on the walls of their home. The free association set her to imagining the image of some curious Loop neighbor discovering the remains of Sergeant Wally Smith's chin somewhere on the street. Watching Eden Colson staring at the elongated dark anchovies on her slice, Tiffany knew exactly what the woman was thinking. But she was hungry, and Angelo's made one hell of a pizza. She ate.

When Greg Colson asked his wife how her day went, it seemed Eden might lose it. The woman clearly didn't know where to begin. She managed one whopping lie before she touched her first slice.

"You know, a little gardening, a neighborly visit to the Campbell house, not much else."

"I saw a police car parked by the excavation," Greg said.

Tiffany tried for the save. "Neighbors said there was some sort of domestic disturbance, some yelling. Not sure what house." Eden caught her eye and managed a subtle partners-in-crime nod of approval.

Greg went at his pizza. "We're learning new stuff about our neighbors every day, aren't we? Speaking of which, Tiffany, do you have family in Glenn Echoes?"

The question rattled her for a moment. "Used to. After my father died my mother remarried and I didn't see much of her after that. She sends me checks for school and calls sometimes, but mostly — well, it's not like with you guys."

"Yeah," Zack said. "We're all super close, aren't we Mom?" He shot Eden a glance that made his mother take new interest in her anchovies.

The water's being shut down earned Greg's wife a pass for not preparing dinner, but Tiffany had no idea how the woman would explain the slug-things in their home she had overheard Fred Reefe describe, or her two brushes with men brandishing weapons in her face. Still, Eden Colson so far had succeeded in covering up the craziness. Maybe the woman would pull off her ruse, but only for a short while, because Gregory Colson did not appear to be an idiot.

Tiffany broke the tension. "Hey, Zack. Want to see a trick?" She grabbed a long anchovy from the pizza and took it into her mouth. Pretending to chew it, she pulled it out tied into a perfect knot. "Cool, huh?"

Greg and Eden didn't seem to think so, but the previous subject seemed shelved for now, and Greg appeared happy to move on from Tiffany's tongue tying talents.

"So, Zack, how was your day?"

Zachary smiled. "Tiffany let me ride on her Harley, and we hung around the excavation for a while to watch them dig. They got this loader they call Big Mama." Succinct and to the point, Zack filled his mouth with pizza so he didn't have to elaborate. Still, the boy had difficulty looking his father in the eye. Visiting Jessie Moss would have been a pisser to explain, as would have been just about everything else. His mother hadn't told him to keep mum regarding the day's events — he just knew. And there was plenty he didn't tell *her*. She had enough on her plate.

Eden spoke without removing her eyes from those damned anchovies. "Porcelain in the main bathroom — I spotted some rust in the tub this morning. The builders must have cheaped out. Probably needs a little reglazing, is all." With another whopper, her eyes shifted to her can of Diet Pepsi, but her husband didn't seem to notice her preemptive strike.

"I'll have a look. New tub shouldn't rust without water to rust it," Greg said, reaching for another slice. "Water will be on for a few hours tonight, at least?"

"That's the rumor. But in the morning the well runs dry again. There are problems, apparently."

Mrs. Colson was good, Tiffany thought, but she must have known there were way too many holes in this dike to plug them all. When that dam burst, it wasn't going to be pretty.

Luckily, for now Mr. Colson seemed clueless.

Greg changed the subject. "Phils play the Giants tonight, Zacker. You want to keep the old man company by the ol' Sony? You're invited, Tiffany. Pretzels and chips on the house. Beer is for the Missus and me. Sorry."

"I'm twenty-three, Mr. Colson. I'm legal." Tiffany managed a polite smile. "I'll take a rain check on the game tonight, though, thanks. I've got class in the morning and homework I have to get to."

Zachary broke an awkward silence. "I want to show Tiffany something on my laptop, okay, Dad? We may go out for a while later, but I'll be back before dark to watch the game with you, okay?"

He and Tiffany headed up the stairs. Eden gave her husband a look. "Okay, Mister Liberal. Should I tell our son to keep the bedroom door open? Yerkers and serkers, remember?"

Her husband grinned. "'Yerkers and serkers, they're not the same...'"

*"Door open, Zachary!"* Eden shouted.

★ ★ ★

...but Zachary quietly closed the bedroom door and poked his head through his window. "Squad car is still by the excavation, and it's empty. I'm not liking this. There'll be more cops coming to see what's happening here, bet on it. We'll talk to someone, tell them what we've seen, but first—" Rocky jumped on the bed alongside Tiffany while Zachary opened his lap top. "I want you to look at this. See, I have this thing about bed bugs — had bad dreams and couldn't sleep. So I did some searching online about insects and all their slimy friends, just to get some understanding of the bastards. You only fear what you don't understand, right?" He googled "SLUG SEX", held it for Tiffany to see.

"You feared having sex with slugs? You're a very strange little boy, little boy."

"Just read..."

Slugs are 'hermaphrodites'; they have both male and female sex organs. Two slugs inject each other with sperm, and both slugs can become impregnated.

"That's interesting," Tiffany said. "Kind of like Bruce Jenner — or Caitlin. Now how about a game of Candy Crush?"

"You're missing the big picture." Zachary googled "MAGGOT SEX".

Tiffany shook her head and scrolled down the page. "I don't see anything here about maggot sex. How do the little buggers reproduce?"

"Ahh, now you're getting it. Read this.

Maggots typically migrate to a high and dry location to begin the pupa stage. They make a reddish-brown shell around themselves and stay in that protective environment, the pupa, for three to six days until they develop into flies.

"Maggots are flies?" Tiffany asked.

"They metamorphose into flies. They're born from fly

larvae. There's no such thing as maggot sex — but there *is* slug sex. Put the two together, maybe add some kind of evolutionary process like tree apes-to-man, and what have you got?"

"I don't know. Morlocks? Howard Stern?"

"Tiffany, think outside of the box — or outside of the larvae, in this case. Slugs are sort of incredible things. Did you know if they lose one of their sensory tentacles, they grow another? That means they *regenerate*, they're always intact — like Jessie Moss suddenly recuperating after his skull had practically been halved. Maybe afterwards he was more slug than human! And maybe those slug things my mom saw aren't merely killing people, aren't just sucking out their brains, like with Jessie. Maybe it's more like they're taking something from those people as if to impregnate themselves, since all slugs have that ability. Then over time they metamorphose into something more — something almost human. At least on the inside. A hybrid. They can't *be* human, of course — they're not physically equipped with the right parts like, say, werewolves. But they can *think* like humans. And in time it's like karma — You know the cliché; a bird eats flies, but when the bird dies, flies eat the bird."

Tiffany laughed. "You've seen too many science fiction movies, Zachary. Bed bugs, the sex lives of slugs, karmic payback? Stick with Disney for a while. A little Nemo, maybe some Buzz and Woody."

Zachary slammed his lap top shut, enough to send Rocky scurrying from the bed. "We've seen some bad shit today. Don't you see what's happening here?"

"I see what's happening to you. Listen, it's been a rough couple of days, I understand that, but —"

"Think, Tiffany. Those slug-maggot things Mr. Reefe mentioned, they took something from Jessie Moss and Mr. Smith, probably from the Brimleys too. It made those people not *feel* any more, not care whether they killed someone close to them, or even if they killed themselves. Whatever was human about them, those sluggoty maggoty things took away, probably to use for themselves."

"Took away what? Their memories, maybe their souls? Come on, Zack, this isn't *Invasion Of The Soul Snatchers*?"

"Why not? A few chomps into your skull, and the Grinch has stolen Christmas. Maybe they learned they have to kill whatever might kill them. Survival of the fittest, the Cosmic Plan. Some insects kill their mates after sex; they're programmed to do that. Maybe when those cross breeds lay their eggs, over time those eggs aren't just slugs or maggots. They're both — hybrids — with a little of us thrown into the mix, our senses, intelligence, and memories included. You saw that photo my mom took. That thing was no garden slug, no maggot — it was more, something new and improved."

Tiffany wasn't buying it. "This stuff is going to make your head explode. Species don't just join together overnight like that. Slugs mating with maggots would be like you trying to do the nasty with your cat. If those things in the hole evolved from something else, they needed centuries to develop, just like we homo sapiens. And why all of a sudden are they showing up here, in this place, and why now?"

"Maybe it's not only here, maybe it's not only now. Maybe we're just discovering them. Or maybe, somehow, we've disturbed them and brought them to us. I don't know exactly how they developed or where they came from. But I *do* know how we can find out."

"You want to put a slug and a maggot together and watch them screw themselves stupid?"

"Not quite, Madame Curie..." He pulled out his cellular to check the battery, then grabbed his pocket charger.

Tiffany grinned. "Let me guess. We capture one? You only fear what you don't understand, right? So, you want to play, do you, Zack? You and me? The game is again afoot, Sherlock?"

"Right."

"Boy Wonder, you're back!"

Zachary reached over and kissed Tiffany on the cheek. "Girl, if I were only a little older..."

# SINKHOLE

## GREGORY COLSON

Greg inspected the tub in the family's main bathroom. He didn't need to examine it too closely to determine the damage wasn't what Eden had suggested. There hadn't been enough water for rust to develop. The stains were too dark and the tub smelled of smoke. Eden must have known this. Why would she lie?

*("The builders must have cheaped out...")*

That's what Eden had said, but Greg didn't think so.

A raw and fishy stink lingered from the drain. Greg sniffed the air. Even with the fan on, he detected another odor — a faint whiff of hairspray. The waste basket contained not only his wife's fancy-assed *Garnier Fructis* spray but an emptied tube of his hair gel that had been full this morning. Colson was no detective, but he knew something was wrong here. Okay, there had to be a simple explanation, he told himself. Maybe Eden had some stupid accident that caused the damage to their new bathroom and was too embarrassed to admit it. She could be that way.

In the bedroom, he removed his shoes and socks, slipping into his loafers to watch the Phils' game with his son. Eden was always complaining how he tossed his socks on the floor. All right then, to the hamper with them, he decided. And here Gregory discovered another puzzle, one a lot more disturbing than the tub's damage.

"What the —?"

A man's shirt, mud covered *(or was it — could it be? — blood?)* was stuffed inside the bathroom hamper. Sniffing it, Greg made a sour face. It was a work shirt reeking with sweat, the kind Greg had seen the men at the excavation site wearing.

...the men that Eden had invited into their home for some neighborly refreshment.

Colson replayed Eden's words about her day.

*("You know, a little gardening, a neighborly visit to the Campbell house, not much else...")*

Hadn't his wife told him the Campbell woman was a joke?

**247**

The village slut, she'd called her. Why the visit all of a sudden? Returning to the bedroom, he noticed Eden had changed the sheets, unusual on a day when there was no way to wash them. He checked the hamper again, and there the bed's sheets were.

He shook his head, muttered "Shit." Holding the dirty work shirt, mumbling more curses to himself, he headed back down the stairs.

Gregory Colson had a few questions for his wife.

### FRED REEFE

Quitting time had come for the Reefe Water & Sewer Contractors...

Heavy duty equipment, the pneumatic and hydraulic breakers and jack hammers, went back into the storage lockers inside the huge trailer bearing the construction company's logo, its lettering superimposed on a pristine illustration of Big Mama. The front-end loader hadn't seen the kind of cleanliness as depicted on the trailer since her first day on the job. On most days, Jarmal Besser would thread the huge machine through Glenn Echoes Boulevard traffic to return the behemoth to the company's storage and cleaning facility. Not today, though. He figured the loader could miss its shower for one day since work had ceased early after an especially trying few hours. The other excavation workers, sweaty and dirty, climbed into old vans and trucks headed home to wives and kids — and in some cases to the nearest bars. Supervisor Fred Reefe, however, stayed behind. He had a plan.

Reefe oversaw the proper storage of the company's tools and made certain everything was safely cleaned and securely tucked away for the next day's use. He waited until the last of his workers drove off before reentering the storage trailer and opening one of its lockers to retrieve an especially efficient jack hammer the crew called The Killer. This was the portable 55 pound gas powered model with a full speed impact of 1440 blows per minutes, capable of penetrating the toughest concrete or asphalt within seconds, sending chunks of the stuff flying like so many ping pong balls. Never intended as a weapon, if used in that capacity the tool could do serious damage, turning soft flesh into shredded wheat in seconds. This was the fail-safe part of Reefe's plan.

But there was another part. The Diamond Loop excavation covered a relatively small underground area. If something lurked below the Loop as he suspected — something his diggers had disturbed — then there were other possibilities of serious danger. Probabilities, really. Because whatever had got to Jessie Moss and Sergeant Wally Smith had originated from another place near the hole they had been digging. The water mains held the answer, and that meant there was one place he would have to explore — the local sewers. These, Fred Reefe had easy access to. A crowbar and some determination would be all he needed. That, and The Killer.

The nearest manhole was on Apple Grove Way, hidden by a wall of shrubbery close to the entrance to a small park. Reefe grabbed the necessary crowbar and headed for the aperture. Still in his work clothes, he figured it likely no one would question his reasons for opening the cover and climbing down, even if carrying the huge jackhammer would have made no sense. Passing a strolling couple he smiled casually at them, pried open the lid, and made his way into the tunnel. Several water mains connected where the sewer entrances were located, in one direction the conduit branching out to the various Glenn Echoes communities, in the other direction converging en route to the sewage disposal plant on the banks of the Wellington River. The Diamond Loop branch seemed the sewer's tributary worth searching. Reefe tossed the crowbar, grabbed the high powered flashlight from his belt, and climbed down the thin ladder. He slogged through the sewage.

To most, the stink of the place would have been unbearable, the idea of sloshing through a netherworld of knee deep floating human waste even worse. Fred Reefe was no stranger to the Glenn Echoes underground networks, although he

**249**

hadn't visited this newest section beneath Diamond Loop's excavation. Few had. His flashlight's thick beam sliced through the darkness as he readied himself to expect anything.

Below the Loop area, Reefe's beam revealed long rows of pearly white oblong shaped objects clustered along the sewer's high ceiling. There was little doubt regarding what they were. They were clutches of eggs hanging in thick larvae-like groups, dozens of them in all sizes. The larger ones rivaled ostrich eggs, but more than twice their size, nothing that suggested anything as small as a common slug. If these *were* eggs, some of them could have held creatures as thick as a man's arm, and God only knew how huge they could get. Whatever crawled from those pearly enclosures could do a lot more damage than fucking up a garden. Reefe lifted the jackhammer high over his head and poked the sharp point of its chisel at the largest of the bunch. The egg felt like some kind of thick jelly, but the damned thing wouldn't break. Reefe poked harder.

The slippery egg-thing separated from its clutch and plopped into the sewage at Reefe's feet. He couldn't risk water damage to the jack hammer; that meant he would have to break the egg's jelly coating with his bare hands. Putting on his work gloves and balancing The Killer on the water pipe, Reefe felt his stomach churn. He tore into the half-submerged jelly-egg and ripped it nearly in two. If this thick goo was larvae, it didn't give away its contents easily.

**"Screeeeeeeeee!!!!"**

A dark wormy head peeked through. Prematurely born yet almost as thick as a fire hose, the hatchling appeared unformed and sightless, shrieking and squirming in Reefe's grasp. Its sharp mouth hooks snapped at his throat, and he dropped the hatchling in the sewage. Slithering off like a water snake, it disappeared.

*"Shit!"*

He couldn't allow the others above him to escape — or even to be born. There could be dozens of those things in the clutches, and even more clutches elsewhere. Reefe knew only one way to make sure they never hatched. He grabbed The

Killer and snapped the switch of his jack hammer to let its chisel do the rest. The tool roared awake, puffing smoke like an angry dragon.

The eggs exploded in black goo as the jackhammer ripped one after the other to shreds. Soaked with dark remnants of larvae and blood, Reefe kept the smoking tool going as he took out every last egg. Wiping the black ooze from his eyes, he squinted to see something shark-like drifting towards him in the raw sludge. Its red eyes beaded on his, a heat seeking missile of slime honing in on its target.

*It was the mother, or whatever had protected the brood he had just fragmented into stinking mounds of dark jelly!*

Reefe sheathed the flashlight but kept its high beam on. The light danced madly around him as he shifted position, holding The Killer before him like a sword. Its motor's roar reverberated throughout the caverns, ear splitting echoes matched by a screeching slug-thing that rose from the sewage like some colossal prehistoric creature towering over him. Reefe held the large drill straight out.

"I got this covered, bitch!"

**"Yoob...Die-em...men...Yoob...diem..."**

The familiar gurgling sounds (words?) seemed clearer than what Reefe had heard earlier through the water mains. He heard them differently now.

Dripping with sludge, the rubbery creature threw itself at him. Reefe snapped the jackhammer's switch to full speed, and its sharp chisel caught the thing practically in midair. Impaled clear through, it shrieked as its innards were ripped to raw and bloody shreds. Buckets of dark guts spilled over him as the jackhammer split the creature in half.

Nearby, the sewer water churned. Reefe knew that more of them lurked under the sewage, and with reptilian stealth they were surrounding him. Another slug creature rose from the water, much fatter than the one he had killed. Enraged, it fell heavily on him like a huge dead weight. Reefe's drill pierced the soft flesh, but its innards were tougher than the first creature's and the chisel slowed, then stopped, stuck inside the shredded entrails of the thing's belly. Pulling itself from him, the creature fell back into the waste water and took the deeply embedded jackhammer with it.

Now weaponless, Reefe spun, looked behind him, and spotted another creature rising from the sewage. He pulled the heavy flashlight from his belt and swung it, connecting with the slug-creature's skull. It fell into the water but three more surfaced, the sewage churning on all sides. Reefe knew others were coming for him.

Sudden sharp pain exploded in his lower leg, as if a serrated blade slashed through his thick work boot to saw into bare flesh above his ankle. Near the water's surface, razor sharp mouth hooks chewed the skin of his leg to the bone, thick rivulets of blood smearing the water. A second lightning bolt of pain struck Reefe's knee tendons. Unable to stand, he went down, the last rays of illumination from his flashlight strobing throughout the dark conduit like lightning flashes. Appearing from nowhere, another slug creature slithered to him, slicing a large flap of skin from his face. It backed off for a moment, then returned for more.

The agitated waste water bled with thick gouts that gave it a sickly muddy color, the sewage churning with the enraged feeding frenzy of a dozen shadowy creatures. They rolled over Fred Reefe and spun in the filth, blood drenched mouth-hooks opened wide seeking their share, shredding clothing and skin to devour every inch of the man's flesh.

### RI

*In the dank **Wogslûk** underworld, Ri watches and waits for the night...*

*When she was a child they had cocooned her, had spun silken webs around her to form a snug chrysalis, and even after many seasons she remains young and beautiful. But regenerated beauty is wasted on creatures who see through much different eyes. She remains young because they want to keep her alive, vital.*

The Wogslûk have no term for "Queen," but Ri speaks to them as one. As a child, she had lived above for only a short while, yet she understands the man-things more than any Wogslûk can. And she knows what those above fear...

*The dark... the grotesque... the unknown...*

*The very embodiment of what the Wogslûk are!*

"Tonight," Ri tells them. Many above will die, many Wogslûk as well, but this night will be a start. A small start, but necessary. They have come a long way to assure this, and to assure tomorrow.

Already, one from above has destroyed many unborn young in the egg. More will come. This, Ri knows.

She has no love for the man-creatures. Sometimes the memories come of her father on his last day, painful memories of a childless and miserable old man. He had seen his young daughter snatched from him and cursed those who had taken her. He would die finding them so that he could kill them.

Instead, he had found her.

He was a fool.

Instinctively, she recognizes the written yellow signs beneath the ground are a warning. She has determined danger lies in this place for those above. The long pipe containing the smell of bad air is the answer. Some must die so others may live. It is that simple.

Ri wants to believe this, tries to believe this.

Tomorrow is theirs. Many tomorrows.

But first...

"Tonight," Ri again tells them.

# CHAPTER TWENTY-TWO

## DOWN DOWN DOWN: JULY 2015
## RATS AND SECOND THOUGHTS

*"You bet your ass I'm scared..."*

**6:35 p.m.**

Leaving the Colson home, Tiffany, wearing a Cheshire Cat grin, turned to Zack. "You told your dad you'll be home before dark. That's bullshit, isn't it?"

"Garden tested," Zack answered, adjusting his backpack. "What am I supposed to say, that we're hunting mutant soul-stealing slugs? That some smiling neighbor may be dismembering kittens in his basement?" His attention shifted to the row of police cars at the excavation site and the cops on foot circling the Hunter home at 618. Several officers were escorting a handcuffed glassy-eyed Dennis Hunter and his equally-stoned teenaged girlfriend to an awaiting paddy wagon. A few Loop neighbors gawked at the blood-spattered pair. Zack and Tiffany exchanged glances. He muttered, "Uh oh..."

"Looks like more of the same," Tiffany said. "Should we speak to the cops, tell them what we know about the other neighbors? We can leave out the slug monsters."

Two uniformed officers stood by the Hunters' front door like sentries while men in suits were going in and out. The two officers that had spoken to Zack's mother earlier were nowhere to be seen, and that wasn't good. No curious neighbors would be sneaking a peek inside, that was damned certain. Zack had the uneasy feeling the floor of the Hunter home displayed several chalk outlines, *CSI: Glenn Echoes* played out in real time.

"This is getting too weird. Those cops will discover what's going on in the other homes soon. They already know about Mr. Smith, and about Jessie Moss and my mom, and old George and Anna were waiting for them. But telling them *why* we think this shit is happening will get us a ticket to the psycho ward. From what I've seen of that Hunter kid, he's flying the friendly skies every day. You're right — our slug story would put us in the same league with the other Loop fruits. Besides, those Glenn Echoes cops have their hands full now. That leaves *us*."

Tiffany nodded agreement. "Okay, I figured those guys aren't going to waste time searching landscaped gardens for monsters, but I don't see what we can do on our own. Mr. Reefe knows what's happening to the water mains. Maybe he can help us."

"Mr. Reefe isn't here. And I'm not sure I like what may be going on with him and my mom."

"All right, fine. *You* tell me how we defeat the Death Star, young Skywalker."

"I considered a Plan B, wise ass. George Brimley had a large gun collection, remember? There were bullets scattered all over the floor, a box full of them. And we saw that those antique pistols still work."

"You're talking about stealing guns? That's illegal!"

"It'll be for a damned good reason. When we bring one of those bastard creatures back, people will have to believe us. Investigative reporting at its finest, right?"

Tiffany looked skeptical. "I doubt Diane Sawyer ever went gunning for monster slugs. A couple of hours ago you were freaked out being in the Brimley house. And cops are crawling all over the place, in case you haven't noticed. Now you want to pack a couple of Old West six shooters?"

"The cops are focused on the Hunter place right now, and

I don't intend to stay inside the Brimley house more than a few minutes, just time enough to load those suckers. Wait here and text me if you spot anyone nearby." Before Tiffany could protest, Zachary headed for the back entrance of 610.

Tiffany waited a very long ten minutes before Zack returned with his backpack containing his pilfered weapons. Expressionless, he handed her an old book, a journal of some sort.

"I found this in Mr. Brimley's book collection. It's a diary or something, written by some nun back in the late 1800's. A nice collector's item for the old guy. Looks like it covers years. See?" He showed Tiffany the signature of Sister Margelle Mallory. "Careful. The pages are worn, and they're stuck together like the book hasn't been opened. I doubt old George ever read it."

Tiffany took the journal. "So you're also a kleptomaniac? Why this book?"

Zack had to think about that. "Don't know. Something told me there's important stuff in it, so I just took it. Who would know Brimley even had it?"

She looked it over, handed it back. "You're a very strange kid. You know that, right? I'd like to read it later to feed my journalistic curiosity."

"Here's something else for your journalistic curiosity." He handed her one of Brimley's old pistols, and she quickly pocketed it. At the excavation Tiffany retrieved the saddle pouch from her Harley and placed the antique gun inside. She slung the pack over her shoulders as a back pack. The deep trough loomed before them.

"So we're going into the belly of the beast?" she asked.

"That's the plan. I saw Reefe's crew bring in a long ladder this morning. After Jessie Moss' accident, Reefe probably wanted to get his guys out of there faster than with the lift they were using. It won't be hard getting down, 'long as you're not claustrophobic. Or scared."

"You bet your ass I'm scared. And claustrophobic too."

Zack looked around, making sure no one was near.

"What's the worst that can happen?"

Tiffany followed him to the yellow warning tape. "You're kidding, right?"

"I promise you shits and giggles, girl." He stopped her from slipping under the tape, hesitant about what he had to say. "Listen, Tiffany. Before we do this, there's something I have to tell you. I mean, we're being honest here, isn't that right?"

"Right. Just don't tell me you're really a forty year old midget. I've had enough piss-my-pants moments today."

"Well, suppose I told you I've fallen crazy in love with you?"

Tiffany's face reddened. "I'd tell you to go back to online porn."

Zachary laughed loud. "I'm putting you on, you dope! Fuck, I'm only thirteen, and I just started getting some real boners. But what I wanted to tell you is — see I know all about Taffy Licks. I mean, I know more than those three jerks at the Colonel's chicken place were talking about. I've seen your videos on YouTube. I watched them before we met. I guess I did more than just watch them." He waited for Tiffany's indignant response, but instead she laughed.

"You and about a thousand other horn dogs scrubbing their nubs, Mr. Colson. I suppose I'm flattered, but I'm glad I'm not laundering your sheets. You're talking about the twerking stuff and the pole dancing, I hope, none of that Whore-of-Babylon crap?"

Zack looked confused. "Of course. There's more?"

"Not 'till you're eighteen, Boy Wonder. But I'm thinking Miss Licks will probably have retired by then. My alter ego won't be shaking her ass at thirty, thank you very much."

"You won't tell my parents?"

Tiffany laughed. "Tell them what? That you're a normal thirteen-year-old kid? Come on. You'll soon be putting those boners to good use. Right now there are slug monsters awaiting our arrival, and you can't catch one while you're nursing a hard-on." Still smiling, she slipped under the yellow warning tape. Zachary watched her body wriggle down the ladder into the hole.

Tiffany had a good point.

She had put on a convincing front, but Tiffany wasn't kidding about being scared. Her heart raced with each descending step into the pit. She hadn't taken time to consider her questionable decision to join in the half-baked plan of a thirteen-year-old. It didn't matter if Zachary Colson's intelligence bordered on genius. What mattered was that she was probably risking her ass for no sane reason except for her own misplaced sense of adventure. Tiffany knew even her airheaded alter ego, Taffy Licks, would have thought twice about this.

She touched the bottom with Zack close behind. He checked both guns, and pulling a high powered flashlight from his backpack he aimed the beam all around and spoke low. "It's tighter here than I expected and smells like yak piss. I don't see anything."

"Run the light up there along the pipeline."

The copper pipe was still shiny and new, but Zack saw it had bent in several places where something had damaged it. "The metal isn't broken, but there's two sharp indentations, like something tried slicing into it, like with a knife. But a knife wouldn't make any sense, would it?"

"Mouth hooks, maybe? Big ones, like from that ugly thing in the photo your mom took? Does that make more sense?"

"Fuck yes. And there's probably more damage along these water mains. That's what caused those leaks."

*"Zack! Look!"*

Something above them skittered across the pipe. Furry and fat, it stopped to stare at the two staring back at it.

"It's only a rat."

Tiffany backed off. *"There's no such thing as 'only a rat'!"*

The rodent squeaked belligerently and seemed about to disappear following the pipeline into a wall of mud. But another dark creature blocked its path before it could. No larger than a toothpaste tube, somehow the thing seemed menacing, mandibles extending towards the rat like the claws of a miniature lobster.

"It's one of them!" Tiffany whispered.

"It's no slug, that's damned certain — and I think it's about to wage war."

The thing-that-was-not-a-slug, while significantly smaller than the rat, proved fearless as a scorpion. Its hooks jutted forward and snatched the rodent by its throat. The rat squeaked loudly, its feet losing their grip on the pipe. The dark opponent lifted it and tore into its belly with a mouth that covered the elongated creature's entire face. Mandibles sliced the rodent's neck cleanly through like twin buzz saws, and its head fell into the dirt. Slurping the blood from what remained of the rat's torso, the creature grew fatter with dark elasticity as it gorged itself.

Tiffany covered her mouth. "I think I'm going to throw up."

"I'll never catch that thing, but —" Performing a juggling act between the flashlight and cell phone, Zachary hit the video feature to record the final remnants of the rat disappearing down the creature's gullet. "Got it! It's like a snake swallowing a baseball. That little fucker ate the whole—"

The fattened rubbery creature fell heavily from the above pipeline into Tiffany's hair.

*"GET IT OFF ME! GET IT OFF!!"*

Zack swung the flashlight and sent the dark thing flying. It bored into the mud, disappearing in seconds.

"You okay?"

Tiffany couldn't stop shaking. "No, I'm not okay! I want to leave! This is a huge mistake! Look, Zack, coming down here was a stupid idea. I'm sorry I pushed this, but I'm the adult here, okay? I want to go now! You have your video—"

A grinding sound came from somewhere near, an echoing like the sharp cutting of metal.

"You hear that?"

"Zack, we have to get out of—"

"*Shhh!* Sound carries inside a hole. It's called diffraction. Learned it in Science class."

"That's nice. Let's go."

"Tiffany, that sound is coming from a short distance." He reached for the copper water pipe, but it was too high. "Touch that pipe. Tell me if there's a vibration or something. It won't be water inside. There isn't any."

"Zack, I don't want—"

"Do it!"

Tiffany reached for the pipe, barely able to extend two fingers on it. "I don't feel anything. No vibrations."

"Water pipes are connected to a main source. No vibration could mean that grinding sound is coming from another line. Jesus, maybe there's a gas line nearby and something is gnawing at it!"

"A good reason to haul ass! If anything blows up down here, these wall supports will tumble like a fucking deck of cards! I don't feel like being buried alive!" Tiffany headed for the ladder.

"Yeah, I think you're right. I'll follow in just a min—" His cell phone rang.

Zachary didn't get to answer it before the major gas line beneath Diamond Loop exploded.

# PART FIVE

## The Sinkhole

*"Tomorrow is promised to no one."*
—**Clint Eastwood, American Actor**

*"Tomorrow. The word hangs in the air for a moment, both a promise and a threat. Then it floats away like a paper boat."*
—**Thrity Umrigar, Author : *The Space Between Us***

*"Tomorrow will be yesterday, when it is the day after tomorrow."*
—**Author unknown**

*"Time can be extinguished like a blown-out flame, and... the laws of physics that we regard as 'sacred,' as immutable, are anything but."*
— **John Wheeler (American Physicist)**

*"...like history regurgitating on itself."*
—**Zachary Colson (age thirteen)**

# CHAPTER TWENTY-THREE

## BOOM TIMES: July, 2015
## SERPENTS IN THE GARDEN

*"Something very bad..."*

**6:42 p.m.**

*elow Diamond Loop a hundred Wogslûk surge. They tear into the thick copper pipeline of the cul-de-sac's supply of natural gas. Like soldiers off to war, many will die.*

*It doesn't matter.*

*There are many more...*

★ ★ ★

**6:50 p.m.**

Carrying the dirty work shirt belonging to Fred Reefe, Gregory Colson joined his wife in the kitchen while Eden filled Rocky's bowl with a heaping mound of Meow Mix. Seeing the shirt, Eden missed the cat's bowl completely and slopped a good portion of Rocky's dinner on the floor. Her anxiety was not lost on her husband.

"You want to tell me what this is about?"

Eden scooped the meaty mess bare handed and bought herself a few seconds. She washed her hands off and managed a casual, "Water's back on temporarily. They use emergency pumps, reserve tanks or something. That shirt — it's Fred Reefe's." She took a deep breath, forced a smile. "He stopped by to explain what's happening with the water mains and wanted to see if there was any leakage in the garden. I offered him a cold drink and he didn't want to get mud all over everything in the kitchen, so I offered him one of your old shirts. Told him I'd clean his. But, well, you know, there's no water." Eden's smile twitched just enough to suggest there was more to her story.

"Uh huh — I noticed you changed the bed sheets today. Not your usual day for that, is it, especially with the water off?" The odd question wasn't incriminating, but it came off sounding like it was.

Eden went pale. "Look, Greg, I've been off my game these past few days, been a little disoriented, okay? All those workmen trudging in and out of the kitchen because I was trying to be neighborly, you know? I guess I bit off more than I—"

The front doorbell rang. Eden felt grateful for the interruption, but if Fred Reefe stood at the door she would have to think fast. She left Greg in the kitchen.

On the stoop with her infant daughter in her arms, Betsy Lewis stood. The young mother appeared disheveled and nervous, not the way Eden remembered her when they had met briefly backing cars out of their driveways before the excavation work began.

"Why, hello," Eden said, not certain why the woman had picked this moment to become neighborly. The mother looked deathly pale and frightened, holding her squirming infant girl that snarled at Eden like a pit bull. This visit couldn't be good.

"Something is happening on the block, Eden. My daughter — I'm sorry, Emma isn't feeling well, but something very bad is..." She stopped herself, whispered. "...and there were police at your house this morning, and that thing with Mr. Smith today in the street. You know it too, don't you? Something bad is hap—" The mother took a moment, collected herself. "Well, that's not why I'm here."

"Would you like to come in, sit for a few minutes?"

"I can't stay. My husband, Carl — he told me he saw your son and some girl hanging around the excavation. He's sure he saw them go into that hole. I thought I should let you and your husband know. I mean, there's been enough excitement on this street today, and that site is dangerous."

Greg came from the kitchen and didn't pretend he hadn't heard. "Zack? I'm sure your husband is mistaken. Our son wouldn't—"

Eden turned to Greg. "He had on his backpack when he left. I thought that was strange. Greg, that girl, that Tiffany... You don't think she and Zack—?

Greg pulled out his cell, speed-dialed his son's number, waited. "No answer. But he's on his damned smart phone all day, taking photos, going online, God knows what else. Probably used up the battery, is all. I'm sure he's all ri—"

A sound like a car's backfire interrupted him. Two more blasts came in rapid succession, thunderous and much more violent. The ground rumbled with the vibration.

"That's an explosion—!" Greg muttered. He stepped outside, Eden behind him.

"Something very bad..." Betsy Lewis muttered to herself. She clutched her infant and pushed past Greg, headed back to her home. She didn't bother saying goodbye.

Eden matched the Lewis woman's hysteria. "That explosion came from the direction of the excavation. Greg, if she's right and Zachary is anywhere near there—"

Another powerful set of eruptions thundered through the Loop and ripped along the cul-de-sac like detonating dominos, sending concrete chunks flying into the air. A massive **KA-BOOM!** shook the Colson home, and the street's surface cracked wide. The Hunter home blew to the four winds, and the Campbell home went next. Nearby, Betsy Lewis staggered near the precipice as if on a tightrope. Clutching little Emma, she lost her balance and disappeared into the ground.

Another explosion...

### *CRA-AAAA-CKKKKK....*

...and a hailstorm of debris rained down on the nearby houses, smashing windows and roofs. The underground water mains blew apart while massive geysers from the reserve tanks sprouted from the ground spraying the sky, a thunderstorm turned upside down. Lawns disappeared in mud, transforming Diamond Loop into a war zone within seconds.

Eruptions continued like cannon fire along the Loop as one home's burst gas main ignited another. Ducking back inside, Greg slammed the door just as the bookcase fell. He pulled Eden beneath the dining room table. Terrified, Rocky found them and scampered there too. The front bay window blew out, showering glass in every direction as if the home had been the target of a dirty bomb.

With a series of loud firecracker pops the explosions grew weaker , finally fading to feeble snaps, then nothing.

*"Jesus..."* Greg couldn't manage more. He held Eden close.

"Something bad *is* happening here, Greg. I have to tell you, something very—" Eden collected herself. Explanations would have to wait. "Zack is out there! Oh God, if he's any-where near that excavation like the Lewis woman said — *did you see?* The ground, it just swallowed her!"

A sinkhole had opened, huge and forbidding, with massive slopes of mud and cracking concrete broadening it even after the explosions had done their damage. The Colson home had been spared, but it sat close to the precipice and there was no telling if the rupture would crack even wider beneath the foundation and claim the entire house.

Still holding Fred Reefe's filthy work shirt, Greg tossed it aside. That problem now seemed a million miles away. "I'll go check to see if Mrs. Lewis and her baby are okay, then go look for Zack."

Eden clung to her husband. "It's not safe out there, Greg."

"He said he'd be back before dark, and it's nearly—*Shit!"*

The couple climbed from under the table, glass shards littering the floor, with books from the fallen case strewn everywhere. Greg opened the door to a living nightmare. In the fading sunlight the remnants of the street appeared worse than a battlefield. As if struck by a missile, most of the remaining concrete had been reduced to scattered piles of debris, and at the entrance to the cul-de-sac, the bumpers of two patrol cars peeked through the crater's lip. The massive sinkhole that extended the entire length of the Loop had swallowed close to half the homes. Others dangled over the precipice ready to tumble. The constant surge of bubbling water from beneath the ruined street made things much worse. Going even a hundred feet seemed impossible.

Greg kissed Eden's cheek and stepped outside. "There's not much street out there, and the ground is probably unsteady. You wait inside the house."

The last of the reserve water spurt from the ground like a small geyser, soaking Greg to the skin. At the edge of the crushed walkway he looked into the muddy hole. It seemed ridiculous to call to the Lewis woman, but Greg took the shot. No answer came, no baby's cries, nothing. "Mrs. Lewis?" he tried again, but he knew no one could have fallen into the deep pit without breaking every bone in their body. The pressure from the rush of water below certainly would have finished the woman and her infant. Greg turned to Eden still at the door. Shaking his head, he took one last look. "Mrs. Lewis...?"

He saw the eyes first, blood-red eyes the size of baseballs blinking from the dark of the chasm. Something moved below, squirming its way out. For one absurd moment Greg thought it might be a neighbor's dog trapped, some poor large canine covered with the sediment of the flooded trench. But this thing was elongated and crawled on its belly through the slippery clay of the incline. Greg backed away towards the house.

Eden stood immobile at the doorway. Greg pulled her inside. "There's something inside that hole, some kind of animal."

Eden didn't need to hear more. She knew.

"It isn't an animal."

The shattered bay window of the family room left them completely vulnerable. Eden handed Greg her cell phone with the photo she had taken in her garden. He stared at the screen, then looked hard at her.

"You knew about these things? I don't under—"

"It's a long story. When this is over, okay? If we—"

**267**

Their attention returned to the window. The entire middle section of the spoon shaped cul-de-sac — its beautifully land-scaped center — was gone, in its place a gaping pit. Slithering one over the other from the sinkhole, a dozen creatures dripping with mud appeared at the lip of the rupture making their way toward the Colsons' home.

*Many Wogslûk lay dead or dying. Leaking dark goo in the flood that has followed the eruption, their remains float in the muddy water filling the fissure. But most of the dead are not whole and their bloody entrails float alongside them.*

*This outcome is worse than foreseen, and perhaps even Ri has died. Those that remain crawl to the surface.*

*This is not defeat. This is the beginning. Weakened, their numbers are decreased, but they know that those who live above are weakened too.*

From the shattered window, Gregory and Eden Colson looked out. Some of the dark things headed towards the houses left standing, but many came for theirs as more rose from the sinkhole and squirmed out.

"Where are the other neighbors?" Greg asked. "There's no one out there."

"*We're* not out there either," Eden said.

"Your garden shears... get them! Kitchen knives too, whatever you can find. My power saw in the garage and the power screwdriver in the large black tool box — Get those too!" Greg pushed the sofa towards the window's smashed glass, placed it on end to block the opening. He did the same with the coffee table and easy chairs. The improvised fort wouldn't hold for long, he knew that. At most it might buy a few minutes. Returning with a pillow case filled with makeshift weapons, Eden didn't look confident. The sun had set, and she flicked the switch of the floor lamp, but nothing happened. The entire street was dark. No surprise there.

"Electricity's out. Your power tools won't be of much use.

Land line's dead and cells aren't picking up the signal. We've got Murphy's Law here. *Fuck!*"

"Go into the bathroom, lock the door, okay? Stay away from the windows."

"You can't fight those things alone. There's no way —"

*"There's no point in both of us dying, Eden! Go!"*

*"No!"*

Greg took the garden shears from the pillow case. "All right, we'll do it your way. Grab the weapon of your choice." He opened the door.

*"What are you—?"*

He slammed the door behind him in the face of his cursing wife. A slug-thing as large as he was crawled along the smashed concrete of the walkway. It stared at him, studied him. The creature stank like a landfill. Greg held the long garden shears straight out, snapping the tool in mimicry of the mandibles facing him.

"Yeah, you're not stupid, are you? You see what I've got here, don't you?"

It saw, and it didn't care. Two others slithered close behind, pushing forward. Greg backed against the door.

From inside, Eden shouted, "Greg, are you all right?"

"I'm okay! Don't open the door!"

A mouth hook snapped near his throat. Greg's garden shears snapped back. It kept one slug-thing away, but a more ballsy creature lunged forward. He thrust the shears at it and caught its eye. The orb popped like a jelly-filled balloon, blood spurting as it shrieked. It was a hollow victory because many more were coming.

Eden opened the door to pull her husband inside. She threw her arms around him, then quickly switched gears, turning all business. "That's enough heroism for now. You need a better plan. The bathroom might be a good idea for both of us, don't you think?"

Greg nodded and headed for the stairs, but the couple stopped before the first step. A dull pounding came from the kitchen, and one look told them a bad situation was about to get worse. A dozen creatures were at the sliding door, thumping hard against the glass until a spidery crack appeared.

Eden went pale. "They're surrounding the house!"

Greg pulled her arm, but she seemed unable to process the insanity surrounding them. Dropping the garden shears, he scooped Eden into his arms, climbing the staircase to the bathroom and locking the door. Her eyes had gone blank. Greg shook her.

"Stay with me! Dammit, stay with me!" He shook her harder.

Eden came out of her funk. "We're going to die, aren't we?"

"No, we're going to fight. I need you to—" Greg's mouth went dry. He'd left the pillow case with the weaponry in the family room downstairs. They had trapped themselves here in their modern Diamond Loop home, inside their spanking new bathroom where maybe they *were* going to die. He held Eden tight, kissed her forehead. "I don't care about Mr. Reefe's work shirt, okay? You don't have to explain anything. I don't care. I love—"

"Zachary is out there somewhere! And...and...where's Rocky? Zack will never forgive us if—"

He held Eden closer. "I know. Fuck, I know..."

The words spilled from her. "I wanted to tell you — I wanted to tell you, but I didn't know how... Everything is just so crazy, I—"

**RRRRRᵣᵣᵣᵣᵣᵣᵣᵣᵣᵣᵣᵣ...RRRRRᵣᵣᵣᵣᵣᵣᵣᵣᵣᵣᵣᵣᵣᵣᵣ ᵣ....RRRRRRRRRRRRRRRRRRR...**

The loud noise came from outside, something near the house. It sounded like some kind of motor, but that would have been impossible because most of the street's surface had disappeared and no vehicle could get through. Of course, dozens of slime creatures clamoring to break into their home would have seemed ludicrous an hour earlier. Now anything seemed possible.

Eden gripped her husband's arm. "What *is* that?"

"I don't know. Maybe Harry Campbell is mowing his lawn. Or maybe—"

"*Shhh...!*"

A thick squishing sound came from the tub. A legion of the smaller slug-things again had found their way to the open drain and were pouring from it. Some were scaling the tub's side. Others fell onto the floor from the shower head.

Greg looked at his wife. "Builders didn't cheap out, did they? What you told me, that was crap, wasn't it?"

"So now you know," Eden said. She kicked off one of the small creatures clinging to her foot. "You think maybe we made a mistake moving here?"

Glass shattered downstairs, the last remaining shards of the bay window. The furniture fortress toppled with a thud, and the kitchen's sliding glass door came next. The slug-things were coming into the house from all sides. Greg kicked away another small creature and pulled the shower curtain from its rod, wrapping it around Eden and himself. The couple sank to the floor holding each other.

A thick and repetitious thumping came from the staircase, and already several smaller creatures crawled along the protective shower curtain like an invading army. Eden punched at them, but they held to the material fast. There wouldn't be much time.

"I'm sorry, Greg. I'm so sorry..."

He pulled her closer. "It's all right. Everything is all right."

That wasn't quite true. The smaller slug-things were only a preview of the nightmare pounding at the bathroom door, the big brothers of those ugly miniatures crawling onto the shower curtain, onto them...

Greg knew their situation was very far from all right.

# CHAPTER TWENTY-FOUR

## NEWS AT 11:00: July, 2015
## BURYING THE LEAD

*"...and burbled as it came..."*

The Phils were getting their asses handed to them by the Giants when the news bulletin interrupted the ballpark slaughter. Inside the Echoes Tavern, Jarmal Besser put his beer down and felt his jaw drop at what appeared on the screen. The Channel 6 news team's helicopter hovered over the excavation site with live shots of what had been the cul-de-sac homes of Diamond Loop minutes earlier, while field reporter Taryn E. Friedman described the explosions in the gas main that had practically leveled much of the new development. Jarmal had known there had been serious problems at the site, and after work he needed a few beers inside him to steady his nerves before heading home. Now a huge sinkhole remained where new homes had stood, and it appeared half of the Loop homes were swallowed or flattened. Darkness had fallen, the cul-de-sac's electricity was out, and with no illumination there wasn't much to see onscreen from the air except smoke and gushing water.

"Turn up the volume," Jarmal said to the bartender.

From the site, the Friedman woman narrated over an eerily darkened screen. "...a massive gas explosion this evening at the Diamond Loop housing development in Glenn Echoes destroying several homes. We have no word on fatalities or injuries. A New Jersey Gas and Electric spokesman speculates that the explosion occurred shortly after a gas line was ruptured by construction workers during a water main excavation located beneath the cul-de-sac area, although initial reports state that there were several additional explosions plus damaged water lines..."

The woman reporter stood near the excavation but could get nowhere close to the sinkhole that traveled the entire length of the Diamond Loop area. Police quickly ushered Friedman away, but she managed to add "I'm told this entire area remains unstable and many homes have fallen into the massive sinkhole, but one officer claims a neighbor saw two young people near the excavation at the time of the gas explosion. There could be people trapped beneath the rubble, maybe two or more — although at this time we're unable to confirm—"

The bartender shook his head. "What would fools be doing in that damn hole at this hour? Don't you construction guys quit at 5:00?"

Remembering the young woman who had snooped around the site earlier with the Colson kid, Jarmal had an idea who might have been dumb enough to climb into that hole after working hours. But to the barkeep he answered, "There's plenty assholes in the world, Cal. Looks like tonight I might have to become one myself."

Jarmal pushed himself from his stool and didn't finish his beer.

★ ★ ★

*"If anything blows up down here, these wall supports will tumble like a fucking deck of cards! I don't feel like being buried alive!" Tiffany headed for the ladder.*

*"Yeah, I think you're right. I'll follow in just a min—"*

*It happened that fast, the explosion, an ear splitting blast quickly followed by a sea of cascading mud...*

The thick wooden upright support and the ladder inside the excavation toppled at the moment of the first explosion, trapping Tiffany and Zachary beneath. The heavy support kept several foul tons of sinkhole sludge from burying them alive, although the resulting mudslide also kept out most of the breathable air. Little space remained beneath the support, hardly room to move at all. In the blackness, on his belly Zachary reached for the girl.

"Tiffany? You okay?"

Nothing for a moment, but Tiffany's sudden raspy *"Fuck!"* indicated she was conscious. She spit out a mouthful of dirt, rubbed more from her eyes, although it was too dark to see anything. The two couldn't even see each other. Tiffany sputtered, "Are we dead?"

"We should be, but no."

"Then I'm open to suggestions."

"How about we start by screaming our guts out for help?"

Under tons of dirt their shouts became muffled, and it seemed unlikely anyone above would hear, if anyone were even near the collapsed excavation. Silence answered them and the two lay flat in the darkness for a long time. Breathing became more difficult, as did talking.

Finally, Tiffany spoke. "We're going to die down here, aren't we?"

Zachary moved closer. "There's probably people looking for us right now."

"No one even knows we're here! We're going to fucking suffocate!"

"Don't talk, okay? We need to conserve air. We need to..." The sound of shifting mud interrupted him, a slushy liquid sound close by. "I think maybe... maybe someone—" Careful not to start a muddy avalanche, Zachary stretched himself and pulled his flashlight from his backpack. Aiming the beam toward the wall of mud just beyond the support, he saw the unsteady dirt barrier move. He knew this wasn't a rescue, but he couldn't budge.

Tiffany muttered some gibberish. *"'Beware the Jabberwock, my son! The jaws that bite, the claws that catch! Beware the Jubjub bird—'"*

"What the fuck, Tiffany?"

She looked at Zachary. "It's from '*Jabberwocky,*' okay?

Lewis Carroll. It's something my mother taught me to say when I was scared. It's just nonsense words that somehow make sense. I was never big on *The Lord's Prayer*."

"I'm betting that's no Jabberwock in the dirt..."

The rampart of mud separated, great clods falling as something huge pushed through. Zachary saw only the head, saw its mouth bleeding profusely, probably a result of the explosion. But the red eyes that emerged were worse than anything his imagination could have conceived, and the creature easily could make a meal of both of them. The flashlight beam disturbed the thing and it backed off, but only for a moment. It had come for a kill.

Tiffany whispered, "*...with eyes of flame, came whiffling through the tulgey wood, and burbled as it came...*"

"*Shhh...*" Reaching into his pack, Zachary pulled out the loaded antique pistol that had belonged to George Brimley. He kept the beam going with one hand, took aim with the other. "I hope this thing works..."

A metallic snap of mouth hooks just missed slicing his hand from his wrist. He aimed between the two blinking orbs inches from his face. His grip was unsteady, but he managed to squeeze the trigger. The slug-head exploded in blood, thick clots of goo spilling over Zachary in a dark shower. He fired again, and the creature fell back into the soft mud, the sediment partially covering its oozing skull. The sludge quickly claimed the thing entirely.

In the flashlight's beam Zachary turned to Tiffany, his face stained with inky goop. "Well, we know old man Brimley's gun works."

"Great, just great. You may want to save one of those bullets for me." Tiffany coughed and muttered something unintelligible.

"Don't talk, okay? Conserve the air." Zachary didn't follow his own advice, and in under a minute shouted again for help. Her throat already raw, Tiffany joined him.

...and then they fell silent. A roaring sound came from above.

*RRRRRRRRRrrrrrrrrrrrrr...RRRRRrrrrrrrrrr rrrrrrr....RRRRRRRRRRRRRRRRRRR...*

Her voice practically gone, Tiffany asked, "Is that some kind of motor?"

Grinning like a mad man, Zachary pumped his arm. *"Yes!"*

The wooden support shielding them shifted as great chunks of mud moved all around, and for one terrible moment the entire mountain of silt almost buried them. Aiming the flashlight beam at the surface, Zachary shouted with what voice he had left, *"We're here! We're down here!"*

Heaping mounds of dirt were scooped from above. Thick beams of light scanned the hole.

*They were flashlights, searching!*

*"WE'RE HEEERE!!"* Tiffany chimed in at the same moment a huge set of metallic teeth appeared above them, chewing into the ceiling of mud.

*RRRRRRRRRRRRRRRRRRRRrrrrrrrrrrr...*

The loud motor-driven sound stopped. A man's voice from above shouted, *"Are you all right? How many of you down there?"*

Tiffany immediately recognized the voice. "That's Jarmal! The guy that works Mr. Reefe's loader!"

Zachary waved the flashlight's beam like a beacon and caught a glimpse of the starry night sky. "That's Big Mama digging us out!!" To those above he shouted again, *"There's just us two! We're here! We're all right! Follow the beam!"*

The front-end loader's bucket descended into the hole, a gigantic version of the arcade claw crane that searched for toys, except in this pit the toys it searched for were human. From above Jarmal Besser shouted back, "Can you both manage to climb into the bucket?"

Jarmal tilted the huge scoop to accommodate its cargo. It proved a tight squeeze crab-crawling to the jagged toothed shovel, but the pair climbed into the huge scoop, Zachary pulling Tiffany aboard. Enough mud covered them to make it difficult to tell one from the other. The metal behemoth called

Big Mama lifted its bucket high above the excavation, carrying both Tiffany and Zachary to safe ground away from the hole's lip. Helped from the bucket filthy but alive, the two met a chorus of cheers from the Glenn Echoes neighbors who surrounded the site. The cop who pulled them out gave a thumbs up to the surrounding crowd, and more cheers followed, a regular baby-rescued-from-the-well moment.

Tiffany rushed to Jarmal Besser, prepared to kiss the man all over his sweat-drenched face. Tonight he had been a hero, but he didn't appear a happy one. Jumping from the loader's cab, he forced a pained grin and waited for the clamor to die down before pulling Tiffany away from the crowd. He pushed past the man holding the intrusive Channel 6 camera.

"Damn stupid to be climbin' down there, you know that, don't you? You got a gun or something with you? Them cops and me, we heard what sounded like shots, and that's prob'ly what saved your sorry asses."

Tiffany wiped mud from her face. She saw Zachary talking with the cop who had pulled them out. "Ask Zack about the gun. I'm taking the fifth. And a shower."

"You a damn wise ass, ain't you? Well, you two in a shit-load of trouble. You see the law standin' here? They got some heavy questions they'll be askin' both of you jugheads soon as this dumb-ass celebration is over. You're lucky that 'splosion didn't blow your tits off. And we still got our hands full with them homes in the Loop, so people gon' to lose interest in you real fast."

Tiffany answered only, "Thank you for that. I mean, for saving our sorry asses." She looked over her shoulder to see Taryn E. Friedman calling to her. The reporter recognized her immediately and gestured to her cameraman to stay behind. Jarmal shook his head in disgust as the woman rushed towards them, arms at the ready for hugging.

"My God! Tiffany Leone, it's you under all that dirt! You were one of my best cubs. You went on assignment with me back in — hell, when was it?"

Tiffany returned the reporter's hug, smearing Friedman's

stylish summer skirt with mud. She shrugged an apology. "Back in 2010, when I was a senior at Roosevelt. You called me Greenie researching that missing boy case — that Socrates Singer kid. You taught me well, Taryn. Anything for a story, right?"

Friedman flashed her best on-air smile, although the cops had insisted she have her man's camera turned off. "We'll have to get you and your friend right now for the eleven o'clock spot."

A nearby cop overheard this and shook his head, a cue for Tiffany to reject that idea. "Not right now, okay, Taryn? I need to pull myself together a little, okay? Zack and I are a little frazzled from all of this."

Friedman held up her finger in a wait-a-second gesture for Tiffany. She spoke through her head set to the news woman in the chopper. "Helicopter is called back because of the gas threat? Okay." She turned her attention back to Tiffany. "No more overhead coverage until further notice. They want the place cleared because the area is combustible and there could be more explosions. I can count on you for the eleven o'clock spot then?" She forced a smile. "Stay muddy for the piece, Greenie! I'll be nearby!" Hesitating for a moment to consider Tiffany's anything-for-a-story comment, she asked, "What story were you two looking for in that hole?"

Tiffany caught Jarmal's stare and noticed Zachary briefly had broken away from the crowd of cops to come to her side. The three exchanged a quick look that told Tiffany to keep the creature feature from the media for now. She managed her own version of a professional façade for the reporter, a difficult feat while she remained drenched in mud. "I'll have to bury the lead until showtime, Taryn. Delaying tactic, I believe you used to call it. You'll get your exclusive. Promise."

"A true journalist. We'll talk. Remember the eleven o'clock spot. Don't you or your friend go too far!" Friedman headed for the news van to prepare for her story. Another reporter waited for her to disappear, then approached Tiffany, microphone in hand. Tiffany waved her off.

Jarmal muttered to the girl, "Maybe you ain't so stupid after all."

Zachary gestured he needed to speak alone with Besser alongside his front-loader. Jarmal didn't seem eager, but he followed. The Colson boy wasted no time.

"Where that sinkhole is — my parents' home is the last one on the Loop. Electricity is out, and it's probably too dark for them to leave with that hole out there, but there's something *else* out there too, something bad. You have to get to them, Jarmal!"

"Something bad? What you talkin'—?"

"I think you know."

"I'm in 'nuff deep shit with Reefe and Company, me havin' made an unauthorized use of this vehicle. Be lucky if I keep my job."

"Where is Mr. Reefe now? Wouldn't something this important bring him here?"

"I called him, damn straight I called him. His wife said he didn't come home after work, and she was gettin' worried. I couldn't fuck around, so I took Big Mama on my own."

Zachary wiped dried mud from his face, studied the filth on his fingers. "There's something dangerous underground, Jarmal. Mr. Reefe knows it. You know it too, 'cause you saw those busted water pipes. Tiffany and me, we've seen some awful things. Look at this." He took out his cell phone and showed the small slug-thing he had captured on video in the excavation.

Jarmal raised an eyebrow. "You talkin' shit now. Is that some scorpion?"

"An open mind, okay? You can ask Tiffany.

"I'm askin' *you*."

"This little sucker swallowed a rat whole! Well, the torso, anyway. The head he bit off."

"You fuckin' with me, right?"

"Here's what I know..."

Zachary told his story quickly. Jarmal said nothing, but he tried calling Fred Reefe again. Besser lowered his voice. "There ain't no signal, so here's the thing. Can't reach your folks and Mr. Reefe ain't here to give me clearance — and I'm not feelin' good about his not bein' here. You say you seen one of them slug things yourself?"

"It didn't like my flashlight's glare, so I was able to kill a big one in the excavation. Those were the shots you heard."

"With the gun you took from the Brimley home — where you say them two old people shot each other."

"Right."

"Same day that sergeant, Mr. Wilson, shot *his*self..."

Zachary nodded.

"And Jessie Moss swung..."

"The worker who said he got bit in this excavation, *yes!* And those are just the ones we know about. These weren't random deaths, not crazy coincidences either. But other people won't see that."

Zachary Colson's story was damned convincing. Besser looked toward the darkness surrounding Diamond Loop. "Too damn dark to see them things out there, *if* they're out there like you say, and maybe they're smart enough to stay in the Loop area and not come by here to ask 'Wassup?' Well, I can't be in any deeper shit with the company than I am already, can I?"

Zachary agreed. "I'm sure there'll be some sort of rescue party soon, but right now there's only you, and time is important. Big Mama can make it through the Loop area, she can get around the sinkhole, can't she? I mean, even if you have to take her all the way down that hole? There's probably people trapped who need help, and right now your loader is the only way."

Jarmal wiped beads of sweat from his forehead. "That's what Mama's built to do, if there's 'nuff solid area left to take her through. I 'spose I can be as big a fool as you and your friend who's showin' off for them t.v. people. Prob'ly goin' to be out of work by morning anyway." He went to climb aboard the high perch of the front-loader's cab.

Zachary stopped him. "I'm coming with you."

"Like hell you are. That hole is a damn fault line, and this ain't no Six Flags ride."

Zachary didn't wait for Jarmal's permission. Scrambling up the tire's thick tread and into the cab, he planted his ass firmly in the seat behind the glass of the front-end loader, arms folded. "You want me off, you'll have to drag me off. That won't look real good with that t.v. camera pointed this way. Wouldn't you rather be the hero who saved the kid and personally reunited him with his family, instead of the black man with attitude?"

Jarmal looked over his shoulder. The guy holding the large Channel 6 television camera was already setting up the shot. "Fuckin' kid, you blacker than me with all that mud on you." He climbed into the glass enclosed cab and revved the engine until it roared. He snapped on the loader's flood lamp.

Zachary caught Tiffany's attention while she was off speaking with another reporter. He gave her a thumbs up and she mouthed a silent "Good luck."

Big Mama headed into the cul-de-sac bumping and dipping every inch of the way.

# CHAPTER TWENTY-FIVE

## NIGHT CALLERS AND MIDNIGHT CRAWLERS: July, 2015
## MAMA'S BOY

*"...like some muddy shark..."*

The terrain couldn't have been less hospitable, and Zack held on tight with no idea how Jarmal kept his grip on the loader's steering wheel. Besser's eyes remained on the questionable surface as if at any moment the ground might collapse from under them. The tires hit a mushy patch and Jarmal's expression convinced Zachary Big Mama had found her resting place. The deeply treaded rubber sank into the silt and the loader tilted precariously, but somehow Jarmal broke Mama free. Her forward motion was slow and it didn't last.

*"STOP!"* Zack shouted. He pointed toward a home that lay almost completely submerged sideways in the sinkhole, its foundation slipped from under it like a magician's tablecloth trick gone wrong. "That's a woman over there! I know her!"

Her tube top dangling below one exposed sludge-covered breast, the woman staggered alongside the sinkhole and toward them, seeming oblivious to the possibility she could fall in. She looked as if she'd been in mud up to her neck. Maybe she had discovered a shallow part of the hole to wade across, or maybe she swam as the water poured in. It didn't matter because here she was approaching Big Mama's lamp beam, her teeth freakishly white against her mud-covered face. The woman didn't appear to notice the two until she stood half dead before the loader's huge turf tires practically twice her size.

"That's Mrs. Campbell," Zack said. "She's married to some old rich guy, but she usually looks a whole lot better." He called to her, "Mrs. Campbell, are you okay?"

Regina Campbell answered with a badly synchronized chorus of "Like A Virgin" and tried mounting the loader, a long kitchen knife held high like a weapon. The toothy smile broadened.

Jarmal muttered, "This isn't good..."

***"...touched for the very first tyy-yyyymmmm...!"***

Zachary reached into his back pack for the ancient pistol, but that proved unnecessary. A huge slug creature squirmed from the mud hole and serpentined towards the loader. Mouth hooks caught Regina Campbell's ankle, but the woman didn't scream, didn't cry out in pain even as she slipped from the loader's side into the clutch of the thing grasping her foot. Dragged into the darkness of the sinkhole, seconds later she was gone as if pulled into a deep surf.

Zachary turned to Besser. "'We're going to need a bigger boat...'"

Jarmal's eyes widened. "I seen it, but I don't believe it...." He kicked the accelerator and Big Mama roared. "Them things must be all over this place. Can't see 'em with this dark 'til they're in front of us. Let's go find your parents." He inched the loader along the sinkhole's periphery. The machine dipped sideways at a treacherous angle, slanting so sharply the loader threatened to topple upside down into the pit, but gravity so far had not betrayed them.

"Did you see her face, Jarmal? She wanted to kill us. Mrs. Campbell knows me!"

"I doubt that woman was Mrs. Campbell anymore. And what was that bad Madonna impression 'bout?"

"It's nuts. I think before they go all wonky that singing makes some connection with whatever's left inside. It happened with Jessie Moss too at the hospital. Different song — *Nothing from noth—*"

"So, you went to the hospital to see Moss. You a ballsy little kid, ain't you? That's good, 'cause you goin' to need those balls toni—" Something thumped hard against the turf tire. Jarmal didn't seem to want to stop the loader again, but he did.

Zachary pulled out his flashlight, pointed it below. Like muddy apparitions, a crowd of Loop neighbors appeared and pounded on the tires, uselessly trying to claw into the rubber and climbing over each other. Zachary couldn't tell how many surrounded the vehicle. Screaming and cursing, trying to scramble onboard, whatever their bizarre cacophony was, this crowd's rationality had left them. Zachary made a silent prayer that his parents were not among them. One man still wearing his golf shirt climbed halfway to the cab. Swinging the flashlight, Zachary caught the guy's forehead dead center, and the man toppled into the mud.

"Hit the gas, Jarmal!"

The loader lurched forward. Besser turned and caught the small crowd with fists in the air. "Ain't only your slug monsters in the Loop want to kill us! I ain't stopping for nothin', 'cept for your folks. Fuck this 'Walking Dead' shit!"

"They're not dead. They've been lobotomized — kind of. Souls taken, rules gone. *Lord Of The Flies* crap."

"Well, that's their problem, 'cause we ain't pickin' up no hitchin' boogeymen. Let's see that gun of yours. You know how to use it? I ain't bein' blamed for allowin' no kid to carry a firearm. So I ain't askin', and you ain't tellin.'"

Zachary pulled the pistol from his backpack and took a last look at the crowd fading in the darkness. Staggering about in pitch black like that he expected the sinkhole would claim them soon enough. "I took the gun on my own because there's more than boogeymen on this street. Well, maybe not when I first took it. It was all shits and giggles at first."

"Shits and giggles? Like you was expectin' a good time?"

"It's something Tiffany says. I guess I got caught up in the adventure. We both did."

Jarmal sneered. "Well, I 'spose a little niblet like you *could* pass for a damned Hobbit."

The loader bumped and shook on the dicey terrain through what remained of the Loop. A hesitant moon crawled from behind dark clouds to reveal the fallen mailbox adorned with the cartoon bees, an image ridiculously out of place. Hanging sideways over the sinkhole's precipice, the mailbox displayed the numerals 613.

Jarmal didn't appear hopeful. "That your home?" Zachary nodded. It was all he could manage, seeing the surrounding devastation. "Well, at least it's still standin'. Not by much, though." The hole's deep drop was only a few feet from the front door, barely enough surface to get the loader through. "The ground here is like oatmeal, and Mama's too heavy for it. Hole will take her if we stay long."

"Our front window is busted, Jarmal. Those things could've—"

"We don't know that. The explosion coulda blew out the windows. You hold on to that gun and wait here. If you shoot, you better mean it. No back talk from you 'bout joinin' me, not this time."

Zachary wouldn't dare talk back now. He gave another nod and handed Jarmal the flashlight. It was heavy and big, but it wasn't much of a weapon.

"Your parents, I'll find them if they're in there. Ground here's unsteady and Mama's weight could topple her, so you keep her runnin' case we need to make a quick getaway. Keep your gun handy too, and don't touch nothin'. Shoot anything that moves that ain't me or your folks. You got that?"

More nods from Zack. Then, "What will you use if—?"

Jarmal gave no answer. He didn't have one. Jumping from the loader, his work boots squishing in the sludge, he disappeared through the broken bay window of the Colson home.

The crowd of neighbors, so threatening moments earlier, had turned silent. Zachary wondered if the lot of them had disappeared into the hole, oblivious to what was happening around them, or completely insane. As Mama's engine grumbled, alone inside the loader's cab Zachary quickly became aware of other sounds surrounding Diamond Loop. Sudden screams came from one home, then abruptly stopped. A man's curses from nearby were followed by the lightning flash of a gunshot, then silence. Across the cul-de-sac, a child was crying, and from inside the Greene home, Debbie Greene's poodle yelped.

Although the summer night was humid, Zachary felt shivers. What would Jarmal discover inside his parents' home? The other residents didn't seem to be doing so well. Zachary held his pistol close.

*"Yoob diem... no....no....diem, yoob...no...no..."*

The voice (if it *was* a voice) startled him. It sounded like a slowed down recording interspersed with a liquid slurping, a grotesque parody of baby talk. Zachary spun around, saw nothing in the illumination of the loader's headlamps.

*"No...diem...no yoob man diem...no..."*

Something moved toward him, but its motion seemed more seal-like than the movements of a snake, a timid and tentative forward motion, yet curious. Still, it was a slug-thing, and Zachary kept his gun pointed as it approached the loader.

*"No...No diem...yoob...mon..."*

The fuckers could speak! The words were a garbled mess but words they *were*, and somehow there seemed no hint of danger in whatever this creature was trying to say. Zachary repeated the one word he recognized. "No..." Without understanding what he was saying, he parroted, "No diem yoob..."

The creature stopped. In the moonlight, its eyes seemed different, brighter and more intelligent than the others he'd seen. It was smaller than the one Zack had shot, probably younger. It made no attempt to climb aboard the loader; instead, it cocked its head like some curious lap dog and made a soft gurgling sound that reminded Zachary of Rocky's purrs.

He spoke as if the slug-thing might understand. "My parents and my cat are inside that house, you know. Maybe with some of your friends." He immediately felt ridiculous trying to converse with some wild slug-creature that could be waiting for the right moment to spring aboard the loader and eat him. But Zachary somehow doubted it. Mouth hooks didn't jut forward to threaten him, and the creature remained where it lay like an obedient pet.

*"No...No diem yoob..."*

Zachary restrained the urge to encourage it to come closer, but his voice was gentle when he spoke, as if he were speaking to his cat. "You don't look like those others. You're smarter, aren't you? You don't want to hurt me, do you?"

The next moment Zachary knew why. A scream came from inside the house.

*His mother...*

During the spring of 2013, Fred Reefe's construction crew wagered that Jarmal Besser was not the expert loader driver he claimed to be. He took the bet that, while driving Big Mama, he could lift a shiny new dime from a large pile of soft dirt and deposit that dime into a coffee mug — both with one try. Money exchanged hands, most men doubting Jarmal's talent. Besser fooled them all and enjoyed a very decent steak dinner that night.

Jarmal had an eye for details, and once inside the Colson home, he spotted plenty. The furniture piled to block the broken window had toppled, and there were thick snail-like mud tracks on the carpeted floor leading to the stairway. This wasn't rocket science. The slug-things had visited this house, and maybe they were still inside. A pillow case filled with garden tools and those taken from a man's workshop didn't require much deduction either. These implements had been hastily gathered and were meant as weapons, but the Colsons clearly were in a hurry and had left them.

Because the Diamond Loop homes had no basements, the couple's escape from the house seemed unlikely because the creatures also had entered through the garden entrance. That meant the two probably were in the house and upstairs.

Whether they remained alive was another matter, and if their circumstances resembled the knife wielding Mrs. Campbell's, their remaining alive wasn't a good thing. Jarmal listened but heard nothing. If the creatures were in the house, they were stealthy bastards.

It would be foolish to call out their names if anything else lurked inside with him. He saw the garden shears at the foot of the staircase and noticed a black inky substance clung to the blades, another detail that didn't add to his confidence about the fate of Zachary's parents. The shears in one hand, the flashlight in the other, he started up.

Jarmal could be stealthy too. He flipped off the flashlight and moved slowly. The silence was interrupted by a rubbery sound coming from just above the top of the stairs, plus a soft thumping against what probably was the bathroom door. It was too dark to make out what was there, but Jarmal expected he knew. He sent a thick beam of light along the hallway.

A dozen or more of the creatures wriggled in a thick pile, crawling over each other in a writhing pyramid attempting to push through the locked bathroom door. Their efforts were clumsy but forceful, and Jarmal felt certain that soon they would be inside. He heard Eden Colson scream.

*"COLSONS!"* he had to risk calling out. *"You in there?"*

A male voice answered, *"Yes! We're in here! We're all right!"*

They weren't going to be all right for long, and they must have known that. Their kid had mentioned the slug-thing he saw didn't like the light. Well, then...

Jarmal aimed a thick beam at the squirming living mass battering the locked door. Several let out a shriek as if burned. Others turned towards him, their mandibles open for business. From the mound's top, two dropped off and headed for him. They seemed smaller, but still the size of pythons. Jarmal held out the garden shears as one slug-thing, blinded by the glare, ran directly into the blades. The impaled creature's blood spurt all over him.

The other seemed more cautious but just as blind. Jarmal

took the offensive, raised the shears high above him, and drove the twin blades into its brain. The head burst like a blood-filled sack, and this got the attention of the others. He pulled the shears from the dead slug-thing and snapped it at the pile of them. Recognizing that the gnashing movement of the weapon seemed as lethal as their own mouth hooks, their pyramid tumbled to the floor.

Jarmal sensed his advantage. Shouting, he charged forward, an army of one storming the castle. The slug-things scattered, but Jarmal knew this was only a brief retreat before they regrouped.

He pounded at the door. "It's okay! I'm one of Reefe's guys! Open up!"

Greg opened it a crack for him, then slammed it shut as soon as he got inside. Jarmal gaped at the image of Eden Colson crouching beneath a shower curtain covered with dozens of the smaller creatures.

"Jarmal Besser. How you folks doin'?"

"They'll be all over us again in a minute," Greg said. "There's hundreds, I think. We can't—"

"Your hamper, it's in the closet here?" Jarmal asked. Eden nodded, and he dropped the shears. Grabbing the entire curtain, he and Greg balled it up, shoved it into the basket and shut the lid — but several of the slug-things skittered across the floor tile. Besser's heavy work boot stomped two of them into a black paste, but the others shimmied under the door. "Zack is safe outside, but *we* got to leave now!" He handed the flashlight to Greg, kept the shears for himself. "They don't like light. Shine it on them. Your house is full of them big ones!"

Greg discovered that quickly. Several of the fat creatures blocked the staircase but wriggled away when he pointed the high-powered beam at them — like a Jedi warrior's light saber, Zachary might have said. He stopped at the front door. Pulling a power drill from the pillow case, he handed an electric screwdriver with an elongated bit to his wife. Eden found Rocky cowering beneath the dining table and scooped the cat in her arm. Armed to the teeth with work tools, they followed

Jarmal outside to the waiting loader.
It wasn't there.

# CHAPTER TWENTY-SIX

## A SPIELBERGIAN SLUG: July, 2015
## SHEER MADNESS

*"...dime in the coffee cup..."*

Zachary heard his mother's aborted scream. That meant that she was alive and still in the house, although her bloodcurdling shriek couldn't have been good. Jarmal had been gone for several minutes, but his attempt to rescue Zack's parents had provided the boy little comfort. Having to determine what was happening, he prepared to jump from the loader. *To hell with Jarmal's warning.* The slug creature that had been watching him from the ground blocked his path and wouldn't allow him to abandon the loader's perch.

"...no...no..." The creature's one word was clear, the rest gibberish.

Zachary sat dumbfounded. "You—you understand 'no'...? You don't want me going inside?"

The slug thing stared, observing him. It made no threatening move.

"My parents are in there. Can you understand that...?" Catching himself, Zachary felt ridiculous speaking as if this thing were Spielberg's ET. This overgrown slug was a damned gastropod, at least according to Wikipedia, incapable of comprehending anything other than its own need to survive, to feed — probably to feed on *him*. He had to remember that.

*...if it were a slug...*

"No yoob..."

"Yeah, thanks. That helps a whole lot."

The house went silent. The clamor from neighboring homes had stopped too. There remained only sloshing echoes from the sinkhole below. Other creatures down there were not nearly as friendly as this specimen, and perched upon the loader Zachary was a sitting duck if they surfaced.

"Your friends in that hole would probably chow down on my brains for a midnight snack. You know that, don't you?"

*"Yoob...mon..."*

Upon the unpredictable surface, the loader shifted and dipped wildly to its side. As Jarmal had warned, Big Mama's weight could send her toppling into the hole, and Zachary scrambled to the driver's seat for balance. His 112 pounds were hardly enough to do the job, and the loader tipped precariously in the loose mud, slipping toward the sinkhole. He held fast to the steering column to avoid falling out, but he couldn't stop the progression. The loader's wheels locked, and it slid rather than fell deep into the pit, a wild and filthy coaster ride turning almost sideways along a muddy slope towards a bottom that had filled with thick silt from the exploded water mains.

Too terrified to scream, Zachary held tight and shut his eyes. Like dark snowdrifts, huge glops of mud fell as he slid deeper, covering him and filling the cab until the loader came to an abrupt stop in a pool of black water maybe twenty-five feet down, probably more. Her motor still puttered, but Big Mama wasn't going anywhere. Zack opened his eyes long enough to see moonlight breaking through the aperture from high above, enough to illuminate muddy clumps the size of medicine balls breaking free from the slope in a surging cascade tumbling directly at him. It seemed a stupid thought, but he wished he could have seen Tiffany one more time.

*"Damn..."*

The mud pounded at him, pushing him from the loader's cab. In the pit's darkness, luminescent red eyes beaded in on Zachary. Something slithered alongside him in the liquid filth, curling itself around his torso and holding tight.

The real darkness came.

★ ★ ★

Jarmal stood confounded with the Colsons close behind, staring into the hole's blackness for any sign of the front loader. He hoped maybe the Colson kid had his wits about him enough to jump free, because all evidence indicated Big Mama had been swallowed whole in the expanded abyss before him. He aimed the flashlight into the pit and could make out the loader's top along the side slope. Mama's lights were still on, barely noticeable buried in mud. It appeared her motor was running weakly, but there was no sign of the boy.

*"ZACHARY COLSON! YOU DOWN THERE?"*

Jarmal's voice echoed in the cavern below, but he received no answer. He looked into the faces of the kid's parents and felt like he might throw up. Greg shouted his son's name while Jarmal aimed the light's beam in all directions, illuminating the rubble of Diamond Loop for any trace of Zachary. The beam caught two dark figures near the debris of what used to be the Brimley place.

"I think that's him," Jarmal said. "But... there's something with him..." Aiming the beam directly ahead, he saw what accompanied the Colson kid, and muttered *"Shit!"* He handed the flashlight to Greg. "No, he ain't alone. You wait here and keep your eyes open." He trod along the thin muddy path to the Brimley place, the garden shears held close. "Zachary Colson, that you...?"

In the moonlight Jarmal could see him clearly now. The boy seemed in some kind of funk, but under these circumstances, who wouldn't be? The kid didn't answer, oblivious to the slug creature that stood unmoving at his side like a sentinel.

"Zachary, can you hear me? Your parents, they're over there. You see your father waving the light? They're okay. Can you...?"

The slug creature nudged the boy, a curious move and one that suggested Besser had no time to waste. His shears snapped threateningly. "Move away, Zachary! Move away now!" He slowly approached.

"Jarmal?" Zachary's voice was weak, but he seemed okay.

"It's me."

As if awakening from a deep sleep, Zachary murmured, "...saved me. Pulled me out somehow..."

"Move away from that thing, Zachary. Slowly."

The slug creature moved closer to the boy. Eying the raised weapon, it seemed almost protective of him, but Besser dismissed the thought.

"You don't understand, Jarmal. I was in the hole, I... I almost died. And this thing, it managed to... somehow it brought me back ... Jarmal, it's smart, it's aware..."

Besser's shears snapped. The creature's mandibles extended, and now it stood defiant before Zachary.

*"Yoob..."*

The almost human sound threw off Jarmal's concentration. His overheated brain had to be playing tricks on him. "Zachary, step away. You hear me? I ain't goin' to ask again..."

"He's intelligent. Jarmal, he saved me. He doesn't want to hurt—"

*"...no...diem..."*

"Jarmal, please..."

Besser charged forward with the garden shears held high. Shouting like some banshee warrior, he buried the twin blades deep into the slug creature's brain. It shrieked only once, but it was a maddening sound. Large eyes blinked wildly, then filled with blood. Turning briefly to the boy, it fell dead on the spot.

"You killed him! Jarmal, you don't understand what—"

"Fuck what I don't understan'! Let's go!" He pulled the dripping shears from the creature's brain and carried Zachary in one arm through the ruined terrain to where his parents stood, a journey of a few hundred yards that was the longest of his life. Zachary choked back tears the whole way; Jarmal assumed these were the pent-up tears at having been rescued, but the tears came in earnest when the boy saw his parents. Eden grabbed her son and practically smothered him.

"My God, Zack. I thought we lost you!"

Zachary swiped his eyes, saying nothing of the past few minutes. "I'm okay, Mom. Tiffany's okay too. We—"

Besser interrupted. "Hate to break up the reunion, folks, but—"

He took the flashlight from Greg and sent its beam into the hole. "I may be able to pull Mama from down there. Her motor's still purring. A little feeble, prob'ly waterlogged, but she may be able to dig herself out if I can get down there. We can't go footin' it out of the Loop on our own. Them things are everywhere, and the Loop natives ain't friendly." He looked along the slope of the sinkhole. "I think I can slide down, if I don't drown myself in the mud 'long the way. Angle's sharp, but maybe—" He handed the shears to Greg, turned to Zachary. "You still got that gun?"

Greg turned to his wife, then to his son. *"You have a gun?"*

"Long story, Dad. Later, okay?" Then to Jarmal, "It may be no good anyway. It's all mud covered." He pulled the pistol from his backpack and handed it to Jarmal.

"Those things..." Eden said. "They're still in our house. Suppose they come out?"

Zack turned to Jarmal. "They don't like the light."

"Fair enough," Jarmal said, handing the flashlight back to him. To Greg and Eden he added, "Mama's lamps are on — She's runnin', and I'll bring her back. And you two got your pillowcase full of goodies. Stay away from that hole. Ground ain't steady near here, what little there is."

Zachary's head seemed somewhere else. He spoke low to Besser, "You killed one of the good ones, you know. That one back there, he was okay. He wasn't a monster."

"There ain't no good ones."

"Suppose that gun doesn't work? Then what?"

"It worked once. Anyway, we'll find out soon 'nuff." Jarmal shoved the pistol into his work pants. Crouching alongside the lip of the sinkhole, he dropped himself in for the long slip-slide to the bottom and disappeared into the darkness.

The night remained oppressively hot, but still the Colson

family huddled close. The silence from the sinkhole was terrible, but the waiting was much worse. Then, from deep inside the pit came echoes of the loader sputtering. Jarmal must have managed to start digging out. Big Mama made a roaring racket for a few minutes, but then silence returned and lingered.

Greg and Eden looked at each other, said nothing.

Jarmal's shout came from the pit, or maybe it was a scream.

Then came the shot...

Jarmal Besser's descent didn't go exactly as planned. He hadn't counted on the sharp rocks and debris jutting through the mud on the way down, and a good portion of his skin didn't make the entire journey. His body twisted and tumbled in painful contortions, and on his belly, he headed face first towards the pit's bottom. He could easily have been gutted like a trout, but it didn't happen. Somehow the pistol remained in place, and sloshing through the muck, he climbed aboard the loader, surprised he had made it.

With her huge tires and back end half submerged, Mama's engine sputtered and coughed like a consumptive hag, but she was running. If he could bring her back to life, Besser knew Mama's diesel propulsive engine would rival a locomotive's. He knew also that if anyone could pull her out using the loader's bucket to dig a path to the surface, he could. It might take a short while, but it was doable. This he told himself and tried hard to believe as he slid behind the mud drenched controls.

"Dime in the coffee cup," he muttered to himself.

The loader kicked up mud and silt, but she moved. The incline was much too sharp for a successful climb, but with a little digging Jarmal could do it, assuming he didn't start a mudslide and turn this place into his own grave. He set the bucket to work, filled it with great mounds of dripping mud, and went for more.

*"YES!"* He fist pumped the small victory, a Tim Tebow moment, scoring another one for Philly's Birds. Already, he had plowed a small path as easily as through a newly fallen snow, and Jarmal went for his third bucketful assured and hopeful, even smiling.

His smile disappeared when he saw what wriggled from the mud inside the loader's bucket. Mama had scooped three of the bastard slug things right out of the dirt, and raised high above Jarmal, they seemed good-sized snakes peeking over the bucket's toothy edge prepared to spill on top of him. He thought fast and hit the control valve, dumping the squirming crew back into the mud. The three lay twisted and dazed as Mama's bucket came down heavily upon them, smashing the filthy shits into black jelly that sank back into the sediment.

*"Damn!"* Wiping his forehead, Jarmal reached for the controls again. Illuminated by the glowing panel, a smaller slug-thing the size of a cigar sat on the switch, its belligerent hooks poking at him as if the creature were some overfed scorpion. The thing must have dropped from the scoop unnoticed, but how it arrived didn't matter. Jarmal reached for the pistol, hoping to smash the fucker with its grip if he could manage not to blow his own head off doing it. Holding the long barrel, he raised the gun just as the slug-thing sprang into his face.

He tore at it as it tried to find its way into his mouth, but the snapping creature stuck to his flesh like thick tar and wouldn't budge. Its mandibles bore a hole through his cheek like a corkscrew and the thing disappeared inside his face, the creature's lumpy movement visible even through Besser's dark flesh. Jarmal felt it pulsate alongside his jaw, gnawing its way to his brain. He held his ears against what seemed a runaway train inside his head. His skull felt like it had imploded to mush.

**"Agggghhhhh!"**

Besser spun around. Three large creatures had climbed to the top of Mama's rear tires and were thumping at the glass of the cab. A fourth had made it to the driver's side, crimson eyes on the prize. Jarmal saw the protective glass splinter into a webwork of cracks.

He still held the gun, and the thought occurred that he didn't even know if the damn thing had any bullets left because he'd been too frazzled to check. The Colson kid had fired maybe twice. The weapon was a mud covered antique. Even fully loaded, it held fewer bullets than there were of these fucking creatures.

He repeated the words he had spoken to Zack Colson.

"We'll find out soon 'nuff..."

Jarmal placed the barrel of the ancient pistol into his mouth and pulled the trigger.

The Colsons heard the shot, but after a long silence from the hole Zachary broke the stillness. "I think Jarmal is dead."

Eden answered without seeming convinced herself, "You don't know that, Zack,"

"I was down there too, so I know that, Mom. There's dozens, maybe more—"

"There's one way to find out," his father added. Holding the flashlight he approached the periphery of the sinkhole. Eden held her son tighter.

"Jarmal told us the ground is unsteady, Greg. Maybe you'd better not—"

The spongy surface near the opening seemed like it could give at any moment, and Colson's loafers sank to his ankles. He aimed the light's beam downwards. "I think I see the loader's head lamps. Motor's running, but—" He aimed the beam in every direction inside the pit. "—but I don't see Besser. That loader isn't moving."

Eden added, "Maybe it's stuck. Maybe Jarmal is trying to somehow—"

"Jarmal is dead," Zachary repeated. "He tried the kill one of those things, and the others got him. He fell into the water, and they're probably eating him right now. At least his brains. Just like they're going to do to us."

Eden touched his shoulder. "Zack! Enough, okay? We're going to be all right." She handed Rocky to him. "You think this fur ball would ever let anything happen to you? She knows who feeds her."

Greg dug his loafer from the mud and caught his wife's eye. He took her aside, spoke low. "Pretend you're smiling, okay, because there's more of those things down there. The flashlight slowed them, but it isn't stopping them. We can't stay here."

Eden spoke to him through her forced smile. "There's probably a load of them all over the Loop by now. Greg, what can we—?" She saw Zachary watching them and shut up fast. She approached her son and stroked his cat. "Look how calm ol' Rocky is now. You think she'd let something like this bother her?"

"She's got nine lives, Mom. We've got only one."

Eden hugged him. "I'll give you mine, okay?"

A sound came from above, quickly followed by a wash of bright light. In the next moment Greg Colson waved frantically at the chopper overhead. On its side were three words: GLENN ECHOES RESCUE. His wife and son joined him, *"HERE! WE'RE DOWN HERE!!"*

"Thank God! Oh, thank God!" Eden said, and Zachary muttered the same thing himself. The helicopter spotted them and circled, descending slowly. A guy with a megaphone leaned out from the opened door.

*"We're sending a ladder down. Won't be more than a few feet to climb. You folks stay where you are, okay? We've got you."*

Eden hugged Zachary again. "You see? We're going to be all right. A few minutes..." She watched the ladder fall as the chopper hovered. "You go first, okay? Your dad and me, we'll be right behind." Zachary saw his mother reach for his father's hand and squeeze it. With that gesture, his world finally righted itself.

Zachary placed Rocky inside his back pack and made the climb into the waiting arms of a smiling red-headed State

Trooper. He scrambled into the chopper and found himself holding back tears. It definitely wasn't his style to cry — not anymore. He had done that only once despite all the crap of the past few days. Now here he was, saved, and he refused to lose it again. But the tears came anyway.

"It's okay, son," the Trooper said, as he helped Zack's parents into the craft. The chopper rose high over Diamond Loop. The place was smoking and looked like a war zone. Zachary turned to the other seats inside the chopper. Three passengers had been rescued, and an adult male lay sprawled on a stretcher in the rear. Two of the people seemed vaguely familiar; they were new neighbors he had greeted with morning hellos and evening waves, but Zachary didn't see anyone he knew well. A young girl seated alongside him looked about the same age as Tiffany, and she was probably pretty. It was hard to tell because, like himself, she sat caked in mud.

"A rough day for you folks, eh?" the pilot asked.

"You have no idea," Greg Colson answered.

The chopper headed towards the middle school's baseball field and already was descending for a landing.

"Hello," Zachary said to the girl. "These are my parents. Are you from the Loop?"

She stared blankly at him as if she'd lost the ability to speak, then stared at the ground below with the terror of a child on her first ferris wheel ride. Zachary knew what it meant to be in shock. He figured that's what happened with her.

"She hasn't spoken to any of us," the Trooper said. "We pulled her out of the sinkhole. All those busted water mains, she almost drowned. Don't know who she is, or where she—"

"Hello," Zachary tried again. "I haven't seen you around. I'm Zack. That's short for Zachary." He felt proud he had achieved this new found ballsiness, and he hoped the girl hadn't seen him cry to spoil that image.

"Hello," she said to Zachary. The red-headed Trooper and the Colsons caught each other's surprised glance. The young woman's single word was weak, but she managed a twitching smile. Her voice could have belonged to a child, yet when her eyes set on the boy, she seemed anything but childlike. "Hello, Zachary. My name is Ri. That's short for Riona…"

# CHAPTER TWENTY-SEVEN

## SLUDGE-THINGS: July, 2015
## TIFFANY: SINKHOLES AND ASSHOLES

### "Nuh-huh, Taffy..."

The camera loved Tiffany Leone. She knew this, everyone who knew her knew this, just as they knew how Tiffany seized any opportunity for attention she could find. If this was overzealous ego, then so be it, and she used it to her advantage. Active in the Dramatics Club, captain of the cheerleading squad, during her younger years her proper place always was front and center. Her late father used to brag that the glow of the spotlight was in his daughter's blood, but she would correct him: "No, Dad, it's in my DNA and in the marrow of my bones." It wasn't far from the truth. By college, Tiffany's pursuits had turned academic (discounting her various exploits as Taffy Licks), and media journalism caught her interest. Here was the chance for a legit career and major camera time, the best of both worlds.

Tiffany planned to make the most of her opportunity on the eleven o'clock news, even if tonight's debut would introduce her as both mud-covered and disheveled. But there remained one problem with Taryn E. Friedman's lead story coming out of Diamond Loop: There was a much bigger story than Friedman's sinkhole rescue piece, much bigger than anyone could imagine. And Tiffany Leone, at this moment, had no way to prove it.

Those who knew the truth were nowhere to be found. The slug-things (no, they were fucking slug *monsters*!) were sneaky bastards, concealed in the darkness of night and in the abyss they had created under the posh suburban community. Concealed also was their ability to extract what they took from the Brimleys, from Jessie Moss, and from Sergeant Wally Smith. They stole those people's very souls, sucked them out from their frontal lobes like a 7-11 Big Gulp — but to accomplish *what?* The answer wasn't difficult to figure.

*...To use that human part of them, like H.G. Wells' damned Morlocks, of course! To learn, to evolve! That's what Zachary Colson would have said. "Nature — it's weird sometimes," he had told Tiffany when they met, and tonight had proven the kid was right.*

Wasn't the most basic law of nature just one thing — to survive? Wasn't that what these ugly slug fucks were trying to do, unfortunately on Diamond Loop's turf? Hidden by night, those creatures were probably crawling all over the Loop right now, but by morning they would disappear back into their crevices like the prehistoric roaches they probably were.

Tiffany knew she was sitting on top of one huge news event that would have made the guys at *60 Minutes* envious. There had to be proof nearby. Zachary and Jarmal Besser's rescue mission on Big Mama could result in something tangible that would offer that proof, or maybe some determined neighbor would make it out alive from the cul-de-sac's debris to break the story. But here Tiffany became brutally honest with herself.

She figured Glenn Echoes would be sending a rescue chopper over Diamond Loop when it appeared safe from further gas line explosions. Rescued neighbors would talk about the slug monsters, assuming those creatures hadn't sucked the grey matter from their skulls. Reporters would fall over each other for their stories, a good thing, of course, excepting one small consideration. This was her chance of a lifetime, Tiffany understood this. And...

*...and during Taryn E. Friedman's eleven o'clock spot, Tiffany Leone planned to first break the real story about the Diamond Loop sinkhole.*

★ ★ ★

Tiffany had no desire to return to the subterranean world of the slug creatures, but if she hoped to find evidence of them, she would have to put her investigative talents to the test. The gas explosions had probably sent those maggoty things scattering underground in every direction. That meant they could be anywhere below, hidden and undetected within a short radius near the Diamond Loop development. The Loop, after all, was a cul-de-sac, a contained area where the slug-things, undetected, could risk sampling the local inhabitants. Such plentiful hunting grounds would prove more difficult away from the Loop's fish-in-a-barrel layout.

Tiffany checked her camcorder in her Harley's glove box. It looked good to go, and she still carried the old pistol in her pack. She had a few hours before go-time on the Channel 6 news, and although she had promised Friedman an exclusive at the excavation site, she hopped onto her bike with a plan to make that news spot rival the shooting of bin Laden, or at least the birth of Kate Middleton's fucking baby. **MONSTERS AMONG US**, she pictured as the morning's headline, and she had to smile even if the story itself was grim. All she needed was her own video of even a small creature, and voila! — *PROOF!*

Firing up her Harley, Tiffany had several stops in mind. Apple Grove Way led to Glenn Echoes' orchards, and that meant an abundance of food for the slug things, plenty of the windfall apples there for the taking. Failing that, there was the sewage disposal plant on Wellington River, a likely sludge-filled place that could serve as a virtual water park for the slug-fucks. And there were grates and sewer openings along the way, certainly possibilities for the curious bastards to peek their ugly heads through. But Tiffany dismissed all those places when, stopped at the light, she spotted the half opened manhole partially hidden by shrubbery near the small park off Apple Grove Way. It was an odd thing to see; any passerby certainly would have recognized the danger and reported it, or at least someone would have managed to close it. Then again, much of Glenn Echoes' curious citizenry were at the excavation site tonight.

Tiffany snapped into investigative mode. Maybe someone had the same idea as she had, someone who figured the sewer below Diamond Loop might be a good place to catch one of the suckers — or maybe kill a few. (...and wouldn't it be someone who knew the underground system well? Someone like — *like Fred Reefe, whom no one had seen since the close of the working day!)* Tiffany looked around, spotted a discarded crowbar in the nearby shrubbery — the tool of a worker! If that crowbar had been tossed, then whoever climbed down this hole must have carried a weapon with a lot more punch.

It seemed logical. Reefe knew about the slug-monsters and ventured into the sewers to find them, and he had access to enough power tools to make puppy chow of any slug fuck. Tiffany looked deep into the manhole, but it was too dark to make out anything. The cost of her camcorder had kept Taffy Licks twerking for many hours, but it paid off now because the cam had an infrared attachment for night shoots. Maybe she could chance climbing down a few rungs — nothing too risky, just enough to have a look around. Would Taryn E. Friedman expect her to do less?

Tiffany knew she smelled terrible enough already and was filth covered too. Tonight would be one hell of a photo-op for her. Well, then...

"Down the rabbit hole," she muttered.

She squeezed in through the half-opened hole without having to move the heavy cover. The stink of the dark water below stopped her before she made it to the third rung, and Tiffany had second thoughts about the wisdom of this decision. Aiming the infrared light through the tunnel she saw nothing suggesting a threat. Maybe another step down, or maybe two.

She heard something squeak, saw a tubby brown rat dart along the nearby pipeline. It ignored her, but still Tiffany gagged. Okay, this *was* a bad idea. Starting back up, she made it half through the aperture when she noticed three shadowy figures in dirty sneakers standing in the darkness. They surrounded the hole.

"Hello Taffy..." one guy said.

Another added, "I'll bet you'll want to show us your tits now, won't you?"

It took a moment to register. These were the three kids that had harassed her at the Colonel's chicken place yesterday, when Zachary had intervened. But Zachary wasn't here now, and these three punks were.

The big nosed kid spoke. "We recognized your Harley and saw you climb into the hole here. Just what the fuck are you doing at night in the sewer? Giving underground blow jobs?"

Fat Kid added his opinion. "Maybe you had something to do with those underground explosions over at Diamond Loop? A real bad ass, aren't you? Getting naked online give you some daddy issues, maybe? Pissed off at the world, are you?"

Tiffany tried climbing out, but Fat Kid put his foot on her head.

"Nuh huh, Taffy..."

"Look, guys, I don't have time to—"

"You don't smell real good now, so maybe you belong in the sewer," Ugly Big Nose added. "I wouldn't fuck you on a dare. Your little friend with the bucket of wings anywhere around? Tell the little creep I'm really enjoying his bike."

Pimpled Kid remained silent, but when Tiffany tried again to squeeze through, he pushed her back. Stronger than he looked, he unzipped his pants while his pals cheered him on.

*"Lick Taffy Licks! Lick Taffy Licks!"*

"Listen, you stupid pricks. There's something down this sewer that's really bad. That sinkhole at the Loop, it unearthed some—"

Now Fat Kid was whipping out his unimpressive man-hood.

"Stink hole? Is that what you said, cunt? You have a really bad stink hole that reeks like a sewer?" He bent down to let Tiffany have a good look at his junk, tried pressing it against her face. She considered taking a huge bite of his pencil dick, maybe even sinking her teeth into those sorry looking batwing testicles, but she lost her balance on the small wall ladder and tumbled backwards into the dark water below. It wasn't very deep, but it broke her fall and its stink was foul. Above, she heard the three boys laughing themselves sick. Struggling with the weight of the manhole cover, they managed to seal her in.

*"Fucking assholes!!"*

Tiffany still held her camcorder, and thank Christ it was waterproof. Pulling herself to her feet, she aimed the cam all around and looked through the viewfinder.

*(...damned morons...)*

She thought she saw something in the water, and turned her attention to the more pressing problem. "You ugly suckers are down here, aren't you? I know you are..."

*(Fuck!!)*

Something floated by, and for that moment Tiffany felt the ice travel up her spine. It wasn't alive, thank Christ. She reached for it, and held an orange colored work shirt, the same one Fred Reefe wore that afternoon a million years ago, but now it was shredded and filthy with dark stains she knew was blood. She had the sinking feeling this was probably all that was left of him.

Tiffany pulled out her cell phone, dialed Zachary's number. His face came on the screen.

"Where the hell...?" he asked.

"Don't say anything, Zack, just listen. You're at the school shelter, right? If I don't come back by morning, I'm under that small park, in the sewer. You may have to ask the police to come look for me. Okay?"

"What the fuck, Tiffany?"

*Something floating, near...*

"I can't talk." She hung up

She still had the antique gun that Zachary had given her. She pulled it from her pack, but the weapon was soaked.

A spongy object bumped against her leg. Fighting the urge to scream, Tiffany searched through the viewfinder again. A legion of wriggling lumps like muddy sharks appeared on the screen. Nearby, the dark water churned. There were too many of the slug things, but she aimed the pistol at the closest and pulled the trigger. It clicked dully, but nothing happened.

*"Oh damn..."*

Kicking up sprays of filth, a dozen creatures twisted through the sludge towards her.

# CHAPTER TWENTY-EIGHT

## RIONA AND ZACHARY, A WORKOUT IN THE GYM: July, 2015
## MIDDLE SCHOOL CONFESSIONS

*"I know these creatures..."*

Shortly before 10:00 p.m. the rescue chopper touched down on the Glenn Echoes Middle School field where a makeshift shelter had been set up inside the gymnasium for the Loop's displaced residents. Only a handful had been found, and these few were disoriented and silent. The chopper would return to the Loop area for more, but considering the area's devastation, prospects seemed grim. Disembarking, Zachary had made a new friend of the young woman who called herself Ri-short-for-Riona. A girl of few words, she didn't volunteer much, but she did listen to what Zack had to say. He liked that.

"...tossed a bucket of chicken wings on the ugly kid's head, but then the creeps stole my bike, and that was just the start of it. There was this girl I met at the KHC, and she rode a Harley, this girl Tiffany..."

Most of the residents had escaped with only the clothes on their backs, and for now the Colsons were homeless. Cots and blankets awaited those flown from the evacuated area, showers too and some clean clothing donated by Glenn Echoes residents and missions. Once showered and settled in, Riona (wearing possibly the most frumpy dress in the clothing bin) seemed interested hearing what the others had experienced, but no one appeared willing to share and she volunteered nothing about herself. Certainly, no resident mentioned dark slug-like creatures, but with no electricity to illuminate the Loop area, Zachary figured maybe they hadn't seen any, even with the occasional wash of moonlight. Maybe like his own parents, adults simply preferred to keep that kind of information to themselves for the time being. More likely, those who had seen the slug-things hadn't lived long enough to talk about it.

Zachary joined Riona at the far end of the gymnasium, where she had pulled her cot far past the basketball court's center circle, some distance from the other people. He held Rocky, but the cat seemed to make the girl uncomfortable and she backed away.

"Not a cat person, huh?"

"Animals scare me."

Rocky seemed just as scared of her. Fortunately, the cat seemed the only pet in the place since not many people made it out. Zachary placed Rocky on the floor where she promptly curled up and fell asleep.

"You're not from Diamond Loop, are you? How come you were in the area?"

Riona considered the question. "I was lost."

"Are you a runaway?

"I didn't run."

She didn't seem to understand. The girl wasn't local, that was certain; her strange accent confirmed that. But Zachary needed to talk and she was a good listener.

"I'm supposed to attend this school in the fall. I never saw this gym when they gave us new kids orientation a few weeks ago. It looks decent. See, my family just moved here."

"I had a father a long time ago. Aidan Hannigan, he was. He — he died. I didn't understand about fathers then. I was so young, and I never really knew my mother." The girl shook her head as if she didn't believe her own words. "What are these markings on the floor, Zachary?"

She had to be yanking his chain. "That? It's a basketball

court. That circle, it's where the two teams jump for the ball, and there's the foul line. Damn, don't tell me you don't know this stuff." But Riona clearly *didn't* know what he was talking about. "Fuck it, it doesn't matter."

There seemed something sad and touching about this girl. Like a frightened forest animal uncertain of a man's trustworthiness as it approached, she had risked being honest with him, and this encouraged Zachary to do the same.

"Can I share something with you, Riona? I'm not sure what these other people saw tonight, but I know what *I* saw in that sinkhole. My parents too. Maybe it sounds too crazy for these people to talk about. I guess when something traumatic like those explosions happens, it's hard to think straight or to believe your own eyes, especially in the dark when you're scared shitless."

"I was shitless too. I saw something also — in the sinkhole, like you called it."

The girl spoke with an inflection Zachary couldn't place, but she had a childlike directness that he liked. "What did you see?" he asked.

She shook her head. "You tell first."

He was about to, when his cell phone chirped. Tiffany's image came on its screen.

"Don't say anything, Zack, Just listen. You're at the school shelter, right? If I don't come back by morning..."

"What the...?"

Tiffany explained her whereabouts and hung up. Zachary turned back to Riona. The girl stared at him as if the boy had performed some astounding magic trick.

Zachary spoke very low. "Okay. That was my friend Tiffany. She's about your age and maybe a little insane — well, I'll explain about her later. What we saw is kind of nuts, but I swear it's true. See, there's these ugly black things out there — Tiffany and my parents and I, we all saw them. I don't know what they are. Here, take a look."

Holding out his cellular that had somehow survived his muddy adventures, he showed her the video of the rat-swallowing creature in the excavation. Riona seemed more curious than amazed, more intrigued by the phone itself. Zachary found a nearby outlet and pulled the charger from his backpack. "Thank Christ the electricity is still on here. Don't know how long that will last."

Riona watched him, seeming to have no idea what he was doing, but she muttered, "Yes."

"Anyway, those things were probably stirred up by the digging and then by the gas explosions. They're like worms but bigger than jungle snakes. I don't know where they came from, but they made our neighbors crazy, probably killed some of them. Other people maybe saw them, but they're probably dead, or will be. The air conditioning has been shut off for the summer and that probably will make people here a little testy, not a good thing in an already stressful situation. Shit, I'm not telling this real good, am I?"

"I like you, Zachary." Riona tossed the non-sequitur at him as if she believed every outrageous thing he'd just told her.

Zack liked this girl too. He moved closer and risked telling her everything; she listened without saying a word. When finished, he asked, "You believe me, don't you? You saw the video. Others will believe too when those floating dead slugs start showing up, don't you think?"

"They won't be there, Zachary. The dead ones, I mean. The sun makes them go, the heat, the light..."

"I don't follow you."

"Can I share about me now?"

Her offer seemed remarkable from someone so secretive earlier.

"Sure."

"Just listen, okay? This is difficult to explain. I know these creatures well, Zachary, these *slug-things,* you call them? Even the one you say rescued you — there are others like that, you know. I've seen real slugs under the ground. The creatures you saw tonight, they're not slugs. They're smarter than those muddy ugly things because they're not from here. They need to survive. They need a home. That's not hard to understand, is it?"

"Roaches want to live in my mom's kitchen. That doesn't mean we should let them."

"It isn't the same. Do you eat what you kill, Zachary?"

He didn't know whether to laugh. Riona sounded serious, so he didn't. "Someone else kills what I eat. I have nothing against cows or chickens, but I'm no vegan." Riona looked at him, confused. "It means — shit, it means I like a good burger, all right?"

"Well, there you have it, don't you? You need to survive. Every living thing does. So you eat your burgers and chickens, and tomorrow for breakfast maybe it will be bacon and eggs, and you will live another day and not think about cows or chickens."

"The slug-things are eating *us!*"

"Only the good parts, Zachary."

Maybe she was putting him on, or maybe the girl had lost some brain cells during the last few hours. Zachary considered himself a decent judge of character, and she didn't seem the type to yank his chain. Like Tiffany had opened up with him from the start, maybe Riona felt confident sharing with a stranger those things she might not have shared with anyone else, those things she *couldn't* share. In her own way, Riona's openness reminded him of Tiffany. Zachary studied the girl's dark eyes to catch any glimmer of deceit. He saw none.

"They're from another place, these 'slug-things.' I know they frighten you, but I know what they are, I understand them. I'll show you something, but you have to promise not to tell."

"Okay."

"Say you promise."

"I promise."

"Swear?"

"All right, all right. I swear."

She turned away from any probing eyes so that only Zachary could see, twisting her face into a distorted grin that made Zachary shiver a little. For a moment nothing happened. Then, the sharp points of dark mouth hooks appeared on either side of her lips, but they disappeared quickly. Zachary immediately recognized those machete-like mandibles.

"I'm much older than your Tiffany friend, Zachary. And there's something else. You won't like this."

"I'm not liking *any* of this!"

Riona frowned. "I caused what happened tonight."

*"Shit, Riona!!"*

"Shhhh..."

*"Jesus! You're one of—?"*

"Remember, you promised. You swore."

"What are you, like their queen? Some fucking queen bee that rules the hive?"

"Something like that."

Zachary struggled for breath. "Okay, okay. Explain all this to me, all right? This is a lot to take in." Her smile returned, but Zachary could never see this stranger the same way. He moved closer, whispered. "Tell me everything, okay? I mean *everything...*"

Riona did.

Someone wheeled a television into the gym, and the small crowd formed a semicircle near the screen to watch the eleven o'clock news. Zachary and Riona lingered behind the rest. Sure enough, the lead story came from Diamond Loop. Taryn E. Friedman remained near the excavation site still wearing her mud stained summer skirt.

*"...no additional details since we first reported the gas line explosions, although police report that casualties are expected, according to..."*

The rescue helicopter appeared onscreen still hovering over the cul-de-sac. That meant no additional survivors had been spotted.

Where was Tiffany? It wasn't her style to pass up the opportunity for journalistic exposure. The field reporter didn't look happy with Tiffany's no-show interview for what would have been Friedman's exclusive.

*"...a few residents have been evacuated by rescue helicopter to nearby Glenn Echoes Middle School. Area residents have been warned to remain indoors because of natural gas leakage in the region..."*

"This is very bad, isn't it, Zachary?"

"Something's wrong. Tiffany wouldn't stand up the woman who was her mentor, she would never miss her shot at appearing on—" He stopped himself. "Damn! She wanted proof! She thinks like a journalist! She went after those things herself!"

Riona lowered her voice. "No, Zachary. Away from that hole, she won't find them."

Onscreen, from Friedman, *"...there's been speculation of sabotage..."*

"Tiffany is smart. She'll find them, or they'll find her! I don't have a good feeling about this. You said you talk with them, that they understand you, and you understand them?"

"Not with words. It's hard to explain."

"It isn't safe for them here either, you know. Once they're discovered they'll all be killed. There are weapons worse than guns."

"I didn't know that this would be so awful, all this death and pain. I had to see for myself before I understood, Zachary. I didn't know—"

"Tiffany, she's searching for them. She's in — *God!* — she's in the sewer nearby. Can you stop them, make them not hurt her?"

"I don't know where your friend is, how to find her."

Zachary thought that over. Police had surrounded the gymnasium, and groups of reporters appeared on the television screen just beyond the school's doors. For tonight the entire community of Glenn Echoes was on lockdown because the periphery around the disaster area had the potential for more danger. Leaving the school could be a problem.

"Her Harley! Tiffany told me she was at that small park near here, climbed into some manhole to look for them!" Riona stared at Zachary, confused. "Harley. It's a motorcycle. A manhole, it's — it's — shit, it doesn't matter. She's somewhere in the sewers! Under the ground near here! Can you find her?"

"No, not her. But I can find *them*."

Riona headed for the door.

# CHAPTER TWENTY-NINE

## RI-PLACEMENT: July, 2015

"...a ridiculous question... "

*Tonight they came for this young woman, the Wogslûk.*
*She is the one.*
*The female was near and she was alone.*
*Frightened, as expected.*
*Ri has gone, probably dead with the others.*
*This new female — human, like Ri.*
*Young and strong.*
*Theirs now.*

★ ★ ★

It wasn't a dream or even a nightmare. Whatever it was, it felt real. The confining space allowed no room to move or breathe. If this was her death, Tiffany's only thought was that she wished she had been cremated, her ashes safe and secure inside a beautiful golden urn. Anything but this...

She had passed out as in one of those old-time horror films where the young girl shrieks and then faints, although Tiffany had no time to scream before they were on her. That was the last thing she remembered. Now she couldn't move, wrapped tight head to toe as if mummified in thick cellophane. She was alive, although not by much. Even her eyelids felt glued shut, but she managed to open them. How long had she been out? Hours? Days?

Swathed in a silken straitjacket, she had only a dim view of where she was. She could make out the dark tunnel, and the thick smell remained strong enough to seep through the silvery wrapping around her. The raw stench of the sewer brought her to full consciousness, and she realized that, in this dank underworld, she had been cocooned alive.

Some rational thought came. It wasn't reassuring. She remembered that Zachary had explained how maggots left the goo of the pupa to become flies. If she ever emerged from inside this chrysalis, would she have metamorphosed into some-thing else? Tiffany felt certain nothing resembling a butterfly would be leaving her larvae prison.

Her mouth felt sealed by sticky threads, but who would hear her scream anyway? Somehow, she could breathe, a marvel in itself. Tiffany had the absurd regret that she hadn't been more religious so that she could have prayed for death.

A murky shadow appeared nearby. No, there were two shadows. People! Who in their right mind would be in this place? She could hear their voices but couldn't make out words. The two tore the encasement, ripping at the silken barrier with their bare hands. Words slowly bled through.

"Is she alive?" A woman's voice.

"Can't tell. She's not moving." A man's voice. No, a young boy's.

"What *is* this thing?"

"Keep tearing! I think she's breathing!"

The silken cocoon tore open, and the pair caught her as she fell. Even the stink of the sewer offered her welcome air and she inhaled deeply, then almost coughed her guts out. The strangers lowered her to her feet into the sewer's shallow liquid. One slapped her lightly to bring her back to reality. Too dizzy to see them clearly, Tiffany finally stood on her own.

The boy spoke first. "Are you okay? How'd you get into this thing?"

Staring at her two rescuers, Tiffany managed a choked "Who—who are—?""

"I think I know how she got into this," the girl said. "Those creatures must be down here. We need to get out of this place before they find us."

Tiffany saw the long barrel of the boy's rifle. "You—you have weapons. You know what's down here, then."

"We know," the boy answered.

Tiffany believed they were safe, at least for now, because the creatures seemed to want her alive. "Then you know about those slug-like things too? They put me inside this cocoon trap, or whatever it was. I thought for sure I was done. I thought — Hell, it isn't important what I thought. *What are you two doing down here?*"

"I wish I could answer that myself, ma'am," the boy said. "It's a long story — not likely one you'll believe. I'm not sure I believe it myself."

Tiffany smirked, wiped goo from her hair. "After what I've been through, I'll believe any damn thing you lay on me." She extended her hand. "Sorry if I'm sticky. I'm Tiffany Leone. Can't remember much about what got me here. Those creatures were the last thing I saw."

"Cole McKenna," the boy said. "This here is Miss Melissa Monahan. Sorry the rest of the cavalry couldn't make it. We heard an explosion nearby and found *you*."

"Another explosion? Maybe more gas mains went. These slug-things down here must've chewed through them. They found me, somehow cocooned me here and—*Shit!* My back pack is gone!"

"Slug things?" The boy turned to Melissa. "So, they *are* here."

"You know about them too?" Tiffany asked. "My cam, my phone, all my videos — every fucking thing is gone because of them!"

The boy and the young woman looked curiously at each other. Melissa hesitated before she spoke. "Can I ask you a ridiculous question, Miss —Tiffany, is it?"

"I have a few ridiculous questions of my own."

"That's good," Melissa Monahan said, "because Cole and I were wondering what year this is?"

# CHAPTER THIRTY

## PAGLIACCI AND OTHER CLOWNS: July, 2015

### *"Voila, boys!"*

**O**nce they're discovered, they'll all be killed! Riona doubted the Colson boy's words would prove true. Still, there would be death, all right.

She couldn't choose sides. How could she? '**Slug-things**,' Zachary called them, but she had lived among them for so long that she belonged to them. Young Zachary Colson and his people were not the enemy. She understood that now. Maybe the thing to do was to find another place to call home — for them, and for herself. 'Fold 'em,' she remembered her father saying when holding what he called a busted poker hand. She didn't understand much about cards, but she certainly grasped the concept of losing.

That hole in the mountain tunnel, it had filled with some mysterious light that seemed more of a doorway to — to where? To this place, yes, because the dryness of the empty desert town of Trementina had not been the place for them. But neither was this Diamond Loop. She didn't need to understand the strange pit that led to this place; she simply relied on its ability to take her and the others away from here. If that doorway remained, if she could find it, then maybe it would deliver them to where they did belong. All living things belonged **somewhere.**

"You're one of them," Zachary had said, but he was wrong. True, she wasn't human, not anymore. But she never was one of **them** either. The truth was, she didn't know what she was. But she knew what many of them were, the ones that spoke with fractured sounds that seemed almost words. No, she was not one of them, but they were part of **her!**

*Riona couldn't tell Zachary this. She couldn't explain it so he would understand. Those slug-things (she hated the term!), she had delivered hundreds of them, perhaps thousands. Those crawling creatures craved Man's world and knew only one way to attain it. She didn't know if the word 'love' applied to her feelings for them. But one thing she did know. They had come from her own body, and she knew only that she was their mother.*

*She wasn't human. Not anymore.*

*But she couldn't choose sides.*

*How could she?*

"...but I can find them," Riona promised Zachary as she headed for the door. Whether she could stop them now, whether she could protect the boy's female friend, she wasn't as certain. She headed towards the school's exit, but leaving the building wouldn't be easy. Two stern faced armed guards stood by the closed door as if the school were a prison. The younger officer approached her.

"Sorry, Miss. We need the Diamond Loop people accounted for, and the surrounding area may not be safe just yet. The air could be combustible. Gas explosions are tricky, and the area may be contaminated with pollutants. Restrictions are only until morning, okay?"

"Yes, morning." Riona hadn't seen the rising sun for as long as she could remember, but she didn't feel certain she wanted to. She nodded as if she understood the man, although many of his words she never had heard before. She knew only that she had to think fast.

"My father lives in the Loop and he isn't here, and I—I..." She tried falsifying tears and watched the uniformed man's expression transform into a sympathetic smile. Riona realized she'd had his attention for other reasons than her panic owing to her alleged missing father. She was an attractive young woman even if her hair remained wet and the donated dress she wore didn't fit. Her sharpened senses detected his arousal.

"The chopper is searching right now, Miss. They'll find your father."

If she could get close enough to give him a little jab — not enough to hurt him, just enough of a hook pinch to put him out for a while — then, she could make a run for it. Probably the nearby guards wouldn't shoot her, but the men carried guns and she would have to be quick.

"I'm not feeling well. I think I might—" Riona fell into the young man's arms, a calculated risk. He didn't notice her study the thin vein in his temple, didn't see the sharp tips of her mandibles extend like small sabers.

From the nearby gym, some other man, one of the Loop's rescued, sang out loudly. The guard became distracted and turned from her. The words coming from the singer sounded strange and badly out of tune."

**"Ridi Pagliaccio, sul tuo amore infranto! Ridi del duol che t'avvelena il cor!"**

The girl's mandibles quickly disappeared. The young man shook Riona lightly to bring her back. The other guard peeked into the gym and called out, "It's only some geezer singing opera, Jimmy! *Italiano!* Sounds like he's doing Pagliacci—" A woman's screams interrupted him, and he looked inside the gymnasium again. "Christ! The old guy is having convulsions on the floor!"

*...and the man kept singing!*

The officer named Jimmy allowed Riona to stand on her own, steadying her although she wasn't at all wobbly. "You okay? We have to go!" The two guards disappeared and others followed.

"Polly-ah-chi..." Riona repeated to herself with no idea what the word meant. Her attention returned to her task. The school's exit leading to the ball field remained unattended. The thick door was heavy, but she pushed hard.

**"Ridi Pagliaccio, sul tuo—-"** The old guy's personal opus from the gymnasium cut off cold.

But already Riona had gone.

★ ★ ★

Swirling vapors from the natural gas explosions followed a high-tension wire from Diamond Loop that led to the small park less than two miles from the cul-de-sac. A thick smog of gas crawled along the wire, a flickering fuse that threatened to become an all-consuming flamethrower at any point. The fuse required only a nearby spark to turn a combustible object into a keg of dynamite capable of catapulting everything nearby sky high. Three boys hoping to drive off Tiffany Leone's Harley provided that spark.

Earl, the fat one, had the idea to hot wire the girl's cycle, as it would prove a much bigger prize than the nerdy kid's bike they had pilfered the day before. His two friends quickly agreed but had no idea how to do it. Nelson, the pimpled one and the most mechanically savvy of the three, did.

The boys watched the lights of the rescue helicopter as it headed towards the Diamond Loop evacuation area. Glenn Echoes' police department had their hands full tonight. That made the boys' task easier.

"Lend me your pen knife, Norm," Nelson addressed the big nosed kid, and he set himself to work prying off the Harley's ignition cap. The cap was welded very tight, but the three had all the time in the world and the Harley's owner wouldn't be escaping the sewer any time soon. Finally, the cap fell, and Nelson twisted the ignition and battery wires together to send electric power back to the bike's ignition. Nothing happened. Nelson shrugged, twisted the red and green wires again, and finally the wires sparked. The shock knocked the pimpled kid flat on his ass.

Fat Earl grinned. "Best out of three?"

Big nosed Norm sniffed the air. "You smell something funny?"

"Earl probably farted," Nelson offered. He gave the red and green connections another try, and this time sparks shot upwards near the vapors surrounding the high-tension wire. The flash startled the three, but the Harley's motor revved loud and clear. "Voila, boys!" Nelson said with a huge smile. "Now let's see what this baby can—"

It was the last thing the pimpled Nelson ever said as a thunderous blast furnace sent him and his pals twenty feet into the air. Earl's ass struck the promenade dead on and snapped his spine in half, while Norm's ugly big nose morphed into a misshapen melted candle along with most of his face. For a full three seconds, Nelson managed to stay in one piece as he landed in the bushes; then the blown manhole cover crashed down and crushed his skull.

*Riona pushed the exit door and was out...*

She hadn't admitted it to Zachary, hadn't really admitted it to herself until now. She was scared.

Zachary had practically begged her to protect his friend against the — ***slug things***. The words echoed in her head. Riona knew they were not that at all. She knew also that they would return soon, that next time they wouldn't be satisfied with the small patch of homes called Diamond Loop. They would want the entire town and its people unless she stopped them.

*(...if she **could** stop them...)*

She pressed past a group of reporters and disappeared into the darkness of the ball field. Even the humid night air of Glenn Echoes beat the musty confines of the middle school's gymnasium. Once onto the sprawling field, Riona took a deep breath of the summer breeze, allowing the sensation of freshly cut grass to fill her lungs. The familiarity of the earthy smell briefly strengthened her, but her invigoration didn't last. Something wasn't right. She felt dizzy and her stomach churned. Weakened, finding it difficult to breathe, she made it to the nearby stands and collapsed on a bench, hidden in the night's shadows.

"...*stop them*..."

Riona lay there for many hours. The rescue helicopter that touched down in the ball field during the predawn didn't spot her.

It carried a single mud-drenched passenger.

Surrounded by the phlegmy snorts of sleeping neighbors, Zachary Colson lay still on his cot. Two cops had carried out the elderly opera singing man, another victim of the Diamond Loop crazies. The old guy had gone pale on the stretcher and was probably already dead. Zachary hoped no other neighbors tonight decided to break into song.

Sleep finally came only because exhaustion did. In a strange bed surrounded by people acting strangely, Zachary's dream proved strange also...

### BOYS HAVE YERKERS, GIRLS DO NOT. GIRLS HAVE SERKERS, AND BOYS DO NOT.

*The dream's soundtrack features his own words, and the heavy drum beat seems the sort heard inside the sleazy strip clubs Zachary has seen only on cable. The thumping percussion reverberates inside the sleeping boy's brain.*

*Tiffany (no, she's Taffy Licks!) twerks on her pole again, gyrating to the drumbeat like a slithering snake. No pasties this time — Taffy is completely naked, but something about her is not so arousing. Her silky skin slowly morphs into something slimy and ugly.*

*"Yoob, Zachary. Me diem, yoob diem..."*

*Now a dark slug-thing has replaced Taffy, and the she-creature slithers along the stripper's pole deep inside some stinking sewer. She turns to Zachary, sees him. A vent beneath her tail opens wide (like a sinkhole!), making an ugly slurping sound. The creature speaks again — in Taffy's voice!*

*"No yoob, no Tiff-a-me..."*

### ...GIRLS HAVE SINKHOLES, AND BOYS DO NOT!

*The vent beneath the slug-thing spreads wide. She is giving birth, but she drops no eggs! Instead, a hundred tiny slug-things crawl from her. Seeing them spread on the floor*

*around him, dream-Zachary mutters, "No...no...impossible!"*
*...because each of the small slug-things has Tiffany's face...*

Zachary snapped awake. Bathed in sweat, he squelched his own scream, scratching at his body as if a hundred bed bugs crawled beneath his skin. Sleep no longer seemed an option. Grabbing his backpack and Rocky, he found Riona's empty cot on the far end of the gym and slipped hidden beneath its covers. He knew only one way to get through this night. Retrieving the old 1800's journal he had taken from the Brimley home, he snapped on the flashlight to have a look at what its author, Sister Margelle Mallory, had to say.

After its first page Zachary knew he wouldn't be putting the old nun's journal down any time soon. In some New Mexico town called Trementina the nun had seen the slug-things too, she and three others! *Wogslûk*, the Sister had christened them, her own fancy-assed term for what some old guy back then had called the Wag-sloogs. During the summer of 1866, the four had tracked them down to a train tunnel and tried blowing the fuckers up; following that, Margelle had spent the rest of her life hunting them herself. She had never found them again, nor had she found her three companions either; the Sister assumed the Wogslûk *had*. But the lapsed nun found her divine calling again *(praise Jesus!)*, thanks to those slime things she believed were sent from Hell. She raised some money and set up a mission where an old ranch had been, the McKenna Ranch — the source of George Brimley's gun collection and Sister Margelle's journal!

The born-again Sister's knowledge of the creatures may have seemed a bizarre coincidence, but Zachary didn't think so. Despite the seeming randomness of events, he believed a sense of purpose was operating. He'd been meant to find this journal, meant to find Riona Hannigan and the slug-things too, or whatever the old nun called them. A pattern was working here, and whatever game Fate was playing, she had chosen these cards for him, leaving it for him to play them out. One question beat all the others Zachary had, and it was a whopper.

*Why him?*

# CHAPTER THIRTY-ONE

**SISTER MARGELLE CONFESSES: July, 2015**

*"...a regular slug fest..."*

Morning took its time coming, but inside the Glenn Echoes Middle School's gymnasium the hour was impossible to determine. After the long night, Diamond Loop's newly homeless milled about, some even socializing. Most said little or nothing at all. From the school's kitchen wafted the smell of frying bacon as volunteers prepared breakfast for the Loop residents who had made it to the shelter.

Slipping in unnoticed, the mud-spattered young woman approached Zachary Colson's small cot, noticed the black cat nestled there, and shook the bedcovers.

"Are dreams of middle school camel toes dancing in your head under those sheets?" The boy poked his head from beneath the blankets. Tiffany Leone stood grinning at his bedside. "Good morning, Boy Wonder. Glad I didn't have to play 'Where's Waldo?' to find you. I see you made it out, but how come you and Rocky are camped so far from the other Loopers?"

Zachary pushed the tumble of hair from his eyes. "Long story. What time is it?"

"Almost time for Reveille. What's the military expression? 'Grab your cocks and put on your socks'? Can't go anywhere for another hour. The school is on lockdown until it's safe out there."

"I didn't hear from you after you told me where you were. Nothing."

"Lost my phone. It's probably inside some slug-tard's belly."

"Well, I should remind you that your blackface minstrel look is politically incorrect. Were you in that sewer all night? Aw, fuck it, you're safe." Smiling, Zachary reached to kiss her cheek but stopped. "*Pee-yeww, woman!* Who died?"

"Yeah, I need a shower, but I wanted you to take a whiff of me first. Got a hell of a story for you, real Rod Serling stuff if you promise not to think I've gone mentally deficient. I made a couple of new friends last night to add to our shared nightmare. Care to hear?"

"Oh yes! I want to hear all of it. I guess I should tell you *our* friend Jarmal, he didn't make it. Sinkhole got him, and those things crawling inside it. But he helped get me and my parents out. It was hairy."

"I'm sorry. He was an all right guy. We wouldn't be here if not for him. It looks like a few of your neighbors didn't make it out."

"Yeah, I'll fill you in later. You went looking for those slug-things last night, didn't you, you dope? Is that Eau de Sewer your wearing?"

"I love the smell of sewage in the morning. Your three Jar-Jar bicycle thieves trapped me underground with those things. Those slugs, they're all over the place."

"I figured that. They surrounded the Loop last night, crawling from that sinkhole. Speaking of which, look at this." Zachary held up the tattered journal. "You'll find this interesting and disturbing. I stayed up reading about this nun, Sister Margelle, from her journal I took—"

"Stole, you mean."

"Okay, stole. What's crazy is, this Margelle knew about the slugs doing their thing a hundred and fifty years ago. It's all here, a regular slug fest!"

Tiffany looked confused. "Zack, I heard that nun's name from the two who found me last night — a kid and a girl, Cole and Melissa. They appeared from nowhere and saved my ass, as if they had been taking a casual stroll in the sewer in the middle of the night! You're not going to believe—"

"Well, hold on to your teeth, Tiffany, 'cause I know their story. I skipped around the journal a bit — there's too much to read in one sitting, but I got the gist of it. Cole McKenna and Melissa Monahan, right? They hooked up with that nun along with an old guy named Hannigan, and the four went slug hunting. Found a nest of them in some tunnel. But that was in 1866! They're in this journal — both of them!

Tiffany's eyes widened. "I was with them last night!"

Zachary didn't appear surprised. "The nun, she knew them, and they saw what we saw. Sister Margelle—she called the slug-things Wogslûk—wrote how searching for those creatures led her back to God because she believed they must have come from Hell, but she got that part wrong because I found out where those things really came from. This girl with me in the chopper, Riona, she told me — *Riona Hannigan!* Sound familiar? Well, I met her tonight, and she's in the nun's journal too! Damn, everything is tied together."

Tiffany and Zachary stared at each other. "Something very squirrelly is happening here, Zack. Last night, maybe a dozen of those slug fucks —"

"—*Wogslûk* fucks..."

"...wrapped me like a human cannoli inside some silk-worm type of cocoon, but I've no idea what for. These two, Melissa and Cole, found me. The manhole cover blew off, the one I came through, and we found the way out. We heard the explosion, but they didn't want to go any further with me. The kid said they were looking for a way back. I had no idea what he was talking about, and they wouldn't tell me. But the girl asked me what year it was and said they weren't sure they had much time." Tiffany scratched her head. "'Time' seems the operative word here."

"That girl, Riona, had the same story. She says she learned about those Wogslûk things back when she was five. They came through some hole that just disappeared afterwards.

"You know this is nuts, right? Who in their right mind will believe any of this?"

"The nun's journal may be proof. And I have a video. You'll read the journal and we'll talk. I think you'll be interested in how it ends, but I won't ruin it with any spoilers. Anyway, how'd you know to come to the school?"

"Chopper saw me. Lights were searching all over, and I waved like crazy because my Harley was blown to shit and I didn't know how dangerous it was out there. I think those three goons from the Colonel's chicken place were dumb enough to hot wire my bike where the gas was thick. They looked very dead to me. There was plenty of dying going around last night, I guess. Maybe Cole and Melissa were right to stay in the sewer. This town isn't exactly Bedford Falls."

Zachary rifled through the journal's pages and pointed. "In the summer of 1866. Melissa Monahan and Cole McKenna got together with the Sister and with that old guy, Aiden Hannigan. They blew up some train tunnel trying to kill the Wogslûk things. Margelle searched for those creatures for the next thirty years until she died, set up a mission near some dirt water town, Trementina, where the McKenna Ranch used to be. She wanted to be buried there, so I guess that's where she is."

Tiffany leafed through the nun's book. "Cole McKenna, he's about your age, Melissa Monahan about the same as mine. They told me the Wogs-things came from some huge hole, a few holes, really. One was inside the exploded train tunnel — they didn't know what it was, just that it somehow brought them here. That's what they were looking for when I left them, some hole that lit up like a beacon. The girl said it was their only way back. So? Getting the heebie-jeebies yet?"

"Same as the sinkhole at the Loop, maybe? Same as what Riona said. There's a crazy connection working here, Tiffany, like history regurgitating on itself. Riona Hannigan sat on this cot last night. She's the old man's daughter, that guy Hannigan you mentioned. For someone a hundred and fifty years old, she looked damned good to me. Cleaned up, she could be the next Taffy Licks."

"Where is she now?"

Zachary shook his head. "Long story. She went looking for you — and for *them*. I can't tell you more than that, okay? I'm not sure I know what she's about."

Tiffany ran her fingers through sopping hair. "Curiouser and curiouser, Zack. This is even weirder than I thought. We have some notes to compare, you and me."

Zachary fanned the air with the old journal. "Yeah, we'll do that, but only if you take a shower first. No offense, girl, but *Yecch!*"

# CHAPTER THIRTY-TWO

## COMING CLEAN: July, 2015

### *"It's the cosmic surprise party!"*

**T**iffany bee-lined to the girls' shower room sporting a reek pungent enough that sniffing it on herself turned her stomach. Relieved that the school's showers remained empty, she slipped out of clothes she knew she would never wear again. She hoped this stench wasn't like the spray of a skunk that lingered for weeks, but if it persisted, at least she would get a seat on a crowded bus, assuming life in Glenn Echoes ever returned to normal. The warm water felt invigorating, and she enjoyed watching the mud dribble from her skin and disappear down the drain like a bad memory.

Soaping up, she broke into unexpected song, *"This is the way we wash our face, wash our face, wash our —!"* Water cascading through her hair, Tiffany shut up. What brought the song on? It was only a stupid kids' jingle, she told herself.

*(Everyone sings in the shower. It doesn't mean anything.)*

She continued with a little less enthusiasm, *"This is the way we scrub our tits, scrub our tits, scrub..."* and stopped again, turning off the water, addressing no one. "Yeah, that's probably what Jessie Moss told himself, and that Sergeant Smith." A disquieting thought occurred.

*(While she was cocooned and out cold, could one of the Wogs-fucks possibly have—?)*

Tiffany had no time to consider an answer. At her feet, the clogged drain belched and bubbled with soap. Sliding her foot across the duct to allow the rushing water through, she froze where she stood. A small slug creature the size of her thumb emerged from the froth. Before she could react, it pounced and clung to her ankle. She shook it off, but more surfaced. They were fast, and several already were scaling her leg. Brushing these off, she backed against the wall. But now other drains were spouting suds filled with them.

More tiny projectiles sprang on her. She shook her leg, but the new arrivals were more persistent, and they clung like leeches to her thighs and arms while some crawled on her stomach. She waited for the needle-point sting of a dozen mouth hooks, but that didn't happen.

*"Get off me!!"*

Her skin itching with their touch, the slug-things *(Wogslûk things!)* dropped to the shower floor hearing her voice, striking the wet vinyl like tossed marbles. Tiffany could only stare at them, astonished that they had found her again. Motionless, dozens huddled together in a dark heap and they stared back. Tiffany felt a strange and uncomfortable sensation, as if the ugly fucks were trying to get through to her, somehow attempting to reach her. She heard — *something*.

*("Yoob...yoob...")*

It was just random noise, high pitched and barely audible, but it also seemed more than noise. Tiffany shook the ridiculous thought from her head.

*"Go away!"*

They scattered quick as roaches, returning to the drains and disappearing within seconds. Tiffany stood cold and wet, unable to move, almost unable to breathe. She had no idea what had just happened, not immediately.

Then again, maybe she did.

They had understood her — no, they had *responded* to her — and something more strange than that...

Tiffany couldn't shake the thought that these tiny Wogslûk things had been waiting for her.

Inside the school lunchroom Zachary stuffed a mess of scrambled eggs into his mouth. Watching Tiffany in baggy jeans and a too-large t-shirt as she pushed her food around on her plate, he knew something was wrong.

"Not happy with the homeless look you're sporting? Maybe you were expecting Eggs Benedict?"

Tiffany smiled politely for the benefit of Zachary's parents nearby. "No, wiseass. I can't talk. Not here. I think the armored guards have left their posts. Let's you and me step outside." She took a perfunctory chomp of bacon, and they walked into the morning air towards the ball field. Already the sun shone and the day was heating up. Tiffany looked over her shoulder, although no one stood near.

"I saw them, Zack. They're here, our Wogslûk friends. A shit load of the smaller ones came from the shower drains. The buggers were all over me, but then they scattered off. The bigger guys can't be far behind."

"They scattered off?"

"I'm not sure why. They could've done a real number on me, but they didn't."

"Riona said she'd try to find them, scare them away from here." This was a minor lie, but Zachary had made a promise.

"Well, that didn't happen. How did your new pal intend to do that, anyway?"

Zachary shrugged. "Dunno. She claimed she had some experience with them as a kid back in Trementina, before she entered the Twilight Zone and arrived here. Don't put her down, Tiff. To tell you the truth, she reminds me of you. She's ballsy too."

"Well, her slug-fucks are probably still gathering in the school right now — or under it! Where did this Riona intend to find them? In the trees?"

"*You* found them, didn't you? I don't know where she went; she just headed out here to the ball field—" His eyes searched the area. Near third base the helicopter's rotaries started up, preparing for a morning fly-by over the Loop area. Zachary flagged the pilot, and shouting at the chopper's open door he described Riona to the cop at his side. The man said he would do what he could, but he didn't appear hopeful. After a night of searching, there seemed no one left to rescue and Zachary doubted the chopper would be coming back. Nearby, the stands were empty, and the two headed towards them.

Tiffany watched the helicopter circling overhead. "I'm so tired, Zack. I can't face those things anymore. Probably hundreds are still underground, and they're viscous fuckers. Diamond Loop looks like Beirut, and I don't know what we're supposed to do — or what we *can* do."

Zachary sat alongside her. "Eloi and Morlocks, Missy Tiff. We have to ask ourselves which we are. We can't just—" A low moan from the bleachers interrupted him. Zachary spun around, but he saw nothing. "I think someone's here!"

*"Unngghh..."*

He jaunted over several rows of seats, Tiffany following. The girl in the familiar frumpy dress lay hidden from the sunlight beneath a long bench, but something seemed very wrong. Her long dark hair had grayed, and it covered a face Zachary knew was Riona's, although she appeared frail and sickly. He brushed aside wispy strands of her hair to reveal translucent flesh, purple veins showing through her temples like broken blood vessels.

Tiffany covered her mouth. "Jesus, Zack! This is Riona? She looks — *old!*"

Somehow it was true. The girl had aged years in the few hours since she had left the school building, remaining alive only barely. Zachary leaned close to her. "Riona? Can you hear me?"

*"Ungghhh..."*

"Riona, it's me, Zack."

Her lips, lined with age, quivered. *"It's the sun, Zachary...Not good here...The air, sun, not good..."*

He grabbed the girl's waist. "We have to move her. We can't let her stay here."

Riona shook her head. "No, don't...Please...don't..." She looked at Tiffany, and her eyes grew wide. "You're—You're

Tiffany? *I know you!*"

Tiffany and Zachary exchanged glances. "That's impossible, Zack. She's delirious."

He tried to move her despite her protests, but the girl's body seemed made of straw. She reached to him, her arm raw boned and shriveled. "Tell her, Zachary. Tell your friend what I told you. You must! The others, they're near, and Tiffany... you're important to them!"

Her face blistered and her body twitched. The ragged material of her dress tore wide, revealing aged flesh that had split in grotesque tatters. Dark organs bubbled, rupturing like overcooked eggs and spilling from her in misshapen lumps. Riona heaved violently, blood the color of ink spurting as if every artery inside her had been severed. Nothing inside her seemed recognizable as human.

Tiffany turned away. "Zack, don't look!"

But Zachary looked.

Riona managed a low gurgle, her twisted expression disappearing in a crush of skin that lost the support of whatever skeletal structure remained. Imploding like a deflated water toy, her flesh wrinkled badly, then caved in folding over itself. A hissing dissolve of skin and bone liquified into a pile of sizzling oatmeal-like goo. On the hot cement, it ossified, turning to gray dust that blew off in the wind, leaving behind the old house dress. In under a minute Riona Hannigan was only a dark smudge.

Zachary watched the girl's wilted remains disappear. Minutes passed before Tiffany spoke.

"You shouldn't have seen that, Zack. It's not the kind of thing you'll want to remember."

He remained crouched alongside the dark ash, his eyes never leaving the crumpled old dress. "Just the death of the Wogslûk's queen bee, is all. I'm thinking this is what Riona wanted. I can't say I blame her."

"Maybe this is what happens when you spend years living in shadows and mud. Sunlight makes you shrivel up and die."

Zachary's eyes met hers. "She told me those Wogslûk

things need to be near water. They hate the light, but it's the sun they fear. That shower in the school, it kept Riona going a while longer, but then she came out here, and the morning sun, it just — *Fuck!*"

"Are you okay?"

Zachary remained lost in his own thoughts. "It's like Lo-Tsen leaving Shangri-La."

"Who?"

"From the novel *Lost Horizon*. Christ, Tiffany, don't they teach you anything in college? Lo-Tsen left Shangri-La, the place where people never aged, and once outside she immediately grew old and turned into a raisin."

"Well, I know Glenn Echoes isn't Shangri-La. Get off your literary pedestal for one minute and explain what happened here that Riona said you can tell me. She said I'm important to the slug-fucks. Why?"

Zachary got to his feet. "No idea. But she felt protective of them for some reason. She said they did to her what they tried to do to you — wrapped her up like a mummy and sprinkled some magic Wogslûk dust on her that kept her from growing old — or maybe it was magic larvae. Whatever shit it was, it worked — until now. They needed her, used her to learn about *us*."

"Us?"

"Us. You and me. Humans."

"She was one of them, wasn't she? I mean, if Riona really was Queen Slug-Fuck..."

"Hell no! She was born in that old Trementina place. But the slug-things wanted her, learned from her. Last night I heard one try to talk, but it was all garbled shit, 'Yoob boob foob,' some gibberish like that."

Tiffany's eyes opened wide with sudden interest. "Yes! I heard that in the shower!"

"They're smart — they picked up on what she said to them. But they could only manage that damned baby talk, so they communicated with her in other ways. Riona thought maybe they came from someplace that must've turned uninhabitable, maybe some planet going nova, some other galaxy over the rainbow we couldn't begin to know about that just went ka-blooey, Krypton-style. Even she didn't know where it was, or what it was. But I don't buy that *'Welcome-to-the-Outer-Limits, Earth-people. Don't-adjust-your-t.v.-set!'* bullshit."

"Did Riona know how her proteges got from Never-Never Land to here?"

"See, that was big reveal in her story. That hole your two friends in the sewer looked for, they couldn't know what it was. How could they? Their world was wagon trains, saloons, and horse poop in the streets. Riona didn't know either, even after she traveled through the thing. But *I* know what it was — or, what it *is*. It couldn't be anything else, and it's every bit as efficient as Wells' time machine. Black holes in space contain worm holes that lead to — *who the hell knows?* Ask Stephen Hawking."

"Or Rod Serling?"

"Einstein believed time is a river, that you could just pass through it. And NASA claims there could be billions of punch holes in the universe, portals from one dimension to another, maybe to some other time and place, and that they can exist anywhere, take you anywhere. No one has any idea what ninety percent of the matter in the universe is, so worm holes could be *anything*. They're unsteady little suckers, and a few of them have opened at our doorstep. For some reason those holes conveniently appeared here at the *right* time, didn't they? Almost like they were giving those Wogslûk a peek at the local real estate.'"

"Screw Google. Next time I need information about anything I'll ask you. Just don't let those slug-shits get a hold of *your* brains."

"Oh, I have much more. Maybe the old puppet master in the sky dropped them off as some cosmic trial and error — or maybe the landlord just wants us out! Suck a few brains, those Wogslûk worms evolve while my neighbors become the Vienna Boys Choir. No little green men, no saucer attacks or fifth column because the aliens are already here. Booga Booga! It's the cosmic surprise party!"

Tiffany's eyebrow raised. "Then they're near, like Riona said. They're not finished learning the ropes here, and they're not finished with *us*. She knew that too, didn't she?"

Zachary touched the tip of his nose with one finger, pointed to Tiffany's forehead with the other.

"And Bingo was his name-o."

# PART SIX

## The Wogslûk

*"Let them be like the snail that dissolves into slime, like the stillborn child who never sees the sun."*
— **Psalm 58:8**

*"The universe is full of magical things patiently waiting for our wits to grow sharper."*
— **Eden Phillpotts, English philosopher (1862-1960)**

*"Nothing is yet in its true form."*
— **C.S. Lewis, English novelist (1898-1963)**

*"The Universe, is it friendly?"*
—**Albert Einstein, theoretical physicist (1875-1955)**

*"The Loch Ness Monster, Sasquatch, UFO's, and now this..."*
— **Zachary Colson, age 13**

# CHAPTER THIRTY-THREE

## FULL COURT PRESS: July, 2015

*"They don't have Wi-Fi in Hell, you know..."*

*Survive. Multiply. The simplest requirements of all living things, the most fundamental instinct...*

*The Wogslûk understand this much. They also understand that there is more to know.*

*But Ri has gone. Another must show them, lead them... and more.*

*Another who will think she has a choice.*

Leaving the ballfield, Tiffany followed Zachary back towards the school. He didn't seem in a great hurry to get there. The morning had been awful, and the day ahead showed no promise of improving. Having slept little, Zachary Colson seemed dead on his feet. For a long while they stood before the school and remained silent. Then...

"I can't get that image of Riona out of my head. If what happened to her happens to every dying Wogslûk, our proof goes blowin' in the wind. Literally."

Tiffany tried on her happy face that would have fooled no one. "We have your mom's photo and your video. Someone must have seen *some*thing. Those people are in the school right now, and maybe there'll be others. The big question is, do we have a plan?"

"The big question is, do we have a future?"

Zachary seemed defeated. Tiffany faked an unconvincing female wrestler stance. "No damn Wogs-fucks will be chowing

**343**

down on my brains without my kicking some slug butts big time." She managed a very poor attempt at a high thrust kick that wouldn't have knocked over a potted plant.

That earned a well needed laugh. "Any Wogslûk chowing down on your brains would go home hungry. You should stay away from wrestling until you can fit into a jockstrap."

Tiffany held him in a weak hammerlock, adding a weaker noogie to the boy's scalp. "The apocalypse may be coming to Jersey, but you still think you're the smart ass, don't you—?"

Zachary's grin evaporated fast. The two stood bolt upright.

### *CRACK—ACK-CK...!!*

A sound like a felled tree came from inside the building. The middle school echoed with a chaos of gunshots and shouts followed by screams.

"This can't be good."

"I'm not ready for more of this, Tiff."

"Something in the building is giving way, caving in, or—"

## *CRACK—ACK-ACK...!!*

This noise was louder, sharper. Zachary shook his head. "My parents are in there! Did you hear those shots?"

Tiffany grabbed his shoulder and held him back. "Something awful is happening inside. We can't go in."

More screams came from inside the building.

"You can wait here if you want." Zachary bolted past the main entrance. Tiffany paused, then caught up with him. The mayhem came from the school gymnasium, but that was no surprise. Standing by the closed gym door, the boy went pale. Something inside was breaking apart.

"You see any of those cops anywhere? There were like half a dozen of them."

"Far as I know, they were the only ones with the guns."

Zachary pushed the door. A massive sinkhole appeared where the gym's basketball court had been. Planks had splintered at center court. They had cracked like an immense egg shell, exposing another huge pit. Only the stands along the sidelines and the scoreboards above remained. A huge cavity seemed to have swallowed the half dozen cops along with a good many neighbors. Cots had also fallen into the dark trench. Diamond Loop residents cowered in the stands from which the exit doors seemed impossible to reach.

"My parents..." Zachary muttered. "Christ, this whole building is going to sink!"

"They were in the cafeteria, weren't they?"

Like a living shadow, the first Wogslûk squirmed from the cavity, and from all sides others followed. The gymnasium's lights flickered, then went out, throwing the entire place into a grey darkness illuminated only by the weak morning sun coming through the small openings of the skylight.

"They cut the electricity! Tiffany, these things know what they're doing!"

From the gymnasium's far end, a dozen Wogslûk headed for the student cafeteria, dragging residents kicking and screaming back and into the pit. Still holding a milk carton a child stood crying on the opposite side of the court, but the creatures slithered past him and let him be.

"They don't want to leave any adults behind who've seen them. We can't stay here, Zack! They'll spot us!"

*Do you see my parents anywhere?*

Tiffany's eyes darted about the gymnasium. She shook her head.

...and then pandemonium came to Glenn Echoes Middle School. In thick piles, the Wogslûk emerged from the sunken floor, going for the nearest Loop adults in the stands, parents uselessly protecting their kids. Mandibles opened like huge ice tongs as coiled creatures dragged adults kicking and screaming into the chasm's darkness. One heavyset resident, squeezed to his limit, spurt his innards like one of the busted water mains. Another man stood with arms raised high to block a Wogslûk's path towards his small daughter. Twice his size, the slug-thing took him, tearing into his skull until bone crunched like dried wood. Agonized screams echoed from inside the fissure, the only recognizable word the repeated shouts of *"No! No!"* The chorus lessened until no sound emerged but the chomping of

**345**

ingested human brains.

Zachary and Tiffany remained at the door unable to do anything but watch. Zachary recognized one of the screaming victims. "I know that girl. She always walks her poodle past our house, and sometimes I stopped to pet— *Damn!*" He knew he wouldn't be seeing pretty Debbie Greene in her cutoff jeans again, and the girl's toy poodle probably never made it to the school with the family. But Zachary had a more urgent concern.

*"My parents! Where are they?"*

Some people remained in the stands, the sinkhole blocking any escape route. Neighbors had salvaged cots' mattresses, retreating behind the makeshift barriers. It seemed impossible to know who hid where, but Tiffany pointed to the overturned mattress near the court's far edge.

"I see a cat's tail behind that one!"

Zachary saw it too. "That's Rocky!"

The cat's head emerged and she hissed. A fat Wogslûk climbed the pole barrier and tried to mount the stands but backed off. Gregory Colson peered out from behind the mattress stronghold and called to his son, "Zachary! We're okay! Don't wait for us! Just run!"

Tiffany saw what was happening. "Those Wog-sluts aren't coming near your parents! They're scared of your cat!"

"Sister Margelle's journal mentioned that they didn't like animals. Riona told me that too."

Noticing Tiffany and Zachary, the Wogslûk turned towards them. Heeding some shared signal like huge earthworms, a dozen crawled along the benches and headed for them.

Tiffany pulled Zachary's arm. "Your parents will be okay as long as Rocky stays with them. I'm not so sure about us."

The first Wogslûk drew near, mouth hooks extended and eyes on Tiffany. It sniffed the air, detecting her scent. Another approached and did the same. More wriggled from the stands. Tiffany caught their stares, crushing palms into her temples as if to drown out the creatures' liquid murmurs.

"They're ignoring everyone else. Christ, Tiffany..."

"Zack, we have to leave now! Just back out slowly." She gave him little choice, tugging his arm hard and pulling him through the exit, latching the door shut. They headed for the school exit, stopping cold on the small patio. Maybe a hundred punctures appeared in the grass of the ball field. The terrain had become pockmarked with manhole sized patches of mud from which more creatures crawled, but their movement was quick for slug-things larger than any seen inside. Slithering between the diamond's baselines, leaving snail tracks in the dirt, some were the length of a city bus, and each headed for the school.

Zachary absorbed the surreal moment. "The Loch Ness Monster, Sasquatch, UFO's, and now this — and no one in sight to see any of it! Who's ever going to believe this, Tiffany!"

"Do you still have your phone?"

"Right! I charged it last night!" Aiming the lens at the oncoming slug-things, Zachary muttered "Smile, fuck wads!" and took a quick video of the creatures. "Done! The others must have called out their big guns, but they have to get out of the daylight. They'll be wanting inside here in another minute!" He slammed the heavy door shut again and threw the latch. Down the corridor the other Wogslûk had pushed past the gymnasium's locked exit and a legion of the creatures crawled toward them. Zachary turned to Tiffany. "So what's the plan?"

"I was hoping you had one."

"*No retreat, no surrender.*' That's Springsteen."

"'*Fuck that!*' That's *me*."

From outside the door thumped heavily with a barrage of a dozen battering rams thundering through the corridors.

"They must be head-butting the metal!" Zachary said. He leaned heavily against the door. "This isn't going to work. Those others are coming."

Tiffany looked about to lose it. "Think we can borrow your cat?"

"Think harder."

The hallway revealed creatures resembling prehistoric

earthworms crawling from their primordial ooze. Blocked on two sides, Tiffany pulled Zachary and sprinted along the lengthy passageway towards the school's auditorium. The entrance was locked, but Tiffany kicked the door anyway.

"Do you know if any of the classrooms are open?"

"New students had orientation here a week ago, but the teacher locked that room afterwards. The staircase is too far at the end of the corridor, and that door is probably locked too, but I think there's an elevator nearby in the next wing. The doors are heavy and if we can make it to another floor they may get discouraged. But school is out so it may not be working."

The main entrance door burst open and black heaps of Wogslûk spilled through. The corridor filled with dozens of them. Tiffany's decision came fast.

"A fine idea! The elevator it is!" They sprinted towards the lift, and Zack punched the button like a mad man. Nearby, a thick liquid gurgling grew louder. The Wogslûk were moving very fast.

Zachary kicked the elevator door. "They cut the electricity, remember? *Fuckfuckfuck!!!*"

"Grab the door. We'll open it by hand. Just hope there's an elevator behind it!" Together they tugged at the small open space alongside the lift's heavy door. "Harder! Give it all you've got!"

"I'm busting a gut here, Tiffa—"

The door opened enough to squeeze into the cab behind it, and the two crammed through the small space. Pushing, they shut the entry tight, and in the lift's darkness Zachary ridiculously pushed the 'UP' button. Nothing happened. A thunderous pounding announced the first of the Wogslûk arrivals.

"Feeling a little déjà vu, are you, Indiana?" Tiffany asked.

"I'm feeling I have to pee."

The metal blistered, the pounding turning fierce. The elevator door was very thick, several minutes passing while Tiffany and Zachary cowered inside exchanging helpless looks. Like a smashed tin can, the door spidered then split, a dark pile

**348**

of Wogslûk squeezing through, their fishy smell thick and pungent. Tiffany pulled Zachary against the cab's back wall, and they huddled close. Reaching for his hand, she held it tight. A pair of mouth hooks snapped near her face.

She mumbled something to herself, *"'And hast thou slain the Jabberwock? Come to my arms, my beamish boy! O frabjous day! Callooh! Callay...!'"*

"More '*Jabberwocky*'?"

"You'll notice I'm not screaming."

"You'll notice I don't have to pee anymore." A wet snout rubbed Zachary's arm and he elbowed it from him. "You've given me an idea!"

"I'm thinking now might be a good time to try it."

He stepped between Tiffany and the gathering crush pushing into the lift. Studying those Wogslûk nearest, Zachary locked eyes and mimicked the nonsense words he recalled from the night before.

*"No...diem...no yoob man diem...no..."*

Tiffany moved closer behind him. "What the hell is that supposed to mean?"

"I have no idea, but I think maybe they do."

She mumbled, "I think maybe they do too..."

The creatures stopped cold, snorting one to the other. Some recognizable words were in their gibberish, but they made no sense. It didn't matter. Something was happening among them, something had changed. The Wogslûk backed away from the lift. Tiffany and Zachary looked at one another, uncertain of what they saw. Staying close, they moved slowly through the dark horde now crowding the entire length of the school corridor. In the swarm some had wriggled on top of others, but they cleared a path while all eyes remained on the two.

Zachary whispered, "Another minute and our brains were going to be lunch. Now they're acting like trained seals."

"You spoke the magic words, Boy Wonder. They've decided we're special, maybe?"

"Or maybe *you're* special? They're looking at you funny,

Tiffany. They could tear us apart like rag dolls if they wanted."

"That gibberish you just said? I thought I heard something like that in the shower room."

Several Wogslûk approached them, sniffing the girl as if tracking a scent. None made an aggressive move.

"Is there something you're not telling me about what happened last night, Tiffany?"

"I don't remember anything in that cocoon before I was rescued except being in some kind of haze. This is crazy, but I'm getting a read on these things. I'm *feeling* something, a vibe — maybe it's stronger because there's so many of them. I think they're trying to get through to me, but I don't know what they're—" The slug-things followed them close as shadows, Tiffany remaining silent until they had reached the school's entrance. "I think you're right. In the shower room they waited for me, and they've searched to find me here with you. They won't hurt you if we're together, but it's me they're after. I'm sure of it. Just look at them!"

Zachary forced a benign grin for the slug-things to see. "Not an extended mouth hook in sight now that they recognize you. This may be a good time to haul ass before they change their minds."

If she were somehow understanding them, there was a good chance they were reading *her*. Stepping through the doorway, on the patio she turned to Zachary. "They won't follow us outside. The sun is really bright this morning, and they'll sizzle like bacon. What were those sounds you made?"

"Let's walk." A short distance from the school, Zachary watched the creatures gather at the doorway. "Tiff, I don't know what I said to them. One muttered that to me last night, the one that saved me back in the Loop. It could have been quoting Shakespeare for all I know, but Jarmal killed it before I could make sense of it."

From the doorway came a liquid gargling that seemed almost a chant.

*"Yoob...Yoob...mon..."*

"You heard that, right? It's like they're trying to—to— *and*

**350**

*look at the ball field, Zack!* Those holes are gone, and there must've been a hundred of them. It's like something is covering their tracks for them. Something—" Tiffany shook her head, freeing the cobwebs. She shut her eyes, her brows knitted with her concentration. When she opened them, her expression changed considerably. "They're scared, and they want me to come with them. I'm sure of it. I got the same feeling when I saw those in the shower room. That sinkhole inside the gymnasium, it probably connects to the sewer system that's under the school, and that probably connects to that wormhole you think is down there."

"—Black hole. A worm hole is what's inside."

"It doesn't matter if it's God's asshole. I think it's where they want me to go with—"

"Nuh huh, Tiffany!" Zachary pulled her further into the ball field's sunlight, and he wasn't gentle about it. "Are you out of your mind? You saw what they did to all those people! You'll be worm food! I liked it better when *you* were scared."

Tiffany's eyes drifted again to the Wogslûk clustered inside. "I *am* scared. But you told me one of them brought you out of that sinkhole last night, and *you* were scared too. You had no choice but to trust it, right? Well, we don't have a choice now. And I must have something they want, or we wouldn't be standing here. They didn't hurt Riona, and they're not going to hurt me. Maybe I can somehow communicate—"

Zachary grabbed her shoulders, shook her. "*Communicate??* Since when do you talk 'slug'? And just to remind you, they *kidnapped* Riona! Do you think you can saddle one up like a pony and ride it into that pit inside? Wake up! I'm thinking we should find some other cops with guns and go whack-slug on their slimy asses!"

Tiffany poked Zachary in the ribs. "Hey, they could've been crawling all over both of us by now! And didn't one of them save *your* slimy ass? That must mean *some*thing."

That caught Zachary by surprise. "Yeah, well, I still think they're planning to step up their game."

"Zack, I'm going back inside."

"That's crazy!"

"Yeah, it is. Let me have your cell phone. I have an idea, if I can channel my inner Taffy Licks." She breathed hard and ran both hands through her hair. Tiffany had made her decision.

Zachary wasn't buying it. "Are you going on the pole for them?"

"Just give me your phone, okay? That pocket charger too."

"They don't have WiFi in Hell, you know." He handed her his cell and small charger, and she pocketed them. "You and I spent the last two days almost getting torn to Kibbles by those fuckers, and now you're planning to be their den mother? Maybe there's a couple good ones among them, but those others are goddamned killers. Christ, Tiffany, do you have any idea what you're saying?"

"I'm making this up as I go along. Call it instinct — or, if I'm wrong, call it crazy. Riona told you she understood them, so maybe some of that stuff rubbed off on me when I was cocooned last night. And someone has to save the world from the evil slug monsters, right? It's what your Katniss Everdeen would do — slug it out, right?"

Inside the school building the burbling chorus grew louder as more Wogslûk gathered at the open door, watching. Tiffany watched them right back.

Zachary watched her watching them. "Katniss would kill the fuckers! Do you have anyone you want me to notify should you become tonight's dinner? A friend, a pet parakeet?"

"Let Taryn Friedman know I went after one hell of a scoop for her, just like I promised."

"That figures."

Nearby, the Wogslûk gurgled restlessly. Zachary expected they wouldn't wait much longer.

"Stay here until I'm gone, give them some time to crawl back into that sinkhole inside, okay? Can't be too careful. Then go find your parents and put in a good word for me. 'For honor, for country,' as the saying goes. Wish me luck, Boy Wonder! I'm off with the Morlocks to try to talk some sense to them so they don't eat us Eloi."

"Can't you talk right here?"

"They don't want that."

Zachary shrugged. "You're really doing this?"

"Shits and giggles, Zacker."

Half smiling he shrugged. He kissed Tiffany's cheek, whispered, "Then good luck, you crazy bitch."

"I'll see you soon. Promise."

Zachary didn't want to say it, but he did. "No you won't."

She kissed his lips, just a peck but enough to make him blush. Reentering the school building, Tiffany turned and smiled. She started a wave, but surrounded by the awaiting creatures she disappeared among them, and they moved together in a dark caravan towards the gymnasium. Zachary shook his head hoping she hadn't seen him wiping his eyes.

"Crazy bitch..."

He waited only a short while and didn't take her advice. Peering into the school gym, Zachary watched Tiffany stand alongside the sinkhole until every last creature had returned. Maybe some of them waited below to assist her descent, or maybe the girl would suddenly sprout wings and float down there like a sylph. Nothing would have surprised him because Tiffany Leone was one determined woman once she set her mind to achieving the impossible. She slipped into the pit last like some self-appointed human sacrifice, climbed down the backboard's support pole and vanished into blackness. Neighbors who saw said nothing. There was a gasp or two, but that was it. The time for heroes had passed, but this hour of impossibilities hadn't.

The swoosh of several tons of dirt sifting through some enormous sieve filled the gymnasium. It seemed that, from below, an invisible Big Mama loaded tons of silt with an expertness that would have impressed Jarmal Besser. A thick mountain of mud emerged to plug the gap like some Hollywood special effect, a bit of consummate dentistry that required only a few minutes to completely fill the huge cavity, burying Tiffany Leone and the hoards of Wogslûk with her.

*("I'll see you soon. Promise...")*

From the stands at the far end of the gymnasium Gregory and Eden Colson waved to their son, revealing exhausted smiles but clearly overjoyed that their boy had safely returned. Jumping from Eden's hold and darting from the benches across the muddy surface, a black cat ran toward Zachary Colson. In a world gone mad, maybe a slither of sanity remained. He scooped his pet into his arms and held her close.

"Hello, Rocky. And how was *your* morning?"

# PART SEVEN
## DIAMOND LOOPHOLES

*"Life feels like a game of Snakes and Ladders, but without any ladders."*
—**David Moody, *Them or Us***

*"This isn't the first time the world has come to an end, and it won't be the last either.*
—**Joanne Harris, *Runemarks***

*"The collapse of civilization...It never happens according to plan."*
—**Mark A. Rayner, *The Fridgularity***

*"How baffling it is that we imagined cities incinerated by alien bombs and death rays when all they really needed was Mother Nature and time."*
—**Rick Yancey, *The Infinite Sea***

*"The bill is due..."*
— **Tiffany Leone**

# CHAPTER
# THIRTY-FOUR
## SISTERS, SAVIORS, AND SLUGS:
## TREMENTINA, 1898

*"My very soul depends on it..."*

San Miguel County, New Mexico: Thirty-two years after the disappearance of Cole McKenna, Melissa Monahan, and Aiden Hannigan

Last Entry from the Journal of Sister Margelle Mallory, Age 58. The Sisters of Our Savior Mission, Trementina, New Mexico

Thursday, October 20, 1898

My Lord, my Savior...

On my deathbed, I ask to be absolved of my sins, for so often I have doubted you. My faith was weak. But now I cough blood nightly and my time is near. This journal entry shall be my last. I can only hope these final thoughts will be coherent.

My three colleagues are gone over thirty years. I have not seen nor heard from them since their encounter with the Wogslûk during the summer of 1866, and I pray for their souls to this day. Since my last confrontation with the creatures, often I wonder where they have gone, but tonight I know they remain living. Evil does not die, and these unholy beings have lived in dreams that haunt my nights. Whether below the ground or in hiding elsewhere, they wait. As I write this, I cling to my rosary because I question why you, my Lord, have chosen to toss these demons into the path of humankind, and into my own.

But I have come to believe I understand why they are here. It is the strong who survive, and this circumstance must continue as long as Man walks this earth, or as long as Wogslûk crawl beneath it. Tonight convinces me of the terror they have yet to bring, and I cling to the hope that Man will emerge the stronger, because I so want to believe that Jesus does love the little children...

*'We should never be discouraged —*
*Take it to the Lord in prayer...'*

How I wish to have faith in the old hymn's words that echo in my ears this very moment! If Man would vanish tomorrow, what purpose could it serve to replace him with such despicable beings as these? I wonder at this logic, question it. Perhaps it is my own lack of faith that causes me to doubt my Lord's wisdom. More likely, although the Good Book tells us otherwise, perhaps it is your wisdom that created Man from creatures that crawled from the sea, and that very wisdom means to send us back to those beginnings to correct our ways. Perhaps we are meant to start over.

I have seen the miserable excuses for human beings that pass through this Mission; I have witnessed the change in the very landscape of our world, change not for the better. The weak are prey to the strong, and the good fall before those who are evil. I question daily why such evil exists, and only one answer comes to me...

To believe in good, I must see evil. To have genuine faith, I must see that faith tested! My very soul depends on the fear of my God, flawed as my soul may be. In that faith lies my strength!

Tonight, I have seen evil. My soul has been taken — no, stolen! — but I retain enough of my senses to understand why after these many years the Wogslûk finally have come for me. I refuse to accept the evil they have placed inside me — or rather, the goodness they have taken. Fortunately, the Mission's Sisters keep a single weapon here in a safe place, a hidden firearm I have not so much as touched.

Until Tonight.
My Lord, for what I must do, please forgive me.

— Sister Margelle Mallory

# CHAPTER THIRTY-FIVE

## HELL HOLE: DIAMOND LOOP
## SUMMER 2015

### *"SKANK PUSSY HO"*

#### July - August, 2015

For much of that summer, Glenn Echoes lawyers' phones rang. Diamond Loop lawsuits were many, and some hefty out-of-court settlements resulted. The township's politicos made certain the Loop's massive sinkhole was quickly filled. This time, it required no miracle beyond the determination of City Hall to act swiftly because an election year was coming. Newly installed water and gas lines were checked, then double checked, and an ambitious young foreman was hired to oversee the fleet of the former Reefe Construction Company's machinery. With Fred Reefe gone, the company's new logo read **Glenn Echoes Construction**, and the cul-de-sac again came alive with the sounds of jack-hammers and monster loaders rebuilding new homes while repairing property damage to the original ones. Washed sparkling clean, the salvaged Big Mama also returned to service, although not one construction worker referred to the huge front end loader by that name, and Mama's moniker disappeared under a new paint job.

The Glenn Echoes Chamber of Commerce informed those Loop neighbors (the ones who chose to return) that the township could confidently assure their safety, and during the last days of August, many residents happily unpacked their *bags. Taryn E. Friedman's news van pulled up, the field journalist interviewing as many smiling residents as she could get on camera. Young mothers mentioned readying their children for the opening of school, husbands spoke about getting back to their workshops, and their kids either giggled or shied away from Friedman's cameraman. Smiles abounded, and life at Diamond Loop returned to a semblance of normalcy.*

*Not one resident mentioned slug monsters. That kind of ranting would never fly if shared with the outside world, and those complaints wouldn't prove beneficial to real estate values either. Gregory and Eden Colson declined speaking to Friedman, privately agreeing that the less said about sinkhole monsters the better. During the late summer, while in her garden, Eden deleted the photo of the slug-thing she had seen. The memory was too painful, and what did it matter anyway? He and his friends seemed to have gone...*

As he had done practically every night since the gas main explosions, Zachary Colson finished another under-the-covers reading of Sister Margelle Mallory's journal entries, wondering if he had missed an important point. He figured the smaller of the slug creatures must have discovered the Mission and chewed into the woman's skull shortly before she died. Maybe they laid a thousand Wogslûk eggs inside her brain before emptying it. On a more theological level, maybe this was her Lord's questionable method of testing poor Sister Margelle one last time.

It wasn't an unlikely possibility. Those lines she wrote about taking your bitchings to the Lord? Zachary Googled them and found they belonged to *'What A Friend We have In Jesus.'* Maybe Margelle's ultimate fadeout was to sing her little hymn into a babbling insanity like Jessie Moss and Sergeant Smith. Some friend, that Jesus, Zachary thought. He wasn't certain why the nun believed she needed to confront evil to test her faith, but by 1898 Sister Margelle had become so obsessed with the Wogslûk creatures she probably already had gone half crazy.

The nun's journal offered many interpretations, but so did something else. Zachary's thoughts shifted to Tiffany Leone.

Tiffany possibly shared some obsession with the late Sister, having followed the Wogslûk into a sinkhole from which Harry Houdini couldn't have escaped. She had insisted on carrying Zachary's cell phone with her, and he had learned why.

*("I have an idea, if I can channel my inner Taffy Licks...")*
Remembering that, Zachary half smiled, because...

### ...*BECAUSE GIRLS HAVE SERKERS, BOYS DO NOT!*

This was technically true, but to Zachary's way of thinking Tiffany Leone definitely had earned herself one honorary balls out yerker. He discovered this weeks earlier in a way he would not readily have admitted to anyone.

★ ★ ★

## THE HOLE STORY

*In early August, The Colsons returned to Diamond Loop, and their son's lap top went online ten minutes following their arrival. The monitor chirped immediately, a familiar image appearing onscreen. Zachary touched the screen, not believing what he saw.*

*"Hello, Boy Wonder. Up late, I see."*

*Zachary's response halted inside his throat. "Tiffany! Is that really you? I didn't think I was ever going to — Everyone said you were dead, but —!" He stopped himself, looked hard at the screen "It sounds like you're talking with some sort of accent. Are you okay?"*

*"Alive and kicking, and our slug pals are gone. The accent thing, I don't know. One day I wake up inside another of their cocoony wraps, and I'm babbling to myself in some kind of Irish brogue. I'm okay — the cocoon thing is harmless as a hammock, just a bit confining, is all. It's crazy, but just about everything down here is. Could've been worse — I*

**362**

*could've woke up and been a Republican."*

*"Coom back and sang me a chorus of 'Cockles and Mussels,' will yer,? Aw, fook it. Just coom back."* Zachary laughed again. *"Yer alive, yer are!"*

Tiffany laughed too. The kid could be clever. *"'Alive, alive-O!' Zacker. Listen, I have to make this fast. Your cell battery is showing one bar and it's a bitch to recharge down here. That describes my energy level too. So you're home and safely under the covers again?"*

*"I am. And I see you're still there in the sewer? You're going to need about ten showers."*

*"You're looking a bit wasted too, Boy Wonder."* She held the phone's screen high. *"Look all around me, kid. See those nasty Wags-fucks anywhere?"*

The image onscreen was dark, but Tiffany provided a complete panorama of the exotic Glenn Echoes sewer system.

*"Nor a one, lass,"* Zachary said.

*"That's because there's another hole down here, and it's big. Guess what went into it?"*

*"Are they really gone?"*

*"Gone as gone can be, Zacker. Want to see me do an Irish jig?"*

*"Maybe later. You're saying they left on their own?"*

*"Drawn back to that worm hole like moths to a flame. You can thank Taffy Licks for that."*

Hearing the name caused Zachary to move closer to the screen. *"I' m a' feared yer lost me, lassie."*

Tiffany giggled. *"I know you can't let Mom and Dad in on it, but you'll want to take a look at Taffy's latest video, although I doubt you can share it with Taryn Friedman either. It's on an adult site and shows more than what you've been peeking at under the covers. You'll need a password—"*

*"Let me guess. 'W-A-G-F-U-C-K-S?"*

*"And Bingo was his name-o, Boy Wonder! And for you, it's free. That ought to get your Irish up. Among other things."*

*"What will I see? I mean, besides a little ass, little lass."*

More giggles.*"Nuh huh, Zacker. You have to watch it*

*yourself. Consider it a learning tool."*

*"I'll check it out. Hey, the Wogslûk are gone. That's all that matters. So you finally found the black hole your 19th century friends were looking for?"*

*"It was very strange. A few days ago down here this massive sinkhole just opens at my feet, sucking in all the sewer water, **GLERP! ...** and long as a city block. Crazy, but it isn't black at all. It's filled with colored lights like Christmas in Times Square. I swear, Zack, I had a religious experience, the whole Hallelujah Chorus thing. Best high I ever had. And those Wogslûk creatures went into it like an Olympic diving team. They're gone, every last one just minutes ago, gone to...fuck, who knows? I'm standing near the edge right now."*

*Zachary felt his heart pound. "Let me see it!"*

*"Can't do that. It sounds nuts, but there's something big happening here, Zacker, and it isn't just random shit. This hole — maybe those others, too — they seem to have a mind of their own, and I don't want this one disappearing by giving away its secrets."*

*"What happens in a black hole stays in a black hole. Hey, mission accomplished, right?"*

*Tiffany turned serious. "It's a little more complicated than that. See, Zack, about those Wogslûk ... It was tricky, like teaching myself a foreign language or learning horse whispering, but once I picked up their vibes, **presto!** — I understood them. And they understood me too! This place, this time, meant death for them. They saw Taffy's video and they changed their minds fast about staying here. They got the point — leave Diamond Loop or die. And I was the Pied Piper." She thought the remark over. "No, I was Big Mama digging another hole just for them!"*

*"Taffy's video changed their minds? I don't get it."*

*"You will..."*

*Nose to the screen, Zachary almost kissed Tiffany's image. "Screw the damn worm hole! I don't need to see it. I can't wait to see **you**, girl! Just don't tell me you have the urge to crawl around on your belly, okay? So, when will you be*

**364**

*returning to terra firma? I want to hear everything, every disgusting detail! I just love the way you pronounce Wag-sloogs!"*

*Tiffany fell silent. Too silent. "Well, see, that's the thing, Zack. I don't have much time. It's why I wanted to speak to you now, before I —"*

*A red flare exploded in Zachary's head. "Nuh huh...no, Tiffany! Don't you dare say it! You did your part!"*

*"You said it yourself at the school. I guess I knew too. I'm following them, Zack. It's what they want. It's what I want. This hole, it's inches from where I'm standing. The bill is due, and I had to see you one last time, even if it's only on this phone."*

*"What fucking bill? Jesus, Tiffany! There's no point—"*

*"You'll understand after you go to my — to **Taffy's** site. I'm sorry, Zack. I can't bring myself to say—" The screen fuzzed as Tiffany's cell battery weakened.*

*"That's not just some damned bungee jump. You don't even know where you'll wind up! You were lucky last time!"*

*"I'm hoping I'll wind up where I'm supposed to. Hell, Zack, look at me! I'm Taffy Licks, with no family and no talent except to dance on a damned pole. I'm some masturbatory fantasy on some pervert's computer screen, and my Taffy videos will probably ruin whatever chance I'd have in the real media. But I can make a difference today, I can do what I'm meant to do!"*

*The screen image flickered again.*

*"No, Tiff! You're meant to steal Taryn Friedman's job from under her ass! And today you might have saved Diamond Loop and possibly all of Jersey from one huge exterminating bill! You've already done what you're meant to do! I can't let you go down that fucking rabbit hole!"*

*"I'm thinking it's more of a trip through the looking glass, and if I'm lucky, I get to see what Alice found there."*

*"Tiffany..."*

*Silence for a moment. Then, "Ten...Nine...Eight..."*

*(Tehn...Ni—yen...hite...)*

*"Tiffany, I swear, if you're fucking with me—"*

*"Go online to Taffy's site. Promise."*

*(Gow oonline...)*

*"Tiff—!"*

*"Six... Five...Four..Three..."*

*"Don't!!"*

*"Goodbye, Zack."*

*Without another word she stepped forward into the hole.*

*"No..."*

*The computer screen went dark*

## TAFFY

*"I don't get it. Fuck! I don't get it!"*

For an hour Zachary lay awake, but past midnight he reopened his lap top. The wormhole probably already had vanished like that pit inside the school gymnasium, eliminating the hope of anyone finding Tiffany Leone. Maybe disappearing wasn't only what she wanted; maybe this was another piece of some cosmic puzzle, something the whole universe wanted. That's what she seemed to think.

For some reason Tiffany wanted him to view Taffy Licks' last posted video. Following the girl's plunge, Zachary had no desire to watch Taffy's suggestive pole gyrations. But he Googled the site and entered the password. The video's title certainly would confuse the pole dancer's loyal following. Who could have any idea of what she meant by **ME AND THE WOGsSLûK GET DOWN**?

Onscreen, Taffy was up to her usual tricks, undulating erotically to the Beatles' "Fixing A Hole," a soundtrack Tiffany must have downloaded in an attempt at dark humor meant especially for him. But then, something else appeared. Zachary muttered to his absent friend, "You wanted me to see this because you wanted the world to see..."

He watched the entire thing, twenty full minutes that turned his stomach. The video was terrible.

*"...You wanted the world to see **this**?"*

He must have missed something, must have misunderstood Tiffany's intent. Zachary watched Taffy Licks' short exhibition again, then again. It seemed worse each time, and Taffy's YouTube viewers' written opinions, although more vitriolic than Zachary's, essentially mirrored his own:

**"you don't be seen me no more, skank pussy ho' "**

**"Dam whore, your way over the line with this fuckin' shit."**

**"TAFFY LICKS? NO, TAFFY SUCKS!"**

**"I want my money back, bitch!"**

Many more critiques appeared the following night. Days later, the YouTube brass removed the video, then shut down Taffy Licks' entire site. But Zachary had downloaded the video to his hard drive, not certain why except that it was all he had to remember of his brief friendship with Tiffany Leone.

Difficult as it was, he forced himself to watch her performance for the remainder of the summer.

# CHAPTER
# THIRTY-SIX

Jabber-Wogslûk: **LATE AUGUST, 2015**

*"Beware the Jabberwock..."*

**T**he night of Zachary Colson's final viewing of Taffy's video came. He held out hope for some nuance he had missed, some secret message. It seemed unlikely he'd find any. Maybe the online display *was* only a cheesy porn video, and a shitty one at that, but the same nagging thought persisted.

Why had Tiffany insisted he watch it? She had encouraged jeers even from the horn dog fans who were her audience. This wasn't merely Taffy twerking her way into men's hearts — and into their pants. No, Taffy's digital farewell went much further. Zachary made a tough decision, not wanting to remember his friend this way. Weeks had passed since Tiffany had contacted him and then disappeared. He would delete her video and try to forget he ever saw it.

*The hour was late. Well, maybe just one more look...*

Onscreen, there she was writhing on her pole butt naked while McCartney sang in an endless loop about the hole he wanted to fix. The double entendre wasn't lost on Zachary, although Sir Paul's ditty also carried a less-than-subtle sexual innuendo. The pole to which Taffy clung wasn't a pole at all; it was some filthy vertical pipe probably connecting with a water main to the surface above the Glenn Echoes sewer system. The location must have seemed an odd choice to her male followers, but watching a seductive girl covered in crud maybe appeared sexual in some creepy way. But what followed *wasn't* sexual to Taffy's viewers, and even the creepiest among them stated as much online.

In shadows, Taffy gyrated like some human Slinky. Several minutes of preliminaries passed, enough time to hook any curious channel surfing male before the tone darkened considerably. The girl made lip smacking gurgling sounds that weren't words, yet they couldn't have been anything else — *and the Wogslûk came!* At first a single small dark creature crawled along her thigh as she pole danced, but several others wriggled over her like elongated charcoal briquettes that stood out sharply against the creamy flesh of her breasts. To any casual viewer, in the gloom of the sewer the creatures could have seemed slugs, maybe maggots — very fat ones. The whole time Taffy continued bumping and grinding, turning upside down to allow more creatures to squirm along her face. One worked itself into her nostril, hanging from it like some sticky discharge. Taffy waved at the cell phone's unsteady camera as a dozen more dark creatures slid along her arms, mandibles extended but, incredibly, not biting. All the while the girl kept smiling and writhing until every inch of her flesh crawled with Wogslûk.

*...even down there, inside her, then out again!*

Had some slug creature obligingly balanced the cellular to get those shots? Had Tiffany managed that much control over them? The thought conjured an impossible image, but *something* was holding the camera.

Lowering herself into the shallow sewage, Taffy splashed in sludge like some school girl enjoying a dip in the ocean. Here Taffy's performance went completely off the rails. The small creatures slithered from her, but a Wogslûk twice her size entered the frame like some grotesque special effect, its torso too elongated to fit the screen. Pausing to study the recording device *(was the creature posing for the camera?)* the slime-thing mounted her while squirming and undulating in rhythm with Taffy's body. As he did every night, Zachary told himself this couldn't be what it looked like. In a million years Tiffany wouldn't — she *couldn't!*

*("I'm fixing a hole where the rain gets in...")*

The filthy water splashed as the behemoth slipped beneath the shallow sewage, then Taffy was on top, moving much more quickly now — up, down, up, down, undulating in twisted contortions as if sharing some wild jackhammer frenzy. On top, then under, then back on top...

Taffy Licks *was* doing ... *that!*

(No, this was Tiffany Leone onscreen — *his friend!*)

Her lips puckered, exaggerating the silent words she spoke so Zachary would have no doubt what she uttered. Tiffany lip synched her message meant only for him.

***"Beware the Jabberwock..."***

The Wogslûk twitched and puckered its thick lips, repeating Tiffany's words in perfect imitation as the girl thrashed under the creature. A great orifice beneath the slug-thing spread wide like a trap door. Something fleshy, long and thick, extended like a garden snake. It spilled stringy dark goo over her...

*...and into her!*

*"Oh God, Tiffany! Christ!"*

Zachary slammed the lap top shut, as he often did at this point of the video. He didn't know what to make of what he'd seen, and he certainly didn't want to further torture himself seeing Tiffany in this way.

*...Tiffany, who had taken her flying leap into oblivion before his eyes, leaving behind this sickening fuck film to remember her by.*

Zachary's eyes filled. He would never see her again, could never ask what he needed to ask. He certainly couldn't offer this video to Taryn Friedman, expecting the reporter to air it. Who in their right mind would even admit watching this?

*"Why show me this—this—?"*

A power surge occurred inside Zachary's brain. The answer came.

***No one*** *would admit watching this! Tiffany didn't WANT him to show the video at all, not to anyone!*

Yes, maybe — but she titled her video ***ME AND THE***

***WOGsSLûK GET DOWN!*** Tiffany knew only he understood what the strange word meant. It wasn't in the dictionary, and to others it would seem a nonsense word like...

*...like Jabberwocky...*

***Or Jabber-Wogslûk!***

*("Nonsense words that somehow make sense...")*

*("...Yoob...man...diem...")*

Zachary connected the dots. The gibberish of the Wogslûk no longer seemed nonsense to Tiffany. She had communicated with them, persuaded them to leave Diamond Loop. Keeping her end of some bargain, *that* was the reason they poured themselves back into the worm hole. They did it because of her!

*("The bill is due...")*

*Okay, then...What did she owe?*

*("I can't bring myself to say...")*

*Something she couldn't tell him? But, paradoxically, something she wanted him to know?*

*(????????)*

The questionable video didn't last online for long. Tiffany knew it wouldn't, knew also that anyone who saw it would hate it. That meant they probably wouldn't share it; therefore, Tiffany's message to him remained safely hidden. It was somewhere in that pornographic exhibition that was not Tiffany at all.

*Why not just tell him? Why the video?*

Maybe deep inside Tiffany didn't want to leave! She realized if he knew her true intentions he might talk her into staying. She was correct about that, and if she reneged on her agreement then the Wogslûk would come back for her — no, for *everyone*! So she let Taffy Licks tell him...

*Nuh huh! There had to be more than that...*

The Wogslûk had to see her intentions were serious, and she needed proof to demonstrate she wasn't shitting them. Taffy Licks' explicit video was living proof! And...

*...and they watched it!*

*("...I was the Pied Piper...")*

Where did the Wogslûk go? Where did Tiffany go?

*No, the question was, to **when** did they go?*

They didn't leave together, she and the slug-fuckers. She waited, and that meant maybe they didn't arrive at the same place. Or, maybe some did and others went somewhere else. It was enough to make you crazy just thinking about it.

*("...and I was Big Mama, digging a hole just for them!")*

Zachary had it! He picked up Rocky, held the cat close while muttering to the wall, "Damn, Tiffany! They wanted you to stay here, but you couldn't! You had to go into that hole behind them, wherever it took you. You got them to leave, but you had to leave too because of what you knew you had inside you! *FUCK!!*"

*She waited! It had nothing to do with where she thought she was going, or where she thought the slug-fucks were going. She had no idea. She knew only she had to get herself away from TODAY!*

The boy pounded his lap top like a madman, sending Rocky jumping for the floor. The truth was there all along, right on his computer screen.

Writhing on her pole, Taffy Licks had communicated with the creatures in a language they would understand. She showed those hermaphroditic Wogslûk not only what she could do for them; she showed them what she *would* do! If they required their new queen, it wouldn't be her. But she could give them the next best thing.

Yerkers and serkers, — and the Wogslûk had both! That meant Tiffany had one hundred percent of their attention.

*(Beware the Jabberwock...)*

*Oh yes, there was a damn good reason to beware the Jabberwock. Maybe not today, maybe not tomorrow, but eventually...*

"DAMN! DAMN! *DAMN!*"

They chose her, wanted her. No one else would do! Zachary saw no other explanation. His friend would keep her promise wherever the worm hole took her, and they would keep theirs by disappearing in time or space wherever that cosmic puppeteer dropped them off. Tiffany had assured them the one thing no other human being would dare or allow.

*She promised them she would breed inside her another queen like Riona!*

Remaining perfectly still while upright in his bed, Zachary Colson sat as Rocky lay half asleep in his lap. He had the entire picture now. The Wogslûk were free to do the one thing Zachary feared most, the one thing the whole damned planet would have feared, if anyone knew. It didn't matter whether she or those slug-shitters in the wormhole went backwards into the past, forward into the future, or wound up in some other dimension, because Tiffany would birth some Wogslûk baby that kicked evolution in the ass. Those cross breeding slug-shits would metamorphose like maggots into flies, but on a significantly larger scale, and the future was fucked. They were already well on their way with all those Diamond Loop brains they slurped down.

What would those things become when they mutated into something else? Maybe Sister Margelle was on the right track, believing the Wogslûk were evolution's cosmic do-over, a way to go back to the start of Man's little dance on this planet to correct his fuck-ups. No fire or flood this time, just sinkholes filled with Wogslûk, and Tiffany was some important part of that evolutionary rewind. Zachary didn't want to think about that, and he certainly didn't want anyone else figuring out what he had. He deleted Tiffany's video.

His mother peeked into his room. Eden Colson's nightly ritual hadn't changed one bit, but that was okay. There was something reassuring in the familiarity of routine and the ability of life to readjust itself. Zachary needed some normalcy.

"Hey, you, it's almost midnight. None of these late shift excuses once school starts, okay?" She picked up Sister Margelle's journal from the nightstand, thumbed through it. "Still reading the old nun's diary, I see. Anything interesting?"

"Only Jesus stuff. Some prayers and to-do lists, not much else. I mean, she was just some crazy nun."

**373**

Eden placed the journal back and gave Rocky a quick pat. "Well, I can't say that sort of thing fascinates me, but I'm glad you've taken an interest in something besides your computer. Anyway, lights out right now, guys. Don't let the bed bugs bite."

Zachary faked a smile that didn't come easy. "Don't you mean the bed slugs?"

Eden said nothing. She kissed her son's forehead and turned off his night light.

# CHAPTER
# THIRTY-SEVEN
## THROUGH THE LOOKING GLASS: 1823

*"No husband, no family..."*

**D**uring the summer of 2015, twenty-three-year-old Tiffany Leone entered a wormhole somewhere beneath a New Jersey town called Glenn Echoes, not far from the cul-de-sac housing development of Diamond Loop. She had plunged into an oddly lit hole feet first like some child cannonballing into a pool, knowing nothing of where she would emerge or even if she would. But she did emerge at the portal's other end, where the Tiffany of 2015 would not be born for another 169 years. The young woman who appeared on a dusty prairie trail remembered nothing of this long-ago Leone woman, nor how she herself had arrived at this place and time. She recalled nothing of tooling around on a Harley with a brainy kid named Zachary, nor of promises made to dark creatures called Wogslûk that crawled on their bellies and had a taste for human brains.

The woman arrived in the year 1823, but most of her memory hadn't made the trip...

Covered with filth, the woman wiped sweat beads from her forehead. She couldn't remain in this heat for long without fainting, although she had no idea where to go. For that matter, she had no idea how she came to this place. She simply found herself on this twisting trail that she hoped led to people. She should have been terrified, but she felt only confusion. Instinct told her to walk, to keep moving and hope for some memory of where she was; more important, to remember *who* she was. By the time she reached the small town, she still didn't know. Several storefront signs indicated the place was called Trementina. The name stirred a dull memory. She had heard of it. That meant something. Maybe.

In her pocket she found an object that felt familiar, although she had no idea what its purpose was. It contained a broken rectangular dark window with a single circular object below like a garment's button. She pressed it, but nothing happened. For some reason she half expected an image to appear inside the window, but the thought seemed absurd and the cracked glass remained dark — as dark as the vague recollection of a deep mud pit from which she had emerged.

No, that couldn't have been what happened. The recollection seemed more like an insane dream, and she dismissed this also as ridiculous. Her memory would come to her, she told herself. Right now her concern was to find some hint of civilization.

She had walked for what seemed miles, finally spotting the small frontier town. A rattling coach was just pulling into a depot, and she stopped before the only place that had any activity. The freshly painted sign above the swinging doors read THE OLD CROW INN. She stepped inside.

Every man in the place turned to look at her, and their stares almost made her retreat back outside. A long balcony revealed a dozen heavily made up women leaning over its railing, and they watched her too. She remained where she stood until a red haired older woman approached her, smiling.

"Well, you look like hell in a hand basket, honey. You searching for someone here, or just getting yourself out of the heat?" Receiving only a confused stare, the woman motioned for the man behind the bar to pour her a drink. "You must be thirsty. I can offer you a beer, if you feel like talking a bit. Or not. Either way, beer's on me."

The red-haired woman gave the distinct impression of someone making a sales pitch, but a beer was a beer and she was thirsty "Thank you. I'm very tired. I just came from — I don't even know from where." She caught her mistake. "I mean, all these little frontier towns look the same to me."

Hearing the girl's accent, the woman's grin spread. "You're Irish, then! Welcome to Trementina, where there's probably more Irishmen than in Dublin!" She extended her hand in lady-like fashion. "I'm Melanie Carter. Fellas here call me Miss Mellie. And you are—?"

It was a good question, but the girl didn't want this obliging matron to believe she was playing with less than a full deck. The name Katniss came to mind, along with something about a black cat, a pet...

*Something...Something...*

"Kat," she answered. She reached for the beer the bartender had poured. A bottle on the counter read McGillis Brand Whiskey, and she silently thanked the Lord for the inspiration. "Well, Kate McGillis is my Christian name." The words just came as if they'd been scripted, her Irish accent and delivery sounding like she had never spoken in any other manner. Right then she decided Kate McGillis was who she was, at least until she remembered more, if she ever did. That much settled, she downed half the beer in seconds.

"You certainly drink like an Irish woman. A young girl wearing trousers is something of a sight in this town, let alone one traveling on her own. Are you from these parts, Katie?"

"I suppose I am now, Miss Carter. I've nowhere to go." She ventured her first smile, knowing she spoke the truth, knowing also she must have sounded pathetic.

"Well, Katie, nowhere is exactly where you've arrived. The stage bring you? I don't see no bags."

"Haven't any."

That should have raised an eye brow. It didn't.

"Alone, then, are you? No husband, family?"

The Carter woman's questions were direct. She deserved a direct answer, but not before the newly christened Kate emptied her glass. The drink made her admission easier.

"No husband. No family."

It was all the explanation she offered, and Mellie Carter didn't ask for more. She gave the girl a hug, stood back and conducted a thorough once over. The Carter woman's forwardness didn't bother Kate at all. If this were pity, she could accept it for now.

"You're a very fetching woman under all that dry mud, Katie. We can discuss details later after we get you freshened up. I'll introduce you to Mr. Hannigan, the Crow's proprietor. If he likes you, then perhaps you'll consider an offer I'm prepared to make. That is, if you're of a mind to stay in San Miguel County, at least for a while. Right now you'll be needing a hot shower and some decent clothes to show off those good looks of yours. Seems like you could do with a little food too. I'll fix you up something. How's that sound?"

Without waiting for a response, she led the girl up the staircase. They met another woman headed down, wearing a fancy red dress that revealed ample breasts that seemed about to break free.

"Good afternoon, Polly. You entertaining Mr. O'Brien today?"

"Can't say I'm lookin' forward to it, Miss Mellie. That man stinks of whiskey so bad I'm about to fall down skunk drunk with just a whiff." She gave Kate the once over. "This a new girl, then? Be careful not to swallow the fellas too forceful with that crooked tooth, Miss."

Mellie Carter laughed and led Kate to a small room, pointing to the shower down the hall. The girl expressed her gratitude, stopping the woman before she headed back to the tavern below.

"Please don't think this a ridiculous question, Miss Carter, but I have to ask."

"Call me Mellie. Ask me anything you please, Katie. We're all friends here. You want to know what this establishment is, I suppose?"

"No. I know what this place is. I have no problem with that."

"Well, then..."

**378**

The girl stammered, then started over. "See, Mellie, I was wondering — I'm not sure I know how to ask this without seeming either stupid or plain crazy, but — Could you tell me what year this is?"

She showered, then stood before the full length mirror wearing a black dress found inside the large wardrobe. It felt like silk, or some material meant to resemble silk. Every garment she saw revealed a good portion of her bust. She chose not to wear the corset she discovered in the drawer; her waist was thin enough without needing to suffocate herself. She felt comfortable dressed like this, even knowing what purpose the seductive apparel served. Tamping a pad of crimson rouge on her face, she liked what she saw reflected. An hour earlier she had no idea who she was. Now it didn't seem to matter.

"Hello, Kat," she addressed her mirrored image, much preferring the name to Katie. There was a feeling of freedom she liked about this Old Crow place. If she was expected to exchange her favors here for cash, then maybe she'd been meant to do this. In any case, there seemed no other option except to find a church to take her in, but that wasn't a decision she could comfortably make now. She sensed that during this past hour God was no longer on good terms with her.

Giving her freshly brushed tresses a flirtatious toss, she twirled before the mirror like a ballerina. Her agility suggested that maybe she had once been some kind of dancer, but the rest of that memory had gone. Still, this cleaned up 'Kat' was a looker, no doubt there. Hungry, she prepared to head to the tavern below but stopped again to glance at herself in the reflecting glass. The seductive mirror image stirred a dim memory, something about a debt owed to —

"Wag...Wags..."

She almost had it, but the word slipped away. The mirror held its secrets, and it wasn't telling.

From the muddy trousers on the floor she pulled out the strange device she had found earlier. For a moment the glass lit, displaying numbers and letters in small boxes. The illumination dulled. It went out, and it stayed out.

"Who am I?" she muttered to her reflection. Touching her rouged cheeks, from deep inside, an answer came.

***Wogslûk!***

She remembered the word! But what did it mean? The reflection in the mirror responded, lips moving while hers remained pressed tightly together.

***You know what it means.***

"I don't know! I don't!"

***You will.***

Inside her head two words reverberated like distant echoes...

*("Goodbye, Zack...")*

The mirror caught her attention again. This small room was very hot, but her reflection was no trick of the prairie sun.

"What the—-?"

The mirror revealed a grotesque abnormality. Her hand ran along the strange protuberances of thick flesh that disappeared for one moment, then reappeared the next. She practically pressed her face against the glass, but what she saw of her mirrored self was no trick of her mind.

She saw hooks, like those of a maggot.

Katie McGillis took to her new profession quickly. As Kat, she couldn't count the men who climbed the stairs of The Old Crow. She didn't know many of them, and most she never saw again. When her belly grew during the late summer of 1824, she had no idea what manner of visitor had put a child inside her. This wasn't surprising.

She remembered nothing of a woman called Tiffany Leone, nothing of a highly questionable video recording the Leone woman had made for a young friend, a recording that would have explained so much. But how could she remember an event 182 years in the future?

It was so much better that she didn't.

# SINKHOLE

*("Beware the Jabberwock, Zachary...")*

In the downstairs tavern a man called Cade O'Brien pulled a hidden ace from his sleeve in yet another game of Poker no man would dare challenge. In Kat's belly rested an unborn infant whose name she would never know. But some months later, shortly after Kat McGillis' misfortunate execution, the infant would have a name.

The child's adoptive father knew nothing of another paternal claim to her. This other father slithered slug-like far beneath the ground awaiting the opportune moment to reclaim its infant, the child whom Aiden Hannigan, the widowed proprietor of The Old Crow, had named Riona.

# CHAPTER THIRTY-EIGHT

## FORECAST: COLD AND WET

*"...everywhere we go..."*

T heir movement through a thousand seasons seemed a simple passing through an open door, followed by a dizzy tumbling into an endless pit. Belonging to an age still awaiting the invention of the lightbulb, neither traveler could have comprehended time's ability to fold over on itself. Measured in physical distance, they hadn't journeyed far from the subterranean world that had been the starting point of their second journey. Measured in time, however, the distance seemed incalculable...

Awakening from a twilight unconsciousness, the boy and the young woman noticed a sky the color of raw eggs. They stood upon a small pile of mud before a broken cluster of strange looking half sunken homes. Familiar only with ramshackle farm cabins and less than elegant ranch houses, to their eyes the dwellings appeared futuristic; yet, the homes also seemed abandoned relics of a distant past long dead. Filthy pools of water added a swampy reek to the entire area. The flooded terrain appeared a place not of this world. Nearby, a rusted street sign read *Diamond Loop*. Those words, and the discolored playing card diamonds that adorned the marker, demonstrated this place *was* of this world — at least at one time.

"You okay?" the boy asked. "I passed out after that first

tumble."

"I'm okay, I think." Melissa Monahan studied the area. "This isn't San Miguel County."

"Not unless the Pacific's come to New Mexico." Cole McKenna wasn't making a joke.

"I'm freezing and I'm soaked." Melissa studied the dripping weapon she held. "You think your rifle still will fire? God knows what's here."

The boy shrugged. "Don't want to risk firing it to find out. We may need the ammo. Keep your pistol handy. This place don't appear friendly." Young McKenna could sense when there was danger even in silence, because not all silences were the same. Cole knew some silences whispered death.

Looking above, Melissa shook her head. "If Hell has a sky, it's got to be that color. Wherever we are, who could possibly live here?"

Cole surveyed the submerged landscape for answers, but he found none. "We've got trouble if everywhere looks like this. That water could be deep. I don't see how we can —"

"—Don't you even think it! We can't stay here, Cole! We need food, we need to find people, if there *are* any. And we need to get back!"

"Back? How? And where *are* the people? Well, if anything here *is* alive, something is keeping it alive, right?" Cole reached to touch the water. "It's damned cold. Stinks from being stagnant. Must've been like this a long time. I doubt anyone could live here, including us."

Melissa froze where she stood and pointed. "I see something moving..."

Near them the water rippled. Beneath the surface dark objects stirred up small breakers that cascaded against the slippery beach of mud on which the two stood close.

"Something's in the water!" Melissa grabbed the boy's arm. He lifted his rifle.

"Don't move. Stay very still..."

A dark form appeared in the shallows, a single creature of incredible length breaking the surface, drawing near. Dripping sludge, its head emerged like a rapidly growing stalk. Two more shadows followed close behind, then a dozen.

Cole returned Melissa's stare. "They're here. Fuckin' sluggots, everywhere we go..."

More emerged, but something wasn't right.

"Look at their faces, Cole! They're...they're different! They're not those things we saw in the tunnel. They're-"

*"Yoob...foo...yoob...mon..."*

The creatures circled them, too many to count. Rising tall from the filth, mouth hooks opened wide as they inched closer. Something was different, all right. They had almost human faces, unformed like melted wax, incomplete sculptures of human beings but not quite human. Moving awkwardly, somehow they stood as upright as trained snakes.

*"Yoob...mon..."*

Melissa spoke in whispers. "Are those words? I can't make out what they're—"

The boy shook his head, grabbed hold of Melissa's hand. "They're not human. Not sluggots either! I don't know what they are!"

The largest moved toward them, struggling like some toddler trying its legs for the first time. Melissa shoved the pistol into her pocket. Raising her arms high, she displayed no weapon in her hand, but there was little chance these things even knew what a weapon was. Her voice cracking, she shouted, "We don't want to hurt you! Do you understand? We don't want — *we don't —!*"

"Where's the people, Melissa? These things are here, but where are the fucking *people?*"

"Cocooned maybe? Like that Tiffany girl?"

Cole looked into the dark eyes of the creature before him. "I don't think so."

The creature tilted its head and formed more meaningless sounds. More human than slug, its mouth hooks extended the length of tusks.

*"Man...yoob...man...foo...diem..."*

Melissa grabbed Cole's arm. "It's trying to tell us

**384**

something!"

"It doesn't understand what you're saying. None of them do! Or they don't care!" Cole raised his rifle, took aim. "There's more here than in that railroad tunnel!"

"Cole, maybe you shouldn't. I'm not sure..."

"*I* am!"

He pulled the trigger.

The Wogslûk have spotted two.

These could be the last of them.

**"...*Where's the people, Melissa?*"**

The boy and the female human carry what seem ancient weapons, and they are pointed towards the advancing swarm. The boy's weapon clicks, but nothing happens. Cursing, he swings it uselessly.

**"*Shoot them, Melissa!*"**

The female's hand shakes. The boy appears angry.

**"*Shoot them!*"**

Again, nothing.

**"*Fuck!*"**

A liquid riot of slurping noise follows. Water splashes. Mandibles open wide.

"*Yoob...man...foo...diem...*"

**"*Don't look, Melissa! Stand behind me!*"**

**"*Cole, listen to them! I think I understand what they're trying to—!*"**

"*Yoob...mon...foo...yoob...diem...*"

**"*Don't look!*"**

"*Yooob...mon...foo...foo..diem...*"

**"*They're words, Cole — I'm hearing something!*"**

The swarm surrounds them. Some crawl over others, each for its place. Some speak. This time the words are clear.

"*Hooman food...Mmmmmmmmmmmm...!*"

The words are all wrong, but their sentiment is there. Soulful...and soul *felt*. This ceremony is as old as time. It isn't much, but it's something.

## KEN GOLDMAN

The Wogslûk are saying Grace.

# EPILOGUE

In early September of 2015, Zachary Colson entered Glenn Echoes Middle School's seventh grade. He immediately signed up for the Computer Club and decided within the first week that there could be a decent career in technology for him, but he also decided he wasn't going to be married to his lap top anymore. In November, he approached a cute and very popular classmate named Josie and asked her to the Wellington Mall matinee featuring the last chapter of *The Hunger Games*. To his surprise the girl enthusiastically said yes, and together over a shared tub of popcorn the young couple cheered Katniss Everdeen's final victory over the Capital's bad guys. In the spring, Zachary tried out for the Junior Varsity baseball team. He made the squad's second string, but that was fine with him, and by this time Josie and he were considered an item by their many friends. Judging from the occasional hickey that appeared on Zachary's neck, it seemed he was doing all right in that department also. With the arrival of June during his first year at Glenn Echoes he made the honor roll, and to celebrate his achievement Gregory and Eden Colson treated their son and his friends to one hell of a backyard barbecue, the largest seen on Diamond Loop. As an added bonus for him, Zachary noticed that pretty Josie's tube top was showing the first signs of a healthy spurt of her ripening womanhood.

Throughout the school year Zachary slept well, enjoying occasional dreams of Tiffany Leone riding her Harley while he held tightly to her waist, helmet off with the wind blowing through his hair. There were no online searches for Taffy Licks or any other twerking wannabes. Somehow, Taffy and Tiffany became two different people inside Zachary's head, and that was the way he preferred to remember his friend. Nightmares featuring crawling bed bugs disappeared. Zachary knew they wouldn't be returning soon, but somewhere in the darker corners of his mind he also understood that, probably long after he was dead and gone, the bed bugs would be coming back. Not today, though, not tomorrow either, but someday. Except they wouldn't really be bed bugs, nor would they be in dreams.

And Zachary knew when they returned they would be biting...

# ABOUT THE AUTHOR

Ken Goldman is a former Philadelphia teacher of English and Film Studies, whose course on Horror and Science Fiction in Film & Literature is rumored to still give nightmares to his former students. An affiliate member of the Horror Writers Association, Ken has homes on the Main Line in Pennsylvania and at the South Jersey shore depending upon the track of the sun and his need for a tan. His stories appear in over 860 independent press publications in the U.S., Canada, the UK, and Australia.

Since 1993 Ken's stories have received seven honorable mentions in *The Year's Best Fantasy & Horror*. He has written five other books: his anthologies of short stories, *You Had Me at Aargh!!* (Sam's Dot Publishers), *Donny Doesn't Live Here Anymore* (A/A Publishers), plus an e-book, *Star Crossed* (Vampires 2 Publications); and a novella,

*Desiree*, (Damnation Books, and currently on Kindle by eXcessica Publishing).

His first novel, *Of A Feather*, was published by Horrific Tales Publications (UK) in January 2014. Ken's stories haven't made him famous yet. He expects that to happen posthumously, or whenever the Mother Ship arrives to take him home. For now, you may find many of Ken's stories online and at Amazon.com. Stop by and scream hello at:

http://www.amazon.com/Kenneth-C.-Goldman/e/B004 QVWTTE

**or**

*https://www.goodreads.com/author/show/3054 969.Kenneth_C_Goldman*

ALSO FROM
# BLOODSHOT BOOKS

### The Specimen (The Riders Saga #1)

From a crater lake on an island off the coast of Bronze Age Estonia...

To a crippled Viking warrior's conquest of England ...

To the bloody temple of an Aztec god of death and resurrection...

Their presence has shaped our world. They are the Riders.
One month ago, an urban explorer was drawn to an abandoned asylum in the mountains of northern Massachusetts. There he discovered a large specimen jar, containing something organic, unnatural and possibly alive.

Now, he and a group of unsuspecting individuals have discovered one of history's most horrific secrets. Whether they want to or not, they are caught in the middle of a millennia-old war and the latest battle is about to begin.

**Available in paperback or Kindle on Amazon.com**

ISBN-13: 978-1495230004

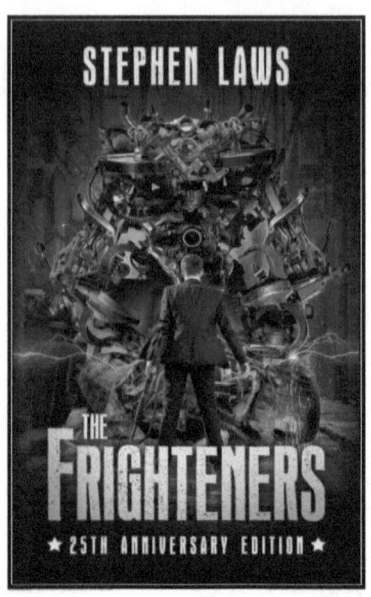

### HOW MUCH DO YOU HATE?

Eddie Brinkburn's doing time for a botched garage job that left Sheraton's brother very badly burned.

### HOW MUCH DO YOU HATE?

When Sheraton's gang burn his wife and kids to death, Eddie soon learns the meaning of hate.

### HOW MUCH DO YOU HATE?

And that's how the prison psycho transfers his awesome power to Eddie. A power that Eddie reckons he can control. A power that will enable Eddie to put the frighteners on Sheraton...

**Available in paperback or Kindle on Amazon.com**

ISBN-13: 978-0998067926

## WELCOME TO THE BLACK
## MOUNTAIN CAMP FOR BOYS!

Summer,1989. It is a time for splashing in the lake and exploring the wilderness, for nine teenagers to bond together and create friendships that could last the rest of their lives.

But among this group there is a young man with a secret--a secret that, in this time and place, is unthinkable to his peers.
When the others discover the truth, it will change each of them forever. They will all have blood on their hands.

ODD MAN OUT is a heart-wrenching tale of bullies and bigotry, a story that explores what happens when good people don't stand up for what's right. It is a tale of how far we have come . . . and how far we still have left to go.

**Available in paperback or Kindle on Amazon.com**

ISBN-13: 978-0998067919

Welcome to the small Midwestern town of Belford, Ohio. It's summer vacation and fourteen-year-old Toby Fairchild is looking forward to spending a lazy, carefree summer playing basketball, staying up late watching monster movies, and camping out in his backyard with his best friend, Frankie.

But then tragedy strikes. And out of this tragedy an unlikely friendship develops between Toby and the local bogeyman, a strange old man across the street named Mr. Joseph. Over the course of a tumultuous summer, Toby will be faced with pain and death, the excitement of his first love, and the underlying racism of the townsfolk, all while learning about the value of freedom at the hands of a kind but cursed old man.

Every town has a dark side. And in Belford, the local bogeyman has a story to tell.

**Available in paperback or Kindle on Amazon.com**

ISBN-13: 978-0692730980

The empty airwaves of the mind...

Welcome to TunnelVision – the premium channel streaming from the imagination of R. Patrick Gates to you!

What happens when you lose sight of the forest for the trees?

Wilbur Clayton has a personal connection with Jesus – Murder! Abused for most of his life, Wilbur and Jesus are out to make amends and take revenge. With Grandma in his head and Jesus on the TunnelVision, Wilbur knows what must be done and who must be made to pay for the sins of the father...

The only thing standing in his way are a cop with a gift for details and deduction, and a young genius whose reenactments of his favorite books are about to become all too real.

TunnelVision – streaming seven days a week, 24 hours a day!

On the air and in your nightmares!

**Available in paperback or Kindle on Amazon.com**

ISBN-13: 978-0998067902

## I KNOW WHAT YOU HAVE HEARD ABOUT ME

You say that I am a madman. You say that I am dangerous. You say that I am the one who has been abducting women, slaughtering them, and burying their corpses all around this city for years. You are wrong, because only part of that statement is true...

## I AM NOT A KILLER

I know that you probably won't believe me. Not now. Not after all that has happened, but I need to tell my side of the story. You need to know how this all began. You need to hear about the birds, but most of all, you need to understand...

## I AM NOT THE BOULEVARD MONSTER

**Available in paperback or Kindle on Amazon.com**

ISBN-13: 978-0998067957

## A NUCLEAR STORM POURS DOWN
## FROM THE HEAVENS

A global disaster strikes suddenly when the Space Shuttle explodes over the Atlantic seaboard, unleashing its toxic payload over thousands of miles. Millions flee. Millions more perish in the deluge . . . and they are the lucky ones. Those who do not die immediately after exposure soon sicken and succumb in horrific agony.

## ON SEA BREEZE ISLAND, A PLAGUE OF UNDEATH
## REANIMATES THE FALLEN

Their minds still function, but their flesh continues to bloat and decay. Ostracized by the fortunate few who have escaped the radioactive rain and quarantined to the water's edge, the "Beachers" are treated as inhuman monsters by family and friends; soon they will become as loathsome in behavior as they are in appearance.

For one particular survivor – a single mother named Sandy – the monster is very familiar. He will put her through a Hell beyond her darkest nightmares, but in order to protect her child, she will endure and do anything. Absolutely anything.

**Available in paperback or Kindle on Amazon.com**

ISBN-13: 978-0998067957

### A MAN IN MOURNING

Still haunted by the death of his wife two years earlier, Derrick Grayson travels with his gifted son Nathan to her hometown of Moss Creek. There, he reunites with her mother, Grace, hoping to bring some peace to his broken heart and to give Nathan a normal childhood.

### A TOWN UNDER THE SHADOW OF EVIL

Moss Creek harbors a dark secret, though. Local children have been disappearing for decades, with no trace of them ever found. When a swath of slaughter and bloodshed cuts its way through the townspeople and Derrick finds himself directly in its path, he must join with a group of kindred souls to hunt down the malevolent specter behind the carnage... a dark figure from a twisted shadowy realm... An ancient unearthly entity known as...

### THE RAGGEDY MAN

**Available in paperback or Kindle on Amazon.com**

ISBN-13: 978-0998067988

### A TERRIFYING HAUNTING

This is the place where the harrowed ghosts of a dozen generations whisper in the shadows of their ancestral home, where one family's dreams of a new beginning turned into a nightmare that ended in tragedy.

### A CURSED BLOODLINE

This is the place where a line of witches bound themselves—in blood—to a primeval entity. Here, nightmare and reality meet beneath frozen skies, and even time and space fall under the power of the demonic being that rules this remote northern wood.

### A CHANCE ENCOUNTER

This is the place where the path of a tormented survivor meets that of an unknowing innocent. Past and present collide, and secrets long buried crawl back into the pallid light of day as the shadow of the Beast falls over them both. But even the bloodiest dreams of that demonic being may pale in comparison to what lies buried within the human heart.
This is the place where evil dwells ...

### ABODE

**Available in paperback or Kindle on Amazon.com**

ISBN-13: 978-0998067988

# ON THE HORIZON FROM
# BLOODSHOT BOOKS

## 2017*

Dust to Dust – M.C. Norris
White Death – Christine Morgan
Red Diamond – Michales Joy
The Organ Donor – Matthew Warner
What Hides Within – Jason Parent
It Sustains – Mark Morris
Shadow Child: 30th Anniversary Edition – Joseph Citro
The Noctuary: Pandemonium – Greg Chapman

## 2018*

Victoria (What Hides Within #2) – Jason Parent
Happy Cage – Gene Lazuta
The Winter Tree – Mark Morris
Blood Mother: A Novel of Terror – Pete Kahle
Not Your Average Monster, Volume 3
Practitioners – Matt Heyward & Patrick Lacey

## 2019-20*

The Abomination (The Riders Saga #2) – Pete Kahle
The Horsemen (The Riders Saga #3) – Pete Kahle
Not Your Average Monster, Volume 4

* other titles to be added when confirmed

# BLOODSHOT BOOKS

# READ UNTIL YOU BLEED!